Forrest Public Library District
301 W. James Street
Forrest, Illinois 61741

DEMCO

ALSO BY SUSAN CRANDALL

Back Roads
The Road Home

MAGNOLIA SKY

SUSAN CRANDALL

NEW YORK   BOSTON

Cover design by Diane Luger
Cover illustration by Rick Johnson
Hand lettering by David Gatti

Warner Books

Time Warner Book Group
1271 Avenue of the Americas
New York, NY 10020
Visit our Web site at www.twbookmark.com

Printed in the United States of America

First Paperback Printing: August 2004

10 9 8 7 6 5 4 3 2 1

For my mother, Marjorie,
who always believed I could.

Acknowledgments

As always, thanks to my critique partners, the ladies of WITTS and Karen White. Appreciation to my husband Bill (who always travels with a plan) for driving all over northern Mississippi with no more direction than my whim. He also gets bonus points for not complaining about the lack of meals, clean clothes or conversation during the month before my deadline. I'm grateful for having such a great team to work with in my editor, Karen Kosztolnyik, and my agent, Linda Kruger.

Chapter 1

The freezing February rain beat steadily on the roof of Luke Boudreau's old Taurus. Through the water-spotted glass, he watched the winter-stripped trees mimic his own unsettled insides as they jerked and twisted in the gusty wind. He hunched a little deeper into his jacket collar and rubbed his chilled fingers against his thighs. Mississippi was the *South*, for God's sake, the Magnolia State. How could it be so damn cold?

He'd been parked here on this levee, watching the storm punish a broad, sweeping bend in the Tallahatchie River for the past hour. The rain slanted in silvery sheets. The clouds hung so low and gray that, despite the fact it was mid-morning, an artificial twilight encompassed Luke's solitary torment.

The moment he'd been both dreading and anticipating for the past five months had come. In all that time, he'd debated long and hard about what he would say, yet had found no words to convey his regret.

This morning he'd changed his clothes between civilian and army uniform three times before leaving his motel in black pants, a sport coat and tie—funeral clothes. He came to Mississippi as a man, not a soldier. Still, he felt as unprepared as if he'd come straight from the battlefield to speak to the mother of the man who shouldn't have died.

Died. He could think of no four letters more powerful, more cutting, more capable of drawing raw emotion to the surface, like blood in a fresh wound. Even so, that word was far from adequate to express what had happened to Calvin Abbott. Abbott had been obliterated. But no one outside his own team would ever know the reality of it.

Each and every time Luke closed his eyes to sleep, he heard the shouts, the garbled static of his communications earpiece, the steady *whomp-whomp* of the helicopter blades, the explosions, the automatic rifle fire, his own ragged breathing—Abbott yelling his name. It was Luke's own private hell, one he couldn't share, even with his fellow Rangers.

Occasionally, a moment in his life allowed the memory to sag to the rear of his mind. But quickly his own body brought it back to the forefront. His fingertips still tingled; every step was marked by a stiff and painful right knee. Today's weather brought a sharp and steady stabbing in his back.

At least he *could* feel. He reminded himself of that every day.

He put the car in drive and bounced along the gravel levee road, each rut and pothole sending a white-hot shaft of pain up through his shoulder blades.

His white-knuckled grip on the steering wheel loosened when he reached the two-lane blacktop that led to Grover. It was odd, he noticed, the way asphalt weathered to an orangish pink here, instead of bleached gray.

Heavy vegetation pressed close to the roadside, making

some stretches look as wild and untamed as it had been in the days of the plantations. Areas that weren't cultivated with cotton supported trees so large and ancient they created a brittle archway overhead. Occasionally, those trees were made grotesque, forming shapes of prehistoric monsters, by the kudzu vines that had engulfed them. All in all, the atmosphere made him feel as if he were driving through an old black-and-white horror picture.

He concentrated on the faded broken yellow line bisecting the lanes, silently ticking off the distance between him and Calvin Abbott's bereaved mother.

Occasionally, dilapidated mobile homes or tin-roofed shanties rose like cankers in the brush beside the road, the rain sheeting off the gutterless roofs to puddle on the ground. Once, a mud-caked mongrel dog shot out from a lane, giving chase for a good quarter mile before he tuckered out and gave up.

Grover first appeared in dribs and drabs along the highway: a car dealer; a field; the John Deere dealer; a field; the Dixie Drive-in, "Home of the Calhoun Burger"; a baseball diamond with a single set of sagging bleachers; a Piggly Wiggly with six cars in the parking lot; a dated yellow-brick high school. Then, tree-lined neighborhood streets with small bungalows and shotgun cottages that soon made way for larger, more stately old homes.

He passed an old brick church whose interior lights shone through the intricate stained glass, a beacon of warmth in the cold, stormy day.

When Luke reached downtown, he was hit with a strong sense of familiarity. The square was still festooned with Christmas lights that draped over the streets between the courthouse dome and the two- and three-story buildings that housed storefronts and offices on all four sides. Browning evergreen wreaths with big red bows that dripped rain and twitched in the wind encircled the globes of sidewalk lampposts.

On the courthouse square was a Nativity scene—apparently separation of church and state hadn't yet been an issue in Grover, Mississippi.

Underneath the superficial differences between his own Yankee hometown and Abbott's southern counterpart (the courthouse was definitely southern, painted white with arched second-story windows that flanked a small balcony over the main entrance; most of the surrounding businesses had galleries that extended over the sidewalk, providing both protection for the pedestrians and porches for the second floor), the small county seats were essentially the same. Same cluster of businesses around the courthouse square. Same dated storefronts. Same untimely removal of tired holiday displays.

It felt just like going home.

Instead of a growing sense of welcoming, the similarities made Luke feel as if he had sand under his skin. He hadn't been home to Indiana for more than a day or two at a time since joining the army over fifteen years ago. Since his release from the stateside hospital a week ago, there'd been a quiet burning in his gut telling him not to go back. He'd decided it was because he couldn't go home and pick up his life—the life he owed to Calvin Abbott—without first seeing Abbott's family.

But in the dark of night, when the truth couldn't be pushed away with mundane tasks, physical therapy and innocuous friendly conversation, a knot of fear replaced that burning, and he knew his life, his identity, *was* the Army Rangers. He was special ops from bone to skin; there wasn't anything else in him.

He turned left at the courthouse and headed west. Calvin's mother owned a greenhouse and nursery called Magnolia Mile, just outside town. Luke was going to take his chances on finding it himself before he stopped somewhere and asked. He had a strong sense of obligation not to speak to someone who might have known Calvin before he spoke to his mother—in the same way the next of kin had to be notified of a death before the general population.

The rain slackened and the windshield wipers began to skip and complain across the glass. He turned them to intermittent.

Businesses fell away in the same sporadic way they'd increased on his way into town. He passed a swampy bog, then moved into a stand of old growth forest. He was just about to decide he was on the wrong road when he saw a brightly painted sign with MAGNOLIA MILE written in fancy script over an ornate gold arrow pointing to the right, down a single-lane chip-and-seal road.

He turned. After traveling that narrow road another several minutes, Luke started to think he'd turned too soon, had missed the part of the sign that said, TURN RIGHT 1/4 MILE. The road bottomed on a low bridge over a creek, then took a near-ninety-degree turn to the left. And there it was, MAGNOLIA MILE written on a sign in front of a very large yellow Victorian house. The ornate white-trimmed front porch made a sweeping curve as it wrapped around the left side of the house. It seemed a little out of place in an area where all of the large homes sported columns and galleries, mimicking antebellum architecture no matter when they were constructed.

A matching story-and-a-half carriage house topped with a large cupola and weather vane sat behind the main house. Luke could see a couple of large, old-fashioned glass greenhouses set yet farther back. He followed the crushed-stone drive to the carriage house, which had MAGNOLIA MILE over a double French door.

Off to the side of the carriage house, a large screen of fancy white trelliswork hid the nursery stock from immediate view. In front of the screen was an artful display of sculpted garden decorations, birdbaths, benches, wrought-iron gates and arches, tiny waterfalls. Even in the miserable weather, it looked inviting. Abbott's mother obviously had a talent for her work.

Abbott had a younger brother, Cole, who was still in high school. Luke supposed it was a bit of cowardice that made him arrive here during school hours. But he allowed himself that. It was going to be difficult enough to face Abbott's mother; facing the youngster who worshipped him would be more than Luke could stand.

He got out of the car and hurried inside, the first couple of steps the most painful; he'd been in the car too long. The first floor of the carriage house had been converted into a shop. It was warmed by a potbellied stove and smelled of old wood, peat moss and fertilizer. Various houseplants hung in baskets from the rafters. The cash register sat on a long counter near the left wall. There was a tent-shaped paper sign beside it that said, IN THE GREEN-HOUSE. C'MON BACK.

Luke had been away from small towns long enough for an unattended cash register to make him nervous.

He went to the back door. It was a good thirty yards to the first greenhouse, and the rain had picked up again. At least the crushed-stone walkway would keep him from sinking knee-deep in mud. He lowered his head and made for the greenhouse at a gimpy trot, trying to avoid the deepest of the puddles.

Two things hit him when he pulled open the steamed-over glass door. A wave of hot air, and Def Leppard rattling the glass panes with "Pour Some Sugar On Me."

"Hello?" He didn't see anyone right away. His gaze scanned over the green leaves springing up from the plant tables. There, in the far corner, he saw two arms with fisted hands making simultaneous circles overhead in time with the music. Occasionally, light hair would bob above the greenery.

Surprise trickled through him. Abbott's mother was . . . boogying?

Luke called hello again, working to reform the image he'd created of Abbott's mother. Luke had imagined a softly rounded body topped with semi-stylish gray hair that smelled of freshly baked cookies, snow-white Keds and a theme sweater. Maybe Yanni or John Tesh. Certainly not Def Leppard.

The dancing continued.

He walked toward that corner of the greenhouse, calling out twice to no avail.

When he reached the aisle where he'd seen the hands, he stopped and stared.

Abbott had said his mother was "unconventional." But no way could Luke see what was before him as a mother. Definitely not Abbott's. A long strawberry-blond braid hung down the tall slender back, swaying as the young woman undulated provocatively with the music. Her short top rode up, showing a curving waist over her low-slung jeans. Those graceful arms bent and she rested her hands on her hair as her head bobbed from side to side. Luke had never seen a sight quite so unconsciously alluring.

Def Leppard continued to beg for little Miss Innocent to sugar them up—and Luke wanted just that.

She spun around. Luke opened his mouth to speak, but her eyes were closed. Her hips moved in a way that he'd forgotten a woman could. Her elbows came forward, her hands still on the back of her head. Her navel winked at him.

Luke's mouth went dry.

You can't just stand here. "Ex—" he swallowed, trying to get some moisture back over his dry vocal cords. "Excuse me!" he shouted.

Her eyes opened. Her hands flew to her heart and she jumped several inches in the air. "Good Lord, man! Are you trying to give me a heart attack?" Her voice held a strong Mississippi accent, but not the backwoodsy sort, more like a southern debutante, sorority girl at Ole Miss. Then her eyes narrowed and she crossed her arms over her chest. "Just how long have you been standing there?"

Luke felt heat come to his cheeks. Jesus, was he blushing? "Not long." He wasn't sure she could hear his denial over the bass beat of the music.

She pinned him with a challenging glare that told him she'd heard just fine. She had beautiful light green eyes that flashed the same fire he'd seen in her dancing. But the way she tugged the hem of her top over her jeans showed just how uncomfortable his spying had made her—no matter what her show of cool.

"I'm—"

"Wait!" She walked toward him, holding up a finger. "Let me turn this music down." She stepped around him and trotted to a table beside the door he'd come in.

As she passed, he caught a scent as sultry as that dance she'd been doing. She dressed in a manner that said she didn't work at looking good—which somehow made her all the more appealing. He tried to figure her age. It was hard to tell; she wore no makeup and had a very youthful spring in her step as she ran to the table. *Much too young for you, Luke, ol' boy.*

She turned down the music and looked at him again. "Now we can talk like regular people. The plants have to have four hours of music a day." Her smile was open and friendly. As he looked more closely at her eyes, he thought perhaps she wasn't so young.

He shuffled his male curiosity back into the closet as he took several steps in her direction. "The plants like rock?"

"The boss lady insists they prefer classical, something with energy. She doesn't like them to hear ballads—makes them depressed. Def Leppard has plenty of energy." She flipped her long braid back over her shoulder and lifted her chin slightly.

Luke thought he saw a hint of blush on her cheeks that belied her rebellious stance. Again, he was drawn to her complex mixture of innocence and spunk.

"I see." He shifted his weight from his bad knee. "I'm looking for M—" he started to say Mrs. Abbott, but knew Abbott's mother had remarried after his father died; Cole was actually his half-brother. Calvin always referred to his mother as Liv, never Mom, or Ma, or Mother. Luke had no idea what her last name was. "For Olivia," he finished. Using her first name felt disrespectful to his military-trained tongue.

"She had to go to town. She should be back in about fifteen minutes. Can I do something for you?"

"No, actually, it's personal." He paused and looked around. "I'll just wait in my car." He started to take a step, but immediately felt his knee begin to buckle. Shifting his weight back to his good leg, he saved himself an embarrassing stumble.

She cast a quick glance at his bad knee, her forehead

wrinkled with a frown. Then her gaze passed over the ugly, jagged scar on the side of his neck. He tensed, dreading her questions, her pity.

Her gaze then connected with his. He wasn't sure what he saw in her eyes, but it wasn't pity. "Wouldn't you like some coffee while you wait?"

"No, thanks. I don't want to interrupt your . . . work. I'll just wait outside for Olivia." He was torn between wanting to be away from the possibility of questions that Olivia had the first right to ask, and the warmth of long-denied feminine contact. There had been plenty of female hands on him in the hospital, but to have *real* interaction with a woman— well, it had been a long, long time.

He started to step around her and she put a hand on his arm. "Please. I'd feel just terrible with you sitting out there in the cold."

He hesitated. Her touch warmed him through the layers of clothing, right to the bone.

"I can tell by your accent you're not from around here," she said. "Maybe you don't know how it works down South." She drew out the words *he-yah* and *down Saauth*, emphasizing her own accent. "We invite. You accept. Otherwise our feelings are hurt." She smiled again. "You're lucky I didn't offer you sweet tea. You Yankees don't seem to have a taste for sweet tea."

He smiled back. It shocked him to realize just how foreign smiling felt. It was almost like the first time he bent his wounded knee after having the brace removed, as if the muscles had to work just to remember how. "I'd be honored to share a cup of coffee with such a lovely flower of the South." He gave her a gallant sweeping bow befitting a Confederate officer. He could hardly believe he was flirting. It felt even more alien than smiling.

"That's more like it." She spun around with a satisfied look on her face and headed toward the door with quick, sure steps.

She was halfway there when she must have sensed that he wasn't right behind her. She slowed her pace, without turning around, without making him self-conscious. God, he couldn't wait for the day when he was himself again.

A little voice in the back of his brain whispered, *You will never again be the man, the soldier, you were.*

He shook off the thought and plunged outside right behind her into the rain. She held back, kept herself from running through the downpour. Her sensitivity to his pride pricked in a way that was almost more painful than other folks' outright sympathy.

Pushing himself to move faster, he nudged her from behind. "Go!"

She broke into a trot. His knee hurt, but he made himself keep up. Even so, by the time they reached the carriage house, they were both soaked to the skin.

Once inside, she spun around, wiping the water from her face, laughing. It was a beautiful sound, bringing to mind warm, soft breezes and church bells.

"Good heavens!" She looked at him. "Oh, my. You're drenched. Let me get something to dry us off."

She went behind the counter that held the cash register and rummaged around while Luke stood dripping on the floor.

"This will have to do." She held up a roll of paper towel and pulled off a long strip. Coming back to Luke, she held it out for him.

"This'll do fine. Thank you." He took the towels, but could hardly mop himself for watching the way she patted her face and throat dry—and the way her wet shirt clung to her curves.

Luke heard a snort from the corner of the room and flinched guiltily. He'd been staring at her as if they were alone. Apparently they weren't.

When he looked around, he saw only a huge red-brown bloodhound curled up in a dark corner.

"That's Rufus, our guard dog."

Luke looked at her in disbelief. "Guard dog? I walked in here earlier and didn't even notice him. I could have carried the place off." He didn't tell her that he was equally remiss. At the top of his form, he'd never have missed the presence of a living, breathing being inside a room. No matter how still it made itself.

The dog let one sleepy eye fall shut.

She laughed. "I doubt that. That's all part of his plan, making you think he's not paying attention. Just try to get near that cash register."

Luke couldn't imagine a dog having a "plan."

"Go on. Try it." She gestured toward the register.

Tipping his head, Luke grinned. "Okay. But just to prove you need to rely on locked doors and not a lazy hound." He walked toward the front door.

Rufus remained snoozing in his corner.

Luke stepped closer to the register.

Rufus didn't move.

Walking right up to the counter, Luke looked at the dog and waited.

One eye opened.

"Not much of a deterrent," Luke said, shaking his head in amusement.

"Rufus just doesn't like to waste a lot of energy carrying on. He knows when to get to business. Try to pick it up." She stood with her arms crossed and a grin on her face.

Luke reached for the register.

In a red-brown blur, the dog leapt across the room in one bound. A deep growl was followed by an equally deep round of barking that rattled the windows, as well as Luke's self-confidence.

Rufus showed an impressive display of sharp white teeth set in a jaw the size of a horse's and maneuvered himself between Luke and the door.

Luke yanked his hands away from the register, his heart hammering in his chest.

The dog inched closer, head low, teeth bared, hackles raised.

"Okay, okay, I let it go," Luke said with his hands in the air, backing slowly away.

The dog still looked ready to pounce.

"Hey, lady, call off Cujo!"

"Rufus, down." She didn't raise her voice at all.

The dog's lips relaxed and he flopped in a wrinkly brown mass to the floor. He blew out a long breath that flapped his lips and watched the woman with adoring eyes.

Luke licked his lips. "Well, okay, then. I'm convinced."

"Actually, poor Rufus never gets to do that; everyone around here already has wind of his reputation." She walked over to the dog, knelt down and ruffled his long ears.

Luke said, "Normally, I get along fine with dogs. Still, if I were you, I wouldn't put my face quite so close to those . . . those fangs."

She laughed. "He won't hurt me—only someone who wants to hurt me."

A large pink tongue swiped across her face. "Yes, I love you, too, big fella."

She stood back up and looked at Luke, extending her hand. "I'm Analise. Cream in your coffee?"

Giving his head a slight shake, Luke caught up with the

change in conversation. He kept his eye on the dog for another heartbeat. He really did like dogs. However, he'd never faced a hundred pounds of snarling teeth and muscle before. "Yes, please." He shifted his gaze to her and shook her hand. It felt strong and gentle at the same time. "And I'm Luke Boudreau."

Her hand spasmed slightly in his. A little breath hitched in her chest. Her lips opened slightly and her eyes widened. Her face seemed to blanch. "Oh." She finally blinked and swallowed. "I'll get the coffee."

She hurried into another room, leaving Luke feeling like he should have recognized her name. Calvin didn't talk much about home—only rarely of his mother and little brother. Luke suddenly realized he'd served beside the man for three years and could count on one hand the personal details he knew about his life.

When Analise returned, color was back in her cheeks. She carried two mugs of steaming coffee. She handed one to Luke and motioned for him to sit at the metal café set near the stove. She sat across the small table from him, concentrating on the steam rising from her cup.

After a few seconds she raised her gaze and looked at him. Her mouth remained relaxed, not reflecting the emotion that Luke thought he caught in her eyes. There was something in her stare that reached right down inside him and grabbed the pit of his stomach. She finally released him from the power of that jade gaze, lowered her lashes and took a sip from her cup.

Luke drank his own coffee, content to let the silence play out.

Analise's long fingers fiddled with the cup that sat in front of her. Luke noticed her fingernails were short and stained from working with plants. She had what looked like a long, narrow burn across the back of her left hand.

After a few minutes she raised her gaze and sighed. "You served with Calvin." It wasn't a question.

He nodded. "I'd really like to wait for Olivia. . . ."

For a second, offense flashed in her eyes, sharp and accusing. Then she said softly, "Of course."

He felt badly, so he tried to initiate polite conversation. "So what about you? Have you always lived in Grover?"

She withdrew her hands from the table and put them in her lap. "No, I grew up around Jackson. Calvin brought me here."

"Calvin?"

Just then, a woman who had to be Calvin's mother came hustling through the front door. She collapsed her umbrella and stomped her feet, which, despite the weather, sported Birkenstocks and white socks. Her gray hair was in an unexpected short-spiky 'do that made Luke think of Annie Lennox. The woman was short, rather box-shaped, with full cheeks, Calvin's slightly-tilted-upward brown eyes and generous mouth, and a virtually nonexistent neck. The big, loose, cable-knit sweater she wore hit her at midthigh, nearly swallowing her up. She moved in a no-nonsense, take-charge way that belied her elfish appearance.

"Oh! Company!" She smiled, and the warmth of it shot right to Luke's scarred heart. This was clearly the face of a woman who never turned a soul away from her doorstep. Still, he doubted her exuberance would last once she knew who the "company" was.

He stood and tipped his head. "Luke Boudreau, ma'am."

Her smile slipped just a little, but she quickly recovered. "You're here about Calvin." Although her smile remained on her face, Luke could see a spark of pain in her eyes.

"Yes, ma'am."

Beside him, Analise made a little hiccup sound. He kept his gaze on Olivia.

She pulled in a deep breath that appeared to add an edge of stiffness to her posture, as if drawing herself up, bracing herself to face something unpleasant yet inevitable. Then she walked toward him, a congenial expression maintained on her face. "I see you've already met Calvin's wife."

Luke's tingling fingers felt like they'd taken a shot of electricity. His heart beat in a chest that suddenly felt cold and hollow. *Wife? How could I not have known Calvin had a wife?*

Chapter 2

The fact that Abbott had a wife ricocheted wildly in Luke's brain. It bounced and slammed against a dozen walls of memory. Never in his entire association with the man, from the time he was assigned to Luke's team until the day he died, had Abbott given the slightest indication he was married. Never even breathed the word "wife." And his behavior *certainly* never reflected it.

Swallowing his surprise, Luke denied himself the long hard look at Analise that he burned to take. He wanted to see her in a different light, to tell himself that all of that lustful chemistry he'd been experiencing was imaginary. But he kept his eyes fixed on Olivia. "Yes, we've met."

He stepped away from his chair and offered it to Olivia, keeping his attention focused solely on her, not permitting Analise even into the periphery of his vision. Years of training allowed him to keep his outward appearance independent from the cascade of emotions running through him. Looking into those lovely green eyes might just prove to be too dangerous at the moment. His earlier thoughts of her were suddenly appallingly inappropriate . . . incestuous.

Olivia took the seat he offered.

Beside him, he heard Analise stand. As she stepped away, she said, "I'll give you some time."

Luke knew he should stop her; she had as much right as Olivia to hear what he had to say. But the woman threw a monkey wrench into the machine of his thoughts. He let her go.

"Please, sit down, Luke." Olivia patted the table in front of the chair Analise had just vacated.

Folding her hands on the table, she waited. Her pause didn't seem heavy and expectant as Luke searched for the place to begin. All of the possible combinations of words he'd been pondering for weeks failed him. He was hobbled by the fact that he could never reveal the truth about Abbott's death. After looking into Olivia's kind eyes, the lies he'd prepared stuck on his tongue.

After a moment, she saved him by saying, "Why don't you tell me a little about yourself? Calvin was never very forthcoming with the details."

You're telling me. Luke bit back a bark of nervous laughter.

She let her gaze dissolve into empty space somewhere between the tabletop and the floor, chuckling with remembrance. "When he was a boy, I used to ask him how his day was when he got off the school bus. Every day it was the same, a shrug and, 'Okay.' Didn't matter what had happened. The school could have burned to the ground or aliens could have landed in the playground, and I would have had to hear it on the six o'clock news."

Luke smiled back at her, nodding. He'd never really thought about it before, but that was exactly how Abbott dealt with everything. He had a straightforward way of skimming over the complexities of the meatier issues, preferring to make the joke, dive into the task.

Still, a wife? How could a guy keep something like that to himself over the course of three years?

Nonetheless, Luke was thankful to Olivia for easing him into conversation. He began with the basics about himself. "I'm from a little town in southern Indiana. Been in the army since I was twenty."

When he paused, unsure how much detail she wanted, she prompted, "Wife? Family?"

"Not married. My dad owns a bar, still lives right where I grew up. I have two sisters, the younger one, Molly, is just about to finish her medical residency in Boston. And Lily used to live in Chicago, but—I guess it's been nearly a year ago now—she moved back to Glens Crossing with her son. She just married an old friend of ours from when we were kids. Great guy, used to be military himself." He shook his head. It still didn't seem possible that after all of these years, Lily and Clay were finally together. She'd belonged with him from the summer they'd first met, but their lives had taken them on a long and difficult road to finding each other.

Suddenly Luke realized the chances of him ever finding a relationship like those two shared had been cast into the range of nonexistent. It set off a hollow burning just beneath his breastbone.

"Is your mother still living?" Olivia asked.

"I haven't been in touch with my mom since I was about eleven—when she left."

"I see." Olivia didn't give him that *oh, you poor child* look that he'd grown to hate. Instead she went on, "I can tell by your voice that you care a great deal for your family." Those gentle brown eyes settled on him. "Especially Lily. That's good. You understand."

"Understand what, ma'am?"

"How it is to have people take a little part of you wherever they go, leave a tiny black hole in your soul that can only be plugged back up when they come home."

He searched her face and could see the underlying questions, the words she wasn't coming right out and saying.

Pulling in a deep breath, he squared his shoulders. "Your son was under my command when he was killed."

She looked at the lividly pink scar on the side of his neck. "And you were injured."

"Yes, ma'am. Calvin was a brave man, a good soldier. I could always count on him to cover my back, no matter what." He swallowed the lump of guilt threatening to choke him. "I was proud to serve with him." He paused. "I can't express how sorry I am that I failed to bring him home safely."

Something in the set of her mouth shifted, reminding him of the way Abbott looked when he thought something wasn't quite kosher. But she reached across the table and put her hand on his. "It was a helicopter crash. Not your doing."

Shame, bright as lightning, sharp as a fresh razor, cut across his heart, when he heard her repeat the official cause of death. *Not my doing? Dear God, if you only knew. Then you wouldn't be looking at me with such caring eyes. You'd be scratching mine out.*

He'd built a career on his ability to detach himself from his thoughts, his emotions. But here in this room, speaking to this good woman, it felt completely immoral.

Pushing the bitter truth away, he said the words he'd traveled hundreds of miles to deliver. "I wasn't able to come—to pay my respects properly at his funeral. I regret that, ma'am." He paused and forced himself to look her in the eye. "More than I can say." Then he stood. "Calvin served with me for over three years. I couldn't have asked for a

better man at my side. You did a fine job raising your son."
His gaze fell to the floor for a brief second, then returned to
her face. "I take full responsibility for his death."

He reached into his pocket. "I just couldn't let them pack
this up and send it with his personal belongings. It was special to him—too special to risk loss in shipping. He had it
with him on every assignment, every mission."

Luke laid the Purple Heart earned by Abbott's father on
the table next to Olivia's hand.

For the longest time, she just sat there, staring at the
medal. Then she picked it up slowly and folded it into her
left hand. She raised her eyes, glistening with unshed tears,
and held him as immobile as if she'd magically drawn away
his will to move. Luke waited, barely breathing, unable to
say more, unable to turn and walk away.

Her chin began to quiver. She pressed her lips so tightly
together they turned white. Finally, her face wrinkled and a
sob escaped her throat. She jumped from the chair and flew
at him.

He braced himself for her assault.

Instead of angry words and furious maternal fists pounding
his chest, damning him and the unfairness that took her son,
she threw her arms around him and pulled him close.

It was worse than being pummeled.

Luke held her and patted her shoulder awkwardly,
waiting for the onslaught of tears to diminish. He felt like
the most despicable man who had ever walked the earth.
First he'd coveted the wife of a fallen fellow soldier. Now he
held a broken-hearted mother in the embrace of a friend—
when he knew her son would be alive if it hadn't been for
Luke's own poor judgment.

Suddenly, she pulled away, cutting herself off in midsob.
Luke's hands fell from her shoulders.

She dashed her tears with a quick brush of her fingers. "Well"—she smiled—"enough of that." She sniffed in a totally unladylike way. "You'll be staying for lunch." A statement of fact, not a question.

"I'm sorry, ma'am—"

"Enough of this 'ma'am' stuff. You're making me feel like Granny Lejeune—Cole's grandma, who's eighty-six and cranky as a wet hen. It's Olivia—or Liv. And no sorry's, either. You'll stay. I'm not much of a cook, but I won't poison you; Ana and Cole survive it." She paused and looked off in the distance, as if a thought had just occurred to her. "Then again, maybe they've built up a tolerance." She patted him on the chest. "No matter. We've got a good hospital."

Analise went to her metal studio in the gabled second floor of the carriage house. She needed to work; she had no time to dwell on personal slights. The fountain she was building needed to be done next week and she had a shipment of copper sprinklers that was due to be shipped this Friday. But, as she gathered her materials, she couldn't keep her mind on either project.

Her insides felt like a film she'd once seen of the inside of a volcano, hot and roiling, toxic vapors and molten rock. It was the same feeling she got every time she thought about her late husband.

She could hear the rise and fall of voices below as Luke and Olivia talked about *her* husband. That guy had some nerve, treating her like she was no more than a stranger to Calvin.

Quickly, her own conscience admonished her. Luke was probably Calvin's loyal friend—she, on the other hand, had betrayed her husband, not in deed, but in her thoughts. She couldn't count how often she'd wished he simply would not come home. Time and again, she'd imagined how much easier her life would be. And now that horrible, horrible wish had been granted. It was too late to take it back.

Why had this man arrived now, just when scabs had begun to form on the wounds in her soul?

Again, her conscience spoke: *Because you deserve no peace.*

Olivia was right about one thing. She wasn't much of a cook. However, by the time they sat down to scorched tomato soup and blackened grilled cheese sandwiches, she'd managed to take the uncomfortable edge off of Luke's mood. She'd chatted and joked and mothered him as she'd worked in her warm, inviting kitchen. He was glad to see she wasn't a fragile woman made of blown glass; Olivia Lejeune was more like a rubber dog toy, appearing all soft and adorable, but tough and resilient when put to the test of teeth. In fact, Luke had been enjoying himself—until Analise came in from the greenhouse and sat down at the kitchen table across from him.

He simply nodded a greeting and tried not to think of her navel.

She smiled back and picked up her spoon. There was something almost fearful in her smile. Which made no sense. If anything, she should be angry over his earlier dismissal of her.

After that, Luke was careful not to look at her. The bright awkwardness bothering him felt much like the time he and a buddy had peeked into their eighth-grade English teacher, Miss Clark's, bedroom window one night and seen her naked. It had been her first year teaching, and every guy in school had the hots for her. Only Luke and Josh had seen her naked. It had been an earth-moving experience—especially since she was really stacked and neither he nor Josh had actually ever seen a real *live* naked woman before. On the way home, feeling like conquering heroes, they'd talked about how they were going to tell everybody—become celebrities in the locker room. But the next day, shame prevented either of them from even bringing it up. From that time forward, they sank low in their chairs during English class and tried not to look at her.

Since then, Luke had never looked at a naked woman who hadn't specifically invited him to.

Still, those feelings he'd had when he first met Analise brought that same sense of dishonor. He couldn't wait to be away from here, so he could put it out of his mind.

"Luke," Analise said, "how long did you serve with Calvin?"

The room seemed hotter than the greenhouse. "We served in the same company for five years, on the same special team for three." He gave her a brief glance; he could hardly speak to her without looking at her at all.

"I see." There was something challenging in her eyes.

Luke knew it was time to apologize. "I meant no disrespect earlier. I'm truly sorry for your loss. I . . ." How was he going to explain that he didn't know she was Calvin's wife, when she obviously was familiar with his name when he introduced himself?

"We were married for eight." The statement hovered over the table between them for a moment, then crashed in the silence like a lead balloon.

What in the hell was he supposed to say to that? He waited for Olivia to save him, but she continued to take quiet sips of soup from her spoon as if alone in the room.

During the following uneasy minutes, both Luke and Analise concentrated over their soup as if it held the answer to world peace in its depths.

Then, out of the blue, Olivia said, "Luke brought Jimmy's Purple Heart home. I suppose Calvin will be getting one, too."

When Luke's gaze snapped to her face, she had a look of calculation deep in her eyes. He forced a crusty bite of sandwich down his throat before it had been sufficiently chewed, then wiped his mouth with a paper napkin. "Actually, ma'am—"

"Olivia," she corrected.

"Olivia." He blew out a quiet breath and dared a glance at Analise. Her sharp green gaze was riveted on him, her spoon stalled halfway to her lips. "The Purple Heart is only awarded to those wounded or killed in combat—at the hands of a declared enemy."

"Humm." Olivia held Luke helpless with her gaze for another moment, then resumed her lunch.

He sensed she was testing him, probing for reaction. By the way her gaze sharpened, he was certain she'd noticed his addition of the word "declared" to the regulations for the Purple Heart. It was as much as he'd be able to give her in confirmation. Any mother of a soldier involved in covert operations would have similar suspicions—and in this case, Olivia Lejeune's were valid. Calvin most definitely deserved the Purple Heart, and probably a couple of other commendations. But often the clandestine work of the Rangers precluded such decorations. Those awards either weren't given, especially posthumously to the next of kin, or were flashed briefly in front of the soldier and then stored away in some vault, never to see the light of day again.

Analise broke the ensuing silence. "It was very thoughtful of you to deliver it in person. That medal was very special to Calvin."

Luke looked at her and offered a nod of thanks. How

could Abbott have treated a medal with more regard than this sparkling, devoted wife? Luke's mind did a quick double take. Where had he gotten the idea that Analise was devoted? He knew plenty of long-distance military marriages were "open," where both parties fooled around at will. Abbott had sure had his share of flings.

When Analise smiled oddly and lowered her gaze, he realized he'd been staring at her as he'd tried to decipher what was impossible to know—and certainly none of his business.

Olivia said, "I think Luke was a good friend to our Calvin." She nodded in satisfaction. "It's good to have a military man in the house again."

For a moment Luke thought of her statement. Were he and Abbott friends? Luke had been as close to Abbott as anyone in their team. They'd protected each other like brothers, shared drinks like fraternity boys, crawled through swamps elbow to elbow; he'd always assumed they were friends. But finding Abbott had a wife tucked away all of these years—well, it made him wonder if anyone really knew Calvin Abbott.

Finally, he said, "Soon to be ex-military, ma'am."

She looked at him thoughtfully. "So, if not for the . . . accident, you'd be career army?"

Her question made him think in a way he hadn't since the "accident." "I really hadn't made a conscious decision— before. I think every Ranger takes each day, each assignment, as it comes. I suppose I would have stuck with it as long as physically possible. Then . . . I guess I'm not sure where I would have chosen to go from there." He absently rubbed his knee. "As for the moment, I'm—uncommitted."

"Do you still have military options?"

"I've been offered a few. I'm officially on extended medical leave, so I guess nothing is certain yet."

"I'm sure you'll make the right choice, when the time comes." She stood and picked up her empty soup bowl. "More soup, either of you?"

"None for me, thank you," Luke said, not having eaten half of what was in front of him already. He noticed Analise had finished hers. The flavor combination of tomato and ash was obviously something of an acquired taste.

"Thanks, Liv." Analise gathered her dirty dishes and got up. "It was great, as usual. I need to get back to my workshop. I have a shipment that has to go out tomorrow and the fountain for the park is only half-finished."

Luke stood.

"It was nice to meet you, Luke. Thank you for your concern for our family."

"Good-bye, Analise." He wondered if she would stay, now that she was a widow, or return to Jackson. He got the feeling that she was at home here: Five months had passed and he didn't see any moving boxes. There was also something in her voice when she spoke of Olivia and Cole as her family that said that she wasn't distancing herself from them just because Calvin was gone.

She deposited her dishes in the sink and left by the kitchen door.

Olivia returned to the table with a half-bowl of soup. "I know I look like a pig, but I'm supposed to bump up my vitamins. I prefer tomato soup to pills."

He sat back down. "Makes sense to me."

Between spoons of soup, she asked him a little more about himself. It felt just like when he was in high school and over at a buddy's house, the mom gently coaxing conversation in the hopes of gathering a single crumb of information about what was going on with her own kid.

He shared a few lighthearted remembrances that included

Calvin, wishing he could answer the unasked question: *What really happened to my son?*

Finally, he slid his chair back and said, "I can't thank you enough for lunch. I should be going."

"Oh, no, you won't. I'm not finished and you can't leave an old woman to eat alone. Sit tight there, I'll get some cookies." She got up and pulled open a drawer.

"I really don't need—"

"Shush." She set a Tupperware container in front of him and peeled off the lid. "Relax, Ana made these, not me."

He was about to argue further when the aroma of the cookies reached him. He hadn't eaten breakfast, and lunch . . . he looked at the half-eaten sandwich and near-full bowl of soup. What wafted from the plastic box was rich enough that it could be used to tempt a man on a hunger strike.

Olivia sat back down. "Don't feel bad, Ana's cookies do that to all men."

Her comment made him realize he'd closed his eyes and inhaled deeply. He reached for the biggest cookie, then took a bite. Oh, sweet Jesus, how could something so simple taste so good?

Olivia chuckled. "She won't tell what's in the recipe— I'm starting to think it's an illegal substance of some sort."

"I might be inclined to agree." He finished that one and reached for another.

"Maybe you should stick around for supper. Ana cooks." She gave him a wry grin. "She's a little more in tune with the finer details of the culinary arts than I am."

"That's a tempting offer, especially after these cookies, but I have to be getting on the road."

Her shoulders slumped slightly. "Cole will be so disappointed he didn't get to meet you."

"You'll have to tell him I'm sorry. Calvin thought a lot of his little brother." Apparently more than he thought of his wife.

Olivia wrapped her hand around her coffee cup and smiled wistfully. "Cole worshiped the ground Calvin trod upon." She sighed and looked into the depths of her coffee. "This has been particularly hard on him."

Luke didn't know what to say. *I'm sorry* was no more than an empty phrase said by everyone who opened their mouth around a grieving family. Instead of talking, he stood and put a hand on her shoulder and gave a warm squeeze.

He was surprised when her hand covered his and she said, "Sometimes, life's a bitch."

"Amen."

He went to the kitchen door. The rain had stopped, leaving the burgeoning greening of the landscape seeming to glow with new life. The chill wind still blew, the clouds scuttling quickly across the gray sky.

Olivia insisted on walking him to his car, her arms folded across her chest against the cold. They picked their way around mud puddles in silence. Just before he opened the door, she gave him a quick hug. "Thank you for accepting all of my misplaced mama hugs—kids may outgrow them, but a woman never outgrows the need to give them."

On impulse, he pulled out a scrap of paper and scribbled a number on it. "I'm not sure where I'm going to be, but this is my cell phone number. If you need anything, give me a call." He was fairly certain an obviously self-sufficient person like Olivia wouldn't be calling anyone for help, least of all a man she'd met only once. Still, offering made him feel better.

A shameful thought skittered across his mind. Maybe that was what this trip was all about—making *him* feel better. It was a thought he didn't want to examine too closely.

Taking the paper, she pressed her lips together, looking like she wanted to say something more.

"What is it?" he asked.

She gave her head a little shake. "It's too much."

Closing the door without getting in, he said, "Probably not. Just ask."

She sighed quietly and the words left her mouth with apparent reluctance. "Cole's father died when he was eight. And, well, you know how he adored his brother. Even though they rarely saw each other—well, maybe a little bit because of that—Calvin took a larger-than-life image in Cole's mind."

Luke braced himself. He'd asked for it, after all.

"If you could just stick around until he gets home from school—spend a few minutes with him. It'd mean so much." Even as she finished, she waved the thought away. "I know you need to go. I just was hoping . . ."

He had been antsy to drive away from this place since the moment he'd learned that Analise was Abbott's wife. In that second he could actually see himself tearing down the stone lane with a billow of dust in his wake, just like a Roadrunner cartoon. But where he was going once he reached the safety of the highway—that was another matter. Eventually he knew he'd end up in Glens Crossing, but planned on taking his time getting there, spending several days on the winding old highways, sorting out his thoughts.

There was no denying he could easily afford a half-day. But no way was he hanging around Analise until the kid came home. "I have a few things to do this afternoon," he lied. "What time does Cole get home?"

Her posture visibly relaxed. "You're a good boy." She

reached up and patted his cheek. He couldn't remember the last time someone patted his cheek like that. The simple gesture reached deep and touched his soul. His own mother had abandoned the family when he'd been in grade school. Maternal affection had left with her.

Olivia pulled her hand back and put it over her own heart. "He has soccer practice until six. So you might as well plan on being here for dinner." Before he could protest she stood on tiptoe and kissed his cheek. "Thank you." She hurried back to the house, as if trying to outrun the returning rain— or his refusal.

Luke drove away from Magnolia Mile feeling like he was stuck in quicksand. He wanted to be free of these women, not to have to look the fallout of his mistake in the eye again. But the more he tried to extricate himself, the deeper he'd been sucked in, that guilt he'd been trying to assuage dragging him down like an anchor.

Now he had to face the kid.

So, buck up, buddy. It's no more than you deserve.

If he could sit through six weeks of English after spying on Miss Clark, he could eat one more meal with Analise, a woman who tempted him to break his own moral code.

He'd see the brother. Then he'd be gone.

Chapter 3

Analise took her metal shears to a fresh piece of copper sheeting, hacking and cutting with furious determination. The rain had returned, drumming on the roof of the carriage house. The sound, normally soothing, only served as an irritant this afternoon.

Olivia certainly seemed smitten with Mr. Boudreau. Analise grudgingly admitted that she, too, might find him attractive—if she could get beyond the fact that just looking at him made her blush with shame. She couldn't help but wonder why, after insisting on discussing Calvin with only Olivia, he made an attempt to apologize to her at lunch.

Well, none of that mattered, she insisted to herself. The man was gone, she'd heard his car start a few minutes earlier.

She'd started to work without her gloves and now noticed her fingers were bleeding in several places. Dropping the metal and cutters onto the workbench with a clatter, she raised her face to look out the window and realized she'd been crying.

"Miz Abbott?"

She swiped the tears from her cheeks and turned toward the stairs. She hadn't even heard the newly hired man come up the steps. He'd stopped on the tread before the top, making his towering bulk less imposing. His pale moon-face made an eerie contrast to the dim light of the stairwell. "Yes, Roy?"

"I done finished unloading them bags of peat." He laid both of his arms on the railing that separated the loft from the stairwell, putting one hand on top of the other, then settling his chin onto them.

"Oh, good. I guess that's all we have for you today, then."

He straightened. A shadow of disappointment crossed his face, quickly transforming his rounded features from bovine to forbidding.

"Tomorrow," she added, hoping to take the edge off his displeasure, "if this rain clears up, we'll need you to shuttle the new nursery stock out to the display area."

His nearly black eyes, which seemed such a stark contrast to his milky skin and sandy hair, bore straight through her. "If'n it's rainin' you don't want me to come?"

His steady stare made her feel exposed, vulnerable. The man was as big as a mountain, after all. And he was looking at her like she was literally taking money from his pocket. "I'm sure we can find a few hours' work, rain or shine."

Roy had come looking for work two weeks ago. Magnolia Mile normally didn't take on extra help this early in the season, but Olivia knew the man was desperate, so she'd hired him. People in this town were always taking advantage of Olivia's good nature, calling her when any form of stray wandered into town. Reverend Hammond, who sent Roy here, was no exception. Olivia had justified hiring Roy saying that with the irrigation project at Hargrove Farms and that new plastics manufacturing plant opening up, there weren't going to be as many men looking for work this spring. They'd better take what they could when it was offered.

Still, she'd made it clear to Roy that the hours would be sketchy at first, telling him that once the season was in full swing, he'd probably be getting overtime. In fact, next week they had their first big job of the season at Holly Ridge County Park.

Analise knew they'd be strapped until sales started to flow next month. But Olivia insisted they'd manage; it would be criminal to turn away a soul in need.

But Analise wasn't so sure about this guy. There was no doubt he was in need. He drove a pickup truck that looked like it'd been the loser in a demolition derby and belched black smoke as it chugged and rumbled along the road. The springs had collapsed on the driver's side, making it look like Roy would be dumped out onto the pavement should the rusty door come open—or, more likely, fall off. Still, Analise had reservations about someone who blew into town on the wind, no matter what his story of woe.

That was another thing. The story. Apparently, Roy had poured his heart out to the reverend, saying he'd come to the Presbyterian church on Center Street because Jesus had guided him. He'd sinned in the past, been plagued by drink. He was from some Alabama dirt road intersection that offered no future. His sickly mama—who of course he'd cared for throughout her long illness—had died, "God rest her soul." Shortly thereafter, the trailer he'd been living in had been turned into confetti by a tornado. He'd taken it all as a sign from God that it was time to leave and find a new, more promising start.

He currently slept under the shell top in the bed of his truck.

Reverend Hammond felt the church should always shine in welcome, therefore the lights were left on behind the large stained-glass window at all times. When Roy drove into Grover and saw light shining through that window, he knew this was where he was meant to be.

Analise always had thought those lights were a bad idea.

Since Roy was just standing there looking at her, she added, "Pretty soon, business will be picking up and we'll be able to give you more hours."

Instead of going down the stairs, he climbed the last step. Moving in his normal, lumbering pace, he crossed the room and stopped right in front of her.

Without thinking, Analise wrapped her fingers around a piece of jagged metal on the table behind her, ready to snatch it up if need be.

He stood there looking at her for a long moment, then his big hand reached for her. "You got blood on your face."

Analise drew in a sharp breath and recoiled as he ran a thumb across her cheek.

"There." His hand dropped back to his side and he took a step backward. "See you tomorrow."

With her mouth dry and her heart beating like a crazed bird against a windowpane, she listened until she heard the shop door close behind him. Until this moment, she hadn't been aware just how uneasy Roy made her.

Hearing his old truck grind to a start, she closed her eyes and willed her heart to slow down. Then she went downstairs to the restroom and washed the drying lines of blood from her hands—and scrubbed her face until she'd erased his rough thumb's touch.

For the rest of the afternoon, Analise focused on shaping copper tubing into fanciful sculptures that doubled as garden sprinklers. As always, she found comfort in the rhythm of her work, in the satisfaction of creation.

She'd just shut off her torch when she heard Olivia call from downstairs.

Analise went to the top of the stairs and called, "I'm up here."

Olivia appeared at the bottom. "I'm running to the Piggly Wiggly. I thought we'd have that *I*-talian chicken Cole likes so much."

"Sure, that's fine." She started back to her work.

"Oh, Ana!"

Peering back down the stairs, she said, "Yes?"

"You'd better come on down early and get cleaned up before you cook dinner. We're having company."

"Reverend Hammond?" The man found more excuses to call at dinnertime. Analise chastised herself. His wife had recently died; he was lonely. The uncharitable thought crept into her mind, *Lonely* and *after Olivia.*

"No." Olivia started to edge away from the bottom of the stairs. "Luke's coming back to see Cole." She disappeared from view.

"Luke . . ."

Olivia's quick footfalls left the carriage house.

Analise closed her eyes. Suddenly Reverend Hammond's quiet yet incessant chatter didn't seem so bad.

Analise stared into her closet, unsure why she was so plagued by indecision. Normally, she reached blindly and wore whatever emerged in her hand. Not that there was all that much variety. Jeans. Knit tops. A few blouses. A pair of khakis. Her black dress slacks. The four "Jackson outfits" she'd brought with her to Grover were wrapped in plastic and shoved to the far end of the closet rod, where they'd been for the past eight years. She had supposed she'd need them for the rare occasion—funeral, wedding or a visit by a foreign dignitary.

She chuckled at that thought. What a turn her life had taken when she'd met Calvin. And, although things hadn't been the happily-ever-after she'd envisioned when she'd said "I do," all in all Calvin had saved her from a life that would undoubtedly have suffocated her, one filled with foreign dignitaries and stuffy political dinners. God, she'd been so close to traveling the road her grandmother had so carefully paved for her. The mere thought made goosebumps rise on her arms.

She rubbed them away, then pulled out a clean pair of jeans and the long-sleeved knit top that was hanging right next to it. After putting on the jeans, she hesitated before she took the top off the hanger. It used to be red, but had faded to a muted shade of rose. She'd bought it as a childish act of rebellion; throughout her entire life her grandmother had reminded her that redheads *cannot* wear red. Grandmother detested red hair. Mostly because her only child, Analise's father, had married a redhead who had asked for a vacation in Hawaii. To celebrate their fifth wedding anniversary, Hugh had given Rebecca that trip. Neither of Analise's parents returned from the island paradise. Their tour helicopter crashed in a mountain valley, killing everyone on board.

After studying the worn red shirt for a moment longer, Analise hung it back in the closet. Since this evening was about Cole, she went to her dresser and pulled out the ribbed turtleneck sweater he'd given her for Christmas. She told herself it had nothing to do with the fact that it was the most flattering piece of clothing she owned, the green just the right shade to intensify her eye color. She wore it for Cole—not company.

When she went down to the kitchen, Olivia was putting away the groceries. She looked at Analise and smiled. "You look very nice."

Analise couldn't decide if the smile was approval or censure. She quickly said, "I thought Cole would like it. He's been so . . . distant lately."

Olivia nodded and set a bottle of white wine on the counter.

"Wine? Are we celebrating something?"

Keeping her hands busy, Olivia shrugged. "Maybe. We'll see."

The woman was up to something. Analise could feel it in her bones. But she knew from experience, nothing would drag it out of her until she was damn good and ready.

After folding the last paper bag and putting it in the pantry, Olivia said, "I think I'll go change, too. My socks are soaked."

"If you'd wear regular shoes in the winter . . . You're going to catch a cold."

"Really, Ana, you know better than that. Colds are caused by a virus—not wet socks. I suppose next you're going to agree with Granny Lejeune that if you wash your hair during your period, it'll give you cramps." She grinned her crafty grin and left the kitchen.

Analise called after her, "I *do* wash my hair during my period and certainly have the cramps to prove it!"

Olivia's laughter echoed through the house. Analise listened to the comforting sound of her mother-in-law's soft footfalls on the stairs with the warm glow of belonging in her heart.

She set about preparing dinner, noticing with some irritation that Olivia had already set the table in the dining room instead of the kitchen. They didn't even eat in the dining room when Reverend Hammond came for Sunday dinner.

Once the chicken was simmering and the salad was chilling, she looked at the clock. It'd been forty-five minutes and Olivia hadn't come back downstairs. Analise wiped her hands on a dish towel and turned the fire down on the stove, then went up to check on her.

Olivia's bedroom door was half-open.

"Liv?" Analise called softly, but got no reply. She pushed the door open fully.

Olivia lay on the bed, dry socks on her feet. Analise paused and studied her for a moment. Did the skin around her closed eyes look more translucent than normal? "Olivia."

Olivia sucked in a deep draught of air. "Oh, my. Guess I drifted off." She sat up and swung her legs over the side of the bed. "Is Luke here?"

Analise shook her head, worry niggling at her. Liv didn't take naps. "Cole isn't home yet, either."

"Maybe practice ran long." Olivia looked at the bedside clock.

Analise glanced out the window. The setting sun was shining from the west, accentuating the dark underbellies of the remaining broken clouds. "Doubt it with this weather. Hope he showers in the locker room, he's going to be covered in mud."

The doorbell rang.

Analise jolted. She both loved and hated the old-fashioned, thumb-turn bell. It oozed Victorian charm and felt more natural in this house than an electronic chime, but the sharp, clattering ring always made her jump nearly out of her skin. This evening she seemed extra sensitive to it.

"That'll be Luke." Olivia hopped off the bed with her

usual sprightly energy and Analise's worry over her mother-in-law's health eased. As Olivia brushed past her, she said, "I'll let him in. You should put on a bit of lipstick before you come down."

"Why would I want . . ." she heard Olivia trotting down the stairs, and finished quietly to the empty room, "to do that?"

Feeling self-conscious about her appearance for the first time in what seemed like years, Analise looked into the mirror hanging over Olivia's dresser. She leaned closer and rolled her lips, biting them to bring in more color.

Lipstick. She snorted.

As she straightened her back, her gaze fell on the framed photograph of her and Calvin on their wedding day. He wore his army uniform. Analise wore a simple cocktail dress of deep purple and a matching bouquet of deep-hued orchids and white lilies. Back then, she'd been more comfortable in full Elizabeth Arden makeup, heels and a cocktail dress than in sneakers and jeans.

She studied Calvin's smiling face and touched a finger to the glass. He'd been the most handsome man she'd ever laid eyes on. When he smiled at her, he literally took her breath away. She remembered the way her heart raced when she heard his voice. How recklessly she'd given herself to him. God, she'd been so young—so naive.

Looking at the photo, her heart ached with shame. She set it back down on the dresser, vowing that Olivia would never know the reality of her son's marriage. Analise loved this family in a way she hadn't dreamed possible while growing up in her grandmother's dispassionate house. But she knew now. Love meant sacrifice. Silence was little enough to give the woman who'd shown her how to live.

Why did Luke Boudreau have to show up now, just when

she'd managed to bury her sin deeply enough that it didn't echo through every waking moment? With his arrival, that sin bobbed back to the surface, making it difficult to look into Olivia's eyes.

Analise left the room, closing the door behind her, looking forward to the end of this evening.

Luke stood on the porch, listening to the water continue to drip from the trees. The sharp pain in his back had eased with the passing of the storm. Since his injury, he'd discovered a new belief in predicting weather by body aches. In fact, he'd found it to be more accurate than most meteorologists.

To his relief, Olivia, not Analise, answered the door. Greeting him warmly, she bypassed the living room, ushering him to the rear of the house.

She motioned for him to take the same seat at the kitchen table that he'd occupied at noon. "I thought we'd sit in here, since Ana has to do"—she waved her fingers in the air—"something or other to the food right before we eat it." She winked. "It's all very complicated."

She poured three glasses of white wine and carried two to the table.

"I'm sure it is. Can't cook myself—other than peanut butter and jelly and microwaving something frozen from a box."

"A man shouldn't have to cook." She paused. "Well, neither should a woman who isn't willing. Luckily, we have Ana."

At just that moment, Analise walked into the room. Luke looked up with a greeting that froze on his lips. She looked incredible in that green sweater and her hair down. All of his mental convincing that he'd imagined the spark she brought to life in him disappeared in a flash of smoke.

"Did I hear my name mentioned?" Analise asked in a light tone. She went straight for the glass of wine Olivia had left on the counter and took a long sip.

"Olivia was just telling me how lucky she is to have you."

Analise's gaze softened. She leaned down and put her arm around Olivia, squeezing tight. "I'm the lucky one."

Luke's heart constricted with something he hadn't felt in years, the disquieting absence of family. He and Calvin had both walked away from the loving warmth of their families, convinced that theirs was a noble duty, a more exciting life. But in leaving, they had distanced themselves in ways they couldn't possibly have predicted. And the two of them had obviously reacted very differently. Although Luke's contact with his family had been sporadic, their constant presence in his thoughts kept him focused, motivated. But Calvin had emotionally detached himself from his home life.

Luke had seen it in many special ops soldiers, men who dealt with the precariousness and inherent danger of the job by isolating their civilian life from their military duties. For some, the thought of someone waiting at home made them too cautious to do the job right.

He watched Analise and wondered yet again how Calvin could have shut her so completely out of his life.

She turned around, wooden spoon in hand, and said, "Dinner's ready. I wonder why Cole's so late."

Olivia looked at the clock. "Maybe I should call Zach's house and see if he's home yet."

"Good idea."

Olivia went to the telephone.

Luke tried to picture Calvin's little brother. Would he be a younger version of Calvin, with Calvin's good looks and ability to charm women without effort? Calvin had been a man's man, but women couldn't keep their eyes—and in many instances, their hands—off of him.

With that thought, Luke cast a guilty glance at Analise, who had her back to him once again, concentrating on her cooking. He just couldn't imagine the freedom in that marriage being a two-way street. Analise seemed much too . . . wholesome. Besides, how do you cheat on your husband in a little town like Grover, while living under the same roof as your mother-in-law?

Somewhere behind his own racing thoughts, he heard Olivia talking on the phone. He couldn't stop looking at Analise, trying to see what was going on inside her.

She must have felt his gaze on her back, because she turned with an expectant look on her face.

Luke shifted in his chair.

"Look," she said, leaning against the counter with her hands behind her, "I'm sorry I snapped at you at lunch—"

"No." He stood. "I'm the one who owes you an apology. I shouldn—" Now he was looking in her eyes and the floor seemed to vibrate under his feet.

She waved his apology away with a smile. "Let's just call things even and have a nice dinner with Cole. He really needs . . ." She sighed, looking distant and more bereft than he'd seen her. "I don't really know what he needs, I guess."

Luke had the strongest urge to take her hand, to comfort her. Instead, he sat back down, putting her out of reach.

Olivia returned to the table and sat down heavily. "Zach's mother said he's been home for an hour. I wonde—"

The sharp clattering ring of the doorbell interrupted her and she jerked her gaze to Analise. Luke didn't miss the anxious, wide-eyed look they gave one another.

Analise started for the door. "I'll get it."

Olivia followed. "Excuse us for a minute, Luke."

He heard the door open. A man's lowered voice drifted down the hall. Then he heard Olivia say, "Thank you so much, Dave."

Luke leaned in his chair, trying to get a view of the front door, but couldn't quite see around the doorframe without getting up.

The front door closed.

Analise sounded like she was giving a quiet, hissing scolding.

Suddenly the crash of breaking glass echoed down the hall, followed by a loud thud.

"Cole!" Olivia sounded frightened.

Luke jumped out of his chair and ran to the front of the house.

Chapter 4

Analise and Olivia were both on their knees beside a tall, jeans-clad form who had to be Cole. The boy lay face down on the braided rug in the foyer. A shattered vase sparkled like ice crystals around him; the marble-topped table on which it used to sit had toppled onto its side.

Luke pulled up just short of the trio.

Neither woman looked up.

Analise grabbed Cole by the shoulders and tried to turn him over. The kid groaned and mumbled something unintelligible into the rug, but didn't move.

Just as Olivia reached to help, Luke stepped in. "Here, let me."

Ignoring his painful knee, he knelt beside Analise and rolled the boy onto his back. The kid's eyes were open, but far from focused. There was a bloody split on his forehead and he reeked of beer.

Olivia let out a little moan. Then she said, "I'll get some ice."

After she disappeared into the kitchen, Luke asked Analise, "He didn't drive like this, did he?"

She raised worried green eyes to meet his. "No. He wouldn't."

Cole tried to sit up, then let his head drop back to the floor and closed his eyes.

Analise put a hand on his shoulder to keep him still. "Dave—he's a county deputy and an old friend of Calvin's—found him parked out at the old Lejeune place and brought him home."

"He was alone?"

She nodded.

Luke heard the sniffle she tried to conceal and decided not to ask how she supposed Cole had *planned* on getting home without driving. "Was it just beer?"

"Dave said Cole swore it was—there weren't any other bottles around." Rolling her lips inward, she paused. "I don't understand it. He's never come home like this. He was supposed to be at soccer practice."

Olivia returned with the ice. She stood there for a moment, just looking down at her son with a troubled expression on her face. "Shouldn't we move him someplace?"

"The couch," Analise suggested. "I don't think we can haul him all the way upstairs." She stood up. "I'll take his shoulders. Liv, you can get his feet."

Olivia started to hand the towel filled with ice to Luke, but he moved to Cole's head. "I'll take his shoulders."

Analise glanced toward Luke's knee.

"Come on," he prompted before she could say something about how he shouldn't be lifting.

She shifted to Cole's feet and grabbed his ankles.

Luke said, "On three." Then he gave the count and they lifted the boy and carried him into the living room.

Two steps before they reached the couch, Luke thought his knee was going to buckle. Sheer determination kept him moving. Six months ago he could have picked this kid up, thrown him over his shoulder and carried him to town without so much as breaking a sweat. Now his face beaded with perspiration after doing little more than dragging him fifteen feet.

Cole landed on the cushions a little harder than Luke had planned. The boy moaned and put his hand to his forehead.

A fat black cat jumped up onto the back of the couch, seemingly coming from nowhere. It folded its paws beneath its chest and peered intently down at Cole.

Olivia knelt and gently moved Cole's hand away from the cut, dabbed the blood from his forehead with a wet cloth, then placed ice on the rapidly rising goose egg. "Well, this certainly isn't making a very good first impression." She said it with a wobbly smile; Luke could hear the slight quiver in her voice that said she was more upset than she was letting on.

The cat growled deep in its throat. The unusual sound of it bothered Luke. When he looked up, the cat was staring directly at him. The message in its green-gold eyes was anything but welcoming.

"Shush, Pandora," Olivia whispered.

Luke cleared his throat and said, "I should be going—let you take care of him."

Olivia jumped to her feet. She must have moved too fast, because she blinked and swayed a little bit, like she was dizzy. After a second, she said, "No. Please stay. Dinner's ready. We can't send you away hungry."

Cole groaned and sat up, the ice falling to the floor with a thump. He lurched to his feet, pushing Olivia aside. Luke could see where things were headed, but couldn't maneuver out of the way quickly enough.

Cole took two steps, then threw up all over Luke.

•   •   •

"Cole really isn't like that," Analise said, pausing to look at Luke at the upstairs bathroom door. She handed him a pair of Calvin's old army sweats that Cole had insisted upon keeping when they gave away the few clothes Calvin had kept at Magnolia Mile.

"Like what?" He was close, looking steadily down at her in a way that made her want to run away and step nearer at the same time. His piercing gaze kept her nailed firmly in place.

"Trouble." She took a deep breath. "He's a decent student—not great, but always manages to keep his grades up for sports. He has a sweet girlfriend. His friends aren't troublemakers. I don't want you to think he's . . . wild."

She waited for him to make some comment, to tell her that he could see Cole was a great kid. But he just stood there looking at her. No, not *at* her, into her.

Finally she said, "The towels on the racks are fresh. Just hand out your clothes once you get them off." As she said it, her gaze ran across his chest and shoulders. It had been a long time since she'd put her hands on a set of well-muscled male shoulders, and Luke's were extraordinarily tempting.

She looked back into his eyes.

Oh, God. He'd seen her thoughts. And why not? Olivia always told her she'd never make a good liar—or politician; her true feelings were always written all over her face.

Luke wasn't going to let her off the hook. He just stood there, looking at her with speculation.

Her cheeks grew warm, but she held his gaze. "Really, you should get in that shower. You stink."

He laughed and it transformed his face. From the first moment she'd met him, his face bore the weight of solemnity, even when he smiled. Now a boyishness she'd never have guessed resided in him burst forth. "You know how to make a guy feel like one of the family." He stepped back and closed the bathroom door.

After a minute, the door opened a few inches and the smelly, folded shirt and slacks appeared. For a moment, she just stared at Luke's lean arm and strong hand.

"Hey, you still there?" he called, moving one sky-blue eye to the crack in the door.

Quickly, she grabbed the clothes. "You army guys— always tucking and folding, never leaving a wet towel in a heap on the bathroom floor."

"You should thank the army. Most women train their men for years to get them this organized."

She grabbed the clothes, a knot of resentment forming in her throat. She hadn't spent enough time living under the same roof with "her man" to even begin to shape his behavior. Not that anyone, or anything, could alter his course once Calvin had set his mind to it. As for *thanking* the army . . .

She must have snatched the clothes more gruffly than she'd intended, because the door opened a bit farther, allowing Luke's head and shoulders to come into full view. Thankfully, he kept the rest of himself tucked behind the door.

He said, "You don't need to go to any trouble. Just throw that stuff in a garbage bag."

Immediately she felt ashamed. "Don't be silly. It's no trouble." She turned quickly and headed toward the stairs, before she lost her battle with the temptation to reach out and touch his bare shoulder.

My God, she wasn't normally like this.

There was a loud thud in the bathroom before she started down the steps. She paused, listening. Had he fallen? With that knee, he never should have been carrying Cole.

Three rapid steps thumped across the bathroom floor, followed by something brushing against the wall.

Nope, he was definitely still on his feet. Analise went back to the bathroom door.

"Shit!" Luke kept the curse mostly under his breath.

What in the hell was he doing in there?

"Come here, you little . . ."

It sounded like he was wrestling something. "Lu—"

"A-ha!" he yelled. "Got you, you little bugger!"

"Luke! Are you all right in there?"

He flung open the door. He stood there, buck naked, holding a wriggling towel like a sack in one hand, with an expression of victory on his face. "I got it!"

"G-got what?" Analise tried to keep her curious gaze from traveling below his chin.

"Rabbit! Somehow a rabbit got in here."

"Oh, no." She dropped his soiled clothes on the floor and reached for the towel.

He moved it away from her grasp. "It might bite. I'll take it outside."

Unable to do more than stutter, Analise put a hand on his chest to keep him from going farther. It was a mistake; warmth shot from her hand straight to the pit of her belly.

It also made him realize he was naked.

He glanced down with an expression of horror on his face. "Oh!" He jerked the bunny-filled towel in front of him and stepped back into the bathroom. "Sorry. I didn't . . ." The door closed.

Momentarily, he returned with a towel around his waist.

The rabbit gave two quick, powerful jerks, drawing Analise's attention away from her embarrassment.

"I-it's S-Skippy." She took the twitching towel with both hands, held it against her chest and knelt down on the floor.

"It's all right," she said softly. The rabbit wiggled wildly, leaping from her arms the second she made an opening for it to escape. It tore down the hall and disappeared down the steps in a flash of brown fur and white tail.

"It lives in the house?"

"Ye—" Analise's voice dried up when she turned her head to look up at him. His shoulders were even more appealing from this vantage point, broad over a slim waist. He put a hand out to help her stand back up.

She was close enough to feel the heat of his breath on her cheek. To keep her gaze from locking with his—which felt much too dangerous at this proximity and his state of undress—she focused on the scar on the side of his neck. It was even pinker from his exertion and pulsed slightly with his heartbeat.

They stood for a long moment. She felt as if she were trying to breathe in a vacuum, the closeness of his near-naked body burning away all oxygen in the atmosphere.

Finally, she forced her eyes to meet his with a light-hearted grin and said, "Don't worry, he's housebroken. Liv found him when he was so tiny he fit in the palm of your hand." She made herself stand there and converse as if she hadn't just seen him naked—as if he weren't still one towel away from being so again. What she felt like doing was running to her own room and locking the door, a little part of her wanting to savor the moment, while her conscience simultaneously scolded her into shame. "She fed him from an eyedropper, he grew up in the house and now he thinks he's a cat. Has a litter box and everything."

Luke looked over his shoulder and perused the bathroom. "Any other critters I should know about before I traumatize more pets?"

Stepping slightly away, Analise said, "The mockingbird

stays in the carriage house, there's a goose Olivia hatched
from an abandoned egg that hangs around the back yard—
that one has a nasty temperament, you might want to steer
clear—we have four cats and, of course, you've met Rufus."

"No gators?" he asked with a smile. Analise noticed for
the first time that he had a dimple in one cheek.

"We don't have gators around here," she said smartly,
and pulled the bathroom door closed. Once it was safely
latched behind her, she sagged against it for a second, her
heart working overtime in her chest. Her hands were trembling and parts of her she'd thought long dead had sparked
to life.

Shame on me. No better than a Peeping Tom.

After a minute, she picked up Luke's clothes and headed
downstairs.

Skippy had a little hutch in the laundry room, which was
located in the old back porch. Analise found him with his
body shoved back in the corner as far as he could manage.
She knelt down and whispered to him, "Yeah, I know just
how you feel."

The rabbit's nose twitched and he turned around, presenting her with his tail.

"Hey, I saved you. He was going to put you outside with
the foxes!"

She started the washer and dropped Luke's soiled clothes
in. Then she went to the stove to see if the dinner was
salvageable.

Moving, she had to keep moving, to prevent her thoughts
from straying to places they had no business going.

Carefully lifting the lid on the pan, she was relieved not
to smell scorched cream sauce. Luckily, the chicken hadn't
overcooked to the point it had to be used as a rawhide for
Rufus. Not that she had any appetite at the moment.

She'd meant it when she'd told Luke that Cole was a good kid. But lately she'd begun to worry. His brother's death weighed heavily on him, that she knew. And he seemed to be deliberately distancing himself from Olivia—more than normal teenage separation. But who could blame him? Love was risky, in ways most people his age never have to realize. His father died. His brother died. It was as if he'd decided to insulate himself from further grief by not caring.

Analise had committed herself to making Cole understand that caring was as essential to life as breathing—and that she'd always be there for him. She supported him, careful to always give suggestions, not recrimination, to listen without judgment. She had to admit that sometimes it stung when Cole worshiped Calvin-the-Flawless, idolizing him in ways that no human could possibly live up to—certainly not the all-too-human Calvin. After all, *she'd* been here with Cole, day in and day out, smoothing out the rough patches, bandaging scrapes. Calvin was more legend than an actual participant in Cole's life. His substance was that of quick visits, stories and photographs. Still, Cole felt his brother's loss, so she'd try to make up for it in any way she could.

Her extra efforts had seemed to be working—at least she'd thought so until today.

Today was just a slip, she assured herself, a misstep. Something had happened to make Cole do this. She resolved to spend the day with him tomorrow and help him sort things out, to get past what was troubling him.

A few minutes later, Luke came downstairs. From the corner of her eye, with his size and in those old sweats, she almost thought it was Calvin come back to haunt her. Then she looked at him fully and the similarity immediately vanished. She breathed out a sigh of relief and took stock of their differences. Luke was nice-looking, well built—her mind flashed the image of him nude—very well built. But Calvin had been heart-stopping, his wide smile the most arresting she'd ever seen.

Her gaze traveled to Luke's feet and she burst out laughing.

He looked down. "What?"

"I've never seen anyone as . . . as *unnerdly* as you wear sweats with black socks and dress shoes."

He looked down, then back up at her with his palms raised and a grin on his face. "'Unnerdly'? Guess I'll take that as a compliment to my masculinity."

"Oh, yeah." It came out as nearly a purr. My God, she didn't *purr*.

In light of their most recent encounter, she really had to measure her tone more carefully. "Um . . . I mean . . ." God, he was going to think she was flirting with him. "Would you like more wine?" *Oh, man, that was worse.* She'd better just shut up before she dug herself a deeper hole.

"I really should get out of here. I've imposed enough. You have your hands full tonight." He cast a glance overhead, toward Cole's room.

"But your clothes aren't done yet." The words came out sounding a little more pleading than she'd intended. As much as she'd wanted him gone earlier today, her curiosity wanted him to stay now. Was it just because she'd seen him naked? Had she become that depraved?

He shrugged. "I can come back tomorrow and pick them up."

Footfalls sounded on the stairs and they both turned toward the hallway. Olivia's energetic pace of just an hour ago had slowed as she entered the kitchen.

She said, "He's asleep. Dropped right off during one of my all-time best lectures." She shook her head. "And I really had a head of steam worked up . . . what a waste. But tomorrow . . ." Looking at Luke, she took a deep breath, then said, "Now that you're clean and comfy, let's feed you."

"I was just telling Analise that I should leave. I can come by tomorrow for my clothes—"

"Nonsense! We're not wasting this delicious meal. And of course you'll come by tomorrow, Cole owes you an apology."

A bit of Skippy's trapped-rabbit look appeared in Luke's eyes. Analise could see he wanted to be finished with his obligation here. And she couldn't blame him. Cole's scene had added to the awkwardness that began building the moment Luke caught her dancing in the greenhouse. Then the Skippy-and-the-naked-man incident. . . . No wonder he wanted to get out of here.

"Dinner does smell great," he said.

Analise gave him points for gallantry.

Olivia took his half-empty wine glass and topped it off. "Just have a seat and I'll get the salad, while Ana takes up the chicken."

As they began dinner in the shadow of the evening's embarrassments, Analise toyed with her salad and kept her gaze lowered. Luke opened his mouth only to compliment Analise on her cooking. He did it so often that she wanted to kick him under the table. Olivia spent the first minutes of the meal in thoughtful silence.

Although avoidance was never Olivia's approach, Analise had begun to think the meal might pass without touchy conversation.

Then Olivia's mood took an abrupt turn. She smiled and

said, "Luke, we didn't get to see much of Calvin during the year before the accident. Maybe you could fill us in on what he'd been up to."

In the first unguarded moment, Analise saw something like panic cross Luke's features. His gaze quickly darted to her face, then just as quickly jerked away. He took a drink of water, then wiped his mouth with a napkin.

Keeping his gaze on Olivia, he said, "I'm sure he would have been in closer contact if we hadn't been deployed most of the year. No sooner did we get back from one assignment than we were ordered to a different part of the globe. We spent a good deal of time in and out of the Middle East and South America."

Olivia put her hand on the table and leaned forward. "No. I didn't mean his work. I want a sense of his day-to-day life, his friendships. Did he read any books, what did he do when off duty, did he still like warm Dr Pepper, was he still playing his guitar? That sort of thing."

Her eyes took on the look of remembrance when she added, "You know, Ana and I gave him a notebook computer for his last birthday, hoping he'd be able to e-mail us." She smiled absently. "He didn't even have time to take it out of the box. It came home unopened."

Luke sat silent for a moment before he answered. My God, hadn't Calvin kept in touch at all? As for his day-to-day activities, Luke could share those without a problem, but it was his nighttime exploits that needed censoring.

He said, "He had a warm Dr Pepper with breakfast every day—even when we were in a place with refrigeration and ice available." He made a look of distaste. Dr Pepper tasted like medicine to Luke, and he viewed *warm* Dr Pepper as a device of self-torture.

The look on Analise's face said she agreed.

"His guitar . . ." Luke paused. Mostly Calvin used the guitar to seduce women. He had a whole Adam Sandler-ish routine he unleashed in bars—got the ladies loosened right up. "He didn't really have much time for it.

"Like I said," he added quickly, "we didn't have a lot of down time."

Olivia nodded, a ghost of a reminiscent smile on her face.

Analise shifted in her chair. The stern set of her lips reminded Luke of his father's when he was disappointed in Luke's childhood behavior.

"Of course," Luke went on, trying to divert the conversation away from Calvin's negligence in family communications, "Calvin was always the practical joker. We counted on him to counterbalance the intensity of the job—to liven up those long boring stretches between activity. One time he actually met a foreign prince with "BillyBob" teeth and an eye patch. Sat through an entire dinner and never once broke." As Luke told the story, he realized that Calvin used his humor as a curtain to hide behind. By diverting the attention to the frivolous, he never had to deal with the deeper emotional issues.

"That's our Calvin," Olivia said with a loving smile. "Ana, tell Luke about how you two met."

Analise bit her lower lip for a moment. Her eyes closed briefly. Obviously, the memory was tainted with sadness now that she was a widow.

"I was at a dinner at the governor's mansion." She directed her gaze to Luke. "Back in Jackson, I was eyebrow-deep in politics. Not a player, just window dressing." She fiddled with her spoon. "Calvin was a special guest, he'd just gotten everyone's attention by whipping a tablecloth out from under a table full of crystal. The next thing I knew, I was acting as his 'beautiful assistant' as he coerced the most stodgy woman in all of Jackson into playing along with a sleight of hand that I never did figure out how he accomplished. He was such a breath of fresh air, so lively and irreverent—"

"And handsome," Olivia interjected.

"Oh, yes, he *was* handsome." She gave her mother-in-law a brilliant smile and patted her hand. "He had me mesmerized from that moment on. We were married three weeks later."

Luke thought "mesmerized" was an odd word to use when describing meeting the love of your life. But what did he know about women's feelings? He said, "Love at first sight. Just like the movies."

Analise sighed and played with the condensation on her water glass. "I guess you could say that. Only without the 'happily ever after.' " She stood abruptly. "I'm going to check on Cole."

Luke stood as she left the room. When he sat back down, Olivia was looking at him curiously.

After a moment she said, "The separation was hard for Ana."

Luke's mouth was dry. "I didn't mean to upset her."

Olivia blew through tight lips and waved a hand in the air. "It wasn't you. Life sometimes deals us a hand we didn't expect. It just takes some getting used to. Ana's still adjusting." She chuckled quietly. "I suppose that's what life is, one big adjustment."

"I guess you're right."

When Analise returned, she'd regained her composure. "He's still sleeping. Probably will until tomorrow." She sat back down across from Luke, but didn't pick up her fork to finish her meal.

Luke took the cue and placed his napkin beside his plate. "That was a fine meal. I really do need to get going."

Analise didn't seem to notice the compliment. She jumped up and began to clear the table.

"Thank you both for dinner." He stood. "I'll help clean up."

Olivia said, "That'd be nice." At the same moment Analise said, "No!"

The two women stared at each other for a long moment. Then Olivia said, "Yes. I suppose we've taken up enough of your time. We really do appreciate your visit."

Some of the tension left Analise's shoulders when she saw Olivia wasn't going to force him to stay longer.

"The meal was great," Luke said for the thousandth time. That urge to kick him was back. But, she reminded herself, he was just being polite. They *had* put the poor guy through the wringer today, and he'd behaved admirably in the situation.

He carried a load of dirty dishes with him as they returned to the kitchen. After setting them on the counter, he moved to the back door—leaving like family, not company. Analise wasn't sure how she felt about that.

Olivia said, "I guess we'll see you in the morning, then."

Analise felt like they were holding his clothes hostage just to get him to return.

"Good night," he said. "And thanks again for the meal."

"Luke," Olivia called to him as he put his hand on the doorknob.

He stopped.

"I really do appreciate you coming. It's been a greater help than you know."

Seriousness again claimed his face as he looked back at them. He paused before he opened the door, looking like he was going to say something. Then he just tipped his head and walked out into the night.

Olivia sighed loudly. "That boy is eating himself alive with guilt."

Analise started to rinse the dishes. "Cole?"

"Oh, no. Not Cole. He's too sick at the moment to think about anything but himself. Luke. And I'm not sure he's going to find his way around it."

"What do you mean?"

Olivia stood thoughtfully for a second, then said, "I'm going to go put his clothes in the dryer, then check on Cole."

"What are you going to do about him?" Analise worried that harsh punishment and gruff words might just drive Cole further away. From the look on his face when Dave brought him to the door, she knew he was sorry for his misbehavior.

"I'm going to make damn sure he understands that lying to me is the very worst thing he could possibly do. The drinking was stupid and dangerous, but the lying . . . Something deeper than experimentation is at the root of this. I'm going to find out exactly what's going on."

She left the room and Analise had no better idea what Cole's punishment was going be than she did five minutes ago. But the look in Olivia's eye warned her not to push right now.

Opening the back door, she called for Rufus. She didn't wait; the dog always took his own sweet time in coming. By the time she had his dish filled she heard a soft chuffing at the door.

"Come on in, big boy."

Rufus paused as he passed her, giving her a long look with those droopy brown eyes. She'd swear she saw accusation there. Lying was the worst affront Olivia could imagine—and Analise had been guilty of that crime for years. Maybe Rufus knew, maybe he could sense what was truly in her heart.

And maybe he's just a dog that happened to look up at you, you idiot. She tried to tone down her imagination, and went back to work on the dishes.

After his dinner, Rufus dozed in front of the stove, where Analise tripped over him every time she put a dish away. For some reason, he was staying uncommonly close this evening.

She hung up the dish towel and realized she still felt too restless to watch TV or read. Olivia had disappeared upstairs after putting the clothes in the dryer and not returned.

"Come on, Rufus. We're going for a little walk."

He opened one skeptical eye and blew out a long huffing breath. Unlike most dogs, the phrase "go for a walk" did not ignite rapture and joy in Rufus's heart. He didn't jump up and prance impatiently at the door while she got her jacket. He didn't whine with eagerness.

He closed his eyes and tried to ignore her.

"Really, Rufus. We're going." She opened the door.

Rufus sighed loudly, then lumbered to his feet.

"Good boy."

Tilting his head slightly, he gave her a grudging half-wag of the tail and went out the door.

Olivia had chosen not to install outdoor lighting around the property, worrying over disturbing the natural habitat more than necessary. So when Analise started down the stone lane, she shuffled along in a state of temporary blindness until her eyes adjusted. Even after, she couldn't make out anything farther away than Rufus's tail.

She remembered the first summer she'd been here, how unsettling the complete darkness had been. Growing up in "civilization," there had always been some form of ambient light. Analise hadn't known what true darkness was until she moved to Magnolia Mile.

Here, you could step away from the ring of light that spilled from the windows of the house and be swallowed completely in darkness. Trees, when leafed out, blocked most of the moonlight even during a full moon. That's one reason she always took Rufus—his nighttime vision was much better than hers, plus he had that bloodhound nose to work with. It wasn't that she feared criminals, not here in Grover. But the wildlife around here was really . . . wild.

They were about half way down the lane to the paved road when Rufus stopped dead in his tracks so quickly that Analise ran into the back of him. He didn't seem to notice her bumping him, but kept his eye on a thick stand of shrubbery off to their right. He growled low and deep in his throat.

"What is it, boy?" she whispered. "Raccoon?"

A rustling much too large to be caused by a lone raccoon, or even a whole family of them, came from the bushes.

Rufus growled louder and pressed himself against her leg. It was obvious he really wanted to tear into the bushes and flush out whatever was hiding there, but she knew from experience he would not leave her alone.

Analise stood perfectly still, listening. Her heart sped up slightly, even as she assured herself there wasn't anything wandering these woods that would cause her harm.

Suddenly whatever it was broke and ran in the opposite direction, crashing like a cow through the underbrush.

Rufus jumped from side to side, baying wildly. He took about three hesitant steps toward the sound, then let loose with his biggest, deepest bark.

"Okay, buddy, I think you've taught that deer a lesson." *It had to have been a deer.*

He walked backward toward her, still sniffing the air and making whining noises. Analise couldn't hear anything moving in the brush.

"It's gone. Let's go." She patted her leg and began walking toward the road.

After a second's hesitation, Rufus trotted to catch up. His ears remained on alert, his nose snuffing loud enough that Analise said, "You're making such a racket with that snout of yours, we couldn't hear if a slavering, growling bear was following us."

He ignored her and kept his vigilant watch.

When they reached the end of the lane, Analise turned to the right, toward the curvy part of the road that led to the creek. Just as they rounded the first ninety-degree turn, she saw lights come on; a vehicle was parked down the road. The brake lights flared, then the reverse light flashed before the driver put the car in drive. It took off so quickly that she heard gravel pinging against the undercarriage.

Rufus howled.

"Shush!" She put a hand on the dog and felt his hackles were up. "It was just somebody fishing down at the creek." *Or could it have been someone nosing around in the woods, sounding like a herd of deer?* She shook off the idea and tried to slow her breathing.

They stood there for a moment longer, Rufus prancing and chuffing, Analise listening and peering into the darkness with her heart still beating a little too fast. "Well, I think that's enough of a walk for tonight." She turned around. "Let's get some exercise and jog back home." She took off and Rufus fell in beside her.

When they reached the lane to the house, she slowed to a walk. *This is ridiculous; I can't even let the dog know I'm scared.* She realized she'd been living behind a façade of self-sufficient stoicism for so long, she didn't even know how to let it down when she was alone with Rufus. She'd thought it would be easier, that she wouldn't have so many secrets to hide, now that Calvin was gone.

But she was wrong.

Chapter 5

It was a good forty-minute drive back to the motel where Luke had spent the previous night. Grover had no motel, so he'd kept the room, unsure how much driving he'd feel like doing once he'd been to see Abbott's family. Now he was glad he'd held on to it, even though it might have made things easier if he'd had his stuff all packed in the car. Then he would have had a change of clothes and wouldn't have to go back to Magnolia Mile again tomorrow.

His intentions had been to pay respects, then head home, get his own life back in order and decide what to do about his future. However, the sense of closure he'd been looking for still eluded him. As he drove back toward the motel, he realized every step seemed to be taking him in quite the opposite direction. He felt the burden of Abbott's death more acutely now than he had yesterday.

Again he asked himself, what had he hoped to gain by coming here? Absolution?

He now knew there would be no absolution. But he also knew he could not have gone on with his life without making this trip. Perhaps if he'd found what he'd expected in Grover, a grieving mother who exhibited only anger and bitterness, it would have been easier to walk away. Maybe that's what he wanted, someone to punish him with hateful words and biting rejection.

Instead, he'd found warmth and acceptance—and a beautiful young widow he hadn't known existed. A woman who sparkled with life, who fired a fierce sense of protectiveness that he hadn't felt in years, not since he and his sisters were young.

Heartburn built just below his breastbone. Absently, he rubbed his chest. His fingers tingled as they ran over Calvin's sweatshirt. He wondered, when was the last time Calvin had worn these clothes? When was the last time the man had held his wife? A woman like Analise deserved to be held and sheltered. And damn Calvin for being such an unfaithful ass. If Analise had been Luke's wife . . .

The thought jarred him. He had no business judging Calvin's personal life, no business at all.

For the next few miles, Luke tried to concentrate on other things. He wondered if he would still feel so out of kilter once he reached Glens Crossing in a couple of days. How would his dad's bar look, now that he'd been forced to remodel after lightning struck during a storm a while back? Did his old friend Peter's summerhouse on the lake still look the same? Was the floating island they used to race to still anchored off the pier? Would Glens Crossing be more timely than Grover and have all of its holiday decorations down and stored away in the courthouse attic?

That thought brought him back to yesterday morning, when the resemblance between his own childhood home and Calvin's had struck him like a fist in the chest. Calvin had ridden his bicycle on those quiet streets, had gone to that high school, made touchdowns on that football field, had first gotten laid when he was a freshman by a senior girl named Candy in the parking lot behind the Dixie Drive-in.

Funny, Luke thought, the only details Calvin had shared about his life were childhood memories nearly interchangeable with those of any small-town kid mixed with the usual bawdy locker-room stories. What Luke wouldn't give to be able to rewind the clock and ask the questions that hadn't seemed important until he met Analise and Olivia.

He pulled into the lot of the Stargazer Motel. As there was only one other car in the lot, he was able to park right in front of room number thirteen. When he'd asked for the room farthest from the office, he'd drawn a suspicious look from the clerk, a small woman who appeared to be in her sixties. When she called her husband from the back office, Luke had been obliged to explain that he had nightmares and didn't want to disturb the owners, whose residence was attached to the office. The woman had then tipped her head sympathetically and handed him the key to room thirteen.

Now, as he glanced at the bold black number spotlighted by the headlight beams on the door, his palms began to sweat and a clamminess crept over him. Since "the incident," as his superior officer called it, Luke dreaded the coming of night. In deepest night, silence allowed the sounds to creep forward from his memory; unguarded regret amplified the chaos of that last mission until he awakened with sweat on his forehead and a scream stuck in his throat.

Now he had even more fuel for his nightmares, a family torn apart, wounded and set adrift by his actions.

Thirteen was well suited to the torment that awaited him when he laid his head on the pillow behind that door. He shut off the engine and went inside with heavy footsteps.

•　　•　　•

When Cole opened his eyes, his room was dark. He squinted at the bedside clock. At first the red numbers were too blurry to read, then they came into better focus. It was only eleven, not the middle of the night as he'd expected. Eleven. Someone was sure to still be up.

He turned onto his side, feeling as if his bed were a swinging hammock. He was queasy and his tongue felt like it was wrapped in a dirty gym sock. Man, was he thirsty.

He didn't dare open his bedroom door to go after a glass of water. If he opened his door, Mom would hear with those bat ears of hers. She'd be all over him within a minute, and this time he wouldn't be able to escape by playing possum. She'd start ragging him, asking questions that he didn't want to think about, let alone answer. Then she'd look at him with disappointment. That was the worst, when she stopped talking and just sat there and looked at him.

It was the same with Coach Douglas. When he suspended Cole from practice, it wasn't *what* he said, it was the look in his eyes that made Cole want to crawl into his locker and stay there.

Then there was Ana. She would ask a bunch of "sensitive" questions about his "feelings," and look like she was going to cry or something. That was almost worse than Mom's lectures. And she'd give him hugs that made him think things he shouldn't about a sister-in-law.

Why couldn't everyone just leave him alone?

He threw an arm over his eyes. If only he could disappear. Maybe he'd wait, slip out in the night and run away, never have to face his mom—or Ana. They'd be better off, anyway, not having such a screwup around anymore.

He sat up. His head throbbed, the bed seemed to lurch under him and his stomach rolled.

Oh, God, don't let me be sick again. The beer had tasted

bad on the way down; coming back up it was even worse. After this afternoon, there couldn't possibly be anything left in his stomach.

He remembered getting sick in the living room. There was somebody else there—a guy. Dave? No, Dave had blond hair. And this guy was much broader than Dave. Who was it? His head hurt too much to think. Cole only hoped he'd never see him again. Oh, God, what if the guy was one of his mom's houseguests? She was always letting some sorry-assed bastard stay here on his way to someplace else. Being sick in front of Ana was about as much humiliation as he could stand. If he had to be introduced to a man he'd barfed on . . .

He heard movement in the corner of his room. Shit. Had his mom been sitting there all this time?

Breathing deeply to avoid throwing up, he waited for her to say something.

She didn't materialize from the dark corner. Pandora, a cat so pure black he constantly tripped over her in the dark, jumped up on the foot of his bed.

Cole kicked his feet, shooing her away. "I don't need any more shitty bad luck."

Mom said Pandora was magical. Sometimes he did think there was something supernatural about the cat—but it was black magic, the Dark Side, the thing that tried to overthrow the counterbalance of good and evil in the universe. She had shown up the day before they got a visit from the army telling them Calvin was dead. Nothing had gone right since. He couldn't believe Mom hadn't made the connection. When Granny Lejeune was here, *she* realized that cat was no good—he could tell by the way she looked at Pandora and avoided being in the same room with the stupid cat. To make things worse, Pandora had attached herself to *him*—spilling all of her bad luck in his lap.

Every night he checked his room to be sure the cat wasn't hiding inside before he closed the door. And every morning, she'd be on his pillow beside his head. It totally creeped him out.

There was a squeak that signaled someone had just stepped on the top tread of the stairs. Cole quickly lay back down and closed his eyes.

Pandora meowed loudly, as if tattling.

The door opened.

"Cole?" Ana said softly.

His throat got tight. He forced his breathing to remain deep and regular, pretending to sleep.

Instead of closing his door and going away, he heard her footsteps cross the room. He felt her presence beside his bed, his skin tingling with her nearness.

Go away. Please, go away.

But she stayed. He could smell the sweet soap she used.

Her cool hand rested on his forehead. "Oh, baby, I wish I could make things better."

He wanted to scream, *It's never going to be better! Life is one big shithole!*

Instead, he kept his breathing slow while his heart thudded like a bass subwoofer in his chest. He felt like he was going to burst out of his skin.

For a long time, she just stood there. Then, finally, she left.

Cole curled into a ball, pulling the blanket over his head. He fell asleep with a burning lump in his throat.

When he awoke, it truly was the middle of the night. He tiptoed downstairs to get a Sprite, carefully stepping over the squeaky top tread. He went back to his room before he opened the drink, muffling the *pop* and *pffft* of the can with his pillow to guard against Mom's superhuman hearing. He remembered once when Joey, his best friend in fifth grade, slept over and they'd planned all day to have a little fun with the telephone once his mom was asleep. They had waited until two A.M. and checked *twice*. She was sleeping like a rock. Still, the second they picked up the telephone in the kitchen to make a few clever calls, Mom yelled down the stairs, "What are you boys doing on the telephone at this hour?"

Man, he thought as he took a long drink from the can, if only something stupid like getting caught making prank calls or forging a signature on a note from the teacher were his current trouble. He didn't know how good he had it when he was a kid.

Lately, his problems seemed to be wielded by a flailing octopus. No sooner did he get a grasp on one part of it than another broke free and hit him in the head. Two days ago, Coach suspended him three practices for "unsportsmanlike conduct." All he did was play the friggin' game. If Coach didn't want to win, he should have put in Timmy Hicks. Hicks never fought for the ball.

Cole supposed he probably shouldn't have argued right there on the sidelines when Coach pulled him off the field. But he'd been so pissed it just came out. He didn't know why he couldn't keep his temper under control lately. *Everything* made him feel like breaking stuff. It was there, like a scream just waiting to be let out.

Last week, he actually did break a window at the old box factory on Vandolah Road; took his hand, wrapped it in an old sweatshirt and drove his fist right through it. Then he yelled. Screamed at the top of his lungs, letting go the curses that had been building inside him for months.

Only it didn't make him feel better. It made him feel stupid.

Even when he was with Darcy, the buzz of anger vibrated just under his skin. Everything she said sounded like fingernails on the chalkboard. And he couldn't understand it. He loved Darcy. She was the coolest girl in the junior class. But lately, he just couldn't . . . connect with her.

In fact, he hadn't talked to her for two days. She told him not to pick her up for school on Tuesday. And today it seemed like she'd been avoiding him.

He grabbed the cordless phone and took it into his closet. He dialed Darcy's cell phone. She always kept it beside her bed, in case he wanted to call in the middle of the night.

It rang twice and her voice mail picked up.

He dialed again.

It clicked once and then stopped ringing.

He called once more.

"Hey." Her tone was flat.

"It's me, Darce."

"I know, I've got caller ID."

"Why didn't you pick up?"

"I was sleeping."

"That's never stopped you before."

"What do you want?" She said it with an irritated edge that she *never* used with him—other guys, maybe, but never him.

"I just wanted to tell you I'll pick you up tomorrow morning." That wasn't at all what he wanted to tell her, but he couldn't make anything else come out.

She sighed. "Listen, Cole, you're a great guy."

His fingers tightened around the receiver and he closed his eyes. *Don't say it. Don't blow me off, Darce.*

She continued, "But I think we need a . . . a break."

Two weeks ago she loved him with all her heart. Now . . . "Why? You interested in somebody else?"

"No." She was much too quick in her denial. It stung his face like a slap. "No, of course not. It's just . . . I need some space."

"Jesus, Darce, space? You need *space*? Can't you come up with something better than that bullshit!"

"Hey!" she said sharply. Now she was mad. "I don't owe you any explanation. You've been acting really weird lately. Everybody's talking about it. I've had enough." She hung up.

Cole dialed again. It switched immediately to voice mail; she'd shut her phone off.

With a punishing grip on his phone, he slammed it into the pile of dirty clothes in the bottom of his closet. He did it three more times, harder each time, before he started to cry.

"I just don't see why he had to go to school this morning," Analise said, putting her coffee mug in the dishwasher. It had been all she could do to keep her mouth shut until Cole dragged himself out the door.

Olivia picked up her jacket and slipped it on. "Because it's a school day."

"Considering what happened yesterday—"

"Is why he took the school bus." Olivia picked up a set of keys off the key rack and held them in the air. "When Luke gets here, ask him if he'll take you to the plantation to pick up Cole's Jeep." She tossed the keys to Analise.

"Where are you going?"

"I have an appointment. I should be back by noon. I'll bring lunch back for the three of us."

"Three?" Was she going to relent and bring Cole home from school? The kid had been practically green when he walked out the door. The bus ride had to have been torture.

"Really, Ana." Olivia shook her head. "You, me *and*

Luke. It's the least we can do after he takes you to get the Jeep."

"He'll probably be gone by lunchtime. I'm sure he's eager to get on the road. What kind of appointment? Doctor?"

"Um-hum. Just a routine checkup." She waved and disappeared out the door.

Analise forced her mind away from Cole's misery and tried to mentally organize her schedule for the shop today. She was on her way to the carriage house when she heard the crunch of tires on the drive. Turning around, she had a peculiar tangle of anticipation and dread in her chest. Disappointment shadowed both when she saw it was Roy.

The very sight of his moon face through the windshield sent an unsettled ripple down her spine. She made herself wave and tried to give him a pleasant smile. He cut the engine and coasted to a stop beside the carriage house. Analise jumped when the truck backfired like a shotgun and a puff of black smoke burped out the tailpipe.

When he got out of the truck, he hurried toward the greenhouse without looking at her. "I'll be gettin' that stock moved, ma'am."

"That's fine. Be sure to put the hydrangeas and hostas under the canopy." Then she realized he probably didn't have any idea what either plant looked like. "They've all got identification tags." As an afterthought, she asked, "You *can* read?"

He stopped in midstride, but didn't turn to face her. "Yes'um. I can read." Resentment resounded in his voice.

"Sorry, I didn't mean . . ."

He walked on without another word.

She stood there for a moment, feeling hurtful and insensitive. She didn't really know why Roy gave her the willies.

It made her ashamed to think it could simply be his appearance and his unfortunate background. She resolved to make more effort to have an open mind where he was concerned.

Rufus came out of the carriage house, sniffing the air.

"Time to get to work, boy." She went inside and he trotted right behind her.

Luke was thankful to see the sun streaming through the narrow opening between the panels of the avocado and orange drapes when he opened his eyes. His relief was twofold. First and foremost, the night was over. It had been every bit as bad as he'd predicted, filled with nightmare after dreadful dream in which he could see disaster coming, but, struggle as he did, could do nothing to avert it. The second was that sunny weather gave no aggravation to his injuries. He arose from the bed with relatively little pain.

He arrived in Grover an hour and a half later and stopped at the Pure gas station on the corner of Center and Maple Streets. It was the newest-looking of the two stations in town. When he got out of his car with his credit card ready to slide into the pay-at-the-pump slot, he discovered this was one convenience of technology that had yet to arrive in this tiny town.

As he entered the station to pay, he was glad to see they had, at least, installed a coffeemaker. He was just adding a good shot of sugar to his Styrofoam Mega-mug, when someone laid a hand on his shoulder. He spun quickly around, fist clenched and ready, unaccustomed to such familiar gestures in an unfamiliar place.

"Didn't mean to make you jump like a bullfrog there," a man in a deputy's uniform said.

Luke relaxed, feeling a little silly for his overreaction.

"You're the Ranger visiting Magnolia Mile." The deputy's

gaze lingered on the scar on Luke's neck. Then he stuck out his hand and said, "I'm Dave Dunston—friend of Calvin's."

"Luke Boudreau." Dave was physically the polar opposite of Calvin—although he was tall, he was thin as a wire, with hunched shoulders, almost fragile looking under his gun belt. His pale hair was cut nearly to the scalp and his Adam's apple bobbed when he spoke. When Dave simply eyed Luke as he shook his hand, Luke added, "It was good of you to deliver Cole home yesterday. Olivia was very grateful."

Dave hitched up his belt. "Well, I like to do what I can for the family. With Calvin gone . . . I feel it's my duty, you know."

Luke nodded and turned to cap his coffee. "Calvin would appreciate it."

"That family's had more than its share of misfortune. Thought Analise'd dry up from all the cryin' she did when she lost Calvin."

Guilt once again pricked Luke's heart. Analise could have been spared those tears. He'd gone against protocol, thinking his was the only life at risk. How wrong he'd been—on all fronts.

Dave asked, "You headed out of town?"

"Yeah, I have to go out to Magnolia Mile before I leave, though."

Something shifted behind Dave's steady gaze. "You didn't stay at Lejeune's? Nearest motel's almost an hour away."

"I know."

A slight gleam of satisfaction shone in Dave's eyes and he crossed his arms over his narrow chest. "Well, being as you're as good as a stranger, it was wise of Olivia not to extend her hospitality too far. Women alone can't be too careful."

Dave sounded much more closely involved with the folks

at Magnolia Mile than Liv and Analise had suggested with yesterday's comments.

Luke said, "Yes, I suppose that's right." He stepped toward the cash register to pay. Dave remained at the coffeepot, filling a cup.

"Morning," the cashier said. "That be all?" She was a tiny woman with a cigarette in one hand and another smoldering in the overflowing ashtray beside the register.

"This and the gas." Luke took out his wallet. "The first pump there."

"I seen." Before she rang him up, she took a long drag on the cigarette. "Twenty-two-seventy-five." She exhaled the smoke with the words. As he handed over his credit card, she said, "So you know Olivia Lejeune?" She nodded toward the coffeemaker. "Heard you talking to Dave over there. I might be little, but my husband says I got the biggest ears in the county. Can't help it. I just hear everything."

"I only met Olivia yesterday. I served with her son."

Pursing her lips, she nodded sadly. "Livvie's my second cousin. Haven't seen her since her boy's funeral, though. City folk think livin' in a small town, you see ever'body all the time—but it's just like ever'place else. Ever'body's busy runnin' in their own circles. Why, I'd never see anybody if I didn't have this job. You from the city?"

"Nope. Small town, like this one."

"Up north."

He nodded and signed the credit receipt.

"Heard it in your voice. The words up there fall hard on the ears—not soft like here in Mississippi."

"Yes, ma'am." He smiled. "I do enjoy listening to you southern women talk." One southern woman in particular came to mind, one whose gentle voice flowed like a warm stream through his veins.

"You tell Livvie that Opal asked after her."

"I'll be sure and do that."

As Luke walked back to his car, he looked over his shoulder and saw Deputy Dave standing at the glass door with his coffee in hand, watching him intently through aviator sunglasses that made him look like a large praying mantis.

Cole sat with hunched shoulders in the back seat of the school bus, keeping his eyes half-closed against the bright morning light. A couple of kids had stared at him when he'd gotten on, but he'd put a stop to that by flipping them off. Nearly made Miss Goody-Two-Shoes, Becca Reynolds, fall right off her seat. She'd probably have to report him to the principal—since she was really into her "social responsibility." Well, that'd be fine. If he was thrown off the bus, he still had to go to school. His mom would have to let him have the Jeep back.

Maybe he'd work on Ana when he got home, she could talk some sense into his mother. It wasn't like taking away the Jeep was going to change anything. Sometimes his mom could be so . . . unreasonable.

The bus hit a pothole, jarring his throbbing head and setting his stomach off again. He closed his eyes and took slow, deep breaths. If he puked right here on the bus . . .

"Are you okay?"

He opened his eyes to see Miss Goody had moved to the seat in front of him and was looking over the back. "Fine."

"You don't look it."

"I'm *fine*." He belched softly, puffing out his cheeks.

"Sure you are." She turned around and rummaged in her backpack. "Here, chew a couple of these, it might help." She handed him a roll of Tums.

He stared at the roll, his stomach in near full revolt.

"Go on, take them," she urged.

Just the thought of the things on his tongue made him gag. "No!"

She flinched and withdrew the Tums, turning around in her seat. "Just trying to help."

That was Becca Reynolds, always the Good Samaritan, the advocate for truth, justice and the American way; always sticking her nose in to fix other people's problems. Did she ever think that maybe nobody wanted her to fix their problems? With all her do-goodliness, you'd think her dad was a preacher, not the owner of the local junkyard—a man known for his Saturday night rowdiness rather than his Sunday morning devotion.

Cole closed his eyes and leaned his head against the window. The vibration buzzed his teeth together and made little knives stab all over his brain. He leaned forward and buried his face in his hands, trying to rub away the pain that danced at the back of his eyeballs. The only thing that was going to make this day worthwhile was seeing Darcy. She had just been in a bad mood last night—he woke her up, after all. Things would be back to normal today.

He put his feet up on the seat, raising his knees. With his arms folded over his knees and his head resting on his forearms, he'd nearly drifted off to sleep when the bus jerked to a stop. He looked up to see the school parking lot still half-empty. That was the one good thing about coming on the bus, he was there before most of his friends. It had become sort of a contest to see who could cut it the closest without being sent to the principal for being tardy. He'd gotten his schedule so precise, he could usually manage to be the very last one in the door of Mrs. Baker's chemistry room before the bell rang. The fact that Mrs. Baker was anal when it came to rules made it all the more challenging. She'd only gotten him once this year.

He looked out the rear window of the bus until he was sure everyone else, particularly Becca Reynolds, was off the bus. Then he picked up his bag and headed to the front of the bus. Before he stepped out onto the curb, he took a fast look to make sure none of his friends were anywhere around. Once he saw the coast was clear, he got off and put distance between himself and the bus as quickly as he could.

"Hey, Lejeune!"

Shit. He spun around to see Rory Johnston hanging out of the passenger side window of Steve Watters's stopped Ford Probe. Since there was a hole in Watters's muffler, everyone within a hundred yards had turned to watch. This would be no drive-by shot, they were going to get him good.

"Did I just see you get off the *school bus*?" Rory's expression held mocking hilarity.

Cole ignored him and walked toward the building.

"Dude! Really—the bus!"

Finally Cole heard the car rumble on. Like Watters had room to talk; until last month, the guy had been riding a bicycle. And Johnston didn't even have his license. Jerks.

He'd almost made it to the front doors when he saw her; Darcy with Travis Benson, a slimeball Cole had hated since first grade. Travis made a career out of stepping on other people. And there Darcy was, leaning into his arm, laughing and flipping her hair over her shoulder. It was clear they'd both just gotten out of Travis's new Mitsubishi.

A boulder landed in Cole's gut. Fighting his urge to disappear, he stood his ground, legs braced for a fight.

When Darcy saw him, her step faltered, just for a fraction of a second. Then she raised her chin slightly and looked right at him.

As they got closer, Cole said, "Really, Darce, you're dumping me for this guy?"

The couple stopped as if someone had hit a switch, shutting off their power. But it was clear by the glitter in Travis's eye that the current was still flowing. "What she does is none of your business."

Cole gripped the handle of his duffel tighter. "I wasn't talking to you, butthead." He looked at Darcy. "Why don't you tell this ass to get lost so we can talk?"

Travis inched closer, but Darcy put her shoulder against him. "We don't have anything to talk about. I told you how I felt last night." She took Travis's hand and pulled him around Cole.

Cole didn't turn, but stalked off, away from the school, unsure where he was headed. He couldn't be *here* anymore.

Chapter 6

Analise had fed the bird and was on her tiptoes watering the hanging baskets when someone said, "Good morning."

"Oh!" She jerked and water dribbled from the watering can onto the floor. Luke was standing in the doorway. "Hello."

He came into the shop. "I didn't mean to startle you."

As he stood there in a shaft of morning sunlight, dressed in jeans and a snug-fitting white T-shirt, his eyes a brilliant blue, he was more than startling. The energy of the sun seemed to amplify his strength, cast shadows into the shallow dips between his muscles. He emitted the same dangerous combination of power and beauty that had initially attracted her to Calvin. That fact froze her with fear. Hadn't she learned anything?

As she stood there, stupidly staring at him, he went behind the counter and pulled out the same roll of paper towel they'd used yesterday to dry off the rain. Then he returned and knelt at her feet, mopping up the spill.

He stood and tipped the dripping spout upright. "I'll get this dried up a lot faster if you stop pouring more on my head."

"Oh . . . gosh . . ." She flashed warm and turned away,

setting the can on the table of the café set where they'd had coffee yesterday morning. Could it only have been a matter of hours since Luke had walked into her life? So much had happened, so many feelings had peaked and valleyed since then. It seemed much longer.

He didn't mock her flustered state. Instead he asked, "How's Cole this morning?"

"Not great. Olivia made him go to school." Her stomach tightened at the thought.

"You sound like you disapprove." He said it smoothly but with puzzlement.

"He was sick! She even made him ride the damn bus."

"Make him think twice before he pulls a stunt like that again, I imagine." There was no spitefulness in his voice, just a statement of fact.

"He won't do it again." She realized how naively defensive she sounded.

Luke stepped a little closer and looked down at her. "Really? You sound sure."

She swallowed and made herself meet his gaze. "I am. I *know* him." She coupled her tone with a defiant lift of the chin. "You don't. He's upset. Losing Calvin—"

"Was almost six months ago. He could use that for an excuse in September, not now." He inched forward and looked into her uplifted face. "And what's to say he won't be 'upset' again? Is this how you think he should handle being upset?"

"I don't suppose that's your concern." Her jaw tensed. She felt like she'd fallen back on childish playground defenses, but couldn't help herself. It *wasn't* Luke's concern.

They stood there for a long moment, frustrated irritation hanging in the air between them.

Luke finally blinked and stepped slightly away. "No. I don't suppose it is." He ran a hand through his hair.

Analise hated herself for noticing it was longer than most military men's. It was oddly appealing, as if it put distance between him and the army.

He blew out a long breath and said, "Not my concern at all." The hard edge had left his eyes, something troubling replaced it. Regret?

She grabbed on to her manners. "I didn't mean to be rude."

He raised a hand and shook his head. "No. You're right." He glanced toward the house and shifted his weight. "I'll just get my clothes."

"Sure." She started toward the door.

He followed, stopping beside his car. "The sweats are in here." He opened the door and pulled them out. "Sorry I didn't have any way to launder them."

She took them and waved his apology away.

When they entered the kitchen, Analise saw the Jeep keys on the table where she'd left them and inwardly cringed. She'd just tried to pick a fight with this guy, now she had to ask him for a favor.

"I hate to ask," she said, "but as you leave, could you drive me out to pick up Cole's Jeep? It's only about five miles from here. Liv had to go into town. Cole's really protective of that car; it used to be Calvin's."

"So protective that he was going to drive it on these narrow, winding roads after a six-pack?"

Her remorse over her bad manners whiplashed around to irritation. She drew in a breath to argue with him, but he raised his hand.

"Sorry," he said. "Again, not my business. Can't keep my mouth shut this morning." He extended his arm, indicating the door. "Let's go get the Jeep."

•　　　•　　　•

Luke drove slowly as Analise directed him along country roads that became progressively narrower and less well maintained. Her instructions were the only sound besides the thud of potholes and vibration of the tires on the washboard gravel road. As there were few turns, Luke had plenty of time for thought.

He was sorry he'd ruined the morning by being confrontational. When he'd left his motel, he'd resolved to maintain his distance, say a pleasant good-bye and be on his way. He'd convinced himself that he could be of no help in healing the wounds he'd inadvertently inflicted here. And nothing he could do or say would relieve his responsibility for the situation. But he'd been unable to keep his thoughts about Cole to himself. Calvin may have been a hell-raiser—but he shouldered responsibility for his actions. Maybe that was all that tempered him, kept him from being dangerous. With Calvin gone, what if no one taught Cole the difference?

"There," Analise said, startling him with the abrupt command. "Turn left there, into that lane." She pointed to a couple of crumbling square brick pillars that looked as if they once supported a pair of wide swinging gates.

Slowing the car, Luke was about to ask, *What lane?* when he saw dual tire tracks through the tall weeds.

He turned. The car crept through overgrowth that made a quiet screech as it scraped along the sides. When Luke glanced at Analise, he saw she had goosebumps on her arms.

She said, "Liv and I come out here once a year to trim the brush back. Looks like we'd better do it soon, or no one will be able to get through here."

"How did the deputy even find Cole back in here?"

"He checks on the old place for Olivia pretty often. Must have been luck that brought him out here yesterday."

Luke didn't respond, but concentrated on following the narrow tracks as they wound around a couple of tight turns. If he was a kid trying not to get caught doing something he shouldn't, this would be just the place.

He had the odd sensation he was actually driving backward in time—to when this land was untamed. "Where are we?"

"This is the original Magnolia Mile, the Lejeune plantation. Established," she said as if a tour guide, "in 1832. Behind all of this wild growth are a few of the old magnolias that lined this mile-long drive."

Her tone became more personal when she added, "Cole's dad owned it. It's in a trust for Cole now."

"Humm," Luke mumbled. Cole's ancestors had been landed gentry—planters. Luke's had been dirt-poor farmers who worked other people's land for a share of the harvest profits. His own father was the first to own his own business. Although still near the bottom of the social ladder in Glens Crossing, Benny Boudreau had taken quite a step up. "What happened to Cole's father?" he asked as they inched their way deeper into the woods.

"About eight years ago, right after I came to Grover, Layton went in for a checkup and the doctor told him he had high cholesterol; said if he didn't get it down with diet and exercise, he was going to prescribe medication. Olivia hates drugs, so she put him on what Layton called a 'rabbit diet' and talked him into running three times a week.

"The second week while he was running, he was hit by a dump truck. Killed him instantly."

"Jesus." Deputy Dave wasn't exaggerating when he said this family had shouldered more than their fair share of tragedy. He looked at Analise, but she was staring out the passenger window, her head turning as if to keep something in sight as they passed. "Something wrong?" he asked.

After a moment, she turned and looked at him. "No. Nothing." Facing front once more, she shouted, "Look out!"

Jerking his gaze back to the road, Luke slammed on the brakes just as a buck deer the size of a moose leapt into their path. They couldn't have missed it by more than six inches.

"That was Jocko," Analise said. "I know he's always around here, I should have been paying more attention. Sorry."

"Jocko? Another pet?"

She laughed and the sound of it wiped everything else from Luke's mind. "Not exactly. But every hunter around here knows if he takes Jocko down, Olivia will make sure he never aims a rifle again. With a rack the size of his, he's a prime target. Liv says he's lived so long because he's smart. I think it's because of her threats."

"I can't imagine a serious hunter passing up a—what is he, a ten-point?"

"Twelve."

Luke whistled.

"Now you know the kind of weight Liv carries around here."

"Guess I'll be watching myself from here on out. She doesn't know about my little run-in with Skippy, does she?"

Analise gave him a wicked grin and a sidelong look. "Not yet."

"I'm shocked. You don't seem like the type of girl to tattle."

"Only if provoked."

"I'll be on my best behavior, then. Don't want Olivia coming after me with a pitchfork." As they laughed together,

Luke realized just how long it had been since he'd laughed—really laughed, not the polite manufactured sound he'd been forcing at the appropriate moments over the past months. It felt good.

He'd read once that laughter releases something that actually changes a person's body chemistry. As he sat next to this woman, blending his laughter with hers, he could believe it. He felt something inside him shift, lighten and carry away a bit of the heaviness that he'd been lugging around in his chest.

Then the house came into view—or, more correctly, what was left of the house—and his laughter stopped. It wasn't replaced by sadness; something more like reverence filled him. What struck him first was the house's massive size. Although one full wing had virtually fallen in on itself, it was among the largest houses he'd ever seen. It was difficult to tell anything about the architecture for all of the vegetation that had sprung up at the foundation and wrapped itself around the structure. Thick, ropy vines wound around glassless windows and through holes in the roof.

He stopped behind Cole's Jeep under a giant gnarled tree.

"Thanks for the ride," Analise said, but it was nothing more than background noise. His gaze remained on the old house as he got out of the car.

When Analise joined him in front of the moss-covered front steps, he said, "There's something about a place with this much history inside. It must have really been something in its day."

"Why are you whispering?" she leaned close and asked in a near-whisper herself.

He hadn't realized that he was. He tore his gaze away from the house and rested it solemnly on her. "It just seems wrong to make too much noise here, like disturbing a final resting place."

She looked at him for a long moment with surprise in her eyes. "That's just what Liv calls it. 'The Lejeune family's final resting place.' It's like all of the hopes and dreams of the people who started this plantation are wrapped inside those crumbling walls. Cole's the last of the Lejeunes."

Looking back at the house, Luke said, "Quite a mixed blessing, a legacy like this. Do you think he'll want to rebuild someday?"

She tilted her head slightly, as if thinking it over. "I really don't know. He does always end up coming out here when he's troubled. I don't know if it's because it's so isolated, or because he feels something for the place. We've never really discussed the future of this land—he's only sixteen."

"Didn't you know what you wanted when you were sixteen?" he asked softly, seeking another glimpse inside the woman she was.

She chuckled and shook her head. "When I was sixteen, I wanted to go to New York City and become an artist, live like a bohemian." She fixed her gaze on him. "Did you know?"

"Sure."

After giving him a moment in which he let the word dangle like bait, she prompted, "Well, what was it?"

"What every sixteen-year-old boy wants: to get a sixteen-year-old girl in the back seat of my car." He winked at her.

"One giant mass of raging hormones, were you?"

He shrugged. "We can't help it. It's programmed in the male genes. Survival of the species and all."

"I'll keep that in mind when I have a teenage daughter."

Turning to face her fully, he fought the urge to reach out and touch her cheek. He'd taken so much away from her. Would she ever have that daughter?

She became very still and finally turned to him. "You look so sad. What are you thinking?"

He pressed his lips together, debating whether or not to be honest about what was going through his mind.

She laid a hand on his forearm. "It can't be that bad. Tell me."

Exhaling a long breath, he decided. "I was just thinking about how much you've lost. Your husband. The future you should have had . . . children." He gave in to the impulse to touch her, resting his fingertips on her cheek. It was an action motivated by sympathy, he told himself. But he questioned his own intent when she leaned slightly into his touch and he felt a sudden rush of intimacy. He dropped his hand back to his side. The feel of her remained on his fingertips. Suddenly he was aware of the scent of her shampoo; the sun warmed the top of her head, intensifying the fragrance.

He took a little step away from her.

"I'm happy with my life. It's not what I imagined, but I have Liv and Cole. I love my work. My life could have turned out a whole lot worse had Calvin not stepped into it when he did."

"If you hadn't met him, where would you be right now?" he asked, finding himself closing the space between them once again.

She gave a wan and distant smile. "Oh, I would have been the good girl and followed the path Grandmother set for me. I'd be married to a senator or congressman, have two immaculately groomed but boring children—preferably one of each sex—a Volvo, a chair in a major charity organization, a solidly booked social calendar and perpetual migraines."

"Ooohh." He gave a visible shiver. "What a horror! The life most women dream about. Well, minus the migraines." He was trying to lighten the moment, but she stared solidly at him.

"I'd be climbing out of my skin and not be able to see the reason why. I'd suffocate a little more every day until there wasn't anything left of me. Calvin saved me from that."

"I wasn't mocking your life—"

"Of course you weren't. I never thought that. I'm just telling you how it is . . . was. He did save me . . . in so many ways."

Her eyes took on the look of distant remembering. She lifted her hand to her heart. "When I met Calvin, he sparked something inside me that had been buried deeply with the death of my parents." Shaking her head slightly, she said, "Grandmother wasn't the type to bake cookies and read bedtime stories. But she wasn't careless about my upbringing. If you wanted to know which flatware to use for which course in a meal, I was your gal. If you wanted to know the proper attire for a gubernatorial inauguration, just ask me. Need someone to pen a condolence letter, an invitation, or a polite, yet scathing reprimand?" She thrust a thumb at her chest. "You guessed it—me. But all of that training was mixed with very little warmth. Oh, I'm sure she loved me in her own way. But that was hard for me to understand as a child.

"Cuddling creased Grandmother's clothes. Hugs messed up hair. Air kisses didn't spoil makeup.

"She considered the other kids at my private school spoiled and rowdy." Analise chuckled, but there was little humor in the sound. "I guess I had to agree with the 'spoiled' part. I had to be on constant guard against raised voices or raucous activity; it was just too stressful to invite kids over. And with dance lessons, piano lessons, tennis lessons, golf lessons and cotillion preparation classes, there really wasn't much time to cultivate outside friendships.

"When I heard Calvin speak of his family, I began to understand that a loving home wasn't just a work of fiction, a fabrication that existed only in movies and books. That there *were* people who made choices based on love—not power, or logic, or security. People who would take a chance, make a risky choice, simply out of love. People who *gave*. I wanted to be one of those people."

Luke wanted to tell her she *was* one of those people—a giver. It showed in everything she did. But he held his tongue, hoping she'd let him see more of her life.

After a long pause, she did. "My marriage to Calvin wasn't what I had imagined. After the first week, we only slept in the same bed a handful of times each year. The separation . . . Calvin wasn't keen on long telephone conversations. Sometimes I felt so distant from him—not just in the physical sense, you know?" Her gaze focused on Luke's face.

He clenched his teeth together and managed to nod. Again he wondered what kind of fool Calvin Abbott had been to disregard a woman like Analise.

She smiled thinly and gave a slight sigh. "I learned to live with what we had. What mattered most was he gave me a completely new view of life and what I wanted out of it.

"This family . . . Olivia and Cole . . . Calvin gave them to me. He saved me—and I'll never be able to repay him for it."

Luke started to blurt out that her remaining faithful to a

man who put no more stock in fidelity than he did telephone psychic readings should have been payment enough, but he bit his tongue. After a moment he said, "I know it doesn't help, but I am sorry. If I could change that da—"

She silenced him by placing a finger over his lips. "Don't say that again." Her finger moved to the scar on his neck. "We all live with what fate deals us."

He wanted to say, fate had nothing to do with it. Bad judgment was the culprit. But once again, he choked back the words as he stared into her green eyes. Besides, he didn't trust lips that were still tingling from her touch to do more than mumble and stutter.

Allowing her hand to linger on his scar, she asked, "Do you want to talk about it?"

"No." The word came out harsh because the question had the same effect as a bucket of cold water over his head. He wouldn't, couldn't talk about that night—ever.

Something closed off in her eyes. She stepped backward. "All right, then." Offering him a handshake, she said, "I guess this is good-bye."

The instant he took her hand, he realized he didn't want to let go. "I guess so." Was she clinging as tightly to his hand as he was hers? She didn't let go, but riveted those green eyes on him. Luke's insides puddled like melted butter. Which was all the more reason he had to leave here now. "Good-bye." He made himself pull his hand back. "Tell Olivia and Cole good-bye for me."

She nodded, then slowly moved in the direction of the Jeep. He waited by the driver's door of his car, watching her. She hesitated with her hand on the windshield frame, looking his way, then gave him a faded smile and climbed in.

He got in his own car and thought, well, that was that.

He'd drive away from here and never see her again. There was a little pinched place in his soul that stabbed with regret. He'd sensed, while she'd held his hand, she felt some connection to him, too. If only he'd met her in a different place, under different circumstances.

The possibility of what might have been between them stung at the back of his eyes. But there was nothing to be done. She'd lost the love of her life, and had come to terms with it. He was going to have to follow her strong example—accept what couldn't be changed and press on.

She started the Jeep and ground the gears as she put it in first. Pulling a wide U-turn on what was at one time a pristine lawn, she held up one hand as she passed back by.

He just nodded, unwilling to take his own trembling hand off the wheel.

Luke swung the Taurus around and followed Analise slowly back out the narrow lane, snaking their original path in reverse. The Jeep's vinyl top was up and the plastic rear window was so fogged and scratched, he couldn't begin to see her behind the wheel.

He rolled down the window, allowing the springlike air to wrap around him. How could it have felt so wintry just yesterday? He'd better draw on the warmth while he could. Tomorrow he'd be back up north where winter still held the land firmly in its grip. Breathing deeply, he smelled the moist earth warmed by the sun and a hint of something near blooming. If only he could stay, not have to return to the cold that would make his body ache and his wounds throb.

At about the spot where the deer had jumped out in front of them, the Jeep's brake lights suddenly flared and it jerked to a stop.

Luke stopped just as suddenly, looking for a sign of Jocko.

Analise climbed out of the Jeep and crooked a finger at him. Her face was serious; there was nothing playful in the gesture. She then stepped into the weeds beside the lane and waited.

Curious, he shut off the engine. When he got out and caught up with her, he could see she stood on a weedy gravel path.

"There's something I think you should see," she said as she started down the pathway through the woods.

"What's back there?" he called after her, his voice sounding harsh against the quiet hum of nature.

"Come on, you'll see."

As she walked away, Luke stood fixed in place, watching her with an unsettled feeling in his belly. She moved gracefully, with light steps and gentle movements that set her long braid to swaying. Occasionally, a sunbeam winked through the heavy mix of evergreen and leafing deciduous, shooting her hair through with brilliant gold.

She turned and looked over her shoulder at him. "You coming?"

He moved through the primeval growth, feeling as if he were walking toward a mystery about to unfold, one that would forever change him.

Ridiculous.

Even as he dismissed the notion, it rose again, stronger this time.

The path curved and went down a slight decline. He momentarily lost Analise from his line of sight. When she again came into view, she was standing in a ray of sunlight beside an ancient, yet recently painted, black iron fence. Her hand rested on the gate as she looked back at him. Beyond her were ten or so tall, aging monuments, some tilted on ground that had shifted long ago. Around them stood smaller markers—some so old and weathered there was no longer more than a ghost of the lettering that declared the dead, some newer, more modern granite headstones.

A slight breeze picked up the hair that had come loose around her face, giving an angelic impression as she stood in the shaft of heavenly light. The certainty that his life was about to change renewed itself. He tried to ignore it, the same as he tried to ignore his growing attraction for the wife of another man.

She didn't move as he came closer, but held his gaze. Again the feeling of leaving the world behind struck him. It was all he could do to keep from reaching out and taking her hand when he got close enough.

He said softly, "Why?" It came unbidden, uncontrolled by thought. And he wasn't even sure what he meant by the question. Why did she bring him here? Why had she stopped and waited with such a somber, yet expectant look in her eyes? Why was he feeling like he was in an emotional free fall?

Turning from him, she opened the gate and stepped through.

As he followed, he looked at a few of the names on the more recent stones: Franklin Coleman Lejeune, Roberta Layton Lejeune, Layton Coleman Lejeune. Then to the stones that looked like worn, bleached bone sticking from the earth: Oscar Milford Lejeune, Stuart James Lejeune, Marianne Lejeune Carson, Robert Patterson Carson, Infant Carson. This cemetery must have been used since the first Lejeune cut down the first tree to till this land.

Analise had stopped by a red granite stone at the far edge

of the burial ground. Luke didn't have to look at the lettering to know to whom it belonged. They stood side by side for a long moment, looking down at the plot of ground that held Calvin Abbott's earthly remains.

"Calvin's father's body was never recovered from Vietnam. Liv wanted Calvin with family, so she put him here, with the Lejeunes—where she's to be buried and she hopes Cole's family will rest when the time comes."

Luke shivered. All of this death, inevitable as it was, cast a chill over him. He closed his eyes.

Abbott's face appeared in his mind, laughing as he often did at a practical joke. Then the smile twisted into something grotesque, a scream of pain came from the contorted lips, shock and pain filling the once-glittering eyes.

Luke realized he must have made a sound, because Analise touched his arm. "Are you all right?" she asked.

He shook his head, words failing to come forth. Would he ever be all right again?

"Is it your knee? I shouldn't have made you walk all this wa—"

"It's not my knee." His voice rasped in a choked whisper.

"The crash," she said as understanding dawned. "I didn't mean to upset you." Her fingers tightened on his arm. "I just thought you'd want to see how peaceful . . ."

Peaceful? Death peaceful? If she knew the reality of her husband's last minutes she would never again associate peace with his death.

He swallowed roughly, wishing he could find something to say. She stepped close enough that her body was pressed against his arm; her hand slid down and held his.

Tears of frustration clouded Luke's view of Calvin's name carved in the stone. After a long while, he said the only thing that he could: "He was a good soldier."

He felt her stiffen beside him. She removed her hand from his. "That's good." She paused. "Because he was a lousy husband."

She turned and walked quickly out of the little cemetery. Stunned by her comment, Luke didn't try to stop her.

Chapter 7

Luke stood, his feet unable to move from Calvin's grave, his mind racing in wild and ever-widening circles. He couldn't tear his gaze from the engraving on Calvin's headstone; the death date, September 6, stabbing into his eyes like poison needles, echoing in his mind in the thunderous roll of automatic weapons fire.

Somewhere under the sounds of the past, he heard the quick squeak of the gate opening, and the drawn-out moan as it drifted back closed. Analise's footfalls were swallowed in the woods, masked by the twitter of birds whose worlds remained as constant as the rising of the sun. But for Luke, constancy was gone, obliterated the moment he'd decided to follow his instincts and not well-ordered rules. From that instant, his world had been rocked with continual aftershocks.

After a long moment, he turned toward the path.

What the hell had she meant? Had she known of Calvin's infidelities? Were there other problems in their marriage? He'd never known Calvin to get rough with a woman, but there were lots of things he was discovering he didn't know about his buddy. A thousand questions circled in his head—and Analise had fled with the answers.

Shaking off the weight of surprise, Luke followed her back toward the cars. His knee was much better today, but on the uneven ground he had to watch his step. When he reached the lane, the Jeep was disappearing around a curve.

For a moment he considered hopping in his car and chasing after her. But to what end? he asked himself. If she'd wanted to explain, she wouldn't be halfway back to Magnolia Mile right now. For a reason that only Analise knew, she wanted him to know just so much and no more.

After a few minutes, he climbed in the Taurus and wound his way back to the main road. Sitting between the ruins of the brick pillars, he stopped and rested his forehead on the steering wheel. His heart demanded he go after her, but his good sense said to leave well enough alone.

Within fifteen minutes, he was on the main highway, headed toward the interstate that would lead him home to Indiana. Over and over in his mind, Analise's words replayed. *He was a lousy husband.*

Somehow Analise made it through lunch without strangling Olivia. It wasn't Liv's fault, which made Analise's nasty impulse that much more appalling. Each time Liv mentioned Luke's name, which seemed to be every other sentence from the moment they sat down at the table—*Why didn't Luke stay for lunch? Cole still needed to apologize to Luke. What do you think Luke's going to do, stay in the army or take a discharge? I wish I had been able to say goodbye to Luke*—shame burned deep in Analise's chest. She had betrayed her family. She'd said the words that she'd kept bottled up inside for more years than she wanted to think about. What had she thought she'd gain by tainting Calvin's memory that way? And right at his graveside. Why had she been compelled to say those words to Luke?

If only she could take them back.

Her single consolation was that she'd never have to see Luke again. He would take those words with him and they would never echo back to Olivia's ears.

Analise tried to put the entire thing out of her mind as she headed to her metal workshop. It was done, there was no recalling the words. As she neared the carriage house, Reverend Hammond's car pulled in the drive behind her. She wasn't surprised when it stopped at the house. He gave her a wave as he went up to the kitchen door—just like he was family. At least he knocked and didn't barge right in.

Olivia answered the door with a smile, apparently glad to see him, and they both disappeared back inside. These visits seemed to be happening more frequently. Was Olivia encouraging the man?

Analise shook her head. Surely not. Olivia had been alone for more than eight years and never given any indication that she'd be interested in dating; the very word, *dating*, seemed much too young and frivolous for a woman Liv's age and twice widowed.

As Analise entered the shop she saw Rufus snoozing in his usual place. He didn't so much as twitch an ear when she walked in.

Roy appeared in the back door. "Miz Abbott?"

The very sound of the man's voice made her cringe. She reminded herself of her commitment to be more open-minded and mentally scolded herself for her harsh thoughts. They seemed to be popping up about everyone around her today. "Yes, Roy?" She even managed a smile.

"I seen the reverend's here." His gaze drifted shyly away.

"I was wondering if I could take a bit to pray with him before he leaves?"

"Of course." She had to be the most uncharitable person in the state of Mississippi. Poor Roy only wanted to get his life back together and she couldn't see anything but ulterior motives.

He nodded and backed out of the doorway, as if she were royalty. "Thankee, ma'am."

A horn honked in the drive. Analise looked out to see Mr. Baker's pickup pulling up in front of the shop. The man arrived just after lunch every March first like clockwork. March second was his wedding anniversary and each year he planted another magnolia tree for his wife, the chemistry teacher at the high school.

Analise met him at the door. "Right on time. I've tagged the best of the bunch for you, but you'll want to look them all over before you make your choice." She couldn't help but smile: The man was a walking, talking contradiction. His gruff manner belied his tender heart and his clothes were the oddest combination Analise could imagine ever assembled on one body. He wore a cowboy hat, a light blue oxford button-down shirt under old-fashioned bib overalls, a Tag Heuer watch, white socks and Teva sandals. Sort of new-moneyed farmer meets outdoor adventurer.

He took off his hat. "This'un will make forty-one."

"Happy forty-first anniversary. That's quite an accomplishment in this day and age. You two should be proud." He nodded in agreement. Analise added, "Running out of places to plant yet?"

He shook his gray head. "Gonna stop when we get an even fifty. Maybe I'll switch to oaks then."

Analise tried to absorb some of the man's optimism. Something she herself was feeling in short supply these past days. Planting slow-growing oaks at his age was a . . . a true statement of faith.

"The magnolias are right out here, in the side lot." She took him out the back door to the display behind the white trellis wall.

"I trust your judgment. Y'all haven't sold me a bad one yet. Not like that bas—that fella over to Oxford."

"Well, they're used to having the university for a customer. They don't have to face the folk they sell to every day, like we do here." Analise stopped. "This is the one." She pointed to the burlap-balled tree she'd spent an hour selecting yesterday.

"Ahhh, yes. That's a good 'un, all right. Lois'll be pleased."

Analise nodded and called for Roy.

He peeked from around the trellis, where he'd obviously been loitering, waiting for Reverend Hammond to reappear.

"Could you get the dolly and load this into Mr. Baker's truck?"

Roy glanced nervously toward the reverend's car.

"I'm sure Reverend Hammond will be here a while yet."

With obvious reluctance and a steady bead on the blue Crown Victoria in the drive, Roy went to retrieve the dolly.

Analise and Mr. Baker returned to the shop to settle the account.

"How's Miss Livvie doing?" he asked as he signed the charge slip.

"She's doing very well. As busy as ever."

"Busy's good. Helps dull the pain."

Analise nodded. Mr. Baker knew what he was talking about; he and Lois had lost a daughter and grandchild to a car accident several years ago. Instead of the tragedy tearing them apart, it seemed to have made their marriage stronger.

They went outside just as Roy was climbing out of the bed of the truck. When he started to put up the rear gate, Analise said, "Wait a minute, Roy. We need to get some of that heavy twine in the back of the shop and secure the tree first."

Roy looked at the reverend's car again.

"He's not out of the house yet. I'm sure you have time to get the twine." Analise realized too late that her tone was much more biting than she'd intended.

Roy hunched his shoulders and went back inside.

While they waited, Mr. Baker started to talk about some trouble his wife was having with a few of the students in her class.

"She keeps threatening to retire. Says kids aren't the same as they used to be. I hate the way it worries her. Just two days ago, there was a break-in at the school. Kids didn't do much but dirty up the place, but once this type of thing gets started . . ."

"Do they know who was responsible?" Her skin tingled with dread.

"Oh, yeah, they're pretty sure they know who, just don't have enough to prove it yet. Shame of it is, seems it's a group of ordinarily good kids."

Analise tuned out everything else around her. Although she nudged and prodded, Mr. Baker was careful not to divulge names.

Roy called out the front door, "Miz Abbott, I cain't find the string."

"It's next to the bags of fertilizer, on the shelf under the window."

"You sure?" He inched farther out the door.

"Yes, I'm sure. I just put it there this morning."

Turning as if his feet were heavy stones, he went back inside.

Analise tried to no avail to get some hint of the vandals' identities. She was still engaged in the conversation when she heard Roy yell, "He's leavin'!"

He dropped the roll of twine in the doorway and took off in a lumbering run after the Crown Vic that was just pulling out of the drive.

Apparently the reverend didn't see Roy in his rearview mirror, because he pulled away and out of sight.

Roy ran out of steam when he got about even with the front porch. He stood there for a bit, his big shoulders rising and falling with his heaving breath. After a long minute during which Analise imagined Roy was trying to draw the minister back with sheer willpower, he turned around and began to return to the carriage house.

Analise watched him walk back. His shoulders were slumped even more than normal and he hung his head so low his chin touched his chest, but his movements were jerky, his step harsh—not the fluid lumbering she'd grown accustomed to seeing. She felt awful for letting the pastor get away. She'd been so caught up in trying to find out if Cole or his friends were involved in the most recent mischief, she didn't even hear the man come out of the house.

Without so much as a pause or a glance in her direction, Roy passed her, saying, "You said I could pray." The words were clipped, from between clenched teeth. His breathing was still ragged. "I need to pray." He hit the doorjamb with his fist as he disappeared inside the shop.

"I'm sorry," Analise called after him. Then she remembered Mr. Baker was still standing next to her. She picked up the twine and returned to the truck. "I'll just get this secured for you—"

Mr. Baker took the twine from her hands. "Nonsense. I

don't need a slip of a girl to tie my tree down for me." He climbed up into the bed of the truck with the agility of a thirty-year-old. After wrapping the twine around the trunk and securing the ends to the truck bed, he jumped down and handed the rest of the twine to Analise. "There, now. That should do fine." Then he nodded toward the shop. "Your man there seemed pretty upset. Want me to go in and talk to him a spell?"

"No. Thank you, though. He wanted to see the reverend is all. He'll be all right in a few minutes. I'm sure the reverend will be back tomorrow or the next day."

Mr. Baker gave a knowing smile. "I 'spect he will."

Had everyone in town noticed the man's interest in Olivia?

Analise and Mr. Baker said their good-byes and then she went inside to find Roy and apologize. From the moment she'd met him, she had been certain his religious fervor was feigned, used only to gain what he wanted. Perhaps she'd been hasty in that assessment.

She didn't see him right away. "Roy?" she called. When there was no answer, she checked the back room, then the greenhouses. He wasn't anywhere to be found.

Glancing out the side window of the carriage house, she saw his truck was still sitting in its parking spot. Maybe he'd gone into the woods to sulk. Irked as she was at his irresponsibility, just disappearing in the middle of the workday, she now realized how important his visits with the pastor were to him.

Unable to do anything about it until Roy decided to show his face again, and totally out of the mood to work upstairs, she went into the stockroom to inventory supplies. Pretty soon there'd be high demand for potting soil and fertilizer; she didn't want to be caught short.

She was shifting bags of peat from one corner to the other when she heard a foot scrape on the floor behind her.

She spun around just in time to hear the door to the stockroom slam shut. With only the light of the small window, it was so dim that she could only see Roy's huge outline against the white door. His expression was hidden in shadow.

Nothing good could be coming of this. She tried to sidle around and maneuver herself nearer the door, yet remain out of reach of those long arms. "What is it, Roy?"

He didn't say anything. He didn't move, either, his bulk blocking the inward-swinging door.

"I'm sorry you missed Reverend Hammond." She kept her voice light and cheerful, though all the while dark thoughts slithered through her mind. "I'm sure he'll be back tomorrow to see Mrs. Lejeune." She couldn't get any closer to the exit without putting herself within his grasp.

Rufus started whining on the other side of the door.

Looking around the room, she could see no weapon of any sort. There was a box cutter, but it was on the far side, dropped inside a box she'd just opened.

"Let's work on unpacking some of those fertilizer stakes. Could you get that box over there?" She pointed across the room, hoping he'd at least move in that direction enough that she could get the door open.

He rotated his big head her way, staring at her for a moment. "I need to pray."

"All right." She swallowed. "I could use a little praying myself." She motioned over by the window. "Maybe we could kneel down over there for a few minutes."

"Momma," he said in a little-boy voice that sparked both hope and dread in Analise's heart, " 'the *devil*,' you said. You *said* . . . I shoulda listened better." The last words trailed off into a near cry.

Analise dared move close enough to touch his arm, thinking to lead him away from the door while he seemed in a vulnerable state.

"No!" he bellowed, jerking away from her touch as if she'd branded him. Then he turned to face her fully and she realized what a horrible mistake she'd made. He leaned over her, forcing her backward.

Rufus howled and scratched at the door.

Roy kept coming forward, until Analise was backed against the wall. "Roy, calm down and let's pray a bit." Analise worked to keep her voice as calm as she could. "We can pray to Jesus."

"Shut up!" he yelled. "You don't say His name!" For a moment she thought he was going to grab her, but he just stood there with his hands balled at his sides. She couldn't tell if he was furious or about to cry.

Rufus bayed and bumped repeatedly against the door. Maybe the latch wouldn't hold. . . .

"Sinner." His voice faded, sounding childlike again. He shook his head. "I'm a sinner."

"God forgives sinners, Roy. You just have to ask—"

The door flew open. Luke grabbed Roy by the back of the neck and said, "Step away from her."

Roy swung his right elbow around. Analise expected to hear the crack of that ham-sized elbow connecting with Luke's face, but instead Roy dropped to his knees with a childlike whine.

Analise quickly stepped away from him.

Rufus had burst through right behind Luke and was bellowing and barking as he jumped from side to side, making such a racket that Analise's ears started to ring. He darted toward Roy, then backed off a step.

"All right, Rufus! Down!" Analise shouted.

The dog mouthed a couple of mute barks, then dropped to the floor. A long thin whine continued to come from his throat.

Luke had a vise-grip on something in Roy's neck that had him mewling like a kitten.

"Luke, it's okay, let go." There was a look in Luke's eye that scared her almost as much as Roy's outburst. It was as if he *wanted* Roy to do something foolish.

Rufus whined.

After a second, Luke looked up at her. His jaw pulsed with tension.

Roy whimpered.

Finally, Luke said, "I'm going to let you go. But don't you move. Got it?"

"Yeeesss." Roy curled into a tighter ball and slurred the word.

Luke released the pressure and Roy rocked to the side and sat with a thud.

"I'm s-s-orry." Now Roy *was* crying, sounding like a repentant child. "I just needed to pray."

"Get up," Luke said.

Suddenly Roy appeared so lost, so much like the child he must still be in his mind. Analise now saw how fragile he was, how much he depended on guidance—which he'd found in Reverend Hammond now that his own mother was gone.

Frightened as she'd been, Analise still moved to help him stand.

Luke stopped her with a firm hand on her arm.

Her gaze snapped to his face.

He didn't say anything, he simply moved her away from Roy.

"Get up," Luke said.

Roy sniffled and slowly got to his feet.

Analise fought her instinct to put a comforting hand on him. He was no more than a child in a man's body.

Luke looked at Analise, "How much do you owe him?"

Taken off guard, she blinked.

He prodded. "Wages?"

"Um, three days . . . around a hundred and forty."

Luke reached in his pocket and pulled out some folded bills. He peeled off five fifties. Grabbing Roy's hand, he stuffed the money into his fist. "That more than covers it. Leave now, and don't even think of coming back here."

"Wait a—"

Luke gave Analise a glare that froze her words in her throat and sent a shiver down her spine. He turned to Roy. "Go."

Roy ran from the room.

"Wait!" Analise followed him, but Roy didn't so much as look over his shoulder before he jumped in his truck. It ground to a start and he whipped it in a circle and headed out the drive in a cloud of dust that left her coughing.

She spun around just as Luke was coming out of the shop. "What in the hell do you think you're doing? You had no right—"

Luke stepped toward her. "That man was attacking you!"

"He was . . . upset. He didn't get to pray with Reverend Hammond. He didn't even touch me. I was handling it just fine until you burst in—"

"And kept him from touching you!"

"He was going to calm down. I didn't realize how child-like he was until just now."

"Childish in judgment—but he has a man's force. I've seen men like that before; he wasn't going to stop until he did some damage. Maybe not this time, but it would happen.

You should stop discounting men's actions because they're 'upset.' "

His insult over her reaction to Cole's behavior stung. But her anger overrode all else.

Before she could say more, Luke asked, "What was your first instinct when he came in the room?"

Looking around, as if she could find the answer flitting about in thin air, she swallowed and said, "I was startled, I guess." She thought of the way her stomach lurched and her skin tingled when she'd seen him there; how panic threatened to rise when he'd slammed the door. But that was before . . . before she knew he was just a child.

"You were scared."

She couldn't deny it.

He said, "You should always heed your first instinct." As if he could sense her doubt and subsequent mental justification he added, "Rufus was raising a ruckus. You said yourself that he never wastes energy carrying on for nothing." He pointed at the dog, now sitting in the doorway to the carriage house. " 'He knows when to get down to business.' "

Again, he was throwing her own words in her face. What pissed her off most was that there was no way to counter it. She *had* said it. Still, Luke had crossed the line. "You had no right to fire him."

"What's going on out here?" Olivia walked quickly toward them from the house. "Roy took off like a bat straight out of Hades."

"Luke just fired him." Analise put her hands on her hips.

Olivia looked from one face to the other, then to Rufus. "I heard Rufus." She said it like that was proof positive that something was wrong.

Analise said, with as little resignation in her voice as she could manage, "Roy *was* getting a little out of hand."

"What do you mean?" Concern creased Olivia's brow.

Luke said, "He had Analise backed into a corner in the storeroom, threatening her."

Analise put a hand on Olivia's arm and shot Luke a nasty glare. "He was upset because he wanted to pray with Reverend Hammond and missed him."

"Oh." Olivia pursed her lips in thought. "Well, we can't have someone around that's unstable. I'd so hoped we could help him. . . ."

Analise wanted Olivia focused on the real problem. Yes, it was too bad they'd failed in getting Roy back on his feet, but there were currently bigger concerns for Magnolia Mile—or they'd need someone to get *them* back on their feet. The bank had already begun to make concerned queries about the financial solvency of the nursery. "Now we don't have help—and next week is the Holly Ridge Park job." Analise turned to Luke. "You had no right to fire him. It's *our* business." She faced Olivia again. "Maybe we can find him—"

Luke nearly shouted, "The man's too dangerous to have around here with just two women—"

Olivia interrupted him with a shush and a raised hand. "We'll just have to find someone else."

"Between now and Monday?" Analise shook her head. "Hargrove Farms has gobbled up almost all of the available manpower around here for that huge irrigation system. Whoever's left has gone to work for the new plastics plant. We can't compete with those wages."

Olivia said, "Cole can help."

"Yes," Analise said. "After school. That cuts me to working with extra muscle for about three hours a day—then it's too dark. Besides, Cole has soccer practice and needs to focus on his grades." She rubbed her temples.

"Don't forget, the contract has penalties for not finishing on schedule."

Olivia grumbled, "I knew when that Clint Braynard got into office he'd start trying to change things—wants to run this county like it's a big city. When have we ever had penalties? Our word has always been enough."

"Maybe we could get several of Cole's friends. Three hours a day with four or five of them might do it—"

"I'll stay."

Both Analise and Olivia turned to Luke. Analise glanced back at Olivia, who had a look of concentration on her face, as if she were weighing the pros and cons of his staying.

He repeated, "I'll stay and help . . . until you find someone else."

Analise said, "Your knee—"

"Won't keep me from digging holes. You've got a dolly for moving the heavy stuff."

She set her jaw. "We can't ask you to stay."

He looked steadily at her. She didn't like the way those blue eyes made her heart beat a little faster and her blood press against her veins.

"You didn't ask," he said. "I offered. In fact, I insist."

"We can't thank you enough," Olivia said with a smile. "I promise to start looking for someone right away."

Analise could see the glitter in Olivia's eye; they both knew there would be no new help until that irrigation system was finished, unless it fell from the sky. Which was practically what had just happened with Luke's unexpected arrival.

"What are you doing back here, anyway?" Analise asked with an edge still in her voice. "I thought you were on your way to Indiana."

The second he riveted those blue eyes on her she realized

her mistake. He looked at her for a long moment. Analise prayed he'd have the decency to keep his mouth shut in front of Olivia.

He finally said, "I just felt we didn't complete our last conversation. I don't like to leave things unfinished. I'm in no rush"—he lifted a shoulder—"so I thought I'd come back and at least say good-bye." He looked sharply at her. "Besides," he added, looking at Olivia, "my knee is much better in the weather down here; maybe I'll wait until spring reaches the North."

Olivia smiled her thanks and said, "I'll get the guest room ready."

At the sound of Analise's indrawn breath, Luke said, "That's not necessary. I'll stay at the motel."

Olivia wrinkled her nose. "I suppose you've been staying at the Stargazer." She said the name like it was a house of ill repute. When Luke nodded, she made noise of disgust. "I wouldn't put Rufus up in that place. It'd have gone under years ago if the married folk around here stayed true. No. I just can't have it. If you're staying on to help, you're staying at Magnolia Mile. The least we can do. Right, Ana?"

Suddenly there was only one image in Analise's mind— and try as she might, she couldn't banish it: Luke standing naked in the bathroom door. Her involuntary reaction to him told her all she had to know—spending too much time with him would weaken her defenses. The attraction she felt to him was dangerously strong. She reminded herself he was only here because Calvin, the husband she'd wished would never come home, had died. There was no way in hell she'd ever be able to reconcile that. His continued presence was going to be like stripping away her skin one square inch at a time. How was she going to undo this without betraying her feelings to Olivia?

In the end, all she could do was agree that he should remain here. She said, "Of course," with numb lips. She realized her voice sounded as if she'd just accepted a long jail sentence, so she followed it with a forced smile. Knowing her eyes would betray her, she kept her gaze on Rufus.

For the second time in the past minutes, Luke inched closer to her heart by saying, "I left my things at the motel." Analise knew this was a lie. She'd seen his duffel in the back seat when he drove her to the plantation. "I'll just stay there for now—since you'll probably find someone in the next day or so. No sense in moving everything out here."

Olivia hesitated.

"It makes the most sense," Analise was quick to say. "We don't need to make him pack up and move for just a couple of days."

Luke nodded, but Analise couldn't tell exactly what was going on in his mind. Maybe he was no more anxious to ensconce himself in their house than she was to have him there.

"What if we don't find someone right away?" Olivia asked.

"Let's cross that bridge when we come to it," Luke said as he walked toward his car. He stopped and looked back at them after two more steps. "And keep those doors locked tonight—just in case Roy has more nerve than he showed this afternoon." He paused just before he got in. "Rufus sleeps inside, doesn't he?"

Analise nodded.

"Good. Pay attention to him."

Olivia waved away his concern. "I'm sure we've seen the last of Roy—judging by his hasty exit."

Luke stared hard at her. "Just the same . . ."

"Not to worry. Rufus is as good as a burglar alarm." Olivia laid a hand on the hound's head.

Luke riveted his gaze on Analise as he walked away. "Later, you and I need to finish that discussion."

Her stomach twisted into a tight knot. She never should have stopped at the cemetery, never should have opened her mouth about her relationship with Calvin. It was both a betrayal of his memory and a disgrace to Olivia. Now she was going to have to explain herself and make things even worse.

She watched Luke drive away, with a mass of confused feelings in her chest that nearly squeezed the breath out of her. How could she be afraid of Luke's staying, yet so reluctant to let him go at the same time?

"I'm going to call the paper and put in an ad for help." Analise had no intention of letting Olivia stall on this; there was something in the older woman's eye that said she liked having Luke around just a little too much. Maybe it was simply because of his connection to Calvin—Luke's presence made her feel closer to her lost son. Which had a significant downside; when Luke left, as he most certainly would, Olivia would have to deal with yet another loss.

"You do that, dear . . ." Olivia said. Analise was certain she heard Olivia whistling as she returned to the house.

Once the ad was placed, Analise went to the soccer field to pick up Cole from practice. He was smiling and sweaty—apparently the workout had been good for him. He seemed more like his old self on the way home. It was as if he'd hit the bottom with his drinking binge and realized he had to get himself together. Maybe this was the turning point, maybe the drama was over and they'd finally get their lives back on track.

As she lay down to sleep that night, she basked in relief:

Cole seemed better; she would find a replacement for Roy—who, in reality, she wouldn't miss one bit; best of all, although she wasn't able to prevent his continued presence, she'd avoided having Luke sleeping under the same roof. Falling into a blissful sleep, the weight of worry drifted away on her soft breaths.

Analise's relief lasted until two A.M., when she was jolted awake by a huge rock shattering her bedroom window.

Chapter 8

Cole was lying awake, worrying. That seemed to be all he'd been doing lately—worrying. The sheets chafed his skin. The darkness pressed on him like he'd been buried in tar. He couldn't find a comfortable position. At first he was too hot, then too cold. He stared at the ceiling, avoiding the chance of seeing those green cat eyes staring at him from a corner of the room. He'd done his usual search for Pandora before he'd closed the door. Although he hadn't found her, he knew she was there, curled up somewhere in the dark, just waiting for him to go to sleep so she could crawl into bed with him.

His life had become so screwed up, he barely recognized it anymore. He tried to picture what his life used to be like—back before Pandora arrived with her black-cat bad luck and changed everything. Back when everything made sense. It seemed as unreachable as childhood Christmases.

How could he look at things the same? Calvin had been strong, able to protect himself. And yet, a stupid accident took it all away—just like Cole's dad. What was the point of standing for your country, trying to do what was right, if in a split second your life could be over?

Losing his dad had been hard, but that was so long ago he had to work really hard to remember more than vague things about him—his cologne, that he liked to fish, the way he'd made Mom laugh. There weren't promises that hadn't been kept with his dad. But Calvin—Calvin was young. Calvin had lots of plans for Cole. He was going to take Cole places after he finished school, just the two of them—guy trips. They were going to go whitewater rafting and mountain climbing. He was going to teach Cole how to surf.

Time after time, something would happen and Cole would catch himself thinking he'd have to ask Calvin about it—only to realize, seconds later, he wouldn't be asking Calvin's advice ever again.

Lately, there just didn't seem any reason to worry about a future that might very well not come. Especially since he had his own personal bad-luck charm that crawled into bed with him every night.

Maybe if he drove that damn cat a hundred miles away and left her, things would shift back to the way they used to be. He wasn't so stupid as to believe that it would bring Calvin back. But maybe soccer and Darcy and school would straighten up.

Closing his eyes so he wouldn't see the cat, he flopped onto his side and pounded his pillow into submission. He heard Rufus whine in the kitchen below like he was dreaming. Even the dog had been having nightmares since Pandora's arrival.

Everything just kept getting more and more complicated and off balance. He'd managed to get by Analise today; she had no idea that he hadn't been at school or soccer practice. It sort of scared him, the fact that he was getting so good at lying. He hardly even felt guilty about it anymore. Even worse, he hadn't been able to bury the feeling of pride that had come when he'd thought to change his clothes, run long enough to work up a sweat and dirty himself up a little before she'd arrived to pick him up. He'd been surprised— and relieved—that the attendance office hadn't called home and snitched on him. Maybe Mrs. Baker had a substitute; no way would she have let his absence go unreported. Old bag.

Thank God tomorrow was Saturd—

The sound of shattering glass mingled with Analise's startled yelp. Cole was off the bed and down the hall in less than a heartbeat. He threw open the door and flipped on the overhead light in Ana's room without a thought.

She sat on the bed, a stunned look on her face. The hand over her heart had a trickle of blood on the back of it. A softball-sized rock lay on the floor in a shower of broken glass; her curtains fluttered out the gaping bottom window frame.

"You okay?" he shouted, even as he started out into the hall.

"Yeah."

He sprinted off, meeting a baying Rufus on the stairs. The dog did an about face, the two of them fighting to get through the front door first.

"Cole! Wait!"

He barely heard Ana yelling. His blood pumped hot. His body burned to punish whoever had hurt her. His bare feet pounded across the front porch and out into the yard. He tore around to the side of the house, where Analise's window was, with Rufus just ahead of him.

Not surprisingly, there wasn't anybody there. Rufus sniffed the ground, following a trail into the woods. Cole checked the edge of the woods, but didn't find anyone hiding in the overgrowth. Then he ran down the drive, the rocks and stones cutting into his feet. When he reached the road, he caught a glimpse of taillights fading in the darkness to the left.

He trotted back toward the house that was now ablaze with light. Analise and his mom stood on the front porch in their pajamas.

He said, "Whoever it was is long gone." He whistled for Rufus to come back.

Analise grabbed him by the upper arm. "What on earth did you think you were doing, running out here like that? Who knows—"

"Your hand is bleeding," he said, taking her hand in his.

"It's nothing. Just a scratch from flying glass." She pulled her hand away and Cole had to overcome the urge to grab it back.

Olivia said, "It must have been Roy." She shook her head and sighed sadly.

Analise said, "Seems like we would have heard that truck of his, as still as it is tonight."

"Rufus was making enough racket to drown out a NASCAR race," Olivia said.

Cole's gaze cut to his mother. "Wait a minute! What happened with Roy?" He *knew* that guy was creepy.

"He went after Ana. We had to fire him."

"What do you mean, went after her?" His stomach knotted further. The rock was bad enough, but if he put a hand on Ana . . .

Analise said, "He was mad because he wanted to meet with Reverend Hammond, but he left before Roy saw him. He was just yelling. . . ."

"Let's get back inside," Olivia said. "A warm day here and there and already the mosquitoes are eating me alive."

"With any luck at all, Roy'll be sucked dry before he gets out of the woods," Cole said, swatting a mosquito himself.

Both he and Rufus cast menacing looks toward the woods before entering the house—just in case someone was hiding out there, watching.

"We didn't expect you until Monday," Analise said, the inhospitable tone stronger in her voice than she'd intended. She finished arranging a large pot of pansies beside the front door of the shop and only glanced at Luke.

He didn't seem to notice her ungrateful attitude. "I assume Roy works on Saturday. Since I'm Roy for the next few days, I'll carry his load. Where do I start?"

Analise was about to say he could start by going away until Monday, but Olivia's voice carried across the yard.

"Luke!" She came closer. "Good gracious! You're just in time."

He turned to Olivia. "In time for what?"

Analise didn't miss the warm smile the two of them exchanged.

"I need you to drive Cole to the hardware store to pick up a new glass pane for Ana's window."

"I said I would take him after lunch," Analise said. She still didn't see the need to keep Cole from driving the Jeep. He'd learned his lesson.

"No sense in waiting, now that Luke's here."

"But he was just leaving."

"He just got here."

"We don't need him until Monday."

"Well, as long as he's already here . . . he has to stay for lunch anyway."

"I really don't think we should expect him to—"

"Wait a minute!" He gave them both a pointed look. "I'll be happy to take Cole into town."

"Oh, good." Olivia grinned at Analise in an uncharacteristically victorious way. "And maybe you can give him a hand replacing the glass in the window when y'all get back?"

"Of course."

Analise inched back toward the shop, hoping to remove herself as inconspicuously as possible.

"There he is now," Olivia said, as Cole came out of the house. She held a finger in the air. "Excuse me a minute." She met him halfway across the yard. After a few brief words, they both came back toward Luke. Analise had successfully disappeared.

Luke studied the boy as he approached. This was the first time he'd seen him sober. It was clear Cole shared Calvin's good looks. But there was something different in Cole's carriage, something missing—Calvin's devil-may-care confidence.

Cole kept his gaze on the ground as he walked nearer. Not until he stopped directly in front of Luke did he make eye contact. He said, "I apologize for puking all ove—"

"Cole!" Olivia's sharp tone cut off his words.

"For my behavior the other day."

Luke nodded his acceptance. "Let's go get that glass."

Some of the tension left Cole's posture. Luke decided to let the subject go altogether; he hoped to make inroads toward helping the boy out of his troubles, and it would be difficult to accomplish from opposite sides of enemy lines. He was going to be around here for a while; no sense in scaring the kid off with probing questions and sermons.

They got into the Taurus and headed toward town. Once out of the drive, Luke said, "Calvin told me you're the best goalie Grover's soccer team has ever had."

"He did?" Cole quickly negated the little-boy wonder with a dose of sixteen-year-old bravado. "I haven't been scored on in the past seven games. I play a little offense, too. Calvin started training me when I was just a little kid. He's a good teacher." He paused and a shadow crossed his face. "*Was* a good teacher."

"He was a good soldier, too. I could always count on him." He paused. "Always." Then Luke added, "That's what makes the difference, you know. You can talk all you want, but if the people who depend on you *know* you'll come through—well, that's the test of a true man."

When his comment was met with silence, Luke feared he'd gotten too preachy. He glanced over and saw Cole was looking steadily out the passenger window.

They traveled without conversation for a couple of minutes, then Cole said, "I've been thinking of joining the army when I graduate. I'd want to be special ops."

Luke nodded. "The army has a lot to offer. What do you like in school?"

"Nothin'."

Glancing at Cole with an understanding smile, Luke said, "Okay, what interests you? Computers? Airplanes? Telecommunications? Mechanics? Engineering? Foreign language?"

"I wanna do the secret stuff, the dangerous things that nobody ever hears about. Sneak around hostile countries. Carry out secret missions. Recover hostages. Like Calvin did."

Luke flinched. "There are lots of avenues that'll give you a better career, more training that'll transfer to civilian occupations."

"Yeah, but they're not as exciting."

Luke shook his head and gave a short chuckle. "The reality is, special ops is about ninety-nine percent mundane activity, one percent excitement." When he looked over, Cole was staring at the scar on his neck. Luke flashed hot.

"Accidents happen everywhere. Scars aren't a badge of honor in the military any more than anyplace else."

Cole looked away and rolled his lips inward.

Luke felt bad for snapping at the kid. "All I'm saying is that you should look at the long term. Pick something with high interest, that'll carry over for the rest of your life." He knew firsthand, as he was being faced with deciding what to do with the rest of *his* life, just how painfully true that statement was. If he could no longer *do* special ops, the only other thing he figured he was fit for was to train and command special ops. And that didn't hold a single iota of appeal. "If you want, I can have some information sent to you, so you can see what kinds of things are offered."

"Okay."

Luke couldn't tell if there was any enthusiasm behind the agreement, or if Cole was just ready to stop arguing about it.

He reduced his speed as they entered the city limits. "Where's the hardware?"

"On Commerce, south of the courthouse."

They parked in an angled spot right in front of the Grover Western-Auto. Luke dropped a couple of coins in the meter and climbed the two steps up to the sidewalk. They went inside, past the bicycles, past the pots and pans, beyond the power tools, to the glass cutting in the rear.

An elderly man with about a half-set of teeth left in his head smiled at Cole. "Say, there, young Master Lejeune." With the missing teeth there was a lot of lisping involved.

"Hey, Mr. Graves. Mom said she called in the order for a piece of glass."

"Yup. Got it right here." He pulled a brown-paper-wrapped sheet of glass from the workbench. "Course you'll be needin' some glazing, too." He added a tube to the order. "Remember, now, gotta chip away all of the old before you replace the glass." As he wrote down the price on a little scrap of paper, he said, "Miss Livvie said y'all got a rock through the old one."

"Yeah. Some guy threw it in the middle of the night. I chased him into the woods. Mom said it was probably the worker they fired yesterday, just trying to get back at them."

Luke felt as if he'd just been doused with cold water. The chill went to his blood. Roy was dangerous—and still sneaking around Magnolia Mile.

They paid for the glass and got back in the car. Luke immediately said, "Tell me what happened last night."

He got an adolescent pumped-up heroic accounting. Which, he imagined, was the polar opposite of what Analise would deliver—the dismissive, *everything's all right* version of the tale. Luke didn't really need either one. He'd set his mind on a course of action. Nothing was going to change it.

Olivia was on her knees pruning some hydrangea bushes in two-gallon black plastic containers when Luke and Cole returned. As she got to her feet, she ran the back of one gloved hand over her nose, driving away the tickle that had been bothering her for the past several seconds. "I thought you two had gotten lost."

"My fault," Luke said. "We went by the Stargazer to pick up my stuff. I've decided to take you up on that room."

"What?" Analise stepped out from behind the trellis wall.

Luke shrugged. "After making the drive this morning, I realized how much more convenient it'd be if I bunked here."

Olivia saw Analise narrow her eyes at Cole, who was getting the new glass out of the trunk.

Analise quickly said, "If this is all about that broken

window, you don't have to worry. Olivia reported it to Dave this morning. He's already been by and is keeping an eye out for Roy."

Luke locked gazes with her. "No. This is all about *me* not driving over an hour a day on bumpy back roads in order to shovel dirt and cart plants."

She shot him a look that said she knew he was lying. Liv knew it, too, but had no intention of saying so. Whatever his motivation, she was thrilled to have Luke under her roof. She needed him—they were all going to need him.

"Good. Good," she said, pulling off her gloves. "You can take the green room."

"What about the downstairs room?" Analise interjected. "That way he'd have his own bath."

"And have him sleep on that lumpy old fold-out? Don't be ridiculous." Olivia looked at Cole. "Take his bag up to the green room."

Cole looked pleased.

Analise looked unhappy.

And Olivia was having a difficult time understanding why her daughter-in-law was so prickly when it came to Luke.

Analise had given Olivia a serious frown when her mother-in-law had suggested they follow their usual Saturday night routine and go to the Boxcar Diner—Luke in tow. But at least if they were in a noisy, crowded place, it would be easier to avoid the questions Luke had returned to ask.

Again and again she cursed herself for the momentary weakness at the cemetery when she'd let those words slip: *He was a lousy husband.* The time was soon coming when she'd have to explain them to Luke. And she'd have to do it in a way that didn't divulge the true reason she'd been compelled to tell him in the first place.

When she'd led him into the cemetery, she hadn't been sure of her motivation—in fact, it wasn't until she was fleeing, praying he wouldn't follow her, that it had come crashing home. She'd wanted Luke to know so he would look at her not as a grieving widow, but as a woman. She'd discovered something about herself that she'd kept walled away for longer than she cared to admit: She wanted a moment, a fantasy in which another man could find her desirable—one who wouldn't be hanging around to complicate her life with Olivia and Cole.

Well, she'd just have to change her perspective now that Luke was staying.

"Ready, Ana?" Olivia called up the stairs.

She wiped off the lipstick she'd just put on. "Coming."

When she got downstairs, Olivia, Luke and Cole were standing by the back door. "Sorry." She looked around. "Is Rufus in?"

"Yeah, and he's been fed. Let's go," Cole said impatiently.

Analise looked curiously at him. Since Calvin had died, Cole repeatedly tried to blow off the Saturday night dinner. Of course, Olivia never let him. This was the first time he hadn't put up a fight in months. "Okay." She smiled. "Let's go."

The Boxcar Diner was actually a cross between a restaurant and a honky-tonk. On Saturday night there was live music—alternating between blues and country—and all-you-can-eat fried catfish. They served beer by the pitcher and had vinyl table covers with black-and-white cow print, railway lanterns over the booths and a toy train that ran around the perimeter of the room on a track suspended just below the ceiling. The windows in the place hadn't been cleaned in a lifetime and were fogged so heavily with grime and cigarette smoke that, once inside, you could hardly see daylight on the brightest day.

Analise could see the pleasure on Luke's face when they walked in. "Your kind of place?" she asked.

"Oh, yeah." He nodded. "Bet they've got sweet potato casserole and chocolate chess pie."

"Best in the county on both counts." She led them to a booth in the back corner.

He sniffed loudly. "There's enough cholesterol in the air alone to clog a man's arteries."

Cole laughed loudly as they followed Analise toward the back of the restaurant.

Most of the tables were filled. Luke glanced back over his shoulder and saw several people waiting near the door. He caught up with Analise and whispered, "Hey, there were people waiting for tables."

She tossed him a smile over her shoulder. "Liv has permanent Saturday night reservations."

Luke realized she was no longer moving along with them. "Where'd she go?"

"She'll get back here eventually. Gotta work the room on her way in."

"Gets really embarrassing," Cole said, sliding into the booth.

Analise waited, letting Luke choose whether to sit beside Cole or on the unoccupied side. Normally, she shared the side with Cole—unless Darcy was along. She realized suddenly that Darcy hadn't joined them for Saturday night dinner in a long while. She'd have to ask Cole about that.

Luke sat next to Cole. Analise breathed a little sigh of relief; she didn't have to choose between sitting next to Luke or having his probing eyes directly across the table from her. She scooted deep into the booth, across from Cole.

"I see we have a visitor tonight," Rosie, their regular Saturday night waitress, said as she set an icy pitcher of beer in the center of the table. It was followed by three frosty mugs and a tall Coke for Cole. "I'll have your onion rings right out." She turned to Luke. "You want anything special added to the appetizers?"

When Luke looked up and smiled at Rosie, who was still riding on the early side of thirty and was very attractive, Analise felt a nip of jealousy.

He asked, "You recommend anything?"

Rosie pursed her lips into a sensual pout and tapped them with her pencil. "Fried pickles are my favorite. Course, the wings are popular."

Luke nudged Cole with an elbow. "What d'ya say? Wings or pickles?"

Analise didn't miss the way Cole sat up a little straighter when being consulted. He said, "Wings with beer."

Luke tilted his head slightly and raised a brow. "And you know this because . . ."

Cole rolled his eyes. "Like I come in *here* and order beer. Wings are more . . . manly. Pickles are for girls."

Luke looked back to Rosie. "A manly platter of wings it is."

She dipped her chin. "You'll have to come back another time for the pickles. Tart and hot." She actually gave a little shiver of pleasure. "I highly recommend them."

My gosh, could the woman be any more blatant?

Luke certainly didn't react like he'd been the recipient of a *let me take you for a wild ride* message. Instead, he turned immediately to Cole. "So this is a Saturday night tradition in the Abbott-Lejeune household? You even have a standing order."

At first Cole's eyes flashed like he was going to respond with a derogatory comment, showing Luke he was too old for "family traditions." But Luke quickly added, "I think this is really cool. Wish I could do something like this with my dad and sisters every once in a while."

"You miss your family," Olivia stated as she slid into the booth. "How long since you've seen them?"

Luke poured beer into the mugs. "It's been a *very* long time since I've been back to Glens Crossing. I try to make phone contact at least once a month. Dad and Lily came to visit a couple of times while I was in the hospital. I'm afraid I wasn't very good company at the time."

If Olivia felt a shred of guilt over detaining Luke from getting home, she didn't show any sign of it.

Rosie delivered the appetizers. "I assume y'all want the usual." She ran her gaze over Liv, Ana and Cole. Then she looked at Luke. "The usual is fried catfish, hush puppies, slaw and fries. You care to try something different?"

Analise gritted her teeth at the innuendo in the woman's voice.

Luke just smiled and raised a hand. "No, thanks. I'll stick with the usual." Then he reached for a wing.

Rosie hesitated for a moment longer. Then, as she started to leave, Luke called her back. "I would like to add an order of sweet potato casserole, though."

"All righty, sugar." She smiled and turned with a provocative toss of her hair.

Once she was out of earshot, Cole said, "Dude! She was totally hitting on you."

"Why, I do believe you're right," Olivia agreed, with a hint of mock surprise in her voice.

"She hits on *all* men." The words were out before Analise could stop them. She sounded adolescent and petty.

"Nuh-uh," Cole said. "Not like that."

"Eat your wings." Analise took a long drink of beer, but didn't miss Luke's wide grin.

She managed better at maintaining her civility throughout the remainder of the meal. They settled into conversations that slid easily from one topic to the other. Luke shared a few stories that had Cole completely rapt. The boy was more lively than she'd seen him in months. After they finished off their meals with chocolate chess pie—on Luke's insistence—and the band was beginning to set up, Luke and Cole went to shoot pool in the alcove that was on the other side of the room. As Analise watched them, she began to feel selfish for being so resentful about Luke's presence. It wasn't his fault she was attracted to him. He seemed to be so good for Cole, and Olivia practically beamed in his presence.

That thought rekindled her original concern. Was Olivia becoming attached to Luke as a link to her lost son? If so, Olivia would be opening herself to more pain. Because the only sure thing in Luke's presence was the fact that he'd be leaving.

The band made some general noise—random drumbeats and cymbal clashes, odd plucked notes and a few stray chords—as they warmed up. Then they began their first set. Tonight the music was country, which Analise preferred to blues. The band wound down on their opening song and the vocalist announced it was time to open the dance floor— which meant the four tables directly in front of the band were removed, crumbs were swept from the hardwood and the lights were dimmed.

As always during the first dance of Saturday night, Dave Dunston appeared to take Analise to the dance floor. It was a habit he'd begun on the first Saturday that they'd returned to their routine after Calvin's death. At first, Analise had been hesitant, but Olivia had encouraged her, saying Dave was just doing what he could to help ease her loss. After all, he and Calvin had been good friends. Since the day Calvin left for the army, Dave had made an effort to fill his absence. Deep down, Analise had been grateful for Olivia's encouragement; she really loved to dance.

Olivia said, "Dave, I'd like you to meet Luke Boudreau. He was in the Rangers with Calvin."

Dave nodded at Luke. "We've met."

"Good to see you again," Luke said as they shook hands.

Dave's gaze quickly switched to Analise. "Ready, darlin'?"

"You bet."

Dave took her elbow and guided her through the tables. Stepping onto the dance floor, Analise saw Dick and Lois Baker, having passed their forty-first anniversary, locking hands for a lively two-step. There was something about seeing those two dance that always made Analise feel hollow and lacking inside. What would it be like to have a life partner who shared your everyday pleasures?

"What are you looking at?" Dave asked as he grabbed her hand and gave her a twirl, sending her unbound hair in a flighty arc.

Normally she left her hair braided when they came out on Saturday night. Tonight, she supposed the same hidden yearning that had made her put on lipstick had also been responsible for the hair. When she faced him again, she had to toss it out of her face. It made her feel unusually flirty. She glanced at the booth.

Luke was talking animatedly to Cole, not looking in her direction at all; she couldn't deny a nibble of disappointment.

"The Bakers," she said to Dave. "They're just so cute together."

"Well, hey, I always thought we were pretty cute

together," he said, a note of teasing in his voice. "Maybe in another twenty years we'll be as cute as they are."

The comment made Analise miss a step. The thought of dancing with Dave, friend of her dead husband, every Saturday night for the next twenty years made her falter.

"Whoa, there; that'd be my toe, little lady."

Analise cringed. "Sorry."

About halfway through "Ain't Goin' Down 'til the Sun Comes Up," and just about the time she was beginning to feel a little breathless from the rapid-paced dance, she saw Olivia spin by.

Startled, Ana did a double-take; Olivia *never* danced. But there she was, laughing, looking like a sprite as Luke tucked her under his arm and swung her out again. Analise nearly stopped midstep, but she managed to keep her feet moving until the song played out.

Stepping away from Dave, fighting the urge to ogle Olivia and Luke, she bowed her head and said, "You're a fabulous dance partner, as always. Thank you."

Dave grinned. "One of these days, I'll get you to dance more than one."

She shook a finger in the air. "One's my limit." It wasn't that she didn't long to dance more, that her toes didn't tap secretly under the table and her feet itch to move with the music. But this was a routine that had certain built-in limits. She wasn't sure she was ready to step beyond those. As it was, everyone knew she danced one dance with Dave, the old family friend, and that was it. She didn't have to deal with curious glances and hushed whispers that Widow Abbott was looking for a new husband.

Dave started to escort her back to her table. But from the corner of her eye, she saw Mimi Adkins inching shyly closer to Dave. "I can find my way back." She gave a discreet nod of her head in Mimi's direction and whispered, "I think you have another partner waiting."

Mimi had probably been the home-ec teacher's pet in school. She exuded a backward wholesomeness that home-ec teachers always seemed to favor. In adulthood, she hadn't strayed far from that field, working at the Heavenly Delight Bakery on Commerce. She was known county-wide for her beautiful wedding cakes. Analise often wondered if perhaps there was a little envy in the placement of the bride and groom atop each cake. As far as she could tell, Mimi didn't date.

She hurried off, giving Mimi a chance to nab Dave before he got away. Mimi had had a crush on him since . . . well, as long as Analise had been in town. From the look in Mimi's eye, it probably stretched way back to when she was learning to bake in eighth-grade cooking class. And of course, as with most males, Dave seemed oblivious. Maybe he was just shy, too, Analise thought as she headed back to the booth.

Maybe he just needed a nudge in the right direction.

She stifled a gleeful giggle at the prospect of playing cupid for those two. Maybe she'd even recruit Olivia. This was just the sort of thing Olivia loved to scheme.

Analise arrived back at the booth before Olivia and Luke.

Cole said, "Did you see Mom?" There was as much stunned wonder in his voice as there had been in Analise's initial reaction.

"She's a pretty good dancer," Analise said.

A breathless Olivia returned on Luke's arm, escorted as properly as if they were at a cotillion instead of a run-down honky-tonk. Her hand fluttered just over her heart as she sat down. "My gracious! I'd forgotten I could do that."

Luke gave her the same gracious bow he'd given Analise

that first day they'd met. Silly as it was, the chivalry of it made Analise's heart trip a little faster.

Analise grinned. "You're great. You should dance more often."

Olivia waved the suggestion away. "I'd need to build up a lot more stamina. Besides, there aren't many men like Luke around here; he knows how to cut a rug."

"It was all my partner's grace." Luke tilted his head. "Care to give it another go?"

"Oh, goodness, no." Then she turned her gaze to Analise. "But Ana loves to dance."

Just as the words were out of Olivia's mouth, the next song started. It was going to be a slow one. The intro played for "It's Your Love" and Analise decided no way was she dancing. That song always made her feel particularly melancholy.

"Liv, I'm sure Luke's had enough."

"Nonsense."

"His knee—"

"Can use the exercise."

"He's tired; he worked all day."

"He seems perfectly—"

Luke cleared his throat loudly. "I don't know if you ladies have noticed, but you're developing quite a habit of arguing about me as if I'm not here."

"See, Ana, you've made him uncomfortable."

Analise sat up straighter. "*I've* made him—"

Her mouth snapped shut as Luke took her hand and yanked her to her feet. "Let's dance."

Chapter 9

Before Analise could regain her breath, she was in the middle of the dance floor, Luke's warm hand on the small of her back. There was a slight tug that said her hair was caught beneath his hand, which for some reason seemed all the more intimate—scandalous.

He swept her right into the dance, leaving no time for her to protest or pull away. He moved pretty well, the stiffness in his knee barely noticeable.

She avoided looking around the room at the familiar and no doubt curious faces, yet she managed not to look into Luke's face, either. All of her repressed desire to dance dried right up. She moved woodenly, feeling like all eyes in the place were on her, judging.

Suddenly Luke gave her left hand a little loosening shake. "Relax a little," he said. "I promise not to trample your toes."

"I'm not worried about my toes." Oops, she made the mistake of looking into those sky-blue eyes. They pulled her over like a rapid waterfall.

He looked deep, his gaze almost palpable, and asked, "What are you worried about?"

She couldn't help but hold his gaze. She tried to sound flippant. "What makes you think I'm worried?"

He snorted—an action that should have been off-putting, but for some reason was oddly appealing, a boyish contrast to the hard-muscled, rugged man.

"The first time I laid eyes on you," he said, "you were dancing—and you certainly weren't moving like a Barbie doll."

She rolled her eyes, hoping her cheeks weren't flaming red as she remembered that moment. "I was supposed to be alone. This is different."

"Really?" He cocked his head slightly to the side, looking as adorable as a puppy. Analise had to remind herself that was how she got sucked in with Calvin. He continued, "You didn't have wooden legs when you danced with Dep'dy Dave, there." He nodded at Dave as they moved past him and Mimi.

Analise noticed Dave didn't appear very relaxed, either.

She shook her head, dismissing the subject, and looked at the band.

"Really, I want to know," he prodded. "What'd I do to make you dislike me?"

Her gaze snapped back to his face. "I don't dislike you." Quite the contrary.

Instead of saying anything else, he just stared into her eyes and pulled her closer as they moved to the melancholy, yet overwhelmingly sensual beat of the love song. She forced herself to hold his gaze, feeling vulnerable and exposed. Could he see what was really in her heart—what a horrible, disloyal woman she was?

Luke leaned a little closer and whispered in her ear, "I didn't come here to upset you—I just want to help."

Shame kept her from responding. Coward that she was,

she tucked her head on his shoulder so she wouldn't have to look in his eyes any longer. If she gave him half a chance, he'd press for the answer to the question he'd returned to ask. And she didn't have the strength to discuss Calvin while in Luke's arms, with Luke's living breath on her cheek.

After a moment, the music's strong emotion melded with her own. The warmth of Luke's body slowly seeped into hers, crossing the minuscule space between them like an arcing current. A change as hot and liquid as melted caramel came over her. She no longer moved stiffly. Her limbs felt heavy and fluid. She knew the reason: Forbidden desire had sparked deep within her.

Closing her eyes, she shut out everything else. She understood the dangerous waters she was treading. And she knew she should never allow herself to go there—never allow herself to be this close to him again. So she gave herself the selfish gift of this moment; to enjoy the feel of his body against hers, relish the little tingle in her lower back where his hand rested, shiver at his breath on the back of her neck, and imagine what might have been in a different place, a different time.

The music finally faded into its last strains. Analise immediately turned away from Luke and started back toward their table. If she looked in his eyes now, he was sure to see.

Just as she left the dance floor she saw Darcy, and the bottom dropped out of her stomach. The girl had danced her way into a dark corner with some guy, who definitely wasn't Cole, and was ending the dance with a very indiscreet, very . . . athletic . . . kiss.

Immediately, she looked for Cole. *Please, please, God, don't let him have seen.*

Olivia was in the booth alone. Analise quickly followed

her mother-in-law's troubled gaze and just caught a glimpse of Cole barging out the door.

Luke stopped her from following right behind by grabbing her arm. "What's with Cole?"

Ana jerked her head toward the corner. "That's his girlfriend."

"Uh-oh."

She started to pull away and go after him, but Luke held tight. "Give him a minute. He can't go far."

"But—"

"If he wanted to talk about it, he'd still be sitting in that booth. Give the kid some time to get himself together."

As much as it galled her to admit it, she realized Luke was right.

Just as they reached the table, Dave came by. "The band's really good tonight," he said. "Analise, how about another turn around the floor?"

"Oh, Dave, I'm sorry, but we have to go." Then she added, when his face clouded, "Next week as usual, though."

"Sure." He smiled. "Next week."

Olivia had already called for the bill. Rosie brought it, stepping in front of Dave as if he weren't even there. She held up the check and cast a curious gaze from Olivia to Luke.

Olivia said, "I'll get it," and at the same time Luke shoved a credit card into Rosie's hand.

As they left the restaurant, Dave, who'd been lingering with small talk, assured them, "I'll be by later tonight. Just to check on things."

Olivia patted him on the arm as she passed. "Thanks so much, Dave. But that won't be necessary. Luke's going to be staying with us."

After a moment, Dave gave a half-smile and nodded.

"Good." He paused. "That's good. I'll still make a pass with the cruiser—just as a deterrent. Police presence sometimes is all it takes to keep the mischief in check."

Analise wasn't able to stand still. Where had Cole gone? She headed toward the door and heard Olivia thanking Dave again.

Once outside, she cast a quick glance around, hoping to see Cole pacing the parking lot. She didn't.

Just as her heart started to speed up, Luke nudged her from behind. "He's in the car."

She looked that way and saw the silhouette of the crown of his head. He was slumped down in the back seat.

A little sigh of relief passed her lips.

As she started toward the car, Luke said, "I'd just let this rest for now."

She spun on him. "I think I know how to handle a boy I've helped raise, thank you very much."

Luke shrugged. "Okay. I was just making a suggestion."

"For your information, I didn't intend to open the door and say something like, *Gee that sucks, Darcy was in there making out with that guy. Should we go get some ice cream to make it all better?*"

Luke chuckled. "No. From the look on your face, you were going to yank open the door and say, *How dare that little bitch dump you like that. Let me go kick her ass.*"

Analise just sputtered and stalked toward the car.

Cole headed straight to his room after the long, silent ride home. His feet thudded up the stairs two at a time. His arrival was announced by a slamming door.

Olivia said, "I don't suppose this would be the best time to tell him that I talked to Mrs. Baker tonight and volunteered him to help at the Kiwanis Rib Fest next Friday."

Luke laughed.

Analise shot him a dirty look.

Olivia *tsk*ed in Analise's direction.

"How can you be so callous?" Analise asked. Then she looked at Luke to include him. "Both of you. Cole's heart is broken."

Olivia stepped closer and wrapped Analise in a warm embrace. "He's sixteen. It's all part of growing up. This won't be the last time. He'll need us to help him keep it all in perspective." She released Analise and turned to Luke. "Do you remember your first heartbreak?"

A nostalgic smile spread across Luke's face. "I can still feel the pain." He clutched his heart. "Amy Whitson. Dumped me for the varsity basketball forward when I was a sophomore." He leaned close to Olivia and added, "To be fair, they *had* just won the sectional. What shallow, self-centered cheerleader could have resisted?"

Olivia giggled like a teenager herself.

Analise wanted to thump them both. "I can't believe you two! Cole's had more to deal with than just simple teenage infidelity."

Luke's voice took on an edge she hadn't heard before when he said, "Sure, the kid's had it rough. But that doesn't mean he can't learn to cope. He has to handle—"

"You don't know—"

He stiffened and leaned toward her. "I do know. All of this 'Poor Cole' crap isn't doing him a bit of good."

"If at sixteen you had—"

"At *ten* my mother took off with some traveling salesman. Walked out the door on an errand and just never came back. She left her husband and three kids in a town that knew the dirty details almost before we did. My dad moved us to an apartment over his bar so we'd be close at night when he worked. You know how many mothers let their kids hang out at your house when you live over a bar? But I never *once* used it as an excuse for my choices."

Analise felt like she'd been slapped.

He looked at Olivia. "No disrespect intended, ma'am."

Olivia fluttered a hand in the air. "I couldn't agree more. Cole has to learn to cope, and to own up to his choices." She gave a great, gaping yawn. "My. I can't remember when I've been so tired. I'm going to bed." She kissed Analise on the cheek and patted Luke on the arm. "Night, you two."

Analise watched her leave the kitchen, the heat of anger still stinging her cheeks. How could the woman remain so calm during a conversation like this? Wasn't she worried about her son? Analise turned around and opened the back door. "Come on, Rufus. We're going for a walk."

When the dog just huffed at her, she let out a strangled moan of frustration and went out alone, slamming the door behind her.

Luke watched out the window as Analise was swallowed by the darkness between the house and the road. *Damn woman. Doesn't she have any sense?* Just last night a rock came crashing through her bedroom window; now she was taking a walk alone in the dark.

He slipped silently out of the house, putting his often-used talents to work. No sense in pissing her off further by letting her know he was following. In the past, he'd tailed men for two days without giving himself away; shadowing a woman so worked up she couldn't see straight, let alone hear someone walk right up behind her, should be a piece of cake. He blended in with the night, moving with a stealth that he'd almost forgotten. He would follow her as long as she wanted to walk, but he wouldn't disturb her.

That conviction held until he heard her first sniffle. Then it wavered, but he held true.

Instead of going directly to the road, as he'd anticipated, she veered off into the yard about halfway there. A hundred tree frogs made a steady succession of ratchety croaks and the crickets were practically deafening; there wasn't much chance of the snap of an unseen twig giving him away. He closed up some of the distance between them.

She settled on a bench he didn't even see until she sat on it—and sniffled.

His conviction to remain unseen crumbled a little more.

There was only the slightest chill in the air, the frigid weather of that first day nothing more than a memory. Although she was wearing a jacket, he saw her rub her arms for warmth. She sniffled again and then buried her face in her hands.

That conviction became no more than a tiny pile of dust carried on the wind.

He took two silent steps backward. Then another two.

"Analise?" he called softly, as if looking for her. Then he tromped loudly in her direction.

She twisted on the bench, looking over her shoulder.

"Are you out here?" he said.

After clearing her throat, she said, "Yes. Over here on the bench."

Luke kept moving toward her. "I can't see a damn thing out here." Had to make it convincing.

She got up and took a couple of steps in his direction. Holding out her hand, she said, "Be careful. The ground's uneven."

He reached out, seeking her with one hand, as if he were as blind as he was pretending to be. When he touched her hand, she grasped it firmly.

"Here, sit down, your knee has to be strained."

They sat on the metal bench; she didn't let go of his hand.

He said, "My knee's getting stronger. The work today was better than physical therapy."

She let go of his hand and covered her mouth to stifle a sob. "I'm so sorry." She snuffed loudly. "I've been so awful to you . . . i-it's in-ex-ex-cusable. You're too good to us."

Too good? Hardly. He could never make up for the damage.

He hesitated, letting his hand hover in the air for a moment before he laid it on her shoulder. "I get the feeling you're used to doing things on your own, carrying the load of this family."

She didn't say anything, but he could feel her shoulder still shaking as she tried to stop crying.

He cupped the back of her head and pulled it to his shoulder. She relaxed against him as she had during the end of that dance. It surprised him as much this time as it had then. Would he ever figure out this woman?

After a moment, he went on, "I told you my mother left when we were kids. My sister, Lily, held us all together— just like you're holding this family together. It wasn't easy, but Lily was tough. I've never seen a little girl with more selfless determination. She never cried, never complained about cleaning or taking care of our little sister. It was like she was trying to fill in the giant space that Mom left with her seven-year-old spirit."

He kept talking softly, feeling her settle more firmly on his shoulder. "We had this special place we used to go to, deep in the woods. One day I found her there—like I found you here, tonight. When she saw me, she swiped the silent tears she'd been crying away. She didn't want me to know. And it made me so mad I could hardly see. I started yelling—not at Lily, but at our mom. I yelled and screamed and finally Lily joined in, too. Then she cried for an hour. I think it was the first time she'd cried since our mom walked out."

"Did it help?" Analise whispered into the crook of his neck.

"Oh, yeah. It helped." He stroked her hair.

As if receiving permission for the first time in her life to cry, the dam burst. Luke held her long enough that pins and needles started to prickle his backside. But his whole ass could fall off, and he wouldn't budge from this spot. Analise needed so much more than she allowed people to give.

Finally, her sobs reduced to ragged sniffles and she raised her head.

He said, "Tell me why you said what you did in the cemetery—just before you left."

She drew a shuddering breath.

"It's all right to tell me, everyone needs to let things out. What you say to me will remain between us." He suspected part of Analise's reluctance had to do with Olivia. She'd unloaded on him in the cemetery only because he would take what she said away with him.

"Oh, there's no helping this," she said in a low, bleak voice.

"I think there is—or else you wouldn't have said anything to me in the first place."

She started to get up, but he grabbed her hand and held her there.

After a long trembling sigh, she looked into the darkness and said, "My parents died when I was three. Grandmother raised me. There were just the two of us in a big old house filled with untouchable antiques, permanently sealed windows and artificial air—no matter what the season." She paused, it was a heavy silence, pregnant with the unsaid, the long-locked-away. "I had the best of everything—clothes, education, travel. I never ran. I never ate with my fingers. I never raised my voice. I never, *never* got dirty. We were very 'civilized,' Grandmother and I. She used the word as a permanent barrier between us and most of the population of Mississippi. We were different—special."

Analise sniffed and shook her head. "I'm making her sound like a wicked stepmother. She wasn't. Now that I look back, I think she was struggling to keep the old South alive, hiding her pain behind rigid rules and proper decorum." Her hand trembled in his. "And, God help me, she was going to make me just like her.

"I remember watching other kids in the park, sliding into home plate with the dust flying." She swooped one hand through the air to show the action. The pale moonlight glinted off her short fingernails, making them appear as delicate as the petals of a flower. "All I wanted was to, just once, roll in the dirt, to know what it was like to have grime under my fingernails, to have skinned knees and gum stuck in my hair, to go to the county fair and come home with my face sticky from blue cotton candy."

Her words picked up energy as they flowed from her lips and Luke knew they'd been a long time in coming. He didn't miss the fact that Analise now made a living by the grown-up equivalent of "rolling in the dirt." She'd taken herself as far away from that antiseptic childhood as she possibly could. He wanted to pat her on the back, pick her up and twirl her around, applaud her strength. He settled for offering her the warmth of his hand, the comfort of his presence.

She glanced briefly at him, then to their interlocked hands. "You already know how I met Calvin. Maybe I grabbed blindly at a chance for change—maybe I wasn't fair to Calvin in that. But I saw something glittering and full of life, and I wanted to be a part of it more than I'd wanted anything in my life.

"Of course, Grandmother disowned me. Our wedding was a far cry from the fabulous social event she'd been planning for years—she'd only been waiting for a qualified groom." She chuckled. "Calvin was anything but what she'd been searching for. So he and I were married by a judge before the end of his leave.

"It was all so . . . so exciting and unpredictable and romantic. I did love him—with everything in me. He made me feel so alive."

Luke forced himself not to pull away from those words. Jealousy nipped at his heart. She'd loved Calvin—and he in turn had given that love no more respect than he would gum stuck to the bottom of a barroom table. In that moment, Luke realized he wanted more with this woman. More than a few weeks of passing acquaintance. But he would never, never use Calvin's infidelities to influence her, to change the purity of her love for her dead husband.

"There were only three months left on Calvin's term of service. Having nowhere else to go, he brought me here, to Olivia." She smiled at him, then bit her lip almost shyly. "She's the only mother I've ever known. There's nothing I wouldn't do for her—nothing." There was a clear message, a certain vehemence in that last statement.

Luke said, "She *is* quite a woman." In the few days he'd been here, he could easily see why the community respected her, why Analise loved her.

Analise blew out a long breath. "Calvin never actually said he *wasn't* going to re-up when his term was over." Her voice had calmed, quieted. Now her words were tinged with disillusionment and regret. "But when we talked about our plans for the future, he never mentioned he was considering it, either. He let me think what I wanted to think. So, just when I was preparing to finally become the wife I'd wanted to be, Calvin called from a bar, drunk as a skunk, telling me he was celebrating his reenlistment—he'd been accepted into the Rangers. Simple as that, no 'family discussion,' no 'Hey, honey, what do you think?' It was done."

"I see." And he did. He saw very clearly. And if Calvin had still been alive, Luke would have kicked his ass up between his shoulder blades. But aloud he said, "Being an army wife is tough."

She gave a sad chuckle, shaking her head. "I wouldn't have minded being an army wife—if I'd been treated like a *wife*. Calvin always had a reason for me to stay here, not move near the base where he was stationed—he was going to be transferred soon, he was deployed for long stretches at a time, the housing around the base stunk. There was always something to prevent me from joining him. After a while, I surrendered. It was clear his life with me would never intersect with his army life."

"It's hard for a lot of men, with the work Rangers do. Sometimes they just have to keep their family life totally separate." Luke said the words with as much conviction as he could muster. It was the truth, although he doubted that had been Calvin's motivation. Still, it might give Analise a bit of peace with the way things were.

This time Analise's laugh was brittle with disillusionment. "Olivia thinks we still loved each other. . . . I carried on with the pretense of regular letters and imaginary phone calls long after the real ones ceased to be. . . . I thought I could go on forever. . . ."

She didn't say more. Instead of talking, she nestled her

head against his shoulder and sat quietly for a long time. Her fingers slipped between his, entwining them in a way that hinted at more than friendly comfort.

Luke drew in the scent of her hair, which tonight was loose and down her back, making her look so youthful it pinched his heart. She was too young to have borne such tragedy. He wanted to do more than hold her hand— and that thought made his shame soar high once again. He was trying to justify his interest in Calvin's widow, because Calvin hadn't lived up to his marriage vows. That line of thinking was no more than cheap, juvenile rationalization.

Earlier he'd been lecturing Cole about standing up for what's right, stepping up and being a man for those who count on you. And here he was, *a man of honor,* wondering if there would come a moment when Analise might cast that green gaze his way and have it be filled with the same adoration she'd given Calvin—her husband, Luke's fellow soldier. The duplicity of it made him sick.

After a bit, she stirred, lifting her face. The hand that wasn't entwined with his cupped his cheek. "Thank you." Her lips brushed his other cheek.

She lingered there, so close he felt her breath against his skin, warm against the night's chill. That warmth penetrated much deeper than it should have, straight to that tiny part of him that was still able to feel good about himself. A part that he didn't know still existed. God, he wanted to kiss her, to tell her she was a treasure, to wrap himself around her, to take away the pain. He knew he shouldn't, but the temptation was strong. It came in waves, weakening his resolve to do the right thing.

In the end, the choice was taken away from him. She tilted her head, sliding those warm lips over his.

All thoughts of honor and guilt and responsibility evaporated with the sweetness of her kiss. Against his better judgment, Luke slid a hand into her hair, pulling her closer. Even so, there was a fragility to their connection, a tentativeness in the kiss.

The moment stretched far beyond the moment when he expected her to pull away. They remained there, in that limbo where passion hadn't taken over all good sense and purity outweighed desire.

The loud snap of a broken branch underfoot brought Luke instantly to his feet.

Something rustled as it retreated in the woods.

"What?" Analise apparently hadn't heard.

"Someone's out there." He started toward the spot where he'd heard the sound. Then he paused, listening intently. He couldn't detect anything beyond the normal night noises.

Analise moved behind him, pressing herself against his back. "Roy?" The name rode out on whispering breath.

Luke turned and put his hands on her shoulders. "Don't know. Maybe it was just an animal. Let's get you back to the house." He turned her around and walked back to the house with his arm around her shoulder.

Just before they reached the light that radiated from the windows, she took a side step, separating their bodies.

She said, "I'm sure Roy's gone now. I haven't heard that anyone has seen him. It had to be an animal."

Luke cast one last glance over his shoulder. "Probably."

They climbed the back steps and went into the kitchen. He started shutting off lights. "You go on up. I'm going to stay down here for a bit."

He followed her to the stairway, turning off lamps on the way.

"You're staying down here in the dark?"

"Just want to watch outside awhile. Don't need any more broken windows."

She hesitated, looking like she wanted to argue, but turned and climbed the stairs. "Good night." She paused and looked over her shoulder at him. "And thank you."

Luke watched her go up the stairs and listened for the closing of her bedroom door. Then he prowled from dark window to dark window for nearly an hour, watching for movement in the night. After that he went out and stood on the front porch for twenty minutes, straining to hear anything untoward over the racket of night creatures. He scanned the darkness with well-adjusted eyes, listened with well-trained ears. Finally, satisfied that if it had been Roy, the man was gone, he returned to the house and locked the front door behind him.

Luke was physically exhausted. The labors of the day had taxed him more than he'd let anyone know. He needed a painkiller and some sleep if he was going to be able to function tomorrow. Painkillers were in plentiful supply, as he took them far less often than prescribed. The sleep, however, was another story. How would he ever manage to fall asleep with the taste of Analise still unfulfilled on his lips? Was that kiss the result of the vulnerability brought about by her emotional state—or was there something deeper?

Come on, Boudreau, you're not a thirteen-year-old getting your first kiss.

No, and he wasn't in a position to take this further in any case. Analise was a new widow; Olivia, whose roof they both slept under, was her mother-in-law. No way could a relationship come of this.

Just let it go.

He repeated that to himself for twenty minutes while he paced the bedroom in the dark. As he passed the window, movement outside caught his eye. He stepped closer and pushed the tied-back curtain aside. Rolling into the driveway with only its parking lights on was a county sheriff's car. Apparently Deputy Dave was making good on his promise to keep watch. Although it should be giving Luke comfort to know someone else was helping to look out for those at Magnolia Mile, the whole idea chafed. Maybe, in his effort to make up for taking Calvin from them, Luke was getting too possessive of this family. Why else would Dave's presence out there bother him?

After idling for a minute or so, Dave backed slowly out of the drive. He didn't turn on his headlights until he reached the road.

Luke finally stripped off his clothes and crawled into bed. The painkillers he'd taken a half-hour before were kicking in, giving him a slight buzz. Which was exactly why he rarely took them. He hated the lack of sharp-witted control. But tonight common sense won out over bullheadedness. There was too much pain in his body, too many emotions in his heart, too much worry in his mind. If he showed the slightest physical effect from today's work, Olivia wouldn't stand for him to lift a finger around here again.

Falling into a doze, the image of long, lanky Dave, wearing his aviator sunglasses, staring out the door of the Pure station, kept popping into Luke's mind. As he slipped deeper into sleep, he dreamed Analise was dancing with Dave at the Boxcar. Suddenly he changed from human into a giant praying mantis. That huge bug turned Analise on the dance floor with flair—then he swallowed her whole.

Luke rushed to her, but it was too late—just as it had been too late for Calvin. People gathered around, yelling at him, pointing accusing fingers. They chanted, "You could have saved her," over and over. The Boxcar spun wildly around him, blurring the faces of those condemning him until he fell into complete darkness.

He was so soundly in drug-induced sleep that he didn't hear anything until Analise shook him roughly.

"Wake up!"

Why was she shouting?

"Luke! Wake up!"

He forced his heavy eyelids open. It was still dark. God, he never should have taken those painkillers. "I'm awake." The words came out raspy. "What's wrong?" He'd already started to move, his legs were over the side of the bed.

She was hurrying around the room, grabbing the clothes he'd taken off and tossing them at him. "Get dressed. Cole's been in an accident."

Chapter 10

By the time Luke had his jeans pulled on, his mind was fully functioning. "Was Cole driving?"

"Jeep's gone—he must have been. Dave came to get Olivia. He didn't have too many details out before he and Olivia shot out the door." Analise twitched impatiently as she watched him grab his tennis shoes. "Put them on in the car. I'll drive." She started downstairs.

He forced his bare feet into the shoes as he hopped along after her, laces flopping against the hardwood floor. "I'll drive." He passed her in the kitchen and walked out the door first.

Once in his car he asked, "Are we headed to the hospital?"

"Oh, my gosh! I forgot to ask. I guess so. Go to the square and turn north on Center."

He put the car in gear, swung it around and started out the drive. "Seat belt."

She gave him a frustrated look.

"We won't get there any faster with it off."

She put it on.

Once out of the lane, Luke pushed his car as fast as he safely could. Analise fidgeted and leaned forward in her seat, as if that would make them go faster.

They didn't make it to town. Just after a sweeping curve on the main road they saw flashing lights—lots of them.

"Oh, my God." The words weren't much more than a rush of air between Analise's lips.

"It always looks worse than it is; they have twice the rescue vehicles needed." He sure hoped that was the case, because there were two ambulances, three police cars and a fire truck on the scene, and Luke heard another siren on the way.

"Stop! Maybe Cole's still here." Panic crept into Analise's voice.

Luke was already pulling the Taurus into the grass beside the road, just short of the emergency vehicles. Analise was out before he got the gearshift into park. He thought she was going to run headlong into the middle of things, so he jumped out of the car as fast as he could. When he reached the front bumper, he saw she was still by the passenger door, bent over with her hands braced on her knees, throwing up.

He stepped close and put an arm around her waist and a hand on her back. He didn't say anything; there wasn't anything that would be more than empty assurances.

As soon as she could move, she did—straight for the ambulances. Luke held her hand tightly as they trotted nearer to the activity.

Analise stopped suddenly and stifled a horrified sob with her hand. Luke saw the Jeep at the same time. It was a good thirty feet from the road, illuminated as bright as day by emergency lights. It lay on its side and looked as if a giant had taken hold of both bumpers and twisted in opposite directions. The mangled steel appeared as if it had given no more resistance to the pressure than an aluminum soda can.

Analise started to run toward the wreckage, but Luke grabbed her from behind, wrapping both arms around her and lifting her feet off the ground. She kept her legs pumping, kicking his shins and struggling to break free.

"Stop! Analise, stop! He's not there!" Luke yelled.

She slowed her fight for freedom.

More quietly Luke said, "There aren't any rescuers by his car. He's not there."

"Where is he?" She began to look wildly around.

"We'll find him. Try to calm down."

Luke scanned the area. He didn't see Dave or Olivia anywhere. The two ambulances both sat empty with their back doors open. Neither one had a paramedic within fifteen feet. He then looked beyond the fire truck and saw another vehicle. It was blasted with the same white light as the Jeep. But this car was wrapped around a tree and crawling with firemen and medics.

The firemen revved up a saw. At the sound, Analise's head snapped in that direction. "Dear God."

Luke felt the strength go out of her. He kept her wrapped in his arms.

The blade threw blue-white sparks and screamed as it cut through the metal. Watching the crew work with that powerful tool to free the passengers was both awe-inspiring and sickening at the same moment. How could someone be left whole in that twisted mess?

Finally, a deputy sheriff noticed them and hurried closer. He had to shout over the whine and shriek of the saw. "Cole already went to the hospital. Dave and Olivia, too."

"How bad?" Analise asked.

Luke loosened his hold, but kept his arms around her.

The deputy said, "He was unconscious when the EMS pulled out. He was thrown from the car."

A little cry escaped Ana's throat. "The others?"

"Won't know until we get them out. Looks like the Benson boy's car, but we can't confirm who's inside yet. May only be the driver."

Luke's own stomach twisted. It was every bit as bad as it appeared from a distance; they couldn't even tell how many passengers were trapped inside.

Turning Analise away from the wreckage, he said, "Let's get to the hospital." He walked her back to his car with his arm around her shoulder. She was shaking and breathing too fast, silent tears trailing on her cheeks. Her burst of adrenaline had run out.

After he put her in the passenger seat and closed the door, he looked across the road and saw a pickup truck not fifteen feet away, parked in the grass on the other side. As focused as he was on the accident scene when they drove up, he hadn't even noticed it.

Sitting on the open tailgate was a gray-haired woman wrapped in a blanket. Luke hurried across the pavement.

"You all right, ma'am?" he asked.

She blinked a couple of times. "Yes." Her gaze shifted back to the accident. "There wasn't anything I could do." Her chin started to tremble. "This is just awful . . . just terrible."

"What happened?"

She pointed to the curve. "I was coming around there. The little car, it was in my lane. I swerved. He swerved the other way and hit the other car. They both went flying. . . ." Her hand demonstrated the tumbling flight the cars had taken from the road.

"Is someone coming to take you home?" He wanted to get moving, but he couldn't just leave the poor woman like this.

She nodded. "My husband."

He patted her shoulder, then ran back to his car.

"What did she say?" Analise asked as he got in.

Luke started the car and pulled back onto the road. "Sounds like they were racing. She came around the curve and one of them was in her lane."

"Racing? Why? What was Cole doing out? He was supposed to be in bed. . . ."

Luke knew she didn't really want to hear the answers to those questions, so he kept silent and drove to the hospital as quickly as he could.

When they entered the emergency room, Luke saw Olivia sitting on an orange vinyl couch, dressed in a nightshirt and slippers, twisting a tissue in her hands. Her spiky hair was flattened on one side from sleeping. Her eyes looked overlarge in her face. She looked even smaller than she had the first day Luke had seen her in that oversized sweater. Dave sat beside her, his arm draped comfortingly around her shoulders.

The second Olivia saw them, she jumped up and hurried to Analise. "We don't know anything yet."

Analise threw her arms around Olivia. They stood there for a few moments, rocking slightly side to side, drawing strength from one another. The sight made Luke ache for his own family. Suddenly he realized he wanted to be a part of this family, too, to give these women comfort, to be with them as they faced whatever news came from behind those emergency room doors. He prayed he would be given the opportunity to help Cole find his way to adulthood.

Let him be all right.

Dave slipped silently up behind Olivia and put a hand on her shoulder. He looked over the women and said to Luke, "I'll stay with them. It might be a long while before we know anything."

Did this guy really think he would walk out of here not knowing how Cole was? "I'm staying."

A nurse appeared with a hospital gown, handing it to Olivia. "You must be chilly. This is as close to a robe as I could find."

Olivia looked grateful as she slipped it around her shoulders.

They settled in on the ugly chrome and vinyl furniture, among the forgotten paper cups of coffee and tattered months-old magazines. Analise and Olivia sat leaning close to one another, clasping hands. Dave took the seat opposite them. Luke paced the speckled-tile floor.

On each revolution of the room, he looked at Analise. The fluorescent lighting amplified her pale and drawn features, the bruised-looking circles under her eyes. Olivia didn't look any better. An ache throbbed deep within him, an ache borne of helplessness, of knowing there was nothing he could do to relieve their suffering. How much more could this family take before the whirling force of heartbreak tore them apart?

An hour later, the doctor emerged from the treatment area. He approached Olivia with an unreadable expression on his face. Luke stopped dead in his tracks, offering up one last prayer that was much too late to be of any help.

Analise and Olivia stood as one. It was clear they were braced for the worst.

"We're waiting on a mobile CT scan to arrive. But by X-ray and my initial examination, I'd say you have one lucky young man in there."

A bit of the rigidity drained from both women's postures. Luke held his own relief in check until he heard the rest.

The doctor continued, "No broken bones. A slight concussion. Pretty bruised and scraped up, though."

Olivia's eyes still held a mother's worry when she asked, "Can we see him?"

"Of course. Keep in mind, his face is bruised and he's got about fifteen stitches in his head. It looks worse than it is."

Olivia nodded gravely, took Analise's hand and followed the doctor toward the double doors. Dave looked like he wanted to follow. After a few seconds he ran a hand over his close-cropped hair and sat back down.

Luke crossed his arms over his chest and started moving restlessly about the waiting area once again.

Analise had thought she was prepared. But her first glance at Cole's battered face caused the blood to drain from her head. Dizziness made her steps falter. Olivia's hand squeezed hers.

This is terrible, I should be supporting her.

She drew a deep breath, forcing away the grayness that threatened to draw her into a full faint. When did she become such a wimp?

Olivia went to one side of the bed, Analise the other. For a long moment, Analise kept her eyes on Olivia's face, avoiding looking at Cole's injuries.

How did Olivia do it? She stepped up to Cole's bedside with dry eyes and a calm expression on her face, the worry of the past hours completely masked with quiet confidence. Had her frequent dealings with tragedy somehow built up an inner strength that Analise still lacked?

Analise mentally gave herself a kick in the ass. She had to be strong for Cole and Olivia—her family. Her thoughts flashed ever so briefly back to her recent confessions to Luke. It had felt so good, so right, to depend on him, to allow him to see her inner pain. If only he were here with her and Olivia now. . . .

He could be. All she had to do was ask. She knew it as surely as she knew the sun was now rising outside these hospital walls. But indulging in her dependence on Luke would be a betrayal to Olivia. Calvin had only been gone five months—

She realized both Olivia and Cole were looking at her. "I'm sorry, what?"

Olivia said, "Cole said you should sit down. You do look pale."

Analise shook her head. "I'm fine." Here was Cole, obviously in pain, and his mother worried sick, and they were concerned over her well-being. She was so ashamed. She drew in a deep breath and tried to find a calm place inside her.

When Cole spoke again, it was with a broken voice, that of a child needing his mother. "I'm sorry, Mom."

Analise's chin trembled and a lump restricted her throat.

Olivia put a hand on Cole's brow, between the blue-black bruise and the recently stitched gash.

He said, "How's Travis?"

"Oh, Cole." Olivia sighed. "It was bad. He was trapped in the car. They haven't brought him in yet."

At that Cole looked really frightened. "How long have I been here?"

"Over an hour."

He turned his head away with a strangled sob.

Analise couldn't stand it. "I'm sure he's going to be fine."

Cole said, in a whimper, "He's dead."

"No!" Analise said quickly.

Olivia gave her a stern look. "We don't know yet." She continued calmly, "Was he alone in the car?"

Cole nodded and winced in pain.

Analise saw Olivia's eyes close briefly as she raised her face to heaven. "Thank goodness," she whispered.

A nurse came through the curtain. "I need to take him for another round of X-rays. I'll let you know when he's back."

"All right." Olivia kissed Cole's forehead. "We'll be waiting."

Cole didn't say anything, but swallowed hard. Analise knew he was afraid to open his mouth for fear of crying. She left the cubicle with Olivia, wishing that they'd not only taken Cole's keys away from him, but had taken the wheels off the Jeep, too.

They paused at the doors to the waiting area and watched the nurse wheel Cole's bed in the other direction.

A siren sounded, coming closer. Both women froze as it wound down just outside the emergency door. In a flurry of frenzied activity, a gurney crashed through the doors. Monitors beeped and blipped. Orders were shouted.

Olivia clutched Analise's forearm. "Travis."

Someone called out over the ruckus, "Lifeline is still sixteen minutes out."

"Shit." That came from the emergency physician—a doctor who didn't look much older than Cole. "Get that crash cart cycled up."

Analise stood in shocked horror. She couldn't see the boy—just the blood. There was so much blood. How could someone survive losing that much blood? She watched as a bright red drop fell in slow motion from the soaked gurney and splattered on the white tile. The imagined splash of impact crashed and echoed in her mind.

An alarm sounded.

The activity exploded with new urgency.

The nurse from the emergency desk came up behind Olivia and Analise. "Let me help you ladies out to the waiting area."

She gently turned them around and pushed open the swinging door.

The last thing Analise heard as the door closed behind her was the doctor, who sounded more panicked than competent. "Where's that damned chopper?"

The sight that greeted her in the waiting room only disconcerted her further. Reverend Hammond had joined Luke and Dave. He quickly descended on Olivia and swept her off to a private corner.

Analise stood there, just outside the emergency room doors, shaken and alone. Without Olivia, she had no place to anchor herself.

It was hard to breathe. She should sit down, but she couldn't make her feet move. Each time she blinked she saw a sea of blood.

Then suddenly Luke was there, his arm around her and a calming voice in her ear. "It's all right. Let's step outside for a minute."

Her numb legs were of no use to her. She leaned heavily on Luke. He as much as carried her down the hall and out into the cool early morning air.

"Just breathe." He moved her away from the building, across the asphalt and into a grassy area. "That's it. I've got you. I won't let you go." He sat them down on a concrete bench beneath a huge old magnolia. His hand went to the back of her head and pushed her forward. "Put your head down for a minute." After a second he said, "Close your eyes. Smell it? There isn't anything that smells like this time of day. The sun's just coming up. Soon the heat of it will change everything."

She breathed in the scent of moist earth, early morning mist and the fragrance of blooms about to burst. She didn't know if the calming came from the earthy scents or from Luke's soothing voice, but inch by inch, it crept over her. She wanted him to keep talking and never stop.

He did stop, but he didn't let her go. Pulling herself back to a sitting position, she rested her head on his shoulder. It felt so right, so natural, to lean on him—just as her confidences flowed easily from her lips when they were alone.

"Better?" he finally asked.

She was tempted not to admit it, for he might suggest they go back inside and she just wasn't ready yet. "Some."

"Here it comes." He pointed to the eastern horizon.

Low over the trees, just above the sinking mists, the sky erupted into a blaze of unbelievable orange-pink that quickly faded into lavender, then slate as her eye traveled skyward. The last stars of morning were eclipsed by the new day. It was a breathtaking sight that happened every day and she couldn't remember when she'd last taken the time to watch the transformation of night to day. "Wow."

Luke chuckled deep in his chest and squeezed her tight. "Very eloquent."

Smiling weakly, she turned her face to his.

Dave's voice cut sharply through the early morning quiet. "Olivia needs you inside!"

All of her calm vanished in the blink of an eye. Her heart in her throat, she ran toward the building. As she hurried through the door with Luke right behind her, she heard the distant thumping of an approaching helicopter.

"The sheriff's here to talk to him," Olivia said. She turned to Luke. "Cole wants you to be with him."

"Me?"

Olivia cut him off. "It's what he asked for. It's a simple questioning to find out what happened. Will you do it?"

Luke nodded. "All right."

He glanced at Analise. Although her eyes said she was hurt Cole had chosen him, her head nodded once in agreement.

"Thank you," Olivia said as solemnly as if Luke had agreed to champion the family in a duel.

"Do we know anything more about Travis?" Analise asked.

"Lifeline's taking him up to Memphis."

"You're sure Cole shouldn't have an attorney instead?" Luke forced himself to bring up the possibility of legal charges. He looked pointedly at Dave.

Olivia's gaze followed Luke's. Dave said, "No need. I've got it under control."

Olivia looked back to Luke. "Good enough for me."

The desk nurse called across the room to them, "The sheriff is ready."

Luke gave Olivia one last look, an opportunity to change her mind.

She didn't.

The sheriff wasn't the beefy southerner that Luke had expected. He was a wiry little whiplash of a man with thin, graying hair and a pencil-line mustache. He made Luke think of the old black-and-white movies he and Lily used to stay up late watching. He had kind brown eyes with laugh lines around them.

"I'm Sheriff Smolek." He extended his hand and Luke shook it. "Folks call me Smug. So that'll be fine for this informal meeting."

"Luke Boudreau."

"I understand you served with Calvin."

"Yes, sir."

"Son, we're country folk here. Smug will do fine."

Luke nodded.

Smug turned his attention to Cole, whose head had been slightly raised by adjusting the bed. "All right, Cole, can you tell me what happened out there?"

The boy's worried eyes sought Luke's. Luke could tell Cole had been given something for pain by the sluggish way he reacted.

Luke gave a nod of encouragement and said, "Just take it slow."

"I-I drove by Darcy's." Cole's speech matched his slow eye movement. "Travis's car was there." He licked his dry, swollen lips. "Could I have some water?"

A nearby nurse said she'd check the orders. In a few seconds she returned holding a clear plastic glass filled with ice chips and a spoon. "Just take a few of these at a time," she said as she handed the glass to Cole.

"Thank you." He took some ice, then licked his lips again. "I drove around for a little while. Then I circled back by Darcy's and Travis was getting in his car."

The sheriff asked, "That's Darcy Thayler, Bob's daughter? Lives over on Jackson Street?"

Cole nodded. "I stopped. I just wanted to talk to him. But he got in his car and peeled out." He paused and took another ice chip; his hand holding the glass trembled. "I went after him." He halted, looking at Luke, not the sheriff.

Luke prompted, "Go on."

Cole stared at the wall for a second. "He pulled into the Dixie parking lot and got out. I did, too. I can't remember exactly what we said, but it got ugly, there was some shoving. Then Travis punched me in the eye. I hit him in the gut. Doubled him over." He paused. "And then I left. I was so mad. I knew if I stayed, I'd kick the living sh—daylights out of him.

"I was on the other side of town, headed home, when I saw headlights come up behind me—really fast. And . . ." His voice faltered and his chin quivered.

"And . . . ?" Luke said.

"I sped up. I can't really remember much after that. It all

happened so fast. I think there was another car, coming at us. Then everything went nuts."

Luke prayed Cole was telling the truth—not that it looked like Travis would be contradicting his story anytime soon. The sheriff's expression was unreadable.

The sheriff said, "All right, son. You get some rest and we'll talk later."

Cole looked at the sheriff directly for the first time since Luke had entered the room. "Was there another car?"

Smug nodded.

"W-was anyone else hurt?" The words were a sluggish whisper.

"Thank the good Lord, no." The sheriff nodded to Luke and left the cubicle.

Luke said, "I'll go get your mom."

Cole said, "Stay. Just for a while. Mom . . . Mom . . . I just can't look at her anymore right now. If Travis . . ."

"Shhh. We just have to wait. Close your eyes and let those drugs do their job." Luke sat on the only chair in the cubicle and rubbed his knee, wishing he had a shot of something himself.

Analise fell into a chair after Luke went back to sit with Cole.

"Here, the caffeine will at least keep a headache away." Dave handed her a cup of hot coffee, then he sat down in the chair that was at a ninety-degree angle to hers. With his long lanky legs, his left knee rubbed against her right.

She doubted her stomach would tolerate it, but she sipped the coffee dutifully.

Olivia perched on the edge of the chair on Analise's left. "I'm going with the pastor to the chapel for a few minutes. Do you want to come?"

Analise looked into her coffee, too ashamed to tell Olivia that she'd given up on praying because sometimes reckless prayers were answered. "I'll wait here—just in case there's a change." She watched the two of them leave the area, the reverend's hand on Olivia's elbow. A bitter little thought bubbled to the surface of her mind: If it weren't for the reverend, she doubted Olivia would be spending her time in the chapel. She'd be right here, in case Cole needed her.

After a couple of minutes, Dave cleared his throat.

When Analise looked at him, it was obvious something was on his mind. "What?"

He looked uncomfortable and pressed his lips together. Then he shook his head. "It's really not for me to say."

Her heart rate spiked. Had he learned something from the sheriff's department that had to do with Cole? Had they found alcohol in the car? Or something worse? She sat up straighter and leaned slightly toward Dave. "Please, tell me," she said quietly.

He shifted in his seat and folded his bony hands between his knees. For a long moment, he just stared at his twisting fingers. Then he said, with obvious hesitance, "I'm just worried about Miss Olivia. She's had so much . . ."

Relief inched its way into Analise's muscles. Not more trouble for Cole. "We're all worried about Liv."

Dave looked down the hall, then back at Analise. "That's not what I mean. I—I just think maybe it's a not a good idea for you to be carrying on with that army fella right under Olivia's own roof. Calvin's only been gone a few months."

She jerked herself up straight. "Carrying on! What are you talking about?"

"I suppose it's not really adultery—but Miss Olivia—"

"Hold on a minute! Where did you get the idea that Luke and I . . . that we're—"

"Come on, now, Ana, I got eyes!" He glanced around, lowered his voice and pointed toward the outside exit. "There you two were, cuddled up on that bench outside for everyone in town to see."

She shot to her feet. "You're being ridiculous."

He grabbed her hand and looked up at her. "Am I, Ana? This is a little town. Things will get back to Olivia. I just don't think she can take any more disappointment and upset right now. Do you really want to hurt her that way?"

Analise sat back down. She'd been vehement in her denial, but what had gone on in the garden last night had undoubtedly made her consider possibilities she shouldn't have entertained for even the briefest second. She said, "Nothing's going on. You don't have to worry." It was probably a good thing Dave had said something to bring her back to her senses before something *did* go on.

"I believe you." He gave her hand a squeeze. "We all just need to keep Miss Olivia forefront in our minds right now."

She nodded, knowing he was right and yet feeling as if something had been taken from her.

It was nearly noon when they decided to admit Cole to a room in the hospital. Luke had spent the bulk of the morning with him. Analise wondered at the relationship that was forming between them. She nipped the little sprout of jealousy as soon as it peeked out from the soil. It was natural for a boy Cole's age to want a male role model with him at a time like this. And it didn't seem to hurt Olivia's feelings that Cole had chosen Luke over them.

As Analise and Olivia sat side by side waiting for Cole to be moved, Analise felt as if she'd been run over by a truck. Olivia's eyes were still alert and her step lively. Someone had given her a set of blue scrubs and she looked like a duty nurse at the beginning of her shift.

Analise asked, "How do you do it?"

"Do what?" Olivia smiled.

"Keep going. You've had so much . . . tragedy, and still you can sit here and smile at me."

Olivia sighed and patted Analise on the knee. "Oh, my dear, it's the fact that I have lost so much—I suppose I see things differently. When you get to be my age, you appreciate every moment, no matter how painful. That means you still have something you care about enough to hurt. I'm grateful for those I have left, they're all the more precious to me. Cole is alive. We didn't lose him. We're still a family. That's what matters."

Luke walked up to them and Analise looked into his eyes once again. He smiled sweetly down at her, making her heart ache in a way she hadn't experienced in a very long time.

Too bad there wasn't anything she could do about it.

Chapter 11

The hospital arranged for a cot so Olivia could spend the night in Cole's room. He'd been pretty doped up most of the day, in and out of drugged sleep. The doctor had confirmed with a CT scan that there was no damage hidden in Cole's brain and he would probably be dismissed tomorrow by noon. Nonetheless, Olivia wanted to remain nearby in case he had a fitful night.

She insisted that Luke take Analise home and make her get some sleep. She assured them that Dave was going to stop by at the end of his shift; if she needed anything, he could take care of it.

Reluctantly, Analise followed Luke out of the hospital. She moved with leaden feet. For the past hour, Luke had noticed her rotating her shoulders as if they were cramping. She looked ready to drop face first on the floor.

Luke's knee hampered his steps as they walked across the parking lot, but he was pretty sure she was too tired to notice. As he neared the car, he glanced at the sky. It was as breath-taking as it had been this morning. He stopped to say something about it to Analise and she ran right into the back of him.

"Oops. Sorry." Her words sounded slightly muffled by fatigue.

He took her by the shoulders and pointed her west. He was now standing behind her. "Look there. We've watched both sunrise and sunset today." He massaged the tight muscles in her shoulders. "Tomorrow will be better."

She leaned back against him, a little moan riding out on her breath. "I hope so."

They stood that way for a long moment. Luke wanted to wrap his arms around her and hold her close to his chest. But the middle of the hospital parking lot was hardly the place, so he finally guided her to the car and opened the door.

As they drove out of town, they passed the site of the accident. Luke didn't slow, but he saw Analise's head turn as she held the skid marks and the deep gouges in the grass in her sight.

She said, "I don't know why Olivia insisted I go home. I'll never be able to sleep."

Luke knew how she felt. It was familiar enough to him. But he also knew that at some point, no matter what the level of stress, the body takes over and gets what it needs. He'd been on three-day missions that required constant movement. On about the second day, at every five-minute breather, he fell completely and totally asleep, sometimes while still on his feet.

"You'll sleep," he said.

Even as she shook her head, he could see her eyelids grow heavier. By the time he pulled in the driveway, she'd fallen asleep against the door. When she didn't awaken immediately when he shut off the engine, he took a few moments to sit in the quiet and just study her. Twilight was deepening, casting a shadow in the delicate hollow of her throat. The sheer vulnerability of that spot made Luke want to taste it, to allow his lips to linger there until she awakened. Would she welcome his advance, or turn him away?

He shook the fanciful thoughts out of his head; it was all moot speculation. He would never dare cross that line with her—unless she deliberately led him across. Fat chance.

Since sunset, a chill had risen. He should get her inside. "Ana?"

She curled deeper into the door.

He shook her slightly. "Analise. We're here."

She mumbled, "Slow down . . . too fast."

He decided he'd just carry her in. But first he had to sit her upright or she'd fall out the door when he opened it. He put his arms around her, pulling her toward him.

She shivered. Then she screamed, "No!"

He touched her cheek. "Ana. It's all right. You're home."

Shaking her head blearily, she said, "I was dreaming."

"Let's get you inside." He unfastened her seat belt.

She fumbled for the door latch like a drunk. He reached across and lifted it for her. He started to straighten back up when she grabbed a fistful of his shirt, stopping him with his face right in front of hers. He became aware of her chest rising and falling with her breath. Was her breathing faster, or was that just his own?

She licked her lips and pulled him slightly closer. "I'm glad you're here," she whispered. "You make me feel safe"—she inched her lips closer to his—"and in danger at the same time."

When she kissed him, it was with none of the tentativeness of the previous night. The way her lips sought his, the way her hands clutched his shoulders, spoke of desperate yearning. He responded with equal hunger when she opened her mouth to him.

This had to stop, he told himself, even as he slid his hands into her hair.

She rolled against him, turning until his back was against the seat and she was cradled against his chest. He cupped the back of her head with his hand and kissed his way closer to that hollow in her throat that had been so tempting just seconds earlier. When his tongue flicked gently there, she buried her hands in his hair, pulling him closer as she dropped her head back, offering more of herself to him.

"Let's go inside," she said breathlessly, her intent clear.

For one brief second, he struggled. But he kissed her lips again, slowly, then said, "All right."

Once out of the car, she took his hand and led him to the back door.

He stopped her just before she opened it. "We forgot to lock it."

She glanced over her shoulder at him. "It's all right. We hardly ever lock this door."

He grunted. "You've never had anyone throw a rock through your window before." He stepped around her. "I'll go first."

She let out a little snort. "This is Grover, not Guatemala."

Snapping his head around to look at her, he said, "Don't be fooled. Crazy people are everywhere."

"Okay. You go first," she said, mocking a dare.

"I'm not joking."

She gave a contrite frown. "Sorry."

He went in, holding her hand and flipping on lights. He kept her with him as he went through the house. Once he was satisfied nothing looked amiss, he returned and locked the back door while she fed the cats, Skippy and Rufus.

The temporary interruption in their passion allowed Luke

to regain his control. Shit, he'd been ready to have sex with her right there in his car. The whole idea made him ashamed. All of his high ideals about how Calvin should have cherished this woman somehow had taken flight. She deserved better than Luke could give—she deserved honesty.

She let Rufus out the back door and relocked it.

When she came back to Luke, she wrapped her arms around his neck and kissed him lightly. He returned the kiss, swearing to himself this would be the last one. Then she took his hand and led him up the stairs.

As she led him through her bedroom door, he stopped.

She turned around, a questioning expression on her face.

"I don't think we should."

She faced him and touched his cheek. "I don't want to be alone."

Oh, God, he didn't want to be alone, either. He wanted to be with *her*.

He looked beyond her, to where the moonlight fell onto her bed—the bed she'd shared with Calvin.

Her gaze followed his. As if she could read his thoughts, she said, "We can go to your room."

"You don't know how much I want to."

"But . . . ?" she said.

"But this isn't the time. You're exhausted, emotionally drained."

She looked down, her lashes casting delicate shadows on her cheeks. "Luke, I really don't want to be alone."

"All right." He took her hand and led her to his room and closed the door on the rest of Calvin's house.

She took her shoes off and lay down on the bed.

Covering her body with his, he kissed her once. Then he rolled them over, so he was on his back and she on her side against him. He pulled her close. "Go to sleep, Ana."

She laid a hand over his heart. "You'll stay with me?"

"Yes." *As long as you need me.*

Analise awakened sometime in the gray hours before dawn; much too early to call the hospital. She was spooned with her back against Luke's chest, his hand draped over her waist. She lay perfectly still, listening to his steady breathing, unwilling to ruin the illusion that she would wake up this way every morning for the rest of her life.

How could this man, this stranger, make her feel more loved, more cherished with one chaste night than her husband of eight years ever did?

With that thought, the guilt, the sense of disloyalty, came crashing home. Olivia and Cole were her family. Her responsibility. She could never openly love Luke in Olivia's household—and she could never leave.

She'd made a bargain, a trade. She'd been over the moon for Calvin, but he'd wrung that love out of her one neglectful day at a time. And she'd decided she would stay anyway. She took what she'd found here, a warm home, a loving family, as a substitute for an attentive husband. For several years, she'd been happy with that trade.

Then Luke had come and awakened things she'd convinced herself no longer existed within her. And now she lay with the heat of him pressed against her back, his gentle caring having guarded her through the night. It would be so easy to love him.

Temptation bloomed, her desire to feel like a woman flaring to bright life. She couldn't have forever with this man, but if she was going to have anything at all, it had to be now. Later today Olivia and Cole would come home. In a couple of weeks, the job for the county would be done and Luke would be gone.

Slowly, carefully, she turned in his arms. She settled her head next to his on the pillow. His eyes opened.

For a long time, he just looked at her, his expression unreadable. Then she put her hand on his cheek. It was rough from two days' stubble. It felt wonderful and masculine. She allowed her fingers to toy with the coarseness, first with the soft skin on the back of her fingers, then with her fingertips. Still he held her gaze, unblinking, not giving anything away.

Her heart sped up with the prospect of what she was about to do; her breath seemed to squeeze through her chest. It had been so long since she'd felt this way, her body throbbing with a single purpose, her heart aching in her chest.

What if he refused her, as he had last night?

For an instant she wavered. Could she stand the humiliation?

Her body answered for her. She knew if she didn't take this chance, she would forever regret it. Humiliation be damned, she was doing this.

Ask him. Four words, that was all it would take. *Make love to me.* If he refused her, she would have lost little. A few days of strained misery—and then he'd be gone.

She gathered her courage and parted her lips to speak the words that, once said, would be irretrievable.

At that moment he finally moved, turning his head slightly, kissing the palm of her hand. He kept his gaze locked on hers as he did it, as if he were gauging her willingness, too.

Biting her lip to keep from begging for more, she waited.

His tongue tasted her palm, then he guided her hand until it rested over his heart. He pressed it flat on his chest until she could feel it beating strongly, rapidly. "See what you do to me?"

She pushed against his chest until he rolled onto his back. Straddling him, she gathered her hair and pulled it over her right shoulder.

He wrapped a length of it around his hand. "Beautiful."

And the way he looked at her, she truly felt she was. Unbuttoning his shirt, she pulled it open and ran her hands over his chest and across his shoulders. "Beautiful."

He laughed, a soft, languid, thoroughly masculine sound that stirred the fires deep within her.

She leaned down and kissed the flesh over his heart. Then she took his hand and placed it over her heart, which felt as if it were about to throb out of her chest. "See what you do to me?"

The heat in his eyes told her that her hesitation had been foolish. His hand cupped her breast through her clothing and she thought she'd burst into flame. How had she gone so long thinking this didn't matter?

She rocked slightly against him, until he grabbed her waist and stopped her. "I want this to last," he said as he cradled her face and drew her down for a kiss. "It has to last." The way he said the words brought tears to her eyes. It was as if he, too, knew this was something that was only going to happen once. And his tone resonated with regret.

With a slowness that bordered on torture, they undressed one another. When she tugged with impatience, he stilled her, whispered calming words in her ears. And then he fired her need all the more with his own unhurried fingers, followed by lingering lips.

He was right. This had to last. Analise gave herself over to wrapping herself in every sensation, every touch, pushing away her driving need to rush to completion.

Once she slowed her pace, Analise explored his body. He was thickly muscled and fit, even though he'd spent a good deal of the past months in a hospital bed. Tenderly she traced every scar—and there were many more than she'd imagined. At first he tensed and started to pull away, but she persisted, loving every wound, every surgical scar, until she felt him tremble beneath her touch. He'd lived a life so far removed from what she understood, a life of hardship and sacrifice. She loved him gently, hoping to compensate for his pain.

His hands on her body began to be less gentle, more urgent. His kisses demanding. She welcomed the change, was thrilled by the prospect that he was as desperate as she to have their bodies truly joined.

Taking her hands in his, he placed them beside her head and raised himself up to look into her eyes as he completed their union. The caring that Analise saw in those eyes stole her breath. She wanted to freeze this moment in time, to have his heated gaze hold her in everlasting love, to remain in this wondrous moment, never to have to come back down to earth.

As the first brilliant rays of the morning sun shone through the window, he took her to the place she'd yearned for, with an intensity and passion she'd never even imagined possible.

The day brightened, illuminating the reality of Analise's life in every detail of the room that surrounded her. She closed her eyes so she didn't have to see the quilt made by Granny Lejeune, or the fresh flowers Olivia had slipped into the room sometime late yesterday, or the shelf that Calvin had made in high school shop class.

She lay in Luke's arms with her head resting on his chest, putting off the inevitable, enjoying the rare feel of masculine skin against her own.

Once her breathing returned to normal and the perspiration on her skin cooled, she said, "I don't want you to misunderstand." Pausing, she waited, hoping that Luke would take it from there and she wouldn't have to explain.

But he didn't say, *I know what a difficult position you're in,* or *I'm really not interested in anything permanent, either.* He stroked her back and remained quiet. She did detect a slight tightening of his muscles, though, as if dreading her next words.

She rolled away from Luke, pulling the covers around her. "I have Olivia and Cole to think of." Although she didn't say his name, Calvin landed on the bed between them. There was no way for them to be together, here in this house, without his ghostly presence. Calvin was their link, his death the only reason they lay together here now.

Luke sighed and picked up her hand. He kissed the days-old burn on the back of it. She'd gotten the injury while working on the bench that she and Luke had shared in the garden last night. She'd only finished it and placed it in the yard the day before he came to Magnolia Mile. It astounded her to see that her life had been totally turned upside down, her heart irrevocably changed, in less time than it took a blister to fade.

He said, "You have a life here—there's no way I'll fit into it. I never thought I would."

She couldn't help the feeling of relief, as if she were a schoolgirl and had just been assured her misbehavior wouldn't be discovered.

He caressed her hand with his thumb, then laid it back on the bed by her side. "I don't want to make things more difficult for you." He paused and she felt him shift on the bed. "But I'm going to tell you right now, I'm not sorry we did this—I'm only sorry if you're going to suffer for it."

She twisted around to look at him. A tightness squeezed her heart. "Oh, I'm going to suffer." When a shadow crossed his face, she said, "I'm going to suffer every time you're close and I can't touch you, every time you look at me like you are right now and I can't kiss you."

He traced his fingers along her jawline. "Would you rather I leave?"

"Yes." As she kissed him, she knew as well as he did, he wasn't going anywhere. Not until the county project was complete—how would Magnolia Mile manage otherwise?

Analise couldn't decide which would create the illusion of innocence more convincingly: if she went back to the hospital alone, or if Luke came with her. In the end, she asked him to come along, mostly because she wanted to spend a few more private minutes with him.

His ability to bury his emotions amazed her. Even though they were still alone, Luke was showing respect for her precarious position and had taken an emotional step back, treating her as if nothing had transpired to change their relationship in the past twenty-four hours. He was so good at it, even she could almost believe nothing had changed.

Even so, she found it hard to look at him, difficult to fall into bland conversation.

As they sat side by side in the silent car, Analise wished she'd made a different decision and left him at home. She could tell, Luke was taking his cues from her; her distance was probably hurting his feelings.

When they arrived at the hospital, Olivia was standing outside Cole's room talking with Dave. He was dressed in his uniform and had a grim look on his face as he used his hands to demonstrate something that looked suspiciously like a description of the wreck. The horrible sight of the twisted vehicles illuminated in the rescue lights flashed fresh in Analise's mind.

Olivia noticed their approach. "Oh, I'm so glad you're here."

Although it was only eight-thirty, Analise felt a little wash of shame for not getting here earlier. She'd taken an extra-long shower before they came, trying to get the feel of Luke off her skin. But it had been useless; he'd ingrained himself much more deeply than skin. She just hoped she was as good at projecting the image of guiltless propriety as Luke seemed to be. She handed a bag containing fresh clothes to Olivia.

Luke asked, "Any word on the other boy?"

Olivia nodded toward Dave. "That's just what Dave was telling me. He's still unconscious. Poor child." Then she added, "Dave's been checking on the accident investigation—"

Dave interrupted her. "Liv, I think we should keep that between us. Don't want any suggestion of misconduct. Even if the investigation absolves Cole of legal charges, Travis's family still could bring civil suit."

Olivia blanched. "I don't see what would be wrong with telling Ana."

Dave looked pointedly at Luke.

Olivia said, "Luke's family."

At that both Analise and Dave looked at her with surprise. She didn't seem to notice and went on sharing what she knew. "Dave said there's a witness that saw Cole take off after Travis from Darcy's house at a high rate of speed."

Since Luke had shared what Cole told the sheriff with both Olivia and Analise after that meeting, Ana knew the story. "That's exactly what Cole said happened."

Dave shifted his weight from one shiny black shoe to

another. "Trouble is, that's the only eyewitness we have. No one saw them at the drive-in, no one saw Cole leave first."

"You're saying the sheriff thinks Cole chased Travis down?" Ana couldn't keep the panic out of her voice.

"We'll have to wait and see what story Travis tells—if and when he's able," Dave said seriously. He put a hand on Olivia's shoulder. "Don't worry. He probably won't remember anything. I can take care of any problems from the inside."

Olivia's eyes cut quickly to his. "I don't want you to do anything you shouldn't—"

"Oh, no, no." Dave looked uncomfortably toward Luke. "That's not what I meant at all."

But, as Analise looked between Luke and Dave, she got the impression that was exactly what he was suggesting.

By noon, Cole was ready to go home. The four of them sat in the car, avoiding talking about the obvious question eating at all of them: Would Travis recover? They'd been spared seeing his parents at the hospital. Mr. and Mrs. Benson were vacationing in Las Vegas. Apparently, Travis had been left at home in the charge of his eighteen-year-old sister. By the time their parents had been located and notified, Travis was already being airlifted to Memphis.

Once back at Magnolia Mile, Olivia and Analise fussed over getting Cole settled in his room. He had no medical restrictions, but the doctor suggested taking it easy for a day or so. He'd prescribed mild medication for the aches and pains, cautioning them to be certain to bring Cole back immediately if he complained of increased headache pain or problems with his vision.

Olivia set a can of Sprite on Cole's nightstand. "Are you sure you don't want something to eat?"

"Yes." There was an edge to his answer that said he wanted to be left alone. Then he softened it by saying, "Maybe in a little while."

"All right. One of us will check back in a bit," Olivia said as she pulled the door closed behind her.

Analise followed her down the hall, unable to keep from casting a glance into the green room. A few of Luke's personal items marked the room as his—his electric razor, his sport coat on a hanger on the closet doorknob, a pair of balled-up athletic socks on the floor. Her gaze ran over the bed and a little shiver of remembered passion coursed through her. Luke hadn't merely had sex with her—he'd made her feel loved in a way she had never experienced, and doubtless would never experience again. She refused to give in to the little tug of regret—not for what she'd done, but for what she was giving up to keep her family whole.

Before they reached the stairs, the telephone rang. Analise hurried into her bedroom to answer it.

"Hi, this is Darcy." There was a pause. "The hospital said Cole had been dismissed."

"Yes, he's home." She pressed her lips together to keep from saying more.

"Can I . . . talk to him?"

Common sense said the accident wasn't Darcy's fault, but Analise couldn't help but hold the girl responsible for setting this all into motion. "I'll get him."

When she knocked and opened Cole's door, he was on his side, facing away from her. "Cole. Darcy's on the phone."

"Really?" There was a bubble of hope in his voice. He sat up and grabbed his head with both hands. "Whoa." Then his face shadowed. "I don't want to talk to her."

Several emotions fought for center stage in Analise's

mind. She would have been truly relieved if she hadn't heard that optimism in Cole's voice right at first. She could tell he wasn't over this girl—which only meant more pain waited around the bend.

Cole passed on dinner, staying in his room. Luke could see Olivia's worry as the three of them ate quietly in the kitchen. He was actually glad for the silence. It made his duplicity seem less offensive.

What made him for one single minute think there was anything right about what he'd done? In his mind he'd justified making love to Analise because Calvin had been an unfaithful husband. Had he thought it was tit for tat—what's good for the goose is good for the gander? Or had he thought he could give Analise what Calvin had not? That thought was almost comical. The only thing he'd done for Analise was to put her in an awkward position in her own home.

He glanced at the two women. He could tell neither had the energy to feed herself, let alone carry on a conversation. When they both stopped eating before their plates were empty, Luke said, "I'll clean up. You two go on upstairs."

The confirmation of their exhaustion came when they both just nodded and left the table.

Once the dishes were done—there hadn't been many, as they'd had turkey sandwiches for dinner—Luke stepped out on the front porch. There was an unusual evening breeze that kept the worst of the early-season mosquitoes away. That probably meant rain. His supposition was further enforced by the ache between his shoulder blades. He rotated his shoulders, trying to work out some of the pain as he sat down on the steps, avoiding the homeyness of the old wicker furniture that sat on the porch. He didn't deserve the comforts of this house.

He'd been sitting there several minutes when he heard the door open behind him. For a brief second he brightened, thinking it was Analise. When he turned he saw Cole's outline against the hall light.

"Mind if I come out?" the boy asked.

"Come on. The fresh air'll do you good."

Cole closed the door behind him and sat on the step next to Luke, groaning a little as he did.

"Getting pretty stiff?" Luke asked.

Cole nodded slowly, as if the action hurt his neck—which it probably did. After a minute, he asked quietly, "Do you think Travis is going to die?"

Luke put his elbows on his knees and laced his fingers in front of him. "No. He'll probably live."

"You said that like it's a bad thing." There was real fear in Cole's voice.

"It could be," Luke said slowly. He decided he wasn't going to sugarcoat this, wasn't going to blindly reassure. Cole needed to see the reality of the consequences of what had happened. "There are things worse than death." *Like causing someone else to die in your place and living with it every day.* "He was hurt pretty seriously."

Cole unsuccessfully tried to stifle a choked sob. Luke let him be for a moment. There was a reason Cole had sought Luke out and not his mother. He wanted the harsh truth, *needed* it.

"Why didn't I stay home?" It was no more than a quivering whisper.

Luke let it ride. Cole didn't really want an answer to that question.

"I tried to walk away." The boy thumped his fisted hands on his knees. "I knew it was going to turn out bad."

"Sometimes, even when you think you're making the right choice, bad things still happen." Luke knew all too well the futile desire to recover one single second and make a different choice.

"He chased me."

"Did you speed up?"

"Yeah." Cole rubbed his face and spoke through his fingers, "I didn't know . . . I thought he was going to try to run me off the road."

"He might have."

Cole's gaze snapped to Luke's face. "So I was right to run?"

Luke shook his head. "There's no right in this, Cole. Right stopped being a possibility when you took that Jeep out on the road after your mother had taken away the privilege."

"Is it totaled?" He sounded completely miserable.

"Can't see how it wouldn't be. It was twisted like a pretzel."

"I promised Calvin I would take care of it," Cole whispered.

"Do you want to talk about it?"

He huffed. "What's the point. I wrecked it."

"Not the Jeep. About Calvin."

For a long while, Cole was silent. He bowed his head, his hair falling over his brow.

Then Luke heard him crying softly. He didn't move to comfort him. This boy didn't need more reassurances, more platitudes. He needed to talk about what was really going on inside.

The twilight moved to darkness; Luke thought that suited

things just fine. It was so much easier to make your confessions to the darkness.

After a long exhalation, Cole said, "Everybody thinks I should be over it." He paused. "At first it was different. Everyone felt really bad, they understood why I felt so awful. Then they just seemed to forget him—even Mom and Ana. It's like he just disappeared from our family and everybody went back to what they were doing. Now everybody thinks there's something wrong with me because I'm not treating Calvin like he went out with last week's garbage. They think I should be over it." He turned and looked at Luke. "How do you get over something like that?"

Luke drew a deep breath. He rubbed his hands together. "You don't." He knew the truth of that firsthand. "Somehow you have to learn to live with the way things are, though."

"Why can't I do that? I'm just so wound up inside all the time. It's like there's something ready to explode just under my skin. Now Darcy's making everything worse."

"Do you think the two are unrelated?"

His gaze snapped to Luke's face, as if he'd never considered such a connection. "You think Darcy dumped me because of Calvin? That doesn't make any sense. She was great. She even stayed here for a couple of days at first, taking phone calls and helping with all of the food everybody brought."

"And then?"

Cole lifted a shoulder. "Things were okay for a few weeks." Anger inched its way into his voice when he added, "Then she started saying I'd changed." He pounded his knee again. "Fuckin' right I changed. My brother came home in so many pieces that we couldn't even open the casket!"

Luke felt those words as if they'd been delivered on the tip of a sword. They were true, too true. "There's no way something like that won't change you. You just have to make sure it doesn't destroy you. From what I've seen, you seem bent on wrecking yourself."

"You're saying I ran Darcy off because I *want* to be alone?" That anger pushed at its boundaries.

"Maybe Darcy isn't ready for the kind of relationship that gets difficult."

"She said she loved me." There was a bitter edge to his words.

"There's a huge difference between love talk and love. Saying you love someone is easy. It's what a person does that speaks the truth."

"She didn't love me. If she had, she wouldn't have left me just because I'm still messed up over Calvin."

"I'm not saying that. I don't think it's that simple. Darcy probably loved you when things were fine and easy. It takes a very special kind of love to stick around, to do things you don't really want to do when things get hard. She's very young; that kind of love takes a lot of maturity." He shifted his weight and straightened out his knee. "But I think you're missing what I meant. I think this goes beyond your relationship with Darcy. You're doing some very damaging things to yourself—by choice."

Cole put his elbows on his knees and ran his hands into his hair. "I can't seem to make sense out of anything. Nothing matters anymore."

"Your mother?"

He fisted his hands in his hair and pulled. "She doesn't understand."

"Well, how about Ana? From what I've seen, she matters to you."

He blew a long breath between his lips. "That feels

upside down, too. I mean, Calvin's gone. What's to keep her here with us?"

Luke measured his words carefully. From what he'd seen, Analise was as dedicated to this family as if she'd been born to it. And yet, Cole was right, she was a young widow. Her life might take a different road in the future. "I guess there aren't ever any guarantees that the people you want beside you will remain close. If circumstances change for either of you—keep in mind, *you* might be the one leaving—and your relationship with Analise has to change, that doesn't mean it will end. It'll be up to you to make it work."

Cole sighed. "I'll just screw it up like I did with Darcy."

"Oh, Cole. Ana and Darcy are on two different planets. Nothing you can do will make her not love you."

"You can't be sure of that."

"Go to bed. Think about what's important to you and what you're going to do to protect those things. We'll talk later."

Cole got up, but didn't move toward the house. "I want to go see Travis."

Luke looked up at the boy. "I don't think they're letting anyone other than his family in right now. Besides, Memphis is two hours away."

Cole put his hands on his hips, looking like he was thinking.

Luke asked, "Were you two friends—before Darcy?"

"No. I hated his guts." At that, Cole went into the house and closed the door behind him.

Well, Luke thought, that put a different complexion on this whole emotional trauma. No doubt, at one time or another, Cole had wished ill upon Travis. Now the two of them had been in the same accident, and Cole as much as walked away, while Travis had been seriously injured.

Luke sat for a while, just staring into the dark woods. Had anything he'd said to Cole tonight made a dent? *It says something that he chose to talk to me.* Maybe something good would come of his being here after all. Maybe the good he could do for Cole would outweigh the unease he'd caused Analise. Maybe.

Chapter 12

It seemed the longer Luke remained at Magnolia Mile, the more complex his entanglements became. All he'd intended to do was offer condolences, express his sorrow over a mother's loss. But Calvin's family was much more complicated than he'd anticipated. In his conversations with Cole, Luke had challenged the boy to take an honest look at himself. In doing so, Luke had been forced to do the same.

He was falling in love with Ana. Everything about her intrigued him. Ana—Calvin's widow. As much as he'd tried to deny it to himself, it was an unalterable fact.

Obligation said he should stay, help fill the void he'd caused. But the longer he stayed, the harder it was to conceal his feelings. He had to leave soon, or Olivia, perceptive woman that she was, would surely see.

The only way Luke found any peace was by pushing his body so hard throughout the day that his mind didn't run him in circles all night long. He'd even begun to sleep without the intrusion of nightmares.

He and Ana were four days into the three-week job at Holly Ridge Park, and already they were two days behind schedule. Late Thursday afternoon, as Analise moved a load of topsoil with a rented Bobcat and Luke shoveled gravel into a trench for a drain, Cole came walking into the park. Luke looked up and wiped the sweat out of his eyes with the sleeve of his T-shirt.

Much to Luke's surprise, Cole had faced his classmates without seeking excuses, going to school on Tuesday despite his bruised face and the uncertainty of Travis's condition. Still, he'd been understandably quiet and pensive all week. A situation which Deputy Dave didn't seem to be helping; he continually stopped by or called with assurances that there "probably" wouldn't be any charges filed. If that was the case, why didn't the guy stop bringing it up and upsetting Olivia and Cole?

As Cole approached, he raised two cans of Coke. "Thought you two could use some refreshment and another pair of hands. I can't go back to soccer practice until the doctor signs a release."

"Thanks." Luke took one of the drinks and looked over his shoulder at Analise. As he raised a hand to get her attention, Cole stopped him.

"Don't call her yet."

Luke leaned his weight on the shovel handle. He'd never admit it out loud, but his knee was screaming by this time every afternoon.

"They announced at school today that Travis is being transferred back to the hospital here in Grover."

"Sounds promising." He waited as Cole's expression said there was more.

"They don't know if he's going to walk again."

"I see. Sounds bad, but it's early yet. I knew a guy whose doctors swore he'd be in a wheelchair for life who made a full recovery."

"That's what coach said, too. Still . . ." After a pause, he said, "Dave said Travis can't remember anything past Saturday morning."

"Probably best for him."

Cole looked slightly surprised. "I hadn't thought of it that way."

"How many times have you gone though that accident in your mind? Having that memory wiped out could be a blessing." If only all horrific memories could be expunged. Luke had one in particular he'd be glad to give up.

Cole nodded thoughtfully. "A couple of guys at school have started saying stuff."

Luke looked Cole in the eye. "What kind of stuff?"

Lifting a shoulder, Cole said, "Like I chased Travis down and ran him off the road, trying to kill him over Darcy. That I planned the whole thing. Can you believe that bullshit?"

"Are people listening to these guys?" Luke asked calmly.

Cole pressed his lips together broodingly for a second. "Some people."

Luke took a long drink of Coke. "Travis was the one in the wrong lane. There's a witness. There are always going to be people who talk without knowing jack-shit. Sooner or later, everyone figures them out."

In a quiet voice, Cole said, "Don't know if I can hold out that long."

"What choice do you have?"

The look Luke saw in Cole's eyes worried him.

"Hey! What are you doing here?" Analise called as she jumped off the Bobcat.

Cole offered her a smile that, although slightly crooked because of the swelling, Luke might have actually bought— if he hadn't seen the pain in the kid's eyes. "I came to help." He held out the other Coke to her.

"Ahh." She pressed the cold can against her cheek, then popped the top and took a long drink. "Thanks. And, no."

"No, what?"

"No, you're not going to help. You're still too banged up."

"Hey, you've got gimpy here working with a shovel."

"Cole!"

"Well, I'm as able to work as he is."

"He's right." Luke handed him the shovel. "I'll get another one. Two gimps will get this drain finished twice as fast." He winked at a shocked-looking Analise.

She shook her head, but didn't argue further.

From the Bobcat, Analise watched Cole and Luke work together, shoveling in tandem. It struck her how close to manhood Cole actually was: He was nearly as tall as Luke, his shoulders had broadened considerably this past year and she could easily tell if he went a day without shaving. It made her long for the uncomplicated little boy who came to her with simple problems, ones she could fix. Lately, she couldn't fix anything—for him or for herself.

She was having a difficult time keeping her perspective with the aftermath of Cole's accident. It seemed that instead of turning to her as he always had, he was looking to Luke for support, for advice. Repeatedly she told herself, a boy Cole's age should naturally turn to a man. And since Cole didn't have a single living male relative, she should be glad that Luke was willing to help him.

Luke was there for Cole in ways that Calvin never had been. Calvin had been great for the fun times, the adventures. But the daily grind of his little brother's growing up hadn't interested him at all.

The only problem was, Luke wasn't going to be around forever.

Analise looked beyond Luke and Cole. Clint Braynard was

getting out of his Blazer. He wore his standard blue business suit and black wing-tips polished to a high gloss—perfect clothes for inspecting a landscaping job. Olivia swore the man had visions of the governorship. Having traveled in those circles herself, Analise could tell Braynard not to waste his time. He worked far too hard at appearing urbane—and his forced efforts were as obvious as the toupee he wore.

She sighed and shut off the Bobcat. She met him halfway with a smile she didn't feel, using precious minutes she didn't have to spare.

"Good afternoon, Mr. Braynard." She took off her glove and offered her hand.

As always, he shook it as if she were made of tinfoil and could easily be crushed by his strong, manly hands. "Mrs. Abbott."

"Please, call me Ana." This had to be the fifteenth time she'd said the same words.

He nodded and gave her his best politician's smile. "Just wanted to take a little look-see so I can report to the council at the meeting this afternoon." He put his hands on his hips and exhaled as he looked around. "Looks like y'all have a good way to go yet."

"It's coming along. It's one of those projects that always makes a bigger mess, then comes together quickly." At least she hoped quickly.

"Don't see the fountain."

"I still have it back at my metal shop. No sense in bringing it out here and risk damage while we're using heavy equipment."

"But it's ready to go?" He looked at her as if trying to ferret out an untruth.

"It won't hold up the completion." That much was true—if she could manage to gather enough strength at the end of one of these grueling days to finish it. She was just about to tell him that she'd get the work done much more quickly if she didn't have to stand here and indulge his curiosity, when his cell phone rang.

"Oh, excuse me, I have to take this call."

"No problem. You might want to head back to your car, though. It's about to get real noisy here."

He was already moving in that direction, putting his phone to his ear.

She got back on the Bobcat and continued the boring job of moving dirt from one pile to another. She couldn't wait until she had the ground sculpted, then the challenging work would begin. This was to be a children's garden, complete with a whimsical fountain that they could splash through on hot summer days.

She hoped it would be the first of many such jobs for Magnolia Mile. It had originally been Olivia's proposal to the county council, but it had quickly become Ana's pet project. Olivia had graciously stepped back and let Analise take the wheel. Projects like this would offer a much better outlet for her creative impulses than simply selling nursery stock and fertilizer. But she had to make this one work first—it had to be done on time and on budget.

If she had to give up sleeping for the next fifteen days, that's just what she would do.

When they entered the kitchen at Magnolia Mile for dinner, Olivia looked pointedly at her filthy son. "I see you're feeling better. Good. Mrs. Baker will be glad. I told her you'd help at the Kiwanis Rib Fest tomorrow night."

"Mom!" He'd finally gotten old enough not to have to go to that stupid dinner, and now his Mom wanted him to volunteer.

As he saw his mother tighten her lips in disapproval, he added, "I was going to stay home tomorrow night."

Olivia looked from under her brow. "On Friday?"

"It's been a long week."

"You can come home early."

"But—"

"No buts. Mrs. Baker needs the help and, thank the good Lord, you're still able-bodied enough to give her some."

Cole glanced at Ana, looking for a little backup. But she was leaving the kitchen without as much as a hint that she was going to come to his rescue. School had been bad enough. Didn't anybody see how awful it was going to be to be busing tables at an event that half the town attended? *Oh, look, Cole Lejeune has a black eye—too bad he crippled poor Travis.*

Luke said, "Maybe I can come and pitch in after Ana and I get done at the park. If Cole's tired, I can just take over for him."

Cole shot him a grateful look. It didn't exactly get him out of it, but at least it gave him the possibility of leaving early—if the gossip and finger-pointing got really bad.

There was something in his mother's eyes that he couldn't quite figure out—she looked . . . satisfied. He'd convinced himself she was going to nix Luke's offer when she said, "All right." She looked at Cole. "If you're too tired to take a full shift, then I can't see that you'll have the energy to do anything else this weekend."

He knew he'd been had. No way around this one. "Yes, ma'am." He didn't feel like hanging out with anybody anyway; all everyone wanted to talk about was the accident. Besides, he didn't have a car.

After dinner he managed to escape to his room without his mom asking a bunch of questions about what was going on at school. It was bad enough going through it once, but to have to have all of his mother's detailed questions and, even worse, her suggestions about how he should handle things would be excruciating.

Maybe he'd blow off school tomorrow.

Cole did go to school. There was no way he'd be able to skip without a whole raft of trouble—especially with his mom *and* Mrs. Baker both at Rib Fest tonight. He still hadn't figured out why there hadn't been a phone call home to report his absence last Friday.

Today, as he walked through the halls of Grover High, the stares and whispers were worse. With the news of Travis's hospital transfer, accident talk gathered new life. Not that Cole wasn't relieved that Travis was improving enough to be moved; it's just that if it had happened on the weekend, the news wouldn't have been so fresh for a school day. Cole's closest friends told him not to let it get to him, but it was hard, especially with Travis maybe not walking again.

Finally, the dismissal bell rang and Cole felt escape close at hand. Then Mrs. Baker passed him in the hallway by his locker. "I'm so glad you'll be helping out this evening, Cole. Do you need a ride to the courthouse?"

He felt like the air drained out of him—no escape after all, just a change in venue. The school week might be over, but now he had to go face the rest of the town. He considered her question. Used to having a vehicle, he hadn't really given a thought as to how he was going to get to the square. Time alone in the car with Mrs. Baker? He shivered. Wouldn't that just be a nut cracker?

"No, thank you, ma'am." He guessed he'd be hoofing it. Which was sort of okay: The longer it took him to get there, the less time he'd be hauling chairs and setting up tables.

"All right, then." She gave him a smile that said she was glad he was finally turning out to be a good boy and pitching in with community activities. "See you in a bit."

As she walked away, he ducked his head inside his locker and made a disgusted face. Not only did he have to work at this dork-fest, he was going to be Mrs. Baker's pet. At least Luke would save him from being stuck there all night.

He took his time gathering his stuff from his locker and loading his bag. He was still using his sport duffel, even though he wasn't attending soccer practice. Only kids who didn't do sports carried backpacks. Besides, it was stupid to switch all his stuff; the doctor said he could practice on Monday. Good thing. They had a big game in a week, and Coach was counting on him playing goalie.

By the time Cole emerged from the building, the buses had all pulled out and the parking lot was nearly empty. He felt a little less edgy about what he had to do; at least he wouldn't have to explain to anyone why he was walking downtown instead of getting ready to go out like everyone else. The afternoon was unusually warm, so he chose to walk on the shady side of the street. It had been a long time since he'd walked to town; he saw all kinds of things that he normally missed when driving by. When he'd been in junior high, the big green house on the corner had had a Rottweiler with a nasty attitude that barked and lunged against its chain when he'd walked past. Now the yard was quiet, the grass growing up where the dog had once worn a large bare patch.

A huge upheaval in the sidewalk tripped him as he looked at the empty doghouse, just as it had tripped him every time he'd walked by in the past while keeping his eye on the snarling dog.

As he crossed the next street, he heard a voice from behind.

"Mrs. Baker said you were going to be helping today. I didn't believe you'd actually do it."

Cole spun around. Becca Reynolds was just a couple of steps behind him. Which meant she'd seen him stumble. He looked at her with heat rising in his cheeks.

"You *are* headed to Rib Fest?" she said.

Of course Miss Goody would be pitching right in. The smug look on her face made him say, "And why wouldn't I help?"

She caught up to him and shrugged. "No ball involved. No cheerleaders. Didn't think you cared about stuff like this."

Geez, she made him sound like a superficial jerk. "I care about . . . stuff."

She gave him a skeptical eye. He was afraid she'd press for specifics, and he had no idea where the money from this fund-raiser was headed—nor did he care.

Instead of giving him the third degree, she studied him for a moment and said, "Your eye looks better."

His hand absently went to the greenish bruise. "I get the stitches out tomorrow."

She started walking and he fell into step beside her. He didn't know why he always thought of her as stuffy and uncool. She dressed pretty much the same as the rest of the girls in school. He gave her a sideward glance. She was cute enough, with shoulder-length dark red hair and a very interesting shade of green eyes, not pure green like Ana's, but green with brown in it.

"Do you always work at Rib Fest?" he asked.

"Usually. My uncle is in Kiwanis. But this year half of the money from the dinner is going to the animal shelter, so I'm working a double shift."

"Where's the other half go?" he asked.

"A bunch of different stuff." She shifted her book bag—

her backpack—to her other shoulder. "Scholarships. The children's hospital. Playground equipment in the park. Stuff like that."

"So you'd only work half as long if it was just for kids and not for animals?" He couldn't keep the teasing edge out of his voice.

She shot him a look of frustration. "No. I'm working *twice* the normal amount because it *is* for animals."

"Same thing."

"Hardly." Then she asked him, "Why are you working?"

Cole gave her a cocky grin. "For the animals."

She elbowed him in the arm and he dodged away. She said, "Really, why?"

"My mom's a friend of Mrs. Baker's; she volunteered me."

She raised her brows and nodded perceptively. "I see."

She didn't see at all. She assumed it had to do with the accident—some kind of punishment. She thought she knew so much about everything. "Why do you always have to act like you're better than everybody else?"

She stopped and looked squarely at him, anger glinting in her eyes. "That's what you think? That *I'm* the snob?"

He stopped, too. "Well, yeah. You don't do the same stuff as most girls. And you always look so . . . so . . . aloof."

Instead of being mad—and he had to admit, he *was* looking to piss her off—she burst out laughing. "Aloof? I didn't even think you had such a word in your vocabulary."

He pointed at her. "See, that's what I mean! You do stuff like that."

She continued to laugh. "I'm sorry. It's just . . . aloof!" She shook her head. "Jesus."

He started walking again. "Sorry I bothered. I see you don't really want to have a conversation."

He heard her trotting on the walk. "Wait a minute." She caught up. "Okay, okay. I don't do stuff with a lot of other kids because I'm just not interested in the same kind of crap most of the girls in my class are. Mostly they bug the shit out of me with their giggling and gossiping and their who's hot for who this week. And the bigger the group, the worse it is."

Cole was a little stunned by her language; he'd always thought of Miss Goody choking before she'd say a word like "shit." "Oh. I guess that explains it." Actually, she was right. He'd always thought of a bunch of girls together as a dangerous herd that could turn on you in the blink of an eye. A girl alone, however, could be trusted to act a little more sane.

She said, "I'm not a weird activist or a lesbian or something. I just don't like wasting my time."

Cole sputtered. He tried never to let anyone know they'd shocked him, but he just couldn't help it; Miss Goody said "shit" *and* "lesbian" in the same conversation.

She looked at him. "What?"

"Nothing. You're just different than I thought."

"Maybe you shouldn't judge people by whether or not they hang out with cheerleaders."

"Point taken."

After they walked in silence for a couple of minutes, she said, "Just for the record, I believe Travis caused that accident."

Without intending to, Cole slowed his step. "Why do you say that?"

She shrugged. "Because, in general, he's an asshole. And, specifically, I can't see why *anyone* would try to kill *anybody* over Darcy Thayler."

In spite of himself, he laughed. The way she said it shed a whole new light on the absurdity of the rumors.

"Well"—she looked at him with mock seriousness—"it's true."

They passed the post office and were nearing the square. The Kiwanis had erected a huge red-and-white-striped tent on the courthouse lawn, which must have been in case of rain, because the square had plenty of big old shade trees. There was a catering truck parked on the sidewalk and a giant barrel-shaped barbeque next to it. A delivery truck filled with tables and chairs took up five of the angled parking slots on one side of the square.

"I heard your mom has a mockingbird in her shop," Becca said, as they stopped on the sidewalk that led to the main courthouse doors.

"Yeah. She's got a ton of animals. They usually are hurt, or somebody dumped them . . . stuff like that."

"I'd like to see it sometime."

After a millisecond to recover from his surprise, he said, "Sure." Was it his imagination, or was she hesitating going her separate way?

"Great." She looked over her shoulder toward the catering truck. "I'm supposed to go cut lemons."

He gave a single nod. "I'm setting up tables."

"Maybe I'll see you around a little later?"

"Maybe."

She gave him a shy wave and headed toward the truck.

"There you are!" Mrs. Baker's voice sent the same grinding irritation through him out here in the open air as it did in the classroom.

He forced a pleasant look on his face. "Yes, ma'am."

As she bustled him off in the direction of the delivery truck, Cole wondered how he could have been so wrong about Becca Reynolds.

•   •   •

Luke had showered and was ready to head into town. He knocked on Analise's bedroom door. She opened it a crack. He could see she was wrapped in a towel.

"You're not ready?" Luke asked.

She pressed the towel against her breasts, an unconscious gesture that told Luke just how much distance she'd put between them. "No. But you go on. Dave's picking Olivia and me up in an hour. We'll meet you there."

"Oh." Here he'd stepped in, offering to get Cole off the hook—which was normally Ana's forte—and she was busy primping, getting ready to go out with Deputy Dave. "Okay."

She quickly eased the door closed.

Somehow they'd managed to make it through the week without tripping over blunders created by their single night of intimacy—mainly because they'd worked until they were both exhausted to the bone. When on the job, there was plenty to keep most suggestive thoughts at bay. Which was just as well; neither one of them wanted to hurt Olivia. And no amount of discussion could change the outcome.

Luke paused as he passed Olivia's bedroom. The door was open a crack. He looked in and saw her lying on her bed, hands folded on her stomach, eyes closed. This had been hard on her, too. With Analise at the job site every day, Olivia had to run the shop single-handedly. He eased back and started to walk softly away.

"Luke?" Olivia called quietly.

He stepped back to the door and pushed it fully open. "Sorry, ma'am, I didn't mean to wake you."

She blew a breath between her teeth. "Don't be silly." She motioned him forward. "Come here for a minute."

Stepping in the room, Luke was struck with a memory that hadn't surfaced in years. He'd been seven years old. His family had been normal then, living in a little house on

Maple Street. He'd tiptoed past his parents' bedroom because his mom and new baby sister were in there napping. His mother had called to him, much as Olivia just had, and drawn him close to her on the bed. She'd kissed the top of his head and said, "Oh, Luke. Your dad and I are the luckiest parents in the world." She'd hugged him tighter. "I love you and your sisters so much. I couldn't ask for more."

Three years later, she left the house—and her children—and never looked back.

That memory had left its mark; Luke couldn't suppress the tiny seed of dread as he entered Olivia's bedroom. He stopped a few feet from her bed.

"For heaven's sake, Luke, come closer. You look like I'm about to boot you out of here."

Luke's breath left in a half-huff, half-chuckle. He stepped to the side of her bed and tried to put himself at ease, but the feeling of irreversible change didn't leave him.

"Now, Ana and I are driving in to the dinner with Dave. But Reverend Hammond is going to be bringing me home. Maybe Ana and Cole could ride home with you. Dave has patrol duty at eleven, I hate to have him hurry to drive them home and report on time."

"All right." He waited for her to say more, but she just settled back on the pillows with a whisper of a smile on her face. He was just about to tease her about having her date pick her up at the door like a proper gentleman, when she sighed and closed her eyes.

"I'm tired. Just going to get a little nap."

She was breathing deeply before he reached the door. He supposed his odd feelings had more to do with his own mother than with anything Olivia might have said to him. Still, as he went down the stairs, that sense that something was about to happen clung to him like cheap perfume.

Chapter 13

By the time Cole saw Luke walking across the courthouse lawn, he'd completely forgotten that Luke had promised to bail him out. The tables and chairs were all set up and Cole was just taping the last of the white paper to the tabletops. He glanced to see how far out of earshot Becca was before he said, "Hey, Luke."

Luke put his hands on his hips and looked around. "Looks like you've got things pretty well set up. Where do I start?"

Cole leaned closer and said in a low voice, "I've decided to just stick with it. You don't need to do anything."

Luke looked surprised.

"It's not so bad," Cole said. "And half of the money is going to the animal shelter."

Luke tilted his head and raised a brow. "The animal shelter, you say?"

"Yeah. So you can go on. I'll finish helping Mrs. Baker."

Becca stopped on her way by with a plastic bag of foam plates. "When you're done with the table covers, Mrs. Baker needs some help lifting that kettle of green beans."

Cole glanced quickly from Luke to Becca and back again. The look on Luke's face said he'd figured out that Cole's staying had nothing to do with Mrs. Baker or the animal shelter. He said, "Be right there."

Luke stopped Becca before she went on. "Aren't you going to introduce me to your friend?"

Oh, man. The quicker he got it done, the sooner Becca and Luke would be out of dangerous proximity. "This is Becca Reynolds. Becca, Luke Boudreau. He was a Ranger with my brother."

Becca smiled at Luke. "Nice to meet you, Mr. Boudreau."

The late afternoon sun cast a bronze glow over her skin and the light glinted in fiery sparks off her hair. Cole's breath got a little tight in his chest.

"Okay, then, see you later," Cole said, urging her on her way.

"And very nice to meet you, Becca," Luke said, offering his hand.

Cole shifted nervously from foot to foot. He had no doubt that if Calvin had been here, he would embarrass Cole to death in this situation. He didn't know what to expect from Luke, so he felt as if he were waiting for a water balloon to be launched at his face.

Becca shifted the bag of plates to her left hand and shook Luke's hand. Cole watched as her hand practically disappeared in Luke's big grasp. Why hadn't he noticed how small she was? She'd always seemed so strong, so sure of herself, that he'd totally missed how delicate she really was.

He realized he was standing there staring when he should be hustling her on her way. He was just about to mention that Mrs. Baker was waiting for those plates when she asked Luke, "Are you going to be staying in Grover long?"

The question recaptured Cole's interest. He'd been wondering that very thing himself.

Luke said, "Probably not. Just until they find someone else to work at Magnolia Mile."

She nodded and bit her lip. "Well, I'd better get these over to the serving line. Mrs. Baker is getting the pre-first-serving jitters." She glanced at Cole. "I'll see you on break."

"Yeah." Cole ducked his head and fiddled with the tape on the table cover, praying Luke wouldn't make a big deal.

"Guess I'm off the hook, then," Luke said. "I'm going to stake out a prime table for me and the ladies. Something near the dessert table, I think."

"See you later."

"Yeah, later." Luke's voice held just a hint of taunting.

Cole ignored it.

Later, just before his break, he noticed Luke, his mom, Ana, Dave and Reverend Hammond laughing at a small picnic table with a mosquito-repellent candle flickering in the middle. Ana sat next to Dave, and his mom next to the reverend. Luke was in a folding chair at the end, looking just a little left out. Cole almost reconsidered his plans to take his break with Becca and go sit with him. But, as he'd just begun to form a friendship with her, he didn't want to ruin it by dumping her—and he sure didn't want to take her to sit with his mom and Ana and all of their questions.

As he watched, the pastor patted his mom on the shoulder and let his hand stay there—just like guys do when they're trying to hook up with a girl. He tried to focus on his mom's face, to see if it made her mad—but she just kept laughing.

Now, that was really weird.

Then it struck him that there was another weird thing tonight. Nobody had asked him about the accident all evening—even with the evidence of it still all over his face.

He'd figured, with all these parents here, there would be a bunch of questions and accusing looks. Nobody even seemed to notice his bruises as he cleared away empty plates and piles of rib bones. He didn't get the feeling that anyone was talking behind his back, either.

"Ready to eat?" Becca said. He hadn't even heard her walk up.

"Yeah." He turned to walk with her and realized he was hungry for the first time in a week.

As they chatted long after the ribs were cleared from the table, Luke watched Ana watching Olivia. Every time Olivia leaned her head close to the minister's in order to share some aside, Analise visibly tensed. He supposed it was natural, her reluctance to see Olivia in a relationship after all these years. The two women had developed a comfortable routine in their lives—without the constant intrusion from men demanding attention. Even so, as much as Ana professed to love Olivia, he thought it slightly selfish to begrudge the woman a loving relationship if one presented itself. And, as Luke watched Reverend Hammond's solicitous behavior, one certainly seemed to be presenting itself.

In fact, watching the warm friendship and comfortable conversation pass between the two, Luke felt a little stab of envy himself. What would it be like to display so freely his feelings for Analise?

He glanced her way. Dave had maneuvered himself between Luke and Analise when they'd seated themselves at the table. A tactic which Luke kept telling himself was actually a favor; it would be very difficult to sit next to her on that bench, smell her shampoo and watch the reflection of the candlelight in her eyes without behaving like the reverend.

Dave brought Luke out of his tormented musings by saying, "I was talking to Clive Buckley out on Cotton Ridge yesterday. He said that he spotted Roy's truck down by the river near his place the day before."

Reverend Hammond's gray eyes looked truly troubled. "I just can't understand it. Roy seemed so harmless. I could understand a show of temper—but to throw that rock through Ana's window . . ." He shook his head. "I'm just more surprised than I can say."

Dave said, "Well, you should be the one who doesn't doubt it—after he came crying to you."

Analise looked at the minister. "Roy came to you?"

Olivia laid a hand on Reverend Hammond's arm. He absently covered it with his as he said, "Just that first day. I found him sitting in the church."

Dave added, "Seems the pervert has a thing for you. He told the reverend here that you were tempting him—that's why he needed to pray."

Luke stiffened and focused sharply on the minister. He doubted the man would give away much verbally, confidentiality and all, but his body language might fill in the blanks.

Reverend Hammond cleared his throat. "Really, Dave, this isn't the place. Besides, it wasn't all as dramatic as you're—"

"Ha!" Dave leaned his elbows on the table. "He's got a sexual thing for Analise, backed her into a corner and would have done who knows what if he hadn't been stopped. Then he sneaks around her house in the dead of night, throwing a rock through her bedroom window. And who knows what he's done that we don't know about? No, sir." He shook his head. "I can't agree. Man's a sexual predator. Analise needs protection."

"Dave! Enough!" Reverend Hammond's face took on a stern line that Luke had never seen.

Analise said, "Reverend, tell me what he said to you, exactly."

The man drew in a breath, as if to shake off his frustration with Dave before he answered her. "Everything he said was pretty jumbled up. If I hadn't just spoken to Olivia about what happened, I might not have been able to piece together what was upsetting him so. He's just a big child, really."

Luke said, "But he said something specific about Analise?"

"Of course, I can't repeat what he told me." He shot a pointed look at Dave. Luke deduced that Dave had been told something in the confidence of the office, not as a friend of Analise. "The poor man's confused, but I don't think it's sexual perversion. His feelings for Analise frightened him— that's why he wanted to pray with me. I still can't see him becoming violent."

Luke said, "There's violence in every man, it just takes the right trigger to release it. In this case, Ana's the trigger." He wanted them to understand that the man had the ability to inflict harm, whether he consciously had the will to do it or not.

Dave quickly added, "He's right. And until we're sure Roy is gone for good, vigilance is the order of the day."

For the first time since he'd met the man, Luke was in total accordance with the deputy.

At eight-thirty Olivia yawned and said, "I think that's it for me tonight." She stood and the reverend helped her step over the bench seat.

Dave started to get up, putting a hand on Analise's arm to do the same.

Olivia said, "You kids stay. Richard's going to run me home."

Richard, is it, now? Analise felt another little prick of resentment.

Olivia didn't seem to notice. "Analise and Luke can wait for Cole, Dave, so you don't have to go all the way out to our place again and race back here to report for duty."

"I really don't mind—"

Olivia waved a hand in the air. "Oh, I know, you're such a gentleman. We've been enough of an inconvenience to you these past weeks. Luke's driving out to our place anyhow, no reason for you both to make the drive."

Luke stood and shook the reverend—*Richard's*—hand. Analise put a smile on her face and tried to force her negative thoughts back into the dark closet she'd built for such things long ago. "Liv, I'll just come with you. I'm pretty wiped myself."

Olivia looked aghast. "And leave Luke here alone to wait for Cole to be finished? I thought you two could go get a beer while you wait. It'll make you rest better tonight."

Analise looked at Luke, trying to sense his reaction. She supposed if Cole was riding home with them, she'd be safe with Luke—that was to say, she'd be safe from her own weakness.

"A beer sounds pretty good to me. How about walking over to the Boxcar while we wait for Cole?"

Olivia said, "That's a good idea. Lois said the kids should be finished by ten." She blew Analise a kiss. "Night, love."

"Good night, Liv." How could anyone remain aggravated with Olivia for more than two seconds? She watched Olivia leave with *Richard,* trying with all of her heart to be glad for her mother-in-law. The woman deserved happiness— Analise just couldn't figure out how that happiness could be brought to such a vivacious woman by a bland man like Richard Hammond.

Luke remained standing, watching them go, too. He had a slight smile on his face and a light in his eye that said he approved of Olivia's new relationship. Of course, it was easy to welcome such a thing when it didn't affect *his* life in any way.

Oh, my gosh! I sound just like those spiteful women who begrudge anyone's happiness. Is that what the future holds for me ... resentment and bitterness? I can't love, so nobody should?

"Ready for that beer?" Luke rubbed his hands together in anticipation.

Analise looked at him. He gave so much and asked for so little in return. Why did he stay? Here he'd slaved away all week long, and she hadn't once thought about something as simple as stocking the refrigerator with beer. "I'll buy," she said, getting up and stepping over the bench.

Dave remained seated, focused on rolling a toothpick between his thumb and forefinger.

"Dave, care to join us?" she asked.

He looked up at her as if her question startled him. "Oh, thanks. I don't drink when I'm going on duty."

"I didn't mean you had to have a beer. You sure you don't want to come?"

"Yep." He unfolded his long legs from under the table. As skinny as they were, when Analise saw him step over the bench, they reminded her of spider's legs.

He paused by Luke and stuck the toothpick in his mouth. Leaning close, he said in a low voice, "You make sure those ladies keep their doors locked. Y'hear?"

Luke nodded. "Not to worry. I double-check them myself."

Dave held Luke's gaze for a moment, then said, "Good, then." He turned to Analise and winked. "Night, darlin'."

"Good night, Dave. And thanks again for the ride."

He raised a hand over his shoulder in acknowledgment as he walked away.

They found Cole up to his elbows in dishwater in the catering truck.

"Hey, there," Analise called in the open rear door. "How are those dishpan hands?"

Cole laughed and held up two sudsy hands. "I'm going to need a gallon of lotion when I get done here."

"We're just going over to the Boxcar for a drink. We'll be back here by ten to take you home."

"Oh, um, Mrs. Baker said she'd give us a ride home when we're finished. She wants to take us to the Dixie for sundaes."

"You're sure she wants to drive all the way out to Magnolia Mile?"

"It's not that far from her place."

"All right." She started to leave, then stopped. "Cole?"

He looked back up from his work. "Huh?"

"I'm proud of you. I know this wasn't your idea of a fun Friday night."

He shrugged. "Ah, it wasn't so bad."

She waved and walked back to Luke, who was chatting with Dick Baker.

"Get that magnolia in, Mr. Baker?" she asked.

"Yep," he said. "And it didn't show a sign of shock. You know how to pick'em."

"Glad to hear it's doing well."

They parted company with Mr. Baker. Analise said, "Looks like we can just go on home. Mrs. Baker's taking the kids out for sundaes and bringing them back."

Luke's gaze cut quickly to her. "Cole's letting a *teacher* drive him home?"

"Yeah. So?"

"Nothing. Just surprised is all."

The way he said it made her think he knew something he wasn't telling her. That slid under her skin like a thorn from a sting weed; just another nettle that said he knew more about what was going on with Cole than she did.

She was about to press further when Luke said, "I thought you said you were going to buy me a beer."

"You're right, I did," she conceded. "Still want one?"

"Is the Pope Catholic?"

About halfway to the Boxcar, Luke asked, "Sure you don't mind going to the same place two nights in a row?"

She raised puzzled eyes to him.

"Tomorrow is Saturday," he prompted.

"Oh, yeah." She waved away the cobwebs. "I'm so tired, I can't even remember what day it is."

He put a hand on her shoulder and began to massage the knot of muscles there. She sidestepped until his hand fell away.

"Sorry," he said. "I wasn't thinking."

She smiled shyly at him. "That's okay. As long as one of us remembers."

They walked in awkward silence from the circle of one streetlight to the next. Thank goodness someone had finally taken down those depressing Christmas wreaths. It seemed to have been a standoff between the street department and the city council to see who would buckle first and tackle the job. Obviously someone had hollered uncle. Or perhaps a frustrated citizen took it into his or her own hands—Liv had threatened to often enough.

When they reached the Boxcar, Luke held the door for

her. It was almost as busy as Saturday night, since everybody had been drawn into town for Rib Fest. She spotted a cramped table with two chairs shoved against the wall and snaked her way through the crowd toward it.

When they sat down, the table was so small, their knees bumped under it. People jostled around, pressing close, making it impossible to pull the chairs out any farther. Although ashamed to admit it, Analise enjoyed the contact.

Luke ordered a draft beer. Analise decided to stick with Coke; too dangerous to let anything impair her judgment while alone with Luke.

There was no live band, except on Saturday night. The jukebox played sporadically. In general, the noise of dozens of conversations filled the place. Analise and Luke had to lean their heads close together in order to hear one another talk.

"Olivia said you made most of the metal sculptures for sale at the shop," Luke said as he methodically wiped the sweat down on his beer glass with the finger and thumb of his right hand.

Analise had been so fixated on his fingers, she had to think a moment to register what he said. If a simple action like that had her thinking things she shouldn't, it was a good thing she'd decided not to drink. "Yes. I made the bench in the yard, too."

The instant she said it, she wished she hadn't. That bench was a link to an intimacy that was forbidden.

He looked thoughtfully into the bubbles in his beer for a moment. "I suppose that was a craft you picked up after you moved here. What made you choose metal?"

She lifted a shoulder. "Our winters are short, but they can get pretty boring when you're in the landscape business. We sell Christmas trees at the holidays, but other than that there's not much to do. We used to purchase the metalwork from someone else. One winter I decided to try my hand at it." She didn't say that was the winter when she'd realized she was going to have to create a full life for herself without Calvin, or go crazy.

"You're really good. I noticed the display the first time I pulled up in front of the shop."

She saw him glance at the narrow burn on the back of her hand. Self-consciously, she slid it under the table—that scar just another link to forbidden intimacy.

"I'm getting better at it," she said. "Some of my first stuff was horrible—like student engineering experiments gone horribly awry. I just refused to give up."

He leaned closer and looked in her eyes. "I admire that in you. You refuse to give up on anything you love."

Suddenly she felt as if he'd sucked the air from her lungs, as in the old stories of the cat in the cradle. *Oh, if you only knew.*

When she recaptured her breath, she dragged the conversation back to her work. "There's a half-finished fountain upstairs for the garden we're putting in at the park. I'm making it in sections that we can transport, then I'll assemble it on location."

His eyes brightened and he leaned closer. "A children's fountain?"

She nodded, wondering why he looked so intrigued.

"What I've seen of your work has been really good--but with you applying that to a children's theme . . . it's got to be fantastic."

She grinned and leaned back in her seat. "Well . . . *fantastic* might be an exaggeration. . . ." Then she added, "It has been fun."

"Does it have dragonflies and whirligigs?" He looked

like a kid asking if there was chocolate cake for dessert— and it shot straight to her heart.

"Dragonflies, whirligigs, a couple of kites, cattails, toadstools *and* a giant bullfrog."

"Can I see?" he asked eagerly.

She tilted her head. "Maybe. I have to work on it over the weekend. You see, since it's in a hands-on environment and children are the main users, I've had to modify several of my techniques to make certain there aren't any sharp edges that could cut. It's been interesting. I just wish I had more time."

He looked perturbed as he nodded and said, "The penalty clause."

"There's that. We bid the project low so we could get the county to commit. Any penalty would really hurt us. But since this is our first project of this kind, we need it to go smoothly so we can use it as a selling point for others."

Luke said, "We're already working Saturdays, but I'm not opposed to putting in time on Sundays, too."

"This Sunday I need to work on the fountain. But you might just find yourself drafted for the next two."

"If you give me enough direction, I can work the site alone on Sunday."

The willingness in his voice made her admire him all the more. Except for this evening, she'd been squeezing every possible hour of daylight out of him, and here he was ready to give more. "We'll see. Forecast is for rain Sunday."

He finished his beer.

Reluctantly, she said, "We'd better be getting home. I want to make sure we're there before Cole." She hated for this evening to end. It had been the most relaxing she'd had in a very long time. Her life seemed to be falling back into some sort of order; she felt like her old self at the barbeque tonight. And sharing a drink alone with Luke topped off the evening nicely. At first she'd been afraid it might be awkward, but her worry had been completely unfounded. She'd like to linger here until they closed the Boxcar.

Luke started to get out his wallet.

"Hey! I said I'm buying."

"Okay. Okay." He raised his hands. "Force of habit."

She grinned. "Gotta watch those habits. Some of them are hard to break."

"And some are worth picking up," he said seriously.

She ignored the innuendo in his tone and paid the tab. She had no doubt in her mind, Luke Boudreau would be a habit with many benefits. Too bad those benefits all had negative side effects.

Cole slid the last folded table into the delivery truck. He pulled the roll-up door down as he climbed out and jumped to the pavement. His shoulders ached and his hands were raw, but he hadn't felt this good inside for a long time. He felt like he'd spent the last months with a buzzing static tormenting his brain, and now silence had finally descended. The feeling that he was about to jump out of his skin was beginning to subside.

He stood there with his hands on his hips for a moment, taking in the quiet of the courthouse square. The tents remained, but the lights had been shut off. Somewhere not too far away, a dog barked. Everyone was gone, except Mr. Baker, who was driving the rental truck, Mrs. Baker and Becca. Suddenly Cole realized he didn't want to go home. What if, in the dark quiet of his room, the buzzing came back? He didn't think he'd be able to stand it.

If someone had told him two weeks ago that he'd have spent an entire evening working with Mrs. Baker and not hated every minute of it, he would have laughed. Even now, if his friends caught wind—and with half the town here tonight, they were sure to—there would be hell to pay. Normally that would bother him, but for some reason he felt ready for the ridicule. They could say what they wanted and it really wouldn't matter.

"Mrs. Baker has to finish counting the cash box, then we can go," Becca said, surprising him with her silent approach.

He turned to face her. She looked as wiped as he felt. "Wanna sit down while we wait?"

She looked around.

He pointed to an old stone bench near the courthouse that was nearly overtaken by a couple of crepe myrtles. She walked toward it and Cole followed. When they sat on the short bench, made shorter by the encroaching foliage, their elbows rubbed. Becca took a little scoot toward her end. Cole was sorry she did. He liked the way her skin felt against his.

Now, there was another factor of this evening he never would have believed two weeks ago. Becca. If his life had been running like always, he probably wouldn't have given her a second thought. Ashamed as he was to admit it, he wouldn't have made much of an effort to be friends with someone as "uncool" as Becca Reynolds. In fact, at a football game last fall Steve Watters had made an offhand comment that he thought she was hot. After all of the hazing he took, Steve never even looked her way again. Cole was just as stuck-up as the rest of them.

How could they all have been so blind, so stupid?

"Bet we made a bunch of money tonight," he said.

"It was a good turnout." She looked out over the trampled grass of the courthouse lawn. "It probably won't be enough to do everything they need at the shelter, though. The county is threatening to close it down."

"What'll happen to the strays if they do?" he asked.

She gave her head a slight shake. "They'll kill them." Then she raised a palm in the air. "Oh, pardon me, they'll *euthanize* them. So much kinder and more civilized."

"No shit? Just like that. No looking for owners or anything?"

"Nope. No place to keep them, so they'll go straight to doggie and kitty heaven. No passing go. No collecting two hundred dollars."

Cole thought about all of the animals around his house. They were all strays. Even Rufus had been dumped at the end of their driveway as a pup. He couldn't imagine someone just killing any of them—well, maybe with the exception of Pandora.

"My mom will never let the county close down the shelter." He said it with heartfelt confidence.

Becca laughed, but it was a bleak sound. "Oh, Cole, unless she has a bucket of money she's going to throw at it, I can't see what she can do."

"You don't know my mom."

Becca sighed. "I hope you're right."

They sat there for a while, just listening to the crickets. Cole thought how nice it was simply to sit in the dark with her. Then he thought of Travis and was ashamed for enjoying anything.

"I'm going to go see Travis at the hospital tomorrow." He didn't know why he said it, it just fell out of his mouth.

"That's good." She fidgeted on the bench, seeming suddenly restless. She started fiddling with the silver ring on her right hand. "I did something that I shouldn't have." She paused. "Something that might have kept you from getting in that accident."

"What are you talking about? What could you have done?" Even as he said it, he sat up a little straighter.

"I took your name off the absent list Friday." She kept her gaze on the lawn and wiped her palms on the thighs of her jeans.

"How could you do that?"

"I pick up the attendance slips and take them to the office. I erased your name."

They took attendance in first and fifth periods—first thing in the morning and right after lunch. Becca must have taken his name off twice. He said, "That explains why I didn't catch hell."

She nodded solemnly. "If you'd caught hell, you'd probably have been grounded and not out on Saturday night."

He didn't tell her that he *was* grounded and had gone out anyway. Instead he asked, "Why'd you do it?"

She pursed her lips, making her look way hot with the light from the street lamps filtering through the leaves. He moved a little closer to her.

Then she shrugged. "I felt sorry for you."

That floored him. Becca Reynolds, daughter of the junkyard man, Miss Goody, felt sorry for *him*, class president, captain of the soccer team—sorry enough to break the rules.

Even stunned as he was at her turning of the tables, he suddenly had the urge to kiss her. Almost more than he'd *ever* wanted to kiss Darcy; he wanted it in a different way.

Then she looked at him and his heart sped up. He touched her cheek and leaned close, brushing his lips gently against hers.

When he pulled back slightly, he left his hand on her face.

She whispered, "What was that for?"

After a couple of heartbeats, he whispered back, "I'm not sure."

Her exhaled breath teased his lips, then she closed the space between them, kissing him. Her kiss was less tentative than his, amazingly self-assured. He could hardly react because he was so surprised by her confidence. He never imagined Miss Goody could kiss like that.

Just as a fire broke out in his belly, she backed away, yet held his gaze. "Don't look so shocked."

"I—I . . ." *Jesus, stop stuttering.*

She smiled. "Don't worry. I won't tell anyone." Then she got up and walked away.

It took a second for him to make his legs move. He sprinted after her. "What the hell does that mean?"

She turned and looked at him over her shoulder. "I know jocks like you don't go for girls like me. I won't ruin your reputation by telling anyone—and I don't expect anything from you. It was just a kiss—don't make a big deal out of it."

What? Did Miss Goody just blow him off?

Mrs. Baker called, "There you children are! Ready for some ice cream?"

Cole was just realizing a brand-new form of frustration. He wanted to tell Mrs. Baker to buzz off. Becca Reynolds had just given him the kiss of his life and Mrs. Baker was talking to them like they were in kindergarten! Besides, he wasn't done dealing with Becca and could hardly discuss anything in front of his chemistry teacher.

Becca said, "I need to pick my car up at school."

"We'll swing back by there and get it on our way to the Dixie," Mrs. Baker said.

Car? If Becca had a car, why in the hell had she walked into town?

Chapter 14

"**A**re you sure you feel up to helping us at the park today?" Analise asked Cole when he walked into the kitchen at seven the next morning. "You don't look so good."

He didn't feel so good. The ice cream he'd forced down last night had landed like a rock in his stomach. Becca practically ignored him the entire time they were at the Dixie. Then she'd gotten in her own car and he'd had to ride home with Mrs. Baker chattering constantly, when all he wanted was some quiet to think about what had happened with Becca. Once he did get to his room and some privacy, his thoughts didn't allow for sleep. Everything in his life seemed to be so upside down. When he did doze, he had dreams about Becca that he only used to have about Darcy or Anna Kornakova.

But he kept all that to himself. "I'm fine. Can we stop by the hospital on our way in?"

Analise stopped pouring her orange juice and looked at him. "Isn't it a little early? Visiting hours don't start until one."

He lifted a shoulder and picked out a box of Honey Nut Cheerios from the cabinet. He really didn't want to have to see Travis's parents; going early was the only way he could see that would reduce the chances of that happening. "I'll be too dirty later. And I don't want to make somebody drive me back after work."

"We could stop when we go back in to the Boxcar," Analise said.

Cole was scrambling to come up with a counter to that when Luke said, "We'd be late for Olivia's reservation."

Cole's gaze snapped to Luke, who gave him an almost imperceptible nod. Thank God someone around here understood.

"We won't be that late," Analise said. "It's not like they're going to give away our table."

Luke looked at Ana and said pointedly, "Don't you think it'd be just as easy to stop on the way this morning?"

After a moment in which she looked like she was going to argue, a change came over her. "Oh," she said with a lifted hand, "I suppose you're right. We'll stop on the way in." Then she said to Olivia, "Should we bring Cole back here to help in the shop this afternoon? It's likely to get pretty busy."

Olivia sipped her coffee. "That won't be necessary. Richard said he'd come by and give me a hand today. Said he needs the exercise."

Cole wasn't sure how he felt about Reverend Hammond's increasing interest in his mom. It wasn't like they were dating or anything—and they were way too old to have sex. He just couldn't understand it. Maybe it wouldn't be so weird if he wasn't a minister. As Cole glanced at Ana, it was clear she didn't know what to make of it, either.

He threw out half of his cereal. His stomach was still funny; he felt like he was about to take a final he hadn't studied for. What was he going to say when he saw Travis? Their usual adversarial greeting of, "Hey, dickhead," didn't

seem quite appropriate. It'd be easier if he just didn't go. But
for some reason, he felt he had to. He didn't know why,
exactly; it wasn't like it was going to change anything.

"Where's Rufus?" Analise asked as she filled his water
dish.

Olivia said, "Let him out early. He was whining and fret-
ting all over the place. Must have smelled something in the
yard."

At the sound of food and water being dished out, Skippy
hopped in from the living room. Cole picked him up and
scratched his tummy. Becca's comments about the fate of
the animals without a shelter came back to him.

"Mom, do you know anything about the animal shelter?"

His mom poured her coffee into the big thermal cup she
took out to the shop with her. "Not much. Just that they're
always on the hunt for funding. Rib Fest should help."

"I heard that the county is thinking about shutting it
down," Cole said.

She made the same grunting sound that she always used
when she didn't believe he hadn't eaten a dozen cookies
before dinner. "County's always making noise about that."
Then she started on her list of grievances against the county
since Clint Braynard came into office. Once she got going
on that, getting her to look at a specific problem was impossible. He knew he'd have to take another run at her later
about the shelter.

She was still grousing when Ana kissed her cheek and
she, Cole and Luke went out to get in the nursery truck and
head to town.

The closer they got to the hospital, the more Cole's guts
churned. He sat between Analise and Luke, worried that
each bump in the road was going to force a gastronomic
explosion of some kind. He nearly told them to forget the

hospital stop twice before they pulled into the parking lot. Ana put the truck in park and Luke got out so Cole could slide across the bench seat and exit.

Cole hesitated for a moment. Analise said, "Would you like me to come in with you?"

He was tempted to ask her to go in *for* him, but one glance at Luke shot that idea out of the air. Cole had to do what was right—which was going inside and seeing Travis.

"No." He slid out. "I'll be back in a few minutes."

Luke gave a nod of approval as Cole left the parking lot. Strange as it seemed, that single look calmed his jumping insides. If Calvin had been in this situation, he would have walked in this hospital and looked Travis in the eye; Cole would, too. He had to keep foremost in his mind that Travis had chased *him,* Travis had been the one to swing out into the wrong lane. He wasn't here to lay blame, but he wasn't going to crawl in, either.

The farther he got from Luke and the closer to Travis's hospital bed, the more that newfound courage began to falter. But Cole pressed on, asking the desk for the room number and taking the elevator to the second floor.

His tennis shoes squeaked against the newly mopped tile as he walked down the hall. The noise seemed abnormally loud, as if screaming to get everyone's attention. A couple of times he looked over his shoulder, certain someone was standing behind him staring, only to find himself alone in the hall.

Travis's door was partially closed. He listened for a moment to see if a doctor or someone was in there with him, but didn't hear anything. With his heart sending reverberations throughout his veins, he knocked lightly.

A sound came from inside, not quite a "Come in," more mumbled than that.

Slowly he pushed open the door and slipped inside.

The bottom fell out of his stomach. Suddenly he couldn't breathe.

He didn't know what he'd been expecting, but what he saw lying in that bed shook him to his bones. If it weren't for the banner with a get-well wish surrounded by dozens of signatures from Grover High hanging on the wall, Cole would have been certain he was in the wrong room.

There wasn't any part of the body in the bed that was recognizable as Travis Benson. His face was bandaged, showing only blackened eyes and swollen lips. Both legs were casted and in traction and one of his arms was in a cast that held his bent arm out from his body. A white sheet draped him from his waist to his upper thigh. Another bandage encircled his chest and ribs. It was like a Looney Tunes cartoon setup of Sylvester the cat or Wile E. Coyote without the laughing.

Travis's eyes shifted in Cole's direction, but his head remained stationary on the pillow. He made a sound, but Cole didn't have a clue what he was trying to say.

Cole forced himself to walk closer to the bed. He'd never felt so lucky, or so miserable, in his entire life. He had no idea what to say, so he just stood there, staring like an idiot.

Travis started making lots of noise and jerking his head from side to side on the pillow.

Cole had just figured out that he was saying, "Get out! Get out! Get out!" when someone grabbed his shoulder from behind.

"What are you doing here? Can't you see you're upsetting him?" a woman who had to be Travis's mother shouted.

Cole took a single step backward. "I just wanted to see him—"

"So you didn't kill him last week and you're trying to finish off the job?"

"No!"

"I want you out of here! Do *not* come back!" She gave him a shove in the direction of the door.

By the time Cole hit the doorway, a nurse was headed in. "What's—" She hurried to Travis. "Settle down, now. Let's not undo all the healing you've done," she said smoothly. "Just relax. You're just fine."

Grayness edged Cole's vision. He managed about four steps toward the elevator when he got so dizzy he had to lean against the wall. He didn't know how long he'd stood there when the nurse came back out of the room and put a hand on his shoulder. She shoved a glass of water in his hand. "Here, drink this."

He started to walk again, and she pushed him gently but firmly against the wall. "Not until I'm sure you're not going to take a nosedive."

Cole slumped against the wall and took a drink of the water. His hand was shaking so much, he nearly spilled it down his shirtfront.

"Don't put too much in what Mrs. Benson said," the nurse said quietly. "This has been very stressful for the family. She's not thinking clearly."

"I just wanted to see him. . . . I didn't . . ."

"Of course you didn't mean to upset anyone. It's not your fault."

But it is. I was supposed to be home. If I hadn't gone out that night, none of this would have happened. Suddenly he could see it all so clearly, how stupid the entire mess had been. No girl, not even Darcy Thayler, was worth the price Travis Benson was paying in there.

He drew in a shaky breath and let it out slowly.

"Feeling better?" the nurse asked.

He nodded and pushed himself away from the wall. "Thank you, ma'am."

Cole walked out of the hospital unsure if his knees were going to buckle with the next step. But he emerged into the sunlight on his feet. When he saw Analise and Luke standing by the truck talking, he wanted to run and throw himself in her arms and cry like he had when he was little. Instead he drew in a deep breath and walked slowly across the parking lot.

The second Analise's eyes fell on him, he knew he was in for a barrage of questions. "You're white as a ghost," she said, stepping forward.

Oh, please, please, don't make me tell you what happened in there.

She hesitated.

Luke said, "Ana and I were just going to run across the street to the drugstore and pick up some Band-Aids." He held up a blistered palm. "You wanna walk with us, or wait here?"

Ana's gaze cut to Luke. She had that look in her eye, the one she'd learned from Mom that said you were in deep shit.

Cole quickly said, "I'll wait here."

"All right." Luke started to walk toward the road.

After a second, Analise huffed under her breath. "You want anything?"

He shook his head as he opened the rear gate of the truck, then sat down on it.

Ana gave Cole one last backward glance before she caught up with Luke at the curb and they crossed the street.

Cole closed his eyes and raised his face to the morning sun. The brightness bleached out all color from the insides of his eyelids. He welcomed the whitewashing of his vision. It kept him from seeing the accident over and over again, as he did each time he'd closed his eyes for the last week. If he could keep the images away, the sounds remained buried, too. He didn't have to hear the squealing tires, the grinding of metal against metal, the sickening thud of Travis's car hitting his, the revving of the engine as his Jeep had taken flight. It had all happened in an instant, yet replayed in slow motion in his mind— giving the mistaken impression that something could be done to stop it.

Why was it everything that tore your life apart happened in a split second? Something so catastrophic that it changed everything about you should have some warning, a buildup so you could get used to the idea that things would never be the same again. Then maybe you'd have time to brace yourself—maybe you could take one last look at life *before*.

But it didn't happen that way. Calvin was forever ripped from them the instant his helicopter hit the ground. The accident with Travis happened in the blink of an eye. If only a person could call back a single second—things would be so different.

He heard Ana and Luke talking as they came back and he quickly swiped away the single tear that had escaped his control. He jumped down to the ground and faced them.

Luke said, "Ready to go to work?"

Cole gave Luke a brusque nod, but avoided looking into Ana's eyes. "Ready."

Luke braced his hands on the tile, leaning under the shower spray. As the hot shower pelted his tired muscles, he focused fully on the undercurrent that had been bothering him all week. Last night, as he'd watched Analise at the community dinner, relaxed and surrounded by those familiar to her, he knew that he was getting far too emotionally attached to her.

Last evening, she'd showed a strong contrast to the ever-increasing strain he'd sensed in her. Outwardly she continued to be friendly and jovial with him—almost too jovial, as if she were covering up the tension with lighthearted humor. It was when she thought he wasn't looking that he saw her anxiety in the tenseness of her mouth, the set of her jaw. They had no future. Her family was too important to her; there was no way she could protect them and have a romantic relationship with him. She had been happy with her life before he came—he didn't want to alter that and leave her longing for something different.

And that road went both ways. Although his life before Grover had been drifting without an anchor, he knew he could not count on these people to save him. He really had to pull back—before he was so attached he'd never be able to let go.

There was no way for him to erase from his mind the time he and Ana had shared in his bed. The sex had been great, but it was the closeness throughout the night that he cherished the most. It was all they would ever have—and God knows, he didn't deserve that. He couldn't shake the haunting fact that the only reason Analise had opened herself to him was because her husband was dead—and Luke had a direct hand in that death. There was something totally perverse in the entire situation—a Shakespearian tragedy in the making. It was up to him to prevent a catastrophic ending.

He got out of the shower and noticed Skippy curled up in a ball behind the wicker hamper. He was really going to miss this place, these people.

He left the bathroom wearing only his jeans, toweling his hair as he walked back toward his bedroom. His knee throbbed and the stabbing was increasing its persistence between his shoulder blades. It was going to rain.

Analise stuck her head out of her room. "Almost ready?" she asked.

He couldn't repress the smile that the sight of her brought; he hid it behind the towel. "I think I'm going to pass tonight. It's been a long week." He wanted to go, wanted it more than he could say. But it'd be better if he started pulling himself back inch by inch.

Her gaze immediately shot to his knee. "A lot of pain?"

"Not really. I just thought I'd watch a little TV and turn in early—just in case it's dry enough to work at the park tomorrow."

She snorted. "I'd hardly call our Saturday at the Boxcar a late-nighter."

"Just the same. I'm not going to be very good company tonight."

She hesitated a moment, then said, "Did you tell Liv?" She tilted her head slightly, looking so beautiful that he wrapped the towel around his hands to keep from reaching out and touching her.

"I was hoping you'd take care of that for me." He grinned sheepishly.

"Oh, no." She waggled an index finger in the air. "Liv doesn't believe in not shooting the messenger."

He laughed. "In that case, maybe I'll send a note attached to Skippy. I doubt she'd have the heart to do damage to something so cute and furry."

"I think Cole already tried that tactic once."

"And?"

"Let's just say Skippy was safe."

"Cole?"

She *tsk*ed, and shook her head gravely. "Don't think he fared as well."

Just then, Olivia came out of her room. She was wearing a purple nylon jogging suit and a pair of New Balance tennis shoes. She looked pointedly at Luke. "I think they have a NO SHIRT NO SHOES NO SERVICE rule at the Boxcar." She winked. "Not that any of the ladies would mind in your particular case."

"Luke's not going," Analise said with a mischievous twinkle in her eye that made Luke want to turn her over his knee—another sure sign that he needed to keep his distance.

"What do you mean, he's not going?"

"He said he's going to watch TV."

"There isn't even anything good on tonight."

"Maybe he's just sick of being with us twenty-four/seven."

"Well, I certainly can't see that," Olivia said. "We're perfectly pleasant people. Is it his knee? You're working him too hard."

"*I'm* working him too hard? Who pressed him into staying?"

"Well, he needs to take better care of himself. It hasn't been that long—"

"Ahem!" Luke cleared his throat loudly. "Again, ladies, I must remind you, I'm standing right here."

The second Olivia swung her narrowed gaze in his direction, he realized he was better off being invisible.

She said, "So, why aren't you going?"

"Honestly, I'm just tired. I can't keep up with you women, working all week and partying all night."

Olivia put her hand on her cheek. A look of regret came over her. "She *has* been working you too hard."

"Liv! Really, I insist he takes plenty of breaks. He hasn't complained—"

"Of course he hasn't. He's a gentleman."

"All right!" Luke threw his hands in the air in surrender and headed toward his bedroom. "I'll get my shirt."

He'd start distancing himself *tomorrow*.

When the dancing started, Luke made certain that he and Cole were at the pool table. He was chalking his cue when he saw Analise and Dave jitterbug past—he supposed it wasn't actually a jitterbug, but a country equivalent that looked nearly as athletic. He looked quickly away.

"Sure you want to play another game?" he asked Cole with raised brows.

"Hey, I can't let you walk out of here without me taking at least one game." He shook his head in disbelief. "I used to think I was pretty good."

"Always play with someone better than you. Only way to improve. I used to play with your brother."

"He was better than *you*?"

Luke grinned. He knew the envy in Cole's voice was aimed at Calvin, not himself—and that's the way he wanted it to remain. "He always kicked my ass."

"Hmm. Was there anything Calvin wasn't good at?"

The question caused Luke to miss the cue ball. He hit it high and to the right, causing his cue to skitter off and the ball to roll slowly to the left, missing any chance at a shot. He stood up and leaned his hip on the table. Truth or lie? Build up the man into a legend, or make Cole see just how human Calvin was? Luke had a sneaking suspicion that part of Cole's current problems stemmed from the fact that he thought he could never live up to his older brother.

"He was good at lots of things—but not everything." *Like fidelity.*

Just as Luke feared, Cole asked, "Like what wasn't he good at?"

"Well . . ." He looked into the air, searching his memory for an appropriate example. "He was a lousy cook. Nearly poisoned us when it was his turn."

"Aw, that doesn't count. No guy can cook."

"He couldn't balance his checkbook. Always took the bank's word."

"That's no big deal."

Luke decided to inch nearer the truth. "Occasionally he broke a promise."

Cole looked serious as he considered that. Then he said, "But it was always for a good reason, right?"

After a moment, Luke said, "No. Not always."

Cole didn't respond, just lined up and took his shot. His game was improving.

They completed the game without much conversation. Luke wondered if Cole was angry with him for saying what he did about Calvin. It was difficult to tell if it was that, or if he was just concentrating on the game—he did win.

When they finished, Luke said, "I'm going to step outside for a minute, it's hot in here."

"Okay." Cole put their cues back in the rack, while Luke retrieved the balls from the pockets.

When Luke looked at him again, Cole was looking toward the door. For a second, he appeared pleasantly surprised—then his face became unreadable.

Luke followed his gaze. The girl from Rib Fest was walking in with a couple Luke assumed were her parents. He gave Cole a pat on the shoulder. "See you in a bit." He wanted to stay as far away as possible from having to make up an excuse not to dance. He couldn't take another bantering exchange between Liv and Ana that would result in his capitulation; he was *not* dancing. That would involve touching Analise, and he couldn't do that and not have his feelings written all over his face. If he used his knee as an excuse, Olivia would start fussing all over again.

He stepped out into the parking lot. It was packed with vehicles tonight, with the overflow parking going onto the street. They'd brought Ana's eight-year-old red Ford Explorer, Olivia having insisted that Ana drive so Luke could rest his knee. It was nearly hemmed in by someone who double-parked. Luke hoped they wouldn't be stuck here when they were ready to leave. The sooner he got home, the sooner he could hide in his room.

The air was heavy and as still as a tomb. Looking to the western sky, he saw the hint of distant lightning. Unconsciously he rotated his shoulders; the stabbing remained.

He took a slow walk around the parking lot. That used up about two minutes. At times like these, he wished he smoked—at least he'd have something to occupy himself as he killed time. After ten minutes of loitering, he decided a beer would be as good as a cigarette. He turned to go back inside, but his attention was drawn to a noisy vehicle on the street. He was surprised to see Roy's beat-up truck chug past. He didn't slow down and didn't seem to be looking in the direction of the Boxcar. Luke had hoped the man had left the area entirely. By all indications, he'd at least been staying away from Magnolia Mile for the past week.

Once inside, Luke stopped at the bar. Analise was standing near the booth talking to a young couple, and Cole was nowhere in sight. For the moment, Olivia sat alone, her elbow on the table, her head resting on her hand. Caught in a moment unawares, her fatigue showed. She was a woman of high animation and her stillness conveyed the weariness she'd been trying to mask. What woman could go through what she had in the past months and *not* show signs of it? One son dead, the other trying to kill himself with dangerous behavior.

The protective streak that had reared its head so often leapt to its feet and roared. Luke would do anything to prevent Olivia—her entire family—from further pain.

First step in that plan was not to cause any more direct harm himself. He remained at the bar and ordered a beer. He lingered there, nursing his drink, waiting to leave. Standing at this corrugated steel and Formica bar, Luke thought of the antique walnut bar in his dad's tavern. Dad had saved it from an old building being torn down to make way for a new fire station when Luke was just a baby. The antique had always been a true point of pride for Benny Boudreau. He said it gave his place character.

Luke looked around. The Boxcar had plenty of what his dad would call character—those little things that a long-established business had accumulated along the way, things that said the people who came here cared: an autographed photo of the one high school basketball player who had gone pro; framed reproduction black-and-whites of turn-of-the-century parades on Center Street; a folded and boxed flag with a plaque that said it had been presented to the owner after his son had been killed during a peacekeeping mission in Africa in the eighties; a wooden pillar that had been the recipient of a hundred pairs of carved initials over the years; the worn section of the floor where who knows how many Saturday nights of dancing had taken place.

Luke was starting to get homesick and only halfway through a longneck when Olivia gathered up her family and started for the door.

Luke took one last swig, then set the bottle on the bar.

Back in the parking lot, he was relieved to see the car that had been pinning the Explorer in was gone.

Then his gaze fell on the windshield of Ana's car. Relief was instantly replaced by vigilance. He stepped closer to Analise, hands on her shoulders, ready to shove her out of danger should it appear.

Just then she gasped as she saw it, too—a childish hand had taken red spray paint to her windshield. One word: JEZEBEL.

Chapter 15

Luke kept his hands on Analise, quickly scanning the darkness around the lot. Then he looked carefully at the cars on the street. Although he saw no sign of Roy or his truck, he remained alert. He wished he'd checked out the truck more closely. He was certain there hadn't been a gun rack in the back, but a rural southern man like Roy most likely had a rifle. A mind as unsophisticated as Roy's didn't seem the type to take potshots from afar, but he also didn't seem the type to walk right into a busy parking lot and spray-paint graffiti on a car, either. Luke had Roy pegged as an emotional responder—not as a calculating aggressor.

"Cole, go back in and get Dave," Olivia said calmly.

The boy disappeared without a word.

Analise reached out to touch the letters, but Luke grabbed her wrist to stop her. "Don't touch it."

She looked over her shoulder with a question in her eyes.

"Maybe there's evidence," he said.

"Like fingerprints?"

"Maybe. Don't want to chance ruining something before the police get a look at it."

She sagged back against his chest. "Who in the hell uses the word Jezebel anyhow?" she asked with disgust. "And why me?"

It was an easy conclusion for Luke. Jezebel was a biblical name. Roy viewed Analise as a wicked temptress. He needed to pray to rid himself of his impure impulses. Luke didn't tell her that he'd seen Roy drive by earlier—that he'd save for telling the police.

Cole and Dave trotted up. Dave said, "Don't suppose you saw who it was?" He directed this question at Luke.

Luke said, "Nobody in sight when we came out."

Dave took a step closer to the Explorer, then put his hands on his hips and looked around. "Reckon it was Roy."

Analise stiffened. "You think so?"

"Who else?" Dave asked, looking around.

Luke wanted to get things moving so he could get Analise home, safe behind locked doors. "I assume this is city's jurisdiction. Let's go back inside and call the police." He started to move Ana in that direction. He didn't feel comfortable with her standing out here like a sitting duck.

"Don't know what they can do, but I suppose a report can't hurt. Might help in court if the day comes."

Luke stopped. "Shouldn't the car be checked for evidence—proof that it was Roy?"

Dave said, "We can look around and get just as good an idea. This ain't the big city; the department doesn't have a lot of fancy equipment just to chase down taggers. Besides, fingerprints would only say that Roy touched this car—which he could have done anytime in the past month."

Luke looked hard at the deputy for a moment. "Just the same, I think we need to file a report."

Nodding and biting his lip, Dave said, "Probably right. I'll go to my car and call it in." He started toward the other side of the lot where his cruiser was parked.

Just then, the first random fat drops of rain plopped against the hoods of the cars.

Luke said, "You and Olivia go back inside and wait."

Analise hesitated. Thunder rumbled closer.

"Cole, keep an eye on them—just in case Roy makes an appearance in the bar."

Cole's shoulders straightened a bit. "Sure." He put a hand on his mother's arm and led her toward the entrance.

The rain was quickly increasing and the wind was picking up. Analise lingered, hair blowing around her face, staring at the graffiti. "Why would Roy do something like this? Why not just go away?"

Luke planned to find out. No more sitting around waiting to see if the man was going to do something else; he was going to find him. To Analise he said, "Go inside before you're soaked."

She hesitated.

"We don't want Olivia coming back out in the rain looking for you."

"Right." Just before she reached the door, the rain cut loose. She ran the last ten feet. Luke stood there, unfazed by the downpour; he'd been in worse.

By the time the local police drove up, the parking lot had a half-inch of standing water and the clouds were sending wicked shafts of lightning straight to the ground. The wind was now driving the rain in sheets. The temperature had dropped at least ten degrees.

The officer pulled his cruiser right up to the Explorer and shone his spotlight on it. Luke and Dave both got inside the car to get out of the rain—Dave in the front, Luke in the back. The young officer introduced himself to Luke as Tommy White.

Dave reported the details of the evening and his suspicions that it was Roy. "I've already run a criminal background check on the man. Nothing."

Tommy—Luke couldn't look at that eager youthful face and think of him as "Officer White"—made rapid notes.

Then Luke said, "I came out here about forty minutes ago. I saw Roy drive past."

Dave's sharpened gaze snapped to Luke. "You didn't tell me that."

"I didn't see any reason to get the women more worked up. Besides, he didn't seem particularly interested in this place as he went by."

"You should have told me." There was a peculiar edge in Dave's voice—Luke attributed it to resentment that he knew something that Dave didn't.

"I'll take a look around the vehicle," Tommy said, as he put on his rain slicker and plastic-protected hat. Then he grabbed his flashlight and got out.

As Luke watched through the rain-streaked window, it was clear Tommy was just going through the motions. Not that there'd be much evidence that hadn't floated away already.

Dave turned to Luke again. "Did you see anything else while you were out here?" Again, the edge was present in his voice.

"Nothing suspicious."

"Anybody see you?"

Luke's brow furrowed. "What do you mean?"

"Just what I said, anybody be able to tell me what *you* were doing out here?"

"Wait a minute. You're suggesting *I* did this?"

"I'm not *suggesting* anything—just gathering the facts. Seems funny that you kept this *Roy-spotting* to yourself until just now. Seems mighty convenient, him 'driving by,' after being damn near invisible for a week."

"Why would I have done something like this?"

Dave gave him a long hard look. "Why would anybody?"

"I didn't."

"Those at Magnolia Mile are very special to me. I plan to put a stop to this."

Luke held his gaze. "Good."

Tommy got back in, dripping water from the brim of his hat. "Not much to see there."

Luke suggested, "Maybe your department could bring Roy in for questioning."

Dave said, "They've got nothing to hang a charge on."

"I know that," Luke said, "and you know that, but Roy probably doesn't. It might be enough to shake him up and make him decide to go on down the road."

Tommy nodded, sending a little river of water sliding off his cap and into his lap. "Might be a good idea."

Dave put a hand on Tommy's shoulder. "Bringing that man in, if you can find him, will be a waste of time. Besides, if he catches on we're after him, it might just push him into doing something crazy."

Now Tommy looked equally convinced in the opposite direction. "I see. Could be dangerous."

Luke shook his head. "Dangerous for whom?"

Dave turned and looked at him. "This ain't the army. I know you're used to doing things different, but we can't just go in with weapons drawn and bully people around. We got rules—constitutional rights. What if we bring Roy in, we got nothing to keep him locked up. He could just as easy go after Analise in a big way as decide to leave town." He shook his head. "Not worth the risk—not until we have something concrete that'll keep him behind bars."

Tommy said, "Deputy Dunston, how should I write it up, then?"

"Criminal mischief—by unknown suspect or suspects. Nothing else we can do."

Luke settled back in his seat. *Bullshit.* There was something *he* could do. And he was damn well going to do it.

It was nearly eleven when they arrived back at Magnolia Mile. Although Analise had sworn she was fine, Luke drove home. It had surprised him that Dave hadn't insisted on escorting them. Luke was having a difficult time deciphering exactly what was going on in the deputy's brain. Had he seriously considered that Luke had painted the car?

No matter. Tomorrow Luke would find Roy and get to the bottom of this himself. He wouldn't be at Magnolia Mile much longer; he had to know the man was no longer a threat.

The wind whipped the trees and rain continued to fall in a steady curtain. The culvert that ran under the entrance to the drive was filled with rushing brown water.

Sitting beside Luke in the front seat, Olivia said, "I didn't know it was going to storm like this. I shouldn't have left Rufus out." She leaned forward, straining to see through the darkness. "I hope he had the sense to get on the front porch."

"There he is!" Cole's finger shot between the bucket seats, pointing out the windshield. Rufus was trotting straight for them in the headlight beams.

"Of all the . . ." Olivia breathed.

Rufus had something hanging out of his mouth.

"Looks like a shoe! Rufus has a shoe," Cole said as the dog stopped right in front of them.

"Cole, climb over here and drive the car the rest of the way to the house," Luke said, then got out.

He stepped directly into a puddle that covered his shoe. He shook off the mud and approached the dog. "Hey, Rufus, let's see what you've got there, boy." He reached for the shoe. Rufus took a step backward and growled deep in his throat.

"It's all right, buddy. We're on the same side." Luke inched closer.

Rufus sat in the muddy drive. The shoe remained in his mouth. The rain pelted them both.

Luke put out his hand. The rain was blinding him, the ground was slick and his knee hurt; he didn't really want to chase this dog all over the yard. "Come on, Rufus, give it up."

One of the car doors opened and slammed shut.

Analise appeared on the other side of the dog. "Drop it," she shouted against the wind.

The dog's mouth opened and the shoe fell with a plop into a puddle.

"Good boy." Analise patted him, her hand slapping against the wet fur.

Luke picked up the shoe. It belonged to a man—a big man. He raised his voice over the wind and told Analise, "Better get back in the car."

She wiped the rain from her face. "I'm soaked and muddy already. I'll walk, too."

Luke stepped out of the way and motioned for Cole to drive past. Then he and Analise and Rufus walked the rest of the way to the house. The rain made a sound like a giant waterfall and the wind whipped words away, so they didn't try to talk. Luke noticed Analise looked at the shoe in his hand often as they walked side by side.

When they reached the back steps, Olivia and Cole were waiting just inside the kitchen door with towels. Analise and Luke took them gratefully. Luke tried not to watch as Analise gathered her hair in her hands and squeezed the water out over the doorstep.

Rufus suddenly shook his huge loose-skinned body, spraying water on everything in a six-foot radius.

"Good Lord, Rufus! Couldn't you have done that outside?" Olivia pointed. "Go to the laundry room!" Then she added, "Cole, get a towel and dry him off."

"But I want to see—"

"It's a shoe, for goodness' sake. Take care of your dog."

Rufus looked particularly pitiful, his head low, his tail hanging straight down, as he walked slowly into the utility room. Cole looked equally put out.

"I think you might owe Rufus an apology," Luke said, holding up the shoe. "Dog was on duty tonight."

"Because he dug up some old shoe and splattered my house with mud?" Olivia said.

Analise said, her eyes riveted on the shoe in Luke's hand, "*Roy's* shoe."

"Noooo . . ." Olivia said with disbelief.

Analise confirmed what Luke had strongly suspected. He looked carefully at the shoe. As kids they'd called them "shit stompers," not quite a boot, not quite a shoe. There were deep tooth marks all down the length of the cracked leather, and blood on the inside at the ankle. "I'd say he took a chunk of Roy, too."

Olivia's eyes widened. "You think he came out here to wait for us to come back? He's still somewhere around here?"

Luke put down the shoe, locked the door behind him, then wiped the worst of the orange-hued mud off his feet and walked around the entire downstairs. When he came back to the kitchen, he said, "I can't see that he was inside; there's no water, no mud. Rufus probably scared him off."

Olivia said, "Should we call Dave?"

"That's up to you," Luke said. "I can't see there's anything to be done tonight that can't wait until morning."

"You're right." Olivia looked pensive for a moment, then said, "Now you and Ana go get those wet clothes off before you freeze to death."

Luke automatically looked at Analise. The idea of them taking their clothes off certainly held a great deal of appeal. A shared hot shower to warm them up. . . .

Analise quickly looked away, apparently able to easily read what was in his mind.

Analise awakened with a start. She sat up in bed and looked around, her breath caught in her throat. After a second, she assured herself it had only been a nightmare; Roy, with his pale round face and giant hands, was not hiding in any of the dark corners of her bedroom.

The storm had subsided, leaving only a gentle rain that pattered quietly against her window. It was a soothing sound, one that always made Analise feel snug and secure when swaddled in the warm covers of her bed. Glancing at the bedside clock, she saw it was just after three. Tonight, sleep had been hard won—her body restless as it yearned for Luke's touch, the warmth and security of him lying next to her, her mind endlessly wondering why Roy didn't just go away.

As she pulled the blanket up to her chin, hoping that somehow she'd be able to slide back into sleep, she heard voices. Sitting up, she listened closely.

Downstairs, Luke's deep voice mingled with Olivia's lighter speaking tones.

What were those two doing up?

Quietly, she slipped out of bed and walked softly to the top of the stairs. The voices came from the living room. The only light was of the night-light that Olivia always left burning in the window there, "A welcoming guide for those spirits trying to find their way home," she'd explained to Analise. Ana supposed it had come about because Calvin's father's body never found its final resting place here at home.

Olivia said softly, but with laughter in her voice, "That's quite a story."

"You know Calvin, so you can believe it's true." Luke's tone matched Olivia's.

"Oh, I believe it."

The rain tapped gently on the roof. Analise could hear one of them shift sitting positions—probably Luke; she'd noticed he always seemed to have trouble sitting still in comfortable furniture.

Olivia sighed.

Analise was just about to head down the stairs when Olivia said, more solemnly, "I have something I want to discuss with you—without all of the other ears listening in this house."

Analise froze. She hadn't intended to eavesdrop, but couldn't resist hearing what Olivia had to say to Luke in private. Did she suspect that they'd slept together? Her throat went dry. Had she risked everything she had here just so she could feel loved one more time?

Luke gave a most respectful, "All right, ma'am."

"You already know what Calvin meant to me and how difficult his death has been; his father and I had such a short time together."

"I understand he never saw Calvin." The warmth and

compassion in Luke's voice made goosebumps rise on Analise's arms. How could someone who'd lived such a hard-edged life, who appeared to be sculpted of stone, have such a gentle side? It gave her an ache in the center of her chest.

"That's right. For a long time, it was just Calvin and me." Olivia paused. "And in all of those years, I never felt alone, never felt the lack of a husband—a lover."

Luke remained silent.

Analise's insides took flight. *Oh, my God, she knows.*

Olivia let that sink in for a moment, the way she always did when she was about to make an important point. Then she said, "Analise is more than an in-law. She's my daughter. Cole depends upon her as his family."

Softly, so softly that Analise could hardly hear, Luke said, "I can see that."

Analise knew she should be an adult and go down there. She should face Olivia and admit what she'd done, apologize for being such a disloyal daughter. Not let Luke take all of the blame. But she couldn't make her feet move. She hid on the stairs like a naughty child.

Rufus walked into the hallway, stopping at the bottom of the stairs. He looked expectantly up toward Analise. When she didn't move down the stairs, he began to whine quietly.

It wasn't much of a sound, but it was enough to catch Luke's vigilant attention. "Just a minute," he said, as Analise heard him get up and start walking toward the hall.

She sucked in her breath and held it.

Olivia said, "What?"

"Not sure. What is it, boy?" Luke asked softly.

Analise pulled herself quickly around the corner and pressed herself against the wall at the top of the stairs.

Rufus whined louder.

"Upstairs?" Then Luke's voice sounded more distant, as

if he'd turned away when he said, "Sit tight, Liv. I'm just going to make sure everything's all right."

When Analise heard Olivia get up and hurry across the living room, she took the opportunity of additional noise to skitter back to her own room and slip into bed. By the time she heard Luke's cautious footsteps at her door, she'd managed to slow her breathing to normal. God, she was *worse* than a naughty child!

Her door opened. She heard Liv whisper loudly from downstairs, "Everything all right?"

After a moment, the door closed again and Luke's steps faded away. She heard him go back down the stairs. After a few minutes, there was noise in the kitchen—the familiar noise of Liv making late-night cocoa.

Then the soft hum of conversation filtered up from the kitchen. They were probably resuming their conversation where they had left off.

I should get up and go down there. She said it over and over to herself, and yet couldn't make herself do it.

Analise was still awake at dawn. She must have at least dozed at some point, because she'd lost track of when the conversation in the kitchen stopped. She put off going downstairs for another hour. Everything was going to be different today and she didn't want to face it. Analise realized then that she'd been harboring the ridiculous hope that, as long as Olivia didn't know that she'd betrayed her by sleeping with Luke under her roof and Luke remained here, somehow things would work out in the long run; her life at Magnolia Mile would somehow go on and Luke would be incorporated into it permanently.

It was clear that was not going to happen—ever. It seemed unfair that to protect one person she loved, she had to sacrifice another. Her breath caught as that thought stopped her cold. *Love?* Did she love Luke?

What difference did it make? She pushed the very thought away. She'd loved Calvin. Trusting that feeling hadn't worked out as she'd planned—and that situation wasn't nearly as complicated as this. Romantic love was overrated, exaggerated by movies and novels. Romantic love didn't last. Family did.

She glanced at her clock. If she waited just a bit longer, Olivia would leave for church. Analise had never taken up the habit of churchgoing in Grover. Olivia had never pressed her about it. Organized religion just didn't do much for Analise. She didn't feel any closer to God after she'd spent the morning in church. She felt close to God when she was working in the dirt, when she was sitting by the Tallahatchie River, when she felt the warm sun on her skin. For her, faith was a deeply personal and private thing.

During her days in Jackson, she'd seen too many people use their Christianity as a tool, an instrument to get what they wanted, a wall to hide behind, not a belief. Her grandmother had insisted every Sunday that they attend both Sunday school and the service—it was the right thing to do. All "good families" went to church.

Now she guessed she had finally become the bad person Grandmother kept threatening she'd become, a person who put her own desire first and hurt those around her.

She got out of bed and went into the bathroom. Her head ached, her eyes were dry and bloodshot. She brushed her teeth and took three aspirin. Then she took the hottest shower she could stand. By the time she went downstairs, Olivia should have been well on her way to church.

But she wasn't. She was sitting at the kitchen table, sipping a cup of coffee, still in her robe.

"Good morning, Ana. Pour yourself some coffee and sit down here for a bit. We have some things to discuss."

That lead ball that had been sitting in Ana's stomach doubled in size and weight. She guessed it was better to get it over with. She'd apologize, beg forgiveness, tell Olivia that this family meant everything to her and hope for the best.

She looked at the empty coffee cup in front of Luke's place at the table. "Where's Luke?"

Olivia lifted a hand toward the door. "Gone."

Chapter 16

"For heaven's sake, Ana, breathe!" Olivia got to her feet.

Analise fought the lightheadedness that made her sway drunkenly. Luke was gone—as he was always bound to be. But . . . she wasn't ready. Not yet, not like this.

Olivia patted Ana's cheek. "What's the matter with you?"

"I . . ." She struggled to gather enough breath to speak. "I didn't get to say good-bye. I know you're upset, Liv, and I'm sorry, but—"

"Upset? What are you talking about?" She guided Ana to a chair. "Here, sit down before you fall flat."

Analise's trembling knees bent and she sat down hard.

Olivia handed her a glass of water. "Drink."

As she took a sip, the water threatened to make an about face at the lump in her throat.

"I had no idea you needed to tell the boy good-bye every time he walked out the door."

"But"—Ana's voice trembled—"this time he won't be coming back."

"Whyever not?"

Analise slowly looked at Olivia. "You said he's gone."

"He is. He went to look for Roy. Wants to get to the bottom of all this." She pointed to the muddy shoe that still sat on the doormat.

"Roy?" Analise blinked, trying to adapt to the change.

Olivia poured Analise a cup of coffee and set it in front of her. "I think you need some caffeine to wake yourself up." She splashed a large amount of cream in the cup and stirred it. "There." A dawning light then shone in Olivia's face. "Oh, dear! You thought he'd left us for good?"

Analise needed to backpedal. She took a long sip of the coffee. How was she going to explain this overreaction? "Well, I . . ." She picked up the spoon and stirred her coffee again, needlessly. "I assumed . . . I was worried about the contract. . . . We're already behind, and without a grown man to help. . . ."

Olivia looked at Analise through narrowed eyes, her mouth drawn up into a suspicious pucker. "I see."

Sitting back down, Olivia said, "I think we need to make some changes around here—at least until things are back to normal. Luke . . ."

Analise concentrated on the little bubbles in her coffee cup. Didn't Granny Lejeune have a saying about bubbles in your coffee? Analise tried to recall, just so she didn't have to hear Liv tell her how disappointed she was in her behavior, how Analise had betrayed Calvin's memory, how Olivia wanted her to behave herself around Luke from here on out.

". . . It was Luke's idea and I'm sure you'll agree."

Oops! If she was going to have to agree, maybe she should have listened. "Of course." Now she didn't know exactly what she was agreeing to.

"All right, then. One of us will be with you at all times."

Didn't Liv trust her to stay away from Luke on her own? She needed someone to babysit her?

Olivia went on, "Of course, Luke might just take care of this today and it won't be necessary."

Analise's stomach started to roll. "No, of course not."

"Why on earth do you sound so disappointed?"

"I'm just trying to figure out how we're going to get the job finished."

Olivia cocked her head and threw a hand in the air. "What does you not being alone have *anything* to do with getting the job done? Luke's always with you at the park anyway."

It took a second for Analise to realize she was following the wrong track in this conversation. What *were* they talking about? Her guilty conscience jumped to a conclusion that nearly had *her* divulging her secret.

Analise cleared her throat and fought the urge to ask just what Luke and Olivia had talked about so long into the night. Instead she asked what she hoped sounded like a logical question: "How's Luke going to find Roy?"

Olivia picked up her coffee cup. "I have no idea. He seemed confident when he left here, though."

Cole came thudding down the stairs. "Mom!"

"You don't have to yell. I'm right here."

He stepped into the kitchen looking better than Analise had seen him in months. Pausing in the doorway with his hand on the jamb, he said, "A friend is picking me up in about five minutes. We're going to go run around for a while." He started to duck away when Liv stopped him.

"Wait just a minute!"

He slowly turned back around.

"Who is this friend and where, exactly, are you running to?"

"God, Mom, I'm not a baby."

"No, but you have to admit, you haven't been behaving in

the most mature manner of late." She lowered her chin and looked at him from under raised brows.

He shifted his weight and huffed. "It's a girl from school. I promised to show her the plantation."

Analise said, "The girl from Rib Fest?"

"Yeah." He shrugged and ran his hand along the woodwork. "It's no big deal. She just likes history and stuff, so I said I'd show her."

"When will you be back?" Olivia asked.

His frustration showed again. "I don't know."

"For lunch?"

He looked away. "She's packing a picnic—sorta to thank me for taking her to see the place. You know girls."

"Oh, yes," Olivia said slyly. "I know girls." Then she added, "Be back by suppertime."

Immediately, he headed for the front door. "Okay."

Once they heard the front door close behind him, Olivia said wistfully, "If only grown-up hearts could heal so quickly."

Analise said, "What do you mean?"

"Last week he was ready to throw himself off a bridge because Darcy dumped him; this week he's going on a picnic with that cute little redhead."

"Liv! It's not a date, you heard him."

"Oh, I heard him—and I saw the look in his eye. There's no mistaking that look in someone's eye—it can't be hidden. I can pick it out a mile away."

Analise didn't respond. She also didn't look Liv in the eye, for fear of what Olivia might see there.

Riding toward the old plantation in Becca's faded old Volvo, Cole had mixed emotions. For years this had been his secret hideaway, the place where he could go and be certain that no one would interrupt his thoughts, a place apart from the rest of his life. He'd never shared it with anyone, not even Darcy.

But then again, Darcy had never asked.

He glanced at Becca. She'd been quiet since she'd picked him up. He didn't know her well enough to know if her silence was normal or not. The hush in the car was getting to him, so he tried to turn on the radio. The knob clicked, but the speakers didn't produce anything, not even static.

"Sorry. Doesn't work," she said.

"How can you stand to drive around without music?"

Keeping her eyes on the road, she lifted a shoulder. "No big deal. Gives me time to think. Dad says radios are a distraction new drivers don't need."

"Hum."

"He's real careful about us kids driving—guess it comes from seeing so many smashed-up cars that come into the junkyard. We all have to drive this car for a year after we get our license."

"Oh." Cole realized *his* car was probably sitting in Mr. Reynolds's junkyard right now. Calvin had driven it for thirteen years and never gotten a scratch on it. Cole had had it for not quite six months and totaled it. His stomach twisted as he thought of what it might look like—he hadn't gotten the courage to go and see it yet.

"Volvo's one of the safest cars on the road," Becca said, apparently unaware of the disturbing image she'd just brought to Cole's mind.

He tried to think of Becca's car, not his. He guessed the safe thing made sense, but he wondered why it had to be an *ancient, old-lady* Volvo.

"How many brothers and sisters do you have?" Cole

asked, trying to replace the thought of the mangled Jeep with *anything* else. He knew she had a brother who was a freshman and an older sister who graduated last year.

"Five. Matt drove the car first, he's a sophomore at Mississippi State; then my sister Natalie, she's going to nursing school in Memphis; then me; Ron is a freshman; Danny is in eighth grade; and Betsy is in kindergarten."

"Kindergarten?"

He noticed her stiffen. "Yeah, kindergarten. It happens."

"I didn't mean that," he said. "There are fourteen years between me and my brother—with *no* other kids. It's just—gosh, will your dad make her drive *this* Volvo?"

Immediately she relaxed and chuckled. "Probably. He said a first car should be a tank—an inexpensive tank."

"Slow down," he said. "The turnoff is right up here."

She braked and leaned slightly forward over the steering wheel, looking for the drive. Her hair fell over her shoulder like it was silk. Becca had incredible hair. Did it feel as soft as it looked? Cole kept his gaze on her, as she drove slowly and concentrated on what was on the outside of the car.

"Oh, look!" she said, stopping and pointing off to the left. "One of the old magnolias. It must be over a hundred and fifty years old." She looked at it for a long time, so long that Cole started to wonder what was so fascinating about it.

He'd never paid much attention to the magnolias. They were just trees. He knew they had been there since the plantation house was built, which made her right, they were over a hundred and fifty years old. Many of them had died, and those that were left had been swallowed up in the overgrowth. He hardly saw them anymore.

She whispered, "Wow." Then, looking at him with a light

in her eye, she said, "Doesn't it just give you goosebumps? Think of all the things that tree has seen. And the whole mile was lined with them on both sides. It must have been gorgeous."

Not only had Cole *not* paid attention to the trees, he'd never even considered what they'd "seen."

"Think about it," she said. "When this plantation was in its prime, lots of the traffic still came by river." She got a funny far-off look in her eye. "The land was worked by hand; every inch taken from the forest was hard-won. They had to fight downpours, tornadoes, droughts, floods and crop-destroying insects.

"If a person wanted to talk to someone farther than the next plantation, they had to write a letter that took forever to get there." She sighed and closed her eyes. "I can almost hear the carriages and wagons rolling down this drive—the soft clop of the horses on the dirt."

Then she turned in her seat and looked at him. "And the people in those carriages were related to *you*. They survived cholera and yellow fever and influenza and broken bones." She started to get really excited. "They took this wild land and tamed it, made it produce. They survived! Can you imagine how incredibly hard just surviving had to be? Your ancestors were tough."

"I guess they were." It was interesting; most girls thought of Scarlett O'Hara when they talked about the plantation, of parties and beautiful dresses. But Becca seemed to have a much more realistic grasp of what it took to survive and make this land work—she saw the beauty in the hardship and the struggle for success.

He now realized, although he rarely thought about such things head-on, those thoughts were all lying in the back of his mind. Perhaps that's why he came here when he needed to gather strength. Knowing that his trials were insignificant compared to those of the people who built this place.

"How much farther to the house?" she asked eagerly.

"You mean *what's left* of the house. I'm afraid you're going to be really disappointed. It's not like those museums, or the houses down in Natchez and Vicksburg. It's rotten and falling down and pretty soon there won't be anything left but the rock foundation."

A pained look crossed her face. "We let so much slip away. Things we should honor."

"Yeah, well, that honor takes a ton of money in this case. I think the last time anyone lived here was before the Depression. Granny Lejeune said it was in bad shape even then."

That pain changed to a look of determination. "How far?"

"We're halfway there."

She pressed on the gas and the car moved slowly forward. He wanted to tell her the lane wasn't that bad, she didn't have to go so slow; but then he saw the way she was looking around as she drove and kept his mouth shut.

"The slave quarters used to be over there." Cole pointed into the overgrowth on the left. "There really isn't anything left of them—but Granny remembers when she was a kid they used to come out here and look for beads and bottles and buttons and stuff buried in the dirt. Once she said they even found an old pistol somewhere near the main house."

Becca said in a breathy voice, "Oh, I want to see. I'd love to find something that hadn't been touched by another human for a hundred years."

Man, she was *really* into this stuff. "We can walk back out here after we look at the house."

Then the lane curved and they circled around in front of the old house.

"Oh, my gosh," she whispered.

"I know, pretty sad, huh?"

"It's magnificent—wonderful."

He scoffed. "The porch has fallen off. There isn't much left of the roof. I don't think there's an unbroken pane of glass in the place. There's even trees and stuff growing in one wing. Can't see anything wonderful myself."

Becca got out of the car. Cole followed her to the moss-covered stone steps that led to a pile of rotten and broken lumber that used to be the massive veranda.

She said, "She's like a really old woman who used to be beautiful. I'll bet she still feels beautiful inside."

Cole looked at her. "You're starting to scare me. I didn't know you were crazy."

She laughed and gave him a sideways shove. "Hey, I just appreciate old stuff."

"I've got a pair of old gym socks from sixth grade; maybe you'd like to see them?" he teased.

She wrinkled her nose. "Nah. But if you can find some of your *great-grandfather's* gym socks . . ."

He laughed. He'd been worried that he would be sorry he'd shared this place with her. But it felt totally *right*.

"If we go around back, we can get inside."

"Inside! Really?"

Geez, she was acting like most girls do when there's a Dave Matthews concert coming. "Yeah, but it's pretty dangerous, you have to stay right with me and step where I tell you."

"No problem. I'm very obedient on field trips."

Looking at her, he'd almost forgotten the impression he'd held of her for years—Miss Goody. "Yeah, I bet you are."

"What's that supposed to mean?"

"Nothing."

She shoved her hands onto her hips. "Hey, I can be as wild and unpredictable as the next girl."

"Sure." He started to walk around to the back.

"Hey!"

He heard her hurrying to catch up. Suddenly her hand was on his arm, spinning him around to face her. Before he knew what was happening, she grabbed the back of his neck, pulling him to her. Her kiss was so startling, he just stood there with his hands at his sides and his eyes wide open.

"How's that for unpredictable?" she asked with a satis-fied look on her face.

"Th-that was really good." It was great, in fact. She left his lips buzzing, wanting more. He reached for her waist and she stepped out of his reach.

"Uh-uh. That would be *too* predictable."

Cole just stood there and watched her walk around the corner of the house, noticing the way her jeans were just tight enough and low enough to be sexy. His palms burned to get hold of her. He wasn't sure what to do; he'd never had a girl walk away from a kiss before.

"You coming?" she called.

Cole took a deep breath and followed the most con-fusing—and amazing—girl he'd ever met.

It took Luke all of an hour and a half, by asking a few of the right questions, to narrow down the possibility of Roy's camping ground to being someplace just south of town. Opal, Olivia's distant cousin who worked the register at the Pure station, cheerfully told him that not only had she sold gas to Roy, she'd seen him camped out near her place just yesterday.

After getting directions from Opal, it took Luke another

forty-five minutes to find Roy's truck-camper, parked near a wide creek that led to the river. He parked the Taurus blocking the muddy lane that led to the campsite, just in case Roy was as ready to speed out of here as he had been the day he'd left Magnolia Mile.

Getting out of the car, Luke looked around. The remains of a fire still smoldered beside the truck. An old aluminum folding lawn chair with frayed webbing sat next to the smoking ash. In front of that chair sat the muddy mate to the shoe Rufus had brought home last night. A dozen or so empty beer cans were scattered on the ground.

Luke moved slowly and silently forward, alert to any sound, any movement. When he reached the truck, he eased close enough to look inside the covered bed. He saw an empty sleeping bag, a pillow and a tattered black-bound Bible. No Roy.

Just as he turned around, a barefooted Roy emerged from the woods, rifle in hand, dead squirrel held by the tail. The instant Roy saw Luke, he dropped both the rifle and his dinner and ran back into the woods.

Luke sprinted after him, gaining ground easily. Roy was big, but not fast.

"Stop!" Luke shouted when he was within grabbing distance of the man.

Roy ran faster.

"Shit!" Luke threw himself forward, tackling the big man. They both hit the ground with a grunt.

Roy immediately tried to kick his way out of the hold Luke had on him. Luke's trained finesse quickly outdid Roy's brutish attempt to free himself. In an instant, Roy was face down in the dirt with all of Luke's weight on him and one arm wrenched painfully behind his back.

"Hold still!" Luke gave the arm a little more pressure.

Roy cried out, but stopped struggling.

"I thought I told you to stay away from Analise and Magnolia Mile."

Roy started to cry, like the bully in the schoolyard when the tables have finally turned. Between sobs, he said, "I d-did."

"Liar!" Luke flipped the man onto his back and stood over him with one foot on Roy's throat. "Don't lie to me!" Reaching down, he pulled Roy's pant leg up to reveal a very nasty-looking dog bite. "You're lucky Rufus only took your shoe. Could easily have taken a chunk of muscle, too."

Roy's mouth was drawn down into a huge clownlike frown; he blew bubbles between his lips as he cried. "Don't hurt me."

Luke kept his foot were it was. "Why didn't you leave?"

"I did."

Luke increased the pressure on Roy's throat. "I said not to lie to me!"

"I—I ain't. I went aw-way . . . like you s-said. . . ."

Easing the pressure on Roy's neck, Luke said, "Don't make me chase you down again. I get real pissed when I gotta chase a guy twice."

Roy gave two quick, jerky nods of his head. "'Kay." He remained motionless on the ground when Luke took his foot away.

"Why'd you come back? You had enough money to get far from here."

Roy's sobs were lessening. "H-had to."

"What in the hell do you mean? There's no reason for you to be in Grover."

"I had to g-get sumthin."

Luke grabbed the front of his shirt and shook him. "I've got a notion to make you go and lick that paint off Ana's windshield."

"W-what paint?"

"Last night." Luke gave him another shake. "We know you painted on Ana's car—just like we know you were out at Magnolia Mile."

Roy's face crumpled, as if he were going to start crying in earnest again. "I wuz at the nursery—never saw Miz Abbott's car, though."

Luke leaned closer and threatened a punch.

"I sw-swear! Swear on my momma's grave!" Roy closed his eyes, waiting for the blow, but didn't raise a hand to defend himself.

The fear in the man's eyes told Luke Roy was telling the truth. Luke let go and stepped back. He stood over Roy and said, "Why do you keep following Analise?"

Roy vigorously shook his head as he remained prone on the ground. "No! I don't wanna see Miz Abbott—not ever! No!"

Luke just stood there staring at him.

Roy reached for the leather string around his neck. He pulled out a crudely carved wooden cross from under his shirt and rubbed it between his fingers. "The devil," he whispered. His eyes widened and he said in a childlike and confidential tone, "She makes me need to pray."

Luke rubbed his forehead. There were pieces of this puzzle that just were not fitting. He blew out a breath and asked, "Why were you at the nursery last night?"

Roy kept rubbing the cross. "My Bible."

"What about your Bible?"

"That day . . . the day I had to—to leave . . . I hid under one of them tables in the greenhouse, a-way at the back, behind some pots. I wuz needin' to pray."

"And?"

"I forgot my Bible there when I had to . . . leave."

"So you waited all this time to come back and get it?"

Roy's chin started to quiver. "I's scairt—you said not to come back . . . but I had to get it."

"Why didn't you just buy a new Bible? I gave you plenty of money."

With a quick, jerky shake of the head, Roy said, "Not the same. Need Momma's Bible."

"Did you get it?"

He nodded. "Then that dog chased me."

"Then why are you still here?"

"Thunder. Don't like thunder. Afraid to drive."

Luke looked at the sky. The clouds were thickening again. "It's not storming now. But you'd better get going because it looks like another one's blowing in."

"Need to eat. Then I wuz going."

"You'd better not come back here—ever. Understand me?"

Roy scooted to a sitting position and nodded. "I won't. Got Momma's Bible. No need to come back."

"Let me take a look at that bite." Luke knelt down beside him. Roy pulled away when Luke reached for his leg. "I just want to make sure you don't need a doctor."

Roy sat still while Luke examined the wound. Roy said, "No doctor. Momma was fine till she saw a doctor."

The puncture wounds were deep, but it didn't appear that the muscle was torn. "Keep this clean. Wash it with soap every day. If you get a fever, you should see a doctor."

"No doctor."

"Suit yourself." Luke started to walk away. "Cook your meal, then clear out of here. I'll be back later to make sure you've gone."

Roy nodded. "I's good as gone now."

As Luke got back in the car and started the engine, he began a mental list of who might possibly have tagged Ana's car last night. The paint had been limited to the glass—where it would do the least damage. Hardly the act of someone truly bent on vengeance.

Someone else was stalking Analise—and Luke wasn't leaving until he discovered who it was.

Chapter 17

Before Analise headed upstairs to her metal studio, she made sure Rufus was downstairs in the shop. It was a compromise with Olivia, who still insisted she shouldn't be alone. Analise guessed that being thirty yards from the house where Olivia was working on the books was considered alone. So she settled Rufus in his favorite corner with a large rawhide bone, which she knew he would rather bury than expend the energy to chew.

"You did good last night, fella. That bastard comes in here today, you have my permission to take more than a shoe."

Rufus blew out a long breath that rattled his flews.

"I'll just be upstairs." She started for the stairway. "Keep the intruders away."

Rufus closed his eyes.

"I know you're just toying with me. You're a killer at heart."

Once upstairs, she turned on the lights and started her CD player. Then she took some time reacquainting herself with the fountain. It was difficult for her to keep a creative flow going when she had several days in a row without being able to work on it. She walked around the half-assembled pieces and rough-cut metal, studied the drawing again, making sure the overall appearance was still pleasing to her. Often, time away from a project really changed her perspective and she had to alter her original plan. But, as she looked at the sketch, she felt assured this design was right. It would fit well with the site work they'd done so far.

She put on her face shield and welding gloves, then lit her torch with a lighthearted joy she only found when working on her metal creations. The music wrapped around her and her mind fell into a single focus. Her first task was to melt and roll the edges of the pieces she'd cut for leaves, so there wouldn't be any dangerously sharp corners.

About an hour later, she stretched her back and looked out the window. The clouds were getting darker, threatening more rain. Being in her studio while it was raining was nearly as cozy and comforting as being tucked in bed. She loved working up there when a storm rattled the windows.

A sense of perfect peace came over her as she resumed working. It was a peace she rarely found these days. One that told her she was in the right place, doing the right thing with her life.

She was bent over her workbench when she felt, more than heard, someone standing behind her. Her heart kicked into high gear.

She kept the torch burning and held it out like a weapon as she spun around.

"Oh!" Her knees weakened and she took off the face shield. "Jesus, Luke, you scared the shit out of me."

Rufus sat right behind Luke, his tail beating happily on the floor. She shook one gloved hand at him. "Shame on you! You were supposed to be on guard duty!"

Rufus's tongue lolled and he put his head under Luke's hand.

Luke obliged the dog by scratching behind one of Rufus's ears. "Hey, don't pick on Rufus. He knows when to get down to business. I'm the good guy." Then he looked contrite. "I didn't mean to sneak up on you, but you didn't hear me and you were so absorbed in what you were doing. You looked so . . . content." He glanced back down the stairs as if checking to be certain they were alone. "Besides, I find it fascinating to watch you work."

She shut off the torch. "Fascinating, huh?"

He stepped closer. "Yeah. You take this pile of copper and change it, give it life."

She laughed. "That's sort of the way I've always looked at it, too." Taking off her welder's gloves, she crossed the room. "You're just in time. I need someone to hold this in place while I weld it." She picked up a giant dragonfly that she'd finished earlier. "It goes up there." She pointed to the top of a long pole with metal "leaves" on it.

"Okay." Luke looked at the pieces she had sitting in the middle of her work space. "Do you have a drawing of what it'll look like when it's done?"

"Over there." She raised a hand toward the far wall. Then she pretended to continue working, waiting for his reaction. She didn't know why, but it suddenly seemed important to her that he like it—no, not like it . . . respect it.

Luke walked over and studied it closely. "Did you sketch this?"

"Yes. I read a few children's books, then tried to adapt and incorporate the ideas and types of characters from them."

He turned back around and looked at her. "This is really, really good."

She grinned, unable to hide her pride. "Thanks."

Looking back at the drawing, he ran a finger along it. "This is the drain we finished Friday . . . all of that dirt-moving you've been doing finally makes sense."

Chuckling she asked, "Did you think I didn't have a plan? That I was just moving stuff around with no purpose?"

"No . . . it's just I couldn't see. Now I do. It's going to be great."

"Thanks." She crossed her arms over her chest. After a moment she asked, "So, did you find him?"

"Him?" He looked at her with raised brows.

"Stop looking so innocent. Olivia told me."

He tightened his lips and shook his head. "I found him."

Her eyes widened and she asked with concern, "You didn't hurt him, did you?"

"I thought the point was to get him to go away."

"Yes, but Roy's just a big kid. You're . . . you're a *professional*."

"You make it sound like I'm a hit man. You really think I'd . . ." He shook his head and let out a breath. Shoving his hands on his hips, he said, "No, I didn't hurt him. I just talked to him."

"And?"

"And he's leaving. He said he came back here last night and got his Bible from the greenhouse."

"What about my car?"

Luke rubbed the back of his neck. "Says he didn't do it. But that doesn't matter now. He's outta here."

Putting her hands on her hips, she asked, "If he didn't, then who did?"

After a moment's hesitation, he said, "I don't know."

She suspected there was something he was holding back—but she didn't want to ruin her one day in the studio, so she let it go. Luke was right, the important thing was that Roy was moving on down the road.

"All right. Let's get to work, then." She rummaged in the storage closet and pulled out another welder's visor and set of gloves. Handing the face visor to Luke, she said, "Put this on."

He took it from her and put it on, then flipped the shield up.

"And these." She handed him the gloves.

As he took them, he said teasingly, "Looks like this could be dangerous."

"Oh, yeah. A man such as yourself, who jumps out of airplanes and can hand-wrestle a bear, should probably quake in his boots."

"Hey, that's different. Just standing here while you try to burn my hands off is something else entirely."

Rolling her eyes, she said, "I'll try to leave you at least one useful charred stub." She handed him the metal dragonfly. It was a real handful with its three-foot wingspan. "Up there. Stand on that stool."

As he walked to the stool, he swooped the giant bug through the air and made buzzing noises with his mouth, like a little boy with a toy airplane.

Laughing she said, "Very macho."

He looked at her with a very serious expression. "That has to be our little secret."

Holding up her hands, she said, "Wild horses won't be able to drag it out of me."

Keeping his grave demeanor, he nodded. Then he buzzed the bug over to the stool and stepped up on it. She pulled a stepladder close enough that she could stand on it and weld the dragonfly in place.

"How do you want it?" He glanced at the drawing on the wall, then held the bug over the pole. "Like this?"

Analise studied it for a moment. "Tilted a little more your way, I think."

"Here?"

"Perfect." She grabbed her torch and lit it. "Put your visor down, then don't move."

He flipped the shield down over his face. A muffled, "Yes, ma'am," came from behind it.

By the time the dragonfly was firmly in place and cool enough to support its own weight, Analise's arms ached. She could only imagine what Luke's felt like. But he didn't complain or wiggle around like Cole did when she recruited him into assisting her.

"Okay, you can let go now."

The little window in his visor turned her way. "You're sure? I don't want to do this again."

"I'm sure." She looked pointedly at the other pieces. "And, sorry, but we're going to be doing this again, and again, and again."

Slowly, as if he feared the bug would take off in flight, he took his hand from it. The pole on which it sat flexed slightly, making the insect bob. "Hey, it looks like it's flying."

Analise smiled. "Exactly."

He pulled off the gloves and visor. "You do amaze me."

There was just enough genuine wonder in his voice to make a believer out of her. She was beginning to see he wasn't the same flash in the pan that Calvin had been. Luke was a much deeper river—which just meant those currents that could easily sweep her under were better hidden.

Deciding to let his last comment lie, she said, "Okay, you've earned a break. There are soft drinks in the little fridge over there. Help yourself, and then rest those arms."

He went to the refrigerator. "You want something?"

"A bottle of water would be good." She closed the valves on the welding tanks.

The CD she'd started when she had come in had long since played out. Luke put on a new one and turned up the volume. He'd picked a CD that Analise had burned herself, putting all of her favorite sentimental ballads on it. It was sixty minutes of yearning and wild emotions and broken hearts. And her body longed to sway with the tunes.

Luke gave her the bottle of water, then held his can of Coke in salute and inclined his head toward the piece they'd just welded. "To childish fantasies come true."

She ignored his double meaning and said, "To successful completion of this job." Then she touched the top of her bottle against the rim of his can and took a long drink.

"You want to sit down?" she asked, motioning toward a pair of old chrome and red vinyl kitchen chairs nearby. Sitting, she wouldn't be so apt to forget and start moving with the music.

He shook his head, keeping his serious gaze on her. "I want to dance."

She sputtered. "You're supposed to be saving your energy to hold heavy objects over your head."

He set his Coke can on the workbench, then took the bottle from her and did the same with it. His voice was soft when he took her hand palm to palm with his, and said, "I want to see you as happy and uninhibited as that first moment I laid eyes on you." He pulled her a little closer. "Dance with me."

Oh, God. Why did he have to pick one of her greatest weaknesses? She missed dancing almost more than anything. Still, she hesitated.

Whispering in her ear, he urged, "Come on, there's no one here to see. No strings attached. Just a dance." With that, he spun her around so her back was against his chest. He kept one arm around her waist and put his other hand on her hip. Then he began to move them ever so slightly with the music.

A chill swept down her spine.

She really shouldn't.

He said no strings, but what if . . .

The plaintive strains of the music called to her; the beat drew a response from deep within her bones; Luke's strong, masculine presence enticed her. He wouldn't be here forever. Once he was gone, she'd be back to dancing solo in the greenhouse and two-stepping with Dave at the Boxcar once a week.

Oh, to just let herself dance freely in Luke's arms. . . .

After a moment, she gave up all resistance. She closed her eyes and laid her head back against the solid warmth of his shoulder. She rested her hands on the lean-muscled arm around her waist. The music filled her, making her body feel fluid against his.

He rested his cheek against her hair and said in a husky whisper, "Let go, baby." His hips moved, hers followed. She laid her right hand over his and entwined their fingers. He responded by grasping tight.

The realities of her life fell away like icicles from a tree branch on a warm spring day. She could nearly hear them shatter as they struck the ground and turned into puddles of nothing. He transported her to a warm place where there was only the sensual feel of the music and the sensation of his body moving in unison with hers. They rocked with the song, her hips and shoulders beginning to take on its rhythm, her feet shuffling with its beat.

He must have felt the change in her, because he whispered, "That's it. Come with me."

And she did.

Keeping her wrapped securely in one arm, he gently undid her braid with his free hand. His fingers ran through the length of her hair until it was free to move with the music.

How could he know? How could he know that part of her freedom lay in the movement of her hair?

She turned her head, pressing her cheek against his shoulder, letting him fan her hair until it fell across her face.

His chest moved behind her shoulders, and she followed, moving in a long languid sway that robbed her of her balance. If not for his solid presence, she would have fallen to the floor. A little buzz of contentment started in her stomach. She actually felt like purring.

Just then, he spun her away from him. She opened her eyes and looked into his steady blue gaze, realizing how dangerous this was, but liking it too much to care. Without missing a beat, he clasped her right hand in his left and slid his right hand around the small of her back. She let herself be pressed against him and they danced heart to heart for the rest of the song. Just before it ended he dipped her back, sweeping her hair against the floor, then he slowly pulled her up face to face with him again.

It was the most erotic thing she'd experienced in years— oddly, it felt even more intimate than sharing his bed.

Then came the tiny beat of silence between songs. She remained still as a doe in the brush; if he broke away now, that was going to be the end. Either he'd ask for something more, or the moment would simply evaporate forever.

He didn't move. He held her patiently, still swaying slightly to the tune that must still be playing in his head, until Bon Jovi began a new song.

They danced almost halfway through the CD, without

talking, without stopping. When Def Leppard ended "Love Bites," he let her go.

His gaze held hers, intense and unreadable. "I think that says it all."

She was so drawn into his eyes that it took her a moment to respond. "What does?"

Giving her a sad smile, he said, "Love bites."

"Yeah." She wanted to look away, but that was too cowardly, too cruel when he'd given her so much. "I guess it does."

In a heartbeat his expression changed, became less intimate. He drew a deep breath and said, "Now, don't you feel more relaxed?"

He'd given her exactly what he'd promised—a moment in time to feel truly free, to allow her body to meld with the emotion of the songs. And he didn't seem to be asking for anything in return.

"Ahhh, yes." She stretched her shoulders. "That was as good as a two-week beach vacation." She put a little more distance between them.

He rubbed his hair roughly and sighed. "Guess we'd better get back to work. There's a frog that needs a crown."

She tilted her head and gave him a slight smile. "Thank you."

He didn't say anything else. He went to the stereo and changed the CD. This time he put in ZZ Top.

"This oughta keep us moving." He picked up his gloves and visor and they gave the Frog King his coronation.

As Cole and Becca entered through the rear of the old plantation house, he took her hand. "I meant it. You have to walk right where I tell you. I fell through to the basement once."

"Oh! Were you hurt?"

"Nope. Scared the shit out of me, though. I was only nine." It had been the year after his father had been killed, the first year he'd started coming to the old place. He'd ridden his bike here back then. It struck him, with no car, he might just have to start riding it here again.

He stepped inside the back door and felt her grip on his hand tighten. He said, "This part was added when they stopped using the summer kitchen. The floor in here isn't too bad."

She pulled him back as he started to walk into the main house. "Wait. I want to look."

"Not much to see. The woodstove went for scrap during World War II. There are some really big spiders in the pantry."

"Are you trying to scare me off?"

"Nope. Just want you to be primed."

She looked around and pointed out a hundred details of the old kitchen that he'd never noticed. And she did the same when they entered the dining room—from the plasterwork on the ceiling to the meaning of the carving on the wood-work around the fireplace. She even identified the vine that had grown in through the window.

When they stepped into the foyer, she gasped. "This stair-case . . ."

She started to step closer, but he pulled her back against him. "Gotta walk around the edge of the room. Floor in the center is rotten."

Her eyes were wide as they looked up into his. "Okay."

Neither of them moved. Then he raised his hand and touched her hair.

She looked a little startled, but didn't look away.

He said, "You've got a cobweb." He brushed the web from her hair, letting his hand feel the softness underneath.

"Oh. Thanks." She touched her hair where his hand had been.

He moved then. "Step where I do."

"Can we go upstairs?"

"No way."

"Have you been up there?"

"Not since I was little and Calvin took me up. It's too dangerous—"

Suddenly she yelped and stumbled to the side. Cole tightened his grip and grabbed the doorframe to the parlor to steady himself. He kept her from falling, but her foot had gone straight through the floor.

"Whoa!" he said, wrapping an arm around her to steady her. "You all right?"

She worked to bring her foot back through the jagged hole in the floor. "Yeah. I was looking at the staircase and not where I was stepping."

He could feel her trembling. "I shouldn't have brought you in here." He started to retrace their steps toward the back of the house.

"But I want to see more."

"Sorry. Not gonna happen."

Just then it started to rain. They could hear it hitting the leaves outside.

She made a point of looking around him, out the front windows. "Now we'll have to stay in here," Becca said cheerfully.

He *humpf*ed. "Just wait a second. This is the last place you'll want to be."

The first drop plopped right on the center of her forehead, startling her. "Oh, I see." She wiped it away.

"Only dry place now is the car." He began to shuffle her backward toward the kitchen.

They made a dash from the rear of the house to the car, Becca's squealing laughter ringing through the rain like a wind chime.

"Whew!" she said when they jumped into the car. "Man, you're soaked!"

Cole blew a drop of water off the end of his nose. "You should talk."

They dried off with the napkins she'd packed in the picnic basket. Then they ate lunch while the windows steamed up. By the time their sandwiches were gone, the rain had slackened to a heavy mist.

"Got any dessert in there?" Cole asked.

She snapped the basket closed. "Yes. I made something special. But you have to earn it."

"Hey, I ate all my sandwich like a good boy. I want dessert."

"I want to find something old first."

He rolled his eyes. "Like dig around in the dirt—mud? It's still raining."

"Like, you're already wet. What difference does it make?"

"I don't want to."

"Fine." She reached for the key. "No dessert. Time for you to go home."

"Man, Becca!"

She grinned triumphantly, then got out of the car and pulled a garden shovel out of the trunk.

As he got out of the passenger seat, he said, "Good thing I didn't see that earlier. I might have thought you were planning on murdering me and burying me out here."

"Ha-ha." She handed him the shovel. "Find me something old."

He knew where the old summer kitchen used to be, so he started there. It only took him about five minutes. Becca followed him closer than his own shadow. When she saw the first edge of the fractured piece of china, she made a noise like people make when they watch fireworks.

Kneeling down, he dug it the rest of the way loose with his fingers. Then he pulled it out of the dirt and held it out to her as if it were a valuable gift. "Your old thing. Now, where's my dessert?"

Back in the car, while Cole ate all four of the black-bottom cupcakes, Becca used a wet napkin to clean her piece of china. It was half of a saucer, with pale-green flowers and gold gilt around the edge. She noted the French marking on the back and speculated the piece's age.

She said, "You're so lucky. I've always wanted a constant."

He looked at her. "A what?"

"A constant. You know, something that remains the same even if everything else in your life changes—even if everyone you love goes away. You'll always be a part of this place, it was born to you. It'll be your constant."

The word sounded funny, but the meaning she'd given it rang true. Maybe that was part of the reason he liked being here. His dad and brother had died, changing things at home, but this place was always the same.

"Yeah," he said. "I guess you're right."

She grinned. "Of course I am." She started the car and put it in gear, but looked at him before she pulled away. "Thank you for bringing me here."

"Sure. I'm glad I did." And, for all his misgivings this morning, he truly was glad. She was right—no matter what happened, he would always have this place, his connection to those who came before.

How could three days with one person change the way he looked at things?

Maybe things were finally turning around for the better.

"There, that section is finished and ready to go," Analise said as she stepped back and got a good perspective on their day's work. "All that's left are a couple of additions to the center section and then the final assembly on-site.

"I could never have finished on time without your help. Thank you." As she said it, she turned to look at Luke.

There were black streaks on his face and his hair stood in a giant cowlick where the band of the visor had been. She wondered if she looked as disheveled.

"What?" he said, trying to flatten his hair with his hand.

"You have something smeared on your face."

He rubbed his cheek, leaving a new, larger mark. "Did I get it?"

She laughed. "Now it's worse." She grabbed a rag from the bench. "Here, let me." She licked the rag and reached toward his cheek.

"Why do women always do that?" he asked as she wiped his face.

"Do what?"

"Spit on something, then wipe *someone else's* face."

She cringed and drew the rag away. "Sorry."

"I didn't say I minded." He took her hand and put it back to work. "I just wondered."

As she continued to remove the streaks from his face, she said, "I believe it's innate. Must have something to do with the double X chromosome."

"Like soft skin and silky hair." He touched her cheek with one hand and laid his other on her hair.

Looking into his eyes, she felt herself falling. It would be so easy to let herself love him. "Luke . . ."

He pulled her into an embrace. "I know." He paused. "I just need to hold you for a minute. I promise—I won't ask for more."

As she wrapped her arms around his waist, she realized she needed it, too. A moment of closure that had never happened to their intimate relationship—a quiet good-bye before the real thing that would take place in front of Olivia and Cole when the park job was finished.

She felt his kiss on the top of her head, the gentle way he stroked her back, and she ached for what might have been.

Then she stepped back. His hands cupped her face, his thumb wiped away a silent tear. "I'm going to miss you." He kissed the wet place left by her tear.

A sharp clatter jerked her attention to the stairs. She just caught sight of Cole as he spun around and ran back down. The picture that had been on the wall now lay on the floor at the top of the stairs.

"Ah, shit!" she said under her breath. "Cole, wait!" she called as she started after him.

Rufus ran out the door with her, and she could hear Luke pounding down the stairs behind her.

Cole was halfway across the back yard when she caught up with him.

"Cole." The only way she got him to stop was to grab his arm and force him. "Let me explain—"

He jerked his arm free, but stood to face her. "There's nothing to explain—I'm not stupid!"

"Luke—"

"Was supposed to be *my brother's* friend!" Cole walked in a little circle, gesturing as he talked. "God! How could you, Ana? How could you do this?" Then he stopped and looked sharply at her. "Does Mom know?"

"I'm trying to tell you, there isn't anything *for* her to know. Nothing is going on. Luke was just comforting me—"

"Is that what you want to call it? Don't treat me like a stupid kid. I saw!"

Analise reached out to him, but he jerked away.

"No! Don't you touch me." He stopped his agitated movements and looked at her with light dawning in his eyes. "The word painted on your car . . . someone else knows— and they're right!"

He started toward the house.

"Cole, wait!"

He paused with his back to her.

She didn't want to ask, but there was so little time before he exploded through the kitchen door. "What are you going to tell Olivia?"

Slowly he looked over his shoulder at her. There was such cold hatred in his eyes that it cut straight to her heart. Then he turned around and walked stiffly back to her.

"You want *me* to be the one to tell her you're screwing Calvin's best friend right under her nose?"

She slapped him. It happened in the blink of an eye and there was no taking it back.

He stood firm, his chest heaving with his agitated breath, staring her in the eye for a long moment.

Then he turned around and walked to the house.

Analise prepared dinner as usual, but what was going on inside her was anything but usual. At least Cole hadn't burst through the door shouting at the top of his lungs that she was screwing Luke. He'd stalked silently through the house and headed to his room.

Still, Analise worried what he might decide to say to Olivia. The longer she thought about it, the angrier she became at herself. If confronted, it would be impossible for her to deny that she'd slept with Luke. Olivia was too perceptive to accept a lie—and lies were the worst affront imaginable in Olivia's book. If it came to the moment of confrontation, how could Analise explain that she'd chosen her family over Luke without making things worse?

She was so stupid. What had made her think she could act so selfishly and not have it come to light?

When Luke came down from his shower, Olivia was outside feeding the goose. He stepped quietly into the kitchen. "Should I try talking to him?"

Slamming the oven door, Analise snapped, "And tell him what? That we had sex right here in this house while he was in the hospital? That it was a good thing he had that wreck so we had the opportunity?"

He looked like she'd slapped him, too.

Closing her eyes, she let out a breath and raised a hand. "Sorry. I just . . ." She threw her pot holder onto the counter, then rubbed her forehead. "I don't think he's in the mood to listen to either one of us right now."

"I know how you feel . . . what's at risk for you. But"—he hesitated—"I want you to know I'm not sorry it happened." He held her gaze. "Nothing could ever make me sorry."

Unable to look at him with her emotions in such an upheaval, she turned her back and braced both palms on the kitchen counter. She wanted to tell him she wasn't sorry, either. But the words just wouldn't come. He was right, there was a lot at stake—the entire life she'd built for herself here at Magnolia Mile. She just couldn't bear to hurt Olivia so deeply.

Analise heard Luke quietly leave the room. Then she busied her hands, hoping to still her weeping heart.

"Poor Cole," Olivia said as she looked at his empty chair at the supper table. "Maybe I should take some tea and toast up to him."

Analise forced the bite of food in her mouth over the lump in her throat. "I'll do it."

Olivia waved a hand in the air. "When a boy's sick, he needs his mother."

Luke's head snapped up. He gave Olivia a look that Analise couldn't read. There was concern, but not the kind of concern that said, *I'm afraid someone's going to tell on me.* It was more sad than worried.

After a moment, she decided she wasn't going to figure it out, so she got up and started to gather up the dishes. "Did you let Rufus in? I normally have to trip over him until he's fed."

Olivia looked toward the back door. "No. He hasn't barked at the door." She huffed. "After that rain, he'll probably come back covered in mud."

She and Luke got up and helped Ana clear the table.

Analise felt awkward in her own kitchen, trying not to get too close to Luke as they shuttled dishes to the sink and leftovers to the counter. Her tension hummed so much higher with both him and Olivia in the same room with her. She was constantly aware of every detail of her behavior, worried that she'd say or do something to give herself away to Olivia. Finally, Luke said he was taking one of the kitchen chairs that had become wobbly out to the carriage house to reglue it, and Analise breathed a sigh of relief.

Olivia put the kettle on for tea that Cole didn't really need and Analise went to the back door to call the dog. Then she started the dishes. When Rufus hadn't barked at the back door by the time she was drying the pots and pans, she began to get worried. Rufus never missed his dinner.

Just as she went to the back door to call him again, Dave pulled in the drive. He was wearing jeans, so he wasn't on duty. Analise whistled again for Rufus and held the door open for Dave.

"Hey, there. What brings you out here this evening?" she asked.

"Just thought I should check on y'all. Olivia called me today and told me about Rufus getting a piece of Roy last night." He stepped into the kitchen and Analise closed the door. "Any more problems?"

Ana shook her head. "Actually, there shouldn't be any more problems. Luke hunted him down today and told him to take off."

Dave's gaze stopped roving the leftovers on the counter and snapped to her face. "He did what?" He pointed to his cruiser. "There's proper channels for this sort of thing. Taking the law into—"

"It wasn't a big deal. He just talked to him. Roy said he came back here for his mother's Bible. He's leaving Grover."

Dave put his hands on his hips, cast his gaze to the floor and shook his head. "I don't like it. He didn't leave last time. That houseguest of yours wants to be a damn hero." He looked at her again. "What if he just pushed a crazy man to do something crazier?"

"I really don't think Roy—"

"Dammit, Ana! What's the man have to do to convince you he's dangerous?"

There was a loud thud against the back door. Analise jumped. "Look, you've got me all jittery," she said as she headed to the door to see what it was.

"Wait!" Dave grabbed her arm. "You just can't be opening doors when things go bump. Roy—"

"It's probably Rufus. I called him for dinner."

Another thud sounded against the door and the knob rattled. "Ana! Open up!"

"Luke?" She hurried and opened the door. Luke stood on the stoop with the big bloodhound in his arms. "Oh, my God! What's happened to him?"

"I don't know. I found him curled up in the bushes. Tried to wake him, but no response."

"Here. Lay him here." Analise shoved the placemats off the kitchen table. "Is he breathing?"

"Barely," Luke said in a strained voice as he laid the heavy dog down. "Call your vet, I'll get the truck."

As Luke started out the door, Dave grabbed his arm. "Goddammit! I was afraid he'd do something like this! You pushed him and now look!" He jabbed a finger at Rufus's still form.

"Shut up and get a blanket on him while Ana calls the vet." Luke ran out the door.

Ana's fingers fumbled as she dialed the number; she had to do it twice. Luckily their vet was an old friend of Olivia's, so she could call him at home. While she waited for him to answer, she said, "There's an afghan on the sofa. Get it.

"Dr. Flynn! This is Analise Abbott, something's happened to Rufus. He was outside. He's not conscious, his breathing is shallow. No external injuries." She glanced at Dave coming back with the blanket. "He may have been poisoned."

Dr. Flynn said, "Keep him warm and get him here as fast as you can. I don't want to risk you doing anything until we know what the problem is."

She slammed down the phone and yelled for Olivia and

Cole. Then she looked at Dave. "You think Roy did something to him?"

Dave's face was grave when he said, "You got any other explanation for a healthy dog dropping in his own yard?"

Luke burst through the back door at the same moment Olivia and Cole arrived at the kitchen. Analise explained as Luke scooped up the dog and hefted him out to the truck.

Chapter 18

They made the ten-mile trip to Dr. Flynn's office in record time, thanks to Dave's cruiser leading the way with lights and siren going. Analise and Cole rode with him. Olivia and Luke went in the truck, with Rufus securely wrapped in a blanket in the bed.

The doctor was waiting at the front door of his clinic. He was a squat black man who looked to be about Olivia's age. He started asking questions as soon as Olivia was out of the truck.

"Do you have any chemicals where he could have gotten into them?" the doctor asked.

Dave helped Luke carry the dog into the examining room.

"No," Olivia said. "Everything that could be harmful is kept in the storage room with the door closed."

"No rat poison out, anything of that sort?"

"No. Could it be a stroke or something?" Olivia twisted her hands in impotent frustration.

"Not likely. Dogs rarely have strokes. Antifreeze—any bottled around, any leakage from your vehicles?"

"I don't think so. None that we've noticed."

Dave offered, "They've been having some mischief out at Magnolia Mile. Could be somebody gave him something."

Dr. Flynn had his stethoscope on Rufus's chest. "I'll check for that first. Now y'all go out and wait in the front. Tildie'll be here in a second to help."

All five of them just stood, staring at the limp dog on the table. Cole put his arm around his mother.

"I mean it." Dr. Flynn moved quickly to gather the things he needed. "Y'all are in the way here."

Slowly, they left the room. Analise collapsed into a chair, burying her face in her hands. Dave sat beside her. Olivia stood looking out the front window, staring at the gathering darkness with one hand across her middle and the fingers of the other over her chin and mouth. Cole hovered near his mother. Luke noticed this was a change from the boy's natural gravitation to Analise, or more recently himself, in times of stress. Cole didn't so much as look at either one of them.

In a few minutes Luke heard a woman's voice in the back and assumed Tildie had arrived.

After pacing the room a couple of revolutions, he stopped in front of Dave, looking down at him. He asked quietly, "So you think Roy poisoned the dog?"

Dave looked at him with earnest eyes and matched Luke's hushed tone, "What else could it be? Maybe he wanted the dog out of the way. Maybe he's planning on coming back tonight."

"For what?" Analise asked. "Why would he come back?"

Dave gave her a pointed look. "The man is not stable. If Mr. Macho here"—he jabbed a finger at Luke—"hadn't backed the guy into a corner, maybe this wouldn't have happened."

Luke glared at Dave, ready to drive home his point. Then he decided to soften his approach, just to see what kind of reaction he might get from the deputy. "You know, I've been thinking about this whole thing. If Roy's so determined to hurt Analise, why did he just paint on the windshield, where it wouldn't leave any permanent damage?" He rubbed his chin. "Got any ideas on that, *Deputy*?"

For the briefest of moments, fear flashed in Dave's eyes. But it was enough to give Luke what he was looking for. Then Dave drew himself up in his chair and said, "Like I said, the man's unstable. Logic doesn't apply."

Luke stared at him for a second before he turned and walked out the door. He needed some air. If he stayed in that confined space, it would be too tempting to put Deputy Dave's head up his ass, where it belonged.

Once in the parking lot, he began to pace. An outdoor light hung on a telephone pole, casting a sickly glow and emitting a steady buzz that soon got on his nerves almost as badly as Deputy Dave.

After a few minutes, Cole stepped out. Luke's expectant gaze immediately cut to the boy.

Cole read the look and said, "No news." Then he shoved his hands into his jean pockets and walked closer to Luke. After a relatively short but uncomfortable silence, he said, "I want you to leave."

Luke cast a glance back toward the waiting room.

"I want you to leave Magnolia Mile and not come back."

Luke waited a moment, sorting out his words carefully. "That was the plan from the beginning. I'll go as soon as the park is finished."

"So you don't love her."

Luke didn't answer.

Cole shifted, suddenly agitated. "What is it with you?"

He threw his hands in the air. "I thought you were my brother's friend—I thought you were *my* friend! You just want to hook up with her, then leave. She's Calvin's wife! How can you be such a jerk?"

Luke tried to explain something that seemed to be beyond his own grasp at the moment. "I came here because I owe your brother. I didn't plan to stay. . . . I didn't plan a lot of things. This situation is complicated. I care for Analise—I care about all of you."

"Oh, save the bullshit for Ana!"

Looking the boy sharply in the eye, Luke said, "Analise loves you. She loves your mother. And she loved Calvin. What more can you ask of her?"

"Are you going to ask her to leave with you?" The set of Cole's chin was challenging. Luke had to give the kid points for facing him down like this.

"No."

"Then you should go now. Staying will just make it harder for her."

"Not until the job is done. Magnolia Mile can't afford to pay late-completion penalties."

Cole sucked in a deep breath that filled his chest. "We can do it without you." There was that challenge again.

"I'm sure you could. But you won't have to. I'm staying."

For a long moment, Cole just stood there, looking like he wanted to punch Luke in the face. Then he turned around and went back inside the clinic, his every move radiating his anger.

Luke stood in the cooling air, glad for the feel of the chill on his face. The boy's resentment hurt—more deeply than Luke could have imagined two weeks ago. He'd come here to put certain things to rest. Everything that had happened since only tied him more closely to Calvin's family. And that was the key—it was *Calvin's* family and always would be. What had seemed so simple when he drove into Grover now wrapped a thousand silken threads around his heart, tying it to these people.

Luke forced his mind away from an emotional dilemma that had only one way it could possibly end: with his leaving. He needed to look at the problem at hand and deal with it. Could his assessment of Roy have been that far off? The man had been genuinely frightened by Luke's visit. Roy was emotionally unstable with uncontrollable anger, but Luke couldn't see him being calculating and vindictive. Roy's world consisted of that which was right in front of him at the moment. Elaborate plans for revenge and criminal plotting just weren't within his grasp. Yes, the man was dangerous, but only in the immediate sense.

Someone else was stalking Ana. And Luke was gaining perspective as to just who that someone was. But he had to tread carefully, or it was all going to blow up in his face.

About fifteen minutes later, Olivia stuck her head out the door. "Doctor's coming out."

Luke hurried inside, but lingered near the door, away from the tight knot of family. He listened as the doctor spoke.

"We've pumped his stomach and run a couple of preliminary tests. Looks like Benadryl. We found an undissolved capsule inside a chunk of beef. Had to have been a lot of them to take down a dog that size. Not much chance of it being fatal, but it's a good thing you brought him in when you did."

Analise gave a little sob of relief. Dave put an arm around her and gave her a comforting squeeze.

Olivia's response rode out on an exhaled breath. "Oh, thank goodness."

Dr. Flynn said, "I want to keep him here for a day or so, just to watch him."

Olivia nodded. "Can I see him before we go?"

The doctor put a hand on her shoulder. "Yes. He's still not conscious and he's got tubes."

"I understand." She followed him back into the examining area. Just before she went through the door, she looked back and asked, "Anyone else want to come in?"

Cole looked at his feet and shook his head.

Analise said, "I think I'll wait until he looks like himself."

Dave patted Ana's back and let his hand remain protectively on her waist.

Luke wanted to rip his arm off.

A short while later, as Luke drove back to Magnolia Mile, Olivia was understandably quiet. Which was fine with him; it left him alone with the thoughts that were quickly gelling into a conviction.

Looking occasionally in the rearview mirror at Dave's headlights, he decided that, once back at the house, he and Dave were going to have a serious discussion.

Olivia decided they should all have some herbal tea to calm them when they got home. She put on the kettle while Ana, Dave and Luke sat down at the kitchen table.

Cole said, "I'm going upstairs."

Olivia cast him a sympathetic look. "Not feeling any better?"

He gave Luke a stony look. "No." Then he left the room.

Luke saw that Dave didn't miss Cole's anger. A little light seemed to dawn in the deputy's eye.

The four of them sat around the table and sipped their tea in silence. Olivia and Analise both looked hollow-eyed and moved with the lead-limbed slowness of the exhausted.

Luke had plenty he wanted to say, just not in front of the women. Dave spent his time giving Luke a gaze that said he was sizing him up—as if they were two gladiators about to go into the ring.

Just as the ticking of the grandfather clock in the hall was beginning to get on Luke's nerves, Olivia set down her cup and said, "I think I'll head up to bed. I'll want to go see Rufus tomorrow before I open the shop."

Dave stood when Olivia got up from the table. To Luke, it didn't look like fine southern manners, it looked like sucking up.

Before Dave sat back down, Luke stood, too. "I'll walk you to your car."

Dave's gaze narrowed. "I think it might be best if I slept here on the couch tonight. After all, somebody drugged that dog for a reason. I'm worried he's going to come back."

Luke shifted his weight and cast an uncomfortable glance at Analise. "Then maybe you and I should take a walk around the property, just to check things out."

Dave gave a shake of his head that said Luke just didn't understand law enforcement. "And leave the ladies and Cole here in the house alone? I don't think so." He nodded toward the back door. "Since you're so highly trained at sneaking around in the dark and all, why don't you go scout the area and I'll stay here just to make sure no one takes advantage of the situation."

Luke gave him a hard stare that didn't seem to faze him. "I think I will." It was either that or he was going to give in to the urge to knock that smug look off of Deputy Dave's face right here in front of Analise.

He grabbed his jacket and went out the door, closing it much harder than necessary behind him.

•   •   •

As soon as Luke was out the door, Analise wanted to follow him. She'd been fighting the urge all evening to lean on him for emotional support. But she knew she had to stand on her own; someday soon Luke was going to be leaving and taking those broad shoulders with him. Besides, there could be no more little lapses in front of Cole.

So, instead of running after Luke, she asked Dave, "More tea?"

"Please. Then sit down. I've been thinking and have something I want to say to you while he's outside."

The enigmatic tone in Dave's voice set her on edge. She got the tea and sat.

His face said he was the bearer of bad news. He licked his lips, then said quietly, "I'm concerned about you three staying out here with that man."

"What? That's ridiculous—"

He reached out and put a hand over hers. "Ana, you know I think of you and Liv and Cole as family. There are . . . warning signs that we just can no longer ignore." He shifted, as if uncomfortable talking about this. "Some men choose to go into the army because they need to be heroes—sometimes when their ability to do that is taken from them, they . . . manufacture situations. Like remember a couple of years back, that firefighter up north that set fires just so he could go in and rescue people?"

Analise furrowed her brow and shook her head. "You're talking crazy here."

"Exactly. Crazy."

"That's not what I—"

He leaned closer. "Listen, Ana, I want to get this out before he comes back. We have to send him away without his knowing we figured it out—who knows what a man like him is capable of doing."

"Figured *what* out?"

"Let's ask ourselves why a man like Luke would just abandon his own life to plant bushes here in our little town. Why did he come here in the first place?"

"He came to offer his sympathy as Calvin's friend."

"A card or a phone call could have accomplished that—" He cut himself off when the back door rattled and Luke came back in.

Dave leaned back in his chair and threw his arm over the back, suddenly the very picture of tranquillity. "Perimeter secure?" he asked Luke in a very belittling tone.

Something very peculiar was going on here. First, Dave's bizarre accusations, and now Luke looked like he was ready to explode. His jaw flexed and his eyes narrowed to slits.

He pointed a finger at Dave. His voice was threatening, yet cool, when he said, "I don't want to discuss this in front of Analise. So why don't you and I step outside?"

Dave dipped his chin slightly at Analise, as if to say, *See, I was just telling you he's crazy.*

Analise said, "What in the hell is going on here? You both are acting nuts."

A look of resignation came over Luke's face. "Fine"—he gave Dave a pointed look—"you want to stay here? Here it is. When I talked to Roy this morning, the man was scared witless; he was leaving. And he didn't know anything about the paint on your car—he's not smart enough to be that convincing of a liar. I don't think he came back here and drugged Rufus."

Dave started to say something, but Luke pointed a finger at him and said, "You'll get your turn.

"I just can't see Roy taking the trouble to go to the drug-store to buy Benadryl—which he's probably never heard of, by the way—to take down a dog, when there are plenty of chemicals around this place that he's quite familiar with that could have done the job. Besides, Roy would have stuffed it in hot dogs, not prime beef."

Dave got slowly to his feet. "You know, those were the same things I was just about to bring to Ana's attention myself. Doesn't seem like Roy at all." He paused. "I'm thinking maybe *you're* the one who wants to keep Analise frightened, make her want you here for protection." He pointed at Luke. "*You* fired Roy, setting this all up. The rock through the window gave you the excuse to move in. Now you just have to keep the threat of danger high enough to have a reason to stick around."

Suddenly Luke looked wary. "You slick bastard! You saw it coming and now you're turning the tables on me."

Dave stepped around the table to stand directly in front of Luke. "What I've seen coming is a hotshot Ranger out of work who needs to feed his ego—a guy who wants this family beholden to him."

Moving slightly closer to Dave, Luke said, "You're much more clever than I gave you credit for. I thought you just wanted them to need you—but you were setting me up."

Dave poked Luke in the chest. "I should haul your ass to jail!"

"For what—"

Analise stepped up and put a hand on each man's chest and shoved them apart. "Enough! This is absolutely ridiculous. I think you're both crazy." She turned to Dave, her anger bubbling over. "I want you to go home and go to bed."

He started to say something and she cut him off by raising her palm in his face. "No! Don't say anything else. Don't make this worse. Rufus is sick because someone deliberately drugged him. If I thought for a single minute that it was *either* one of you, I'd poison you myself. Just go home and we can forget this conversation ever happened."

"You're not safe," Dave said.

"From the sound of things"—she shot Luke a sharp look— "I'm not safe with either of you around. Go home, Dave."

After giving Luke a long, threatening look, he left.

Analise stood with her hands on her hips, breathing heavily, her eyes on the door. She didn't want to look at Luke. If she let loose all of her frustration right now, nothing good would come of it. When she heard Dave's car start and pull out of the drive, she turned and started to leave the kitchen.

"Analise . . ."

She didn't pause or turn. "I don't want to hear it." She went up to her room and closed the door.

For the first few minutes, she stood, staring out the window, rubbing the back of her neck, fighting the thoughts that whirled wildly in her mind. So far Cole had held his tongue, if not his attitude. But he was angry, and an angry teenager was at best unpredictable. He was sure to say something that would tip Olivia off about her relationship with Luke.

And worry over Rufus gnawed at her. The vet said he'd make it, but what if something still went wrong? She knew she should have gone in to see him before they left Dr. Flynn's. But the image of the dog limp in Luke's arms had burned itself indelibly on her mind, which was horrible enough; she didn't want to risk having her last memory of Rufus one in which he was stretched out on an examination table with tubes stuck in him.

Worst of all, that peculiar exchange in the kitchen had her reeling. She could hardly believe Dave and Luke had stood there pointing fingers at one another. What was she supposed to think?

She had stopped them when she should have stood her ground and demanded the truth be dragged out and into the light. Instead, she'd run from the room, like a child with her hands over her ears to keep from hearing something she didn't want to.

She'd like to believe she knew Luke, what kind of man he was. But the fact was, she had only known him a matter of days. She'd thought she'd known Calvin, too. Were there things deep inside Luke that were dark and manipulative?

She wanted with all of her heart to believe that Roy was at the bottom of all of this. If not . . . well, it was just too horrible to consider.

Cole had locked his bedroom door when he came in, just in case Ana or Luke got it in one of their heads to come in and "explain" things to him. There was nothing either of them had to say that he wanted to hear.

He was too pissed to sleep. He couldn't get on the Internet, because his mom had taken away his connection as part of his punishment. She said it wasn't for the drinking, or for taking the car out when he wasn't supposed to. It was because he'd lied to her—broken her trust.

Wonder what she'd do to Ana if she knew the big fat lie she was living? How much more of a breach in trust could there be?

He'd been tempted to tell his mom right away. But thank goodness he'd waited. If he had, who knows what kind of scene would have erupted? Just maybe it would have forced Analise to leave—to take off with Luke. Luke had said he didn't want to take Analise with him, but Cole wasn't so sure—he'd seen the way they were looking at each other in the metal studio.

Mom had taken the telephone out of his room, too.

Luckily, things had been in such an uproar over Rufus tonight, he'd been able to snag the cordless from the living room without anyone noticing.

Someone knocked at the door. "Cole," his mother said softly, "you asleep?"

He held perfectly still, barely breathing, until she walked on and he heard her bedroom door close.

Then he tiptoed into his closet with the handset for the phone. He'd looked up Becca's telephone number in the student directory when he'd first come upstairs. He'd been debating whether or not to call her for the past hour. So much had happened since she'd dropped him off. And for some reason he felt compelled to talk to her about it.

Sitting in his closet in the dark, he felt particularly isolated from his family as he called Becca.

"Hello?" *Damn, it was her mom.*

He battled the impulse to hang up. He asked for Becca in a voice that was unsteady—what was wrong with him?

When Becca picked up the phone, Cole said, "Hey, what's up?" *Lame. Lame. Lame.*

"I was just doing my history for tomorrow."

"Arrrgh. I'd forgotten about that." That's all he needed, was another incomplete assignment.

"It's not too bad. I started it about twenty minutes ago, and I'm almost done."

"Yeah, well, you're a brain."

"Come on, Cole, it's history, not nuclear physics—it won't be a big deal for you either. But if you have trouble, just call me back and I'll help you."

How embarrassing would that be? She'd just said it was easy—if he called he'd really look stupid. "Um, I just called to make sure your foot is okay—after stepping through the floor and all."

"Yeah, it's fine. Thanks again for sharing that place with me."

She called it "sharing"—funny, that's how it felt.

He said, "No problem. It was fun—even the rain." He paused. "After I got home, we had to take our dog to the vet. Somebody drugged him."

"Oh, how awful! Is he all right?"

"He's still at Dr. Flynn's, but he should be fine."

"I just can't believe someone would do something like that." She sounded really mad.

Well, he decided he'd give her a little more fuel for that fire. He dropped his voice and said, "Something else happened, too."

"What?" There was concern in her voice now.

He hesitated.

"Cole, you can tell me. You know I'm not going to tell anyone else."

Suddenly he did know just that. He knew that whatever he said to Becca would stay with her, not like so many of the other girls who just couldn't keep their mouths shut. "You remember that guy who's staying with us?"

"Yeah, Mr. Boudreau. I met him at Rib Fest."

"After you dropped me off, Mom said he and Ana were in the metal studio working on the fountain. Well, I went up there—and"—he swallowed hard—"they *weren't* working on the fountain, if you know what I mean." *There, it was out.* He waited for her to explode with indignation.

After a pause, she said, "He seemed like a nice enough guy."

"Becca! He was kissing my brother's wife!"

"Oh, it was just a kiss?" She sounded surprised; apparently she'd thought it had gone much further, which made Cole flash hot with anger. Then she added, in a light and teasing tone, "I told you, you shouldn't make too big a deal over a kiss."

"Forget it! I thought if anybody . . . I thought you'd understand."

"Wait, Cole! I'm sorry."

He didn't hang up.

She said, "I didn't mean to discount your feelings—it's just . . ."

"Just what?" He couldn't keep the angry edge from his voice.

"Ana's young. Calvin's been gone awhile. Sooner or later it was going to happen. At least it's someone y'all like."

"He's been gone for *five months*! Five stinkin' months!" He realized he was shouting and lowered his voice before he woke his mother. "And you think it's *okay* she hooks up with his best buddy from the army?"

"I don't know that it's okay, that's not for me to say. I said it's understandable."

"I see," he said harshly.

"Hey, don't jump all over me! *I* didn't kiss him."

"No, you kissed *me*. And now I see just how little that means to you." He disconnected the phone.

He sat in the dark for a while. In the back of his mind, he was hoping she'd call him back. She didn't.

He'd thought Becca was different—just like he'd thought Ana was different. Now he knew, all girls were alike—shallow and selfish.

He went to bed without doing his history assignment.

Analise dodged the Roy-Dave-Luke subject all day. It wasn't that it didn't dominate her thoughts, it was just that she didn't want to discuss it with Luke. She realized that was the coward's way, but it was how she had to deal with it, at

least for today. The whole situation had made it impossible
for her to sleep last night, and her nerves were raw as a
result. It was all she could do to cope with the work at hand.
Luke had tried to bring it up once, but she made it perfectly
clear she was not going to discuss it.

At least the man had the sense to realize how prickly she
was today and didn't push it. When they arrived home,
Olivia's car was gone. As the shop had closed a half an hour
before, Analise assumed she'd gone to see Rufus. Ana pre-
ceded Luke through the back door into the kitchen. The mail
was on the kitchen table; she gave it a cursory glance as she
walked by.

Then she stopped dead in her tracks. Lying opened on the
table was a nine-by-twelve envelope from the U.S. Army
addressed to Cole Lejeune. Her mouth went dry as she
picked it up. It was empty.

"I wonder why he got this," she said.

Luke looked at what was in her hand as he passed. "Oh,
I requested some information for him."

She spun around, her mouth hanging open. "You did
what?" The edge in her voice could not be mistaken for joy.

Luke stopped in the doorway to the hall. "He was talking
about enlisting, so I offered to get him some information on
different career opportunities. It's no big deal."

She took two steps closer to him and waved the empty
envelope in the air like an indictment. "You have no business
encouraging him to join the army! He's just a boy—and
things have been difficult lately. This is no time for him to
be making such a decision."

"He brought the subject up. He said he was thinking
about Ranger—"

"Rangers! He's only sixteen."

Luke's face hardened. "Sooner or later you're going to

have to face the fact that he's growing up. One day, in the not-too-distant future, he's going to leave here—whether it's to the army, or college, or to climb mountains. He has to find his own life."

Every muscle in Analise's body went rigid. "He doesn't have to—" She caught herself before the rest spilled out.

Luke encroached on her space a little farther, leaning over her. "Doesn't have to what, Ana? Go ahead and finish it—he doesn't have to *leave*?"

She wanted to hit him. The urge was so strong that she had to ball her hands in the fabric of her jeans to keep from it. Through gritted teeth she said, "You've got your own family. What are you doing down here messing with mine?" She flung an arm to the north. "Why don't you go meddle in their lives and leave my family alone!"

He was breathing as hard as she was. Anger sparked in his eyes and a vein throbbed in his neck, the pink scar there turning red. He said, in a very low voice that told her he was working as hard to hold his temper as she, "*Your* family is falling apart."

"It's my family to fix—not yours."

He stood there, staring at her with so much anger and frustration radiating from head to toe that Analise could almost see the violence she knew he had to be capable of. Then he stalked past her and went out the back door.

Analise took two deep breaths to keep from passing out, then went upstairs to stop this idea of Cole's before it got so far gone that there was no pulling him back. The army. Jesus. Hadn't she and Olivia given enough?

Chapter 19

Luke got in the Taurus and started it. He sat there for a minute with his hands resting on the steering wheel and the engine idling. Then he shut the car off again. Leaning his head back against the seat, he closed his eyes and blew out a long breath.

Analise was right. This wasn't his family, or his problem to solve. He knew it, but his heart would not let these people go. He also didn't know what he could do to make things right.

He had to ask himself, was his reluctance to leave totally self-serving? Was he avoiding making decisions in his own life by deferring his energies to someone else's problems? Analise had said he had his own family—and yet he still felt more compelled to stay here than to go home.

As he sat in his car, watching the light of day begin to fade, he realized for the first time, he was afraid to go home—actually afraid. His life in the army was essentially over. He'd left Glens Crossing so long ago, how could there be a place for him there? If there was, did he want to fill it?

He ran a hand through his hair. He could not build his life

around Calvin's family, he knew that. And yet, the very
thought of leaving made his chest feel tight.

A pecking on the window made him jump. He looked up
and Olivia was peering at him with a curious look on her
face. He nodded toward the passenger seat and she walked
around the car and got in.

"Going someplace?" she asked in her spritely way.

"Yes. But not now. Soon."

"You and Ana had words." She said it as a statement, not
a question.

He shook his head slightly. "It doesn't matter."

Olivia gave a knowing nod. "Rufus is coming home
tomorrow."

Luke looked at her. "That's good news."

"Well, it's about all the good news that's coming our way
right now."

Sitting up straighter, he asked, "Something happened?"

"Travis's parents are pushing Smug to find Cole at fault
in the accident."

"And the evidence says?"

She lifted her small hand in the air. "Smug insists the
worst we'll see is a no-fault. The witness confirms Cole's
account. Travis still doesn't remember anything."

"So you think they'll file a civil suit?"

"Smug said they can, but he doesn't see how they'll win.
Dave doesn't seem so sure—you never know with juries."

"What does your insurance company say?"

She lifted a shoulder. "Wait and see. We're not to worry."

"Sounds like good advice to me. If the sheriff is looking
at no-fault, and with the witness that said Travis's car was in
the wrong lane, I doubt you have anything to worry about."

She nodded. "So you've decided you're going to leave us
soon."

"Yes. When the park job is done."

"That gives me about ten days."

Luke gave her a scrutinizing stare. "You're committed, then?"

"Oh, yes. There was never any doubt in my mind about that. I just have to get the timing right. I know it's a lot to ask, but I do want you to be here when it happens."

"I can't see how I can help."

She reached across and patted his hand. "This family is going to need someone to hold the rudder for a bit once it's done. Believe me, it'll help me more than you'll ever know."

He squeezed her hand. "Then I'll be here."

Cole lay on his bed, looking at the pamphlets sent by the army. He now had mixed emotions about the prospect of joining. It had seemed the perfect answer just days ago. But he didn't want Luke to get the idea that he was in any way trying to be like him.

Overall, he still was inclined to pursue it. He'd talked to his counselor at school and found that he'd have enough credits to graduate early. He'd be eighteen early in his senior year, so that wouldn't complicate anything.

"Cole?" Ana called through his closed door.

"Yeah. Come on in." He stuffed the papers under his pillow, then flipped over on his back and stuck his hands behind his head.

Analise slowly opened the door, as if she were afraid that he was going to throw something at her. Not that he didn't feel like it.

She said, "Feeling better today?"

"You know I wasn't sick."

She looked uncomfortable as she came in and closed the door behind her. "I really think we should talk."

He turned on his side, facing away from her. "Don't worry. I'm not going to tell Mom."

"That wasn't exactly what I came up here to discuss. But since you brought it up . . . Luke and I . . . actually, there is no 'Luke and I,' I guess that's what I'm meaning to say. I needed a friend—someone outside the family—and Luke . . . Well, we're not—"

"Just stop it, Ana. I don't want to talk about *Luke*." And he didn't, mostly because he'd probably say something that would hurt her more—that Luke only wanted her for someone to sleep with while he was here; that she had almost thrown her family away for the wrong man.

Becca's words echoed in his head. What she said made his stomach curl in dread. Analise was young—well, young for a widow. She probably would find someone else and leave Magnolia Mile. The worry that he'd had the first days after they'd learned of Calvin's death—that she might move away—was back.

He heard her step closer. "I saw the envelope downstairs—from the army."

Shit. He'd forgotten about the envelope.

She went on, "Are you seriously considering joining?" There was just enough disdain in her voice to piss him off.

"What does it matter to you if I am or not?"

"Everything about you matters to me."

Right. "I'm thinking about it."

"Cole." He felt her sit down on the bed behind him. "I know you miss Calvin; you want to join the army to feel closer to him again. But you need to choose for you, not to follow in Calvin's footsteps."

He sat upright and turned to face her in one quick, abrupt motion. "Calvin has nothing to do with this!" His defense was vehement, and yet Cole suddenly realized that the entire time he'd been looking at the pamphlets, he'd been imagining how Calvin had done in basic training, wondering if he would be as good a soldier as Calvin. But he'd never admit it to Ana; she'd shown that she didn't care about Calvin any longer.

"Oh, baby." She reached out a hand to touch his cheek, but he jerked away.

"I'm not a baby. Stop talking to me like I am."

After a second, during which she looked like she was either going to cry or slap him again, she said, "Sorry. I just want you to think carefully. You have lots of time to decide."

"If I commit now, I can choose what I want to do."

She stood up and looked down at him. "Don't do this to spite me."

"Why does everything have to be about you? This is *my* decision, my life. And if anybody has a say, it's Mom— not you."

He wanted to bury his face in his pillow so he didn't have to look at her anymore. But he stayed put, giving the coldest glare he could muster. It was hard because she looked so hurt. He reminded himself that's what girls did when they wanted you to do things their way.

Finally, she left the room without saying anything else.

Cole curled up on his side, wishing with all of his heart that Calvin was still alive, that there wasn't a danger that Ana would fall in love with someone else and move away, that people he loved would stop leaving him.

They sat at the dinner table without Cole, once again. He'd told his mother that he'd gotten hungry early—since he'd been sick yesterday and not eaten—so he'd made himself a sandwich. Now he needed to catch up on his homework. In a completely uncharacteristic move, Olivia had agreed to his absence. One of Liv's steadfast rules had always been that everyone sat together at the dinner table every night—hungry or not.

And she seemed preoccupied, Analise thought. Every evening since Luke's arrival, Olivia never failed to make some flattering comment about Ana's cooking, but tonight nary a word.

At least Analise knew Liv's silence had nothing to do with Cole having blown the whistle on her and Luke. She ate in thankful silence.

She never thought she'd admit this, but the lack of conversation was starting to get on her nerves. It was one of those things that she assumed would never bother her. In fact, she'd occasionally longed for a quiet meal—particularly since Luke had joined their table. Now she realized it was only because Olivia always kept some form of conversation going and she'd never really had to face *dinner silence*—which was much more nerve-wracking than ordinary silence. Each fork scrape, glass clink and knife tap echoed like a gunshot in her ears.

Finally, Olivia said, "Oh, Ana, before I forget, I've invited Reverend Hammond for coffee and dessert tomorrow evening."

Analise looked at her mother-in-law with surprise. "Just dessert?"

"Yes. Don't worry about making anything. I'm going to pick something up from the bakery—maybe one of Mimi's Black Forest cakes. That always finishes a meal nicely."

"All right. Any special occasion for this . . . dessert?"

"Richard's been such a help lately, I want to thank him."

The words were simple, but the look in Olivia's eye said there was more to it than that. When Analise glanced back at Luke, he was staring at Olivia with an odd look on his face.

Analise said, "You're sure you don't want to invite him for dinner? I don't mind." Not that she particularly wanted the man here for dinner—or dessert—but this *was* Olivia's house.

"No. Just dessert. I believe he has another commitment earlier in the evening."

One thing about detesting lying as much as Olivia did, it made one a terrible liar. There was definitely something else afoot.

Oh, my gosh! He's asked her to marry him.

Analise's appetite dried up. It hadn't been too keen anyway, with Cole being so upset with her and the park job still behind schedule. To distract her from her meal even further, Luke was sitting right across from her with new color in his cheeks from outdoor work, looking more handsome than ever. She picked at her food, trying not to look at him.

But there he sat, making her love him and hate herself at the same time. Her body temperature rose as she remembered the intimate dance in the studio. She felt like she had a fever—hot and cold fighting for supremacy, just on the verge of breaking out in perspiration.

She glanced at Luke. Big mistake. There was something in his blue eyes that said he noticed the change in her and understood its cause.

Finally, the meal ended. Analise insisted on cleaning the kitchen by herself. The truth of it was, Olivia looked too tired to lift a dishrag and Analise didn't trust herself alone with Luke. She was still angry with him for his interference. Yet there were feelings underneath that anger that were far from antagonistic. Love and hate, two sides of the same sword, mirror images that cannot be separated.

Alone in her kitchen, she tried to find solace in the rhythm of familiar tasks. She tried not to think of Olivia and

Richard's big announcement—and what it might mean to her life in this house. She buried her thoughts in what should be thrown out of the refrigerator and making note of what needed to be purchased during her next trip to the Piggly Wiggly. However, as habit made her reach for Rufus's bowl, that meager comfort vanished.

She sat down hard on a kitchen chair, buried her face in the dish towel she held and cried. She didn't want to. She'd managed to stay dry-eyed for months. But since that night when Luke coaxed the dammed-up tears from her, they'd been ready to fall at the slightest provocation.

After a few seconds of indulgence, she swallowed her tears, sniffled loudly and got back to work.

She hated self-pity as much as Olivia hated lies.

When Analise went upstairs at ten o'clock, there was a light shining from Olivia's bedroom door, which stood ajar. Analise called softly, pushing the door open. Olivia was already in her nightshirt, tucked in bed. The light was burning, but the book Olivia was reading had fallen on her chest, her eyeglasses shielding closed eyes.

Analise walked quietly over to the bed and removed the book from Olivia's chest. As she lifted Olivia's hand, she saw how thin her skin seemed—the skin of a much older woman. After setting the book on the nightstand, she studied her mother-in-law's face carefully. Olivia was such a vibrant woman, always moving, it was rare to get a glimpse of her this still. Her face seemed fuller in the cheeks. Her color appeared slightly ashen. Was it just the light? Analise noticed tissues in the bedside waste can that had been used to remove foundation. Liv never wore makeup.

Gently, Analise removed Olivia's glasses and put them on the night table on top of the closed book. Olivia showed no sign of waking. Analise tucked the covers carefully around her and turned out the light.

As she closed the door behind her, she heard Olivia sigh quietly in her sleep. That tiny sound fell on Analise's ears and wound its way directly to her heart. She loved Olivia, as much as she imagined she would have loved her own mother, had she lived. She shuddered to think of the woman she would have become without Olivia's spirited love. For some reason, the thought brought a heavy sadness with it— as if something were threatening her peace here.

The only things that threatened Analise's peace, she thought, were her own choices. She knew she'd made the right one; she could never leave this family. Still, a little part of her longed for the passion she shared with Luke. But, she reminded herself, passion burned brightly and fast, leaving nothing but ash in its wake. Better to be content with the steady love of family.

She heard the shower running and saw Luke's bedroom door was open. She glanced toward Cole's door and saw there was no light shining beneath. Olivia was so soundly asleep she hadn't known that Ana was in the room with her.

That itch that Luke had set off demanded to once again be scratched. She bit her lip and looked toward the closed bathroom door.

Who would know if she slipped quietly into the shower with him? One more shot at that passion before opportunity faded.

She shouldn't. It would just make things more difficult.

She couldn't make her feet move toward her own room. The mere thought of his rugged body, slick with soap under her hands, nearly made her gasp with yearning. Oh, to have needles of hot water beat down on her skin, while Luke's hands, his lips, attended every inch of her. He'd given her a taste of heaven; who could blame her for wanting just one more nibble before he left?

God in heaven. She turning quickly and went to her own room, closing the door firmly behind her. She had been better off when she didn't know what was within her grasp.

After she heard the bathroom door open and Luke's bedroom door close, Analise slipped quietly to the bathroom herself. The steamy air still smelled of him. She ran her hand over the wet towel he'd used. It was still warm.

Stop it! Stop torturing yourself.

She wiped the steam from the mirror and closed the door on her indecent thoughts. After going through her bedtime routine, she went back to her own room. As she looked at the bed, it seemed much larger than before, a great expanse of cold sheets and empty dreams.

With a sigh, she slid between those unwelcoming sheets. The image that haunted her made her toss and turn, for each time she closed her eyes, she saw Luke's eyes blazing with passion that one blissful morning.

Flopping on her side, she wrapped her pillow around her head, burying her scream of frustration.

Why did she torment herself like this? She needed to grab hold of that flash of anger she'd felt earlier today when they'd fought over Cole. She needed to clutch it tight and somehow make it outweigh everything else.

At some point she must have fallen asleep, because when she heard Luke yell, she bolted upright in bed and looked at the clock. It was three o'clock in the morning.

He yelled again, a strangled sound of suffering.

Analise jumped up and ran to his room, opening the door without hesitation. As her eyes were well adjusted to the dark, she could see him clearly, thrashing, the sheet down to his waist and twisted around his legs.

"Luke!" she whispered loudly.

His head turning from side to side, he continued to mutter words that made no sense. She closed the door behind her, to prevent awakening Olivia and Cole. Then she hurried to his bedside. Putting a hand on his shoulder, she found him bathed in perspiration. She shook him gently.

"Luke, wake up." When he didn't, she tried again. "Lu—" Her words were cut off when he sat straight up and his hand shot around her throat. It happened faster than a snake strike. His grasp was strong, squeezing her airway closed.

Her fingers dug into his wrist, trying in vain to pull his hand away.

His eyes finally seemed to focus and come out of his dream. "Oh, Jesus." He jerked his hand away from her and looked at it with revulsion. "Oh, God." He reached out and tentatively put both hands on her face. "Did I hurt you?"

She worked to swallow, surprised the muscles in her throat still functioned. "No." Her voice was hoarse. "But you sure scared the crap out of me."

The rigidity of his body left on his exhaled breath. He pulled her to sit next to him on the bed and wrapped his arms around her. "I'm sorry. I'm so sorry, baby."

Analise could feel how frantic his heart was beating. "It's all right. You were dreaming."

He buried his face in the crook of her neck. The warmth of his breath teased her skin.

She stroked his hair with one hand and his bare back with the other. "It's all right," she murmured again.

After a few moments, his breathing slowed to normal and he loosened his grip on her. He didn't let her go, but stopped clinging as if he were about to slip into some vast chasm.

She leaned back, and his hands lingered on her sides. Pushing the hair away from his damp brow, she said, "Better?"

He held her gaze for a moment. "I haven't had a nightmare like that since I started sleeping here. Which doesn't make any sense. . . ."

Smiling at him, she said, "Of course it makes sense. You've been in hospitals and hotels. Here you're home."

He put a hand on the one she held to his cheek and closed his eyes. "No. You don't understand. You couldn't understand."

"Then explain it to me. Maybe it'll help."

He lay back on the bed, pulling her with him. She didn't resist. She rested her cheek on his chest and felt the warmth of his arms around her.

"If I talk about it," he said, "*you'll* start having nightmares." There was something uncharacteristically bleak in his tone. It sent a little shiver down her spine.

She whispered, "I'd take them, if it meant you didn't have to have them anymore."

He took a deep breath that lifted her head. "Oh, Ana . . . you don't know what you're saying." After a pause, he said, "I've earned these nightmares."

She put her hand on his chest and rested her chin on it. "I know I can't imagine the things you've seen, the things you've done in service of your country. You're a good man. I see it in you every day, the way you care for Olivia and Cole—people you barely know. You didn't have to come here—and you certainly didn't have to stay."

"You're right." He touched her cheek. "You can't imagine the things I've done."

She started to say more, but he put a finger on her lips and said, "Shhh. It's late."

Unable to resist, she nipped his finger with her teeth, then shifted and kissed his palm.

His gaze held hers while she teased the flesh of his hand.

Then he pulled her up and kissed her mouth in a way that had her body clamoring for more.

At the end of the kiss, he whispered against her lips, "Go back to your room, Ana."

She nibbled on his lower lip and rubbed his chest. "I don't want to."

"You don't want me. If you knew . . . you'd never want to be near me. I'm not what you think I am."

"Will you shut up? I'm not asking you to marry me, just make love to me." She moved her hand lower on his body.

He moaned, then grabbed her wrist.

"Why?" she asked.

"Because . . . because you're making it harder for me to leave."

She nearly said, *Then don't,* but caught herself, the implications of such a thing crashing over her like a cold wave.

He must have sensed her reaction. "I *am* leaving. Doing this doesn't seem right; it won't change anything."

"Exactly." She moved and dipped her tongue in the hollow of his throat. "So why not do it while we can?"

Groaning, he moved so quickly, she was on her back before she even realized he was caving in.

Sometime deep in the night, Analise had the wild notion that if Olivia was going to marry Richard Hammond and bring him into their house, maybe that would pave the way for Luke being added to their family. Perhaps her and Luke's relationship could extend beyond the self-imposed expiration date.

In the cold light of morning, as with so many nocturnal epiphanies, she realized just how foolish that was. Olivia had been a widow for over eight years, not a matter of months. And she wasn't bringing a new husband into

Granny Lejeune's house. It was clear that life with Luke would mean life away from Magnolia Mile. And, as she had a hundred times before, she recognized the fact that she could not leave this family—even if Richard Hammond were added to the mix.

Or could she? As the first streams of sunlight came through her bedroom window, she began to look at things differently. If Olivia married Richard, she would have a full-time companion and someone to help her run the nursery. And, as Luke had so bluntly pointed out to her, the day would soon come for Cole to make his way into the world. Perhaps in a few months her leaving Magnolia Mile might seem the right thing to do.

She rolled onto her side and hugged her pillow to her chest. She was too tired to think straight, and her reason was too fogged by the hours in Luke's bed. Closing her eyes, she tried to fall asleep for at least an hour before her alarm went off and she had to drag herself back to the job site. Normally, she couldn't wait to get to a project. But her emotional energy had been split, as light through a prism, unable to concentrate the fullness of its intensity to any single facet of her life.

As she fell into a light sleep, she worried that might just make it so she didn't do *anything* right.

Today they were loading up the sections of the fountain and taking them to the park. The pieces were large enough that each one had to be taken in a separate trip. It was nearly noon by the time they'd shuttled all of them to the children's garden. As Analise and Luke had grown adept at working together, it didn't require a great deal of talk. They moved in content silence. The only other subject that was pressing forth in Luke's mind was forbidden in the daylight hours.

As they stood there, looking at the sections set in their approximate permanent positions, Luke said, "You have to be proud. You've made something that will last, something people will enjoy."

She shot him a quick grin. "I haven't *made it* yet. And if the electrician doesn't show up this afternoon to wire the controls, I'm in deep do-do."

Luke grinned back. "If he doesn't, I'll go find him and drag his sorry ass here."

"I'm going to hold you to that."

"Hey, when guys have as few marketable skills as I do, we do what we can."

She looked seriously at him. "What *are* you going to do? I mean, when this job's finished, of course."

Rolling in his lips, he shrugged. "Not sure."

"Army?"

With a look of sadness, he shook his head. "Nothing there for me now. I can't do the job I was trained to do."

She gestured one hand to the air. "Now's the time to go for something you want—not just a job, but something that feeds more than your stomach and wallet. With no family to support, you can do as you please."

Her comment struck him as sharply as a stinging whip. The only thing he "pleased," he could not have. It struck him then, he *would* be happy spending his days working outdoors with this landscaping business, helping Analise with her creations. Money didn't motivate him, never had. Feeling useful, completing a job, being productive, that's what powered him. For a long time, he'd thought it was those moments of adrenaline-pumping excitement, the moments when life hung in the balance. But he now saw it wasn't the adrenaline buzz, exactly, it was the rush afterward when he knew he'd done something that made a difference.

He had a taste of that rush now, looking at this fountain.

"Luke?" Analise prompted.

Shaking his head, he said, "I'm one lost son-of-a-bitch."

The wounded look in her eye made him regret the words as soon as they were out of his mouth. He added, "I'll figure it out—eventually."

He thought she'd set the topic aside, but she didn't. "What did you want to be when you were a kid?"

He chuckled. "An astronaut. A pilot. A fireman. A race car driver. A stuntman. A football coach. Not necessarily in that order."

"A very focused child."

"Oh, yeah."

"All pretty edgy professions." She gave him a sideways glance. "You need the thrill."

"Maybe at one time. But not anymore. I've thrilled myself enough to last a lifetime." *Now I want to be a land-scaper.*

"You say that now. But in a few more months, when you're back up to full speed . . . things will look different to you then."

He wanted to grab her by the shoulders, look in her eye and tell her just how that thrill-seeking personality had screwed his judgment. He thought he could do it all and nothing, but nothing, would go wrong. But something went terribly wrong, and there was no undoing it. He did manage to look her in the eye. "No. I'm done."

A flash of comprehension shone in her eyes, which she quickly masked. He could tell she was trying to lighten the mood when she said, "Okay, forget the dreams of youth. What's deep inside you now? What is your secret desire that's just waiting to be explored?"

He gave her a crafty glance, wanting to divert this

conversation away from his future—the only subject that made him as uncomfortable as his recent past. "Well, I thought my desires were pretty clear last night."

She shoved him playfully. "All right. If you're going to start acting like that, it's back to work."

Luke spent the rest of the day surreptitiously watching Analise work, having trouble focusing on his own. She was beautiful in her concentration as she began to assemble the fountain. His heart ached—for himself, for her, for Olivia and Cole, for the future that was about to be rewritten.

Chapter 20

Dinner was every bit as uncomfortable as Analise had feared. Cole made his first appearance at the table since he'd walked in on her and Luke in the studio—and his cool demeanor could not be misinterpreted by a blind man. Analise and Olivia both chattered about banal topics, fueled by nerves and the need to ignore the impending bomb to be dropped. At one point, Analise almost said she'd figured out the news, so there was no need for all of this jumpy secrecy as they awaited Reverend Hammond's arrival. But she couldn't quite muster up the courage to draw the subject out in the open.

The only bright spot was that Rufus was back home, lounging by the stove waiting for his dinner. As Dr. Flynn had assured them, the dog showed no lingering ill effects whatsoever. Analise had firmly decided it had been Roy, after all. Dave's suggestion that it was Luke was ludicrous. And the possibility that Dave was behind it was equally ridiculous; Dave had been a family friend since before she came to Grover. The argument that Roy wouldn't have used prime meat could be easily dismissed—the three hundred dollars Luke had given him was probably more than the man had seen in one lump sum for a very long time. He probably felt flush with cash. Besides, she didn't think Roy was long on decision making—logic might not apply.

As she loaded the dishwasher and threw out the mostly uneaten dinner, Olivia brought out a pink bakery box tied with string. She pulled out her good china cups and dessert plates, then arranged the cake on a crystal pedestal plate. As she did it, she was humming. Very uncharacteristic of Olivia—if she made a musical sound, it was always singing, never this nerve-wracking humming.

After Cole took out the trash, he said, "I'm going up to study."

Olivia's hands stilled in her preparations. "I asked you to stay down here. Reverend Hammond will be here in a minute."

Cole shifted, his feet obviously itching to get away from Analise. "Just call me when he does and I'll come down."

Turning to her son, Olivia's voice was unusually stern when she answered, "You can stay down here. It'll only be a minute. Take this cake into the dining room."

With a sigh of frustration, Cole did as she asked.

Analise's mind was whirling with what was about to happen. She needed to prepare herself so she gave the proper outward reaction to the news. And just what was the proper reaction? Obviously, she wasn't going to gush, overflowing with enthusiasm. That would just be too false. But she had to be supportive, especially in front of Cole. This was going to be a bigger adjustment for him than for her. He had to know they were still going to be a family, even though things were changing.

Through the window over the sink, she saw headlights shining on the carriage house. Reverend Hammond—

Richard, she had to get used to calling him that—was pulling into the drive. Her mouth went dry and she closed her eyes, steeling herself. She would not ruin this moment for Olivia. She would offer her congratulations and welcome Richard to the family.

The doorbell rang, making Analise jump, even though she knew it was coming. She was going to have to do a better job of controlling herself than that, she thought.

Olivia went to the door. Analise heard her and Rev—Richard's hushed voices in the front hall. She drew a deep breath, picked up the coffeepot and took it into the dining room. Cole was sitting at the table, looking at a comic book. He didn't acknowledge her presence.

Luke was standing in the hall, just outside the wide dining room doorway. His gaze was fixed on the front door and the two people standing in front of it.

Analise watched him from the far corner of the dining room, near the door to the kitchen, her heart beating a little faster at the masculine sight of him. She saw him smile slightly as he greeted the reverend. Then she realized she was staring and Cole was right there, so she turned around and returned to the kitchen.

She came back a few seconds later with her emotions under better control and the cream pitcher in her hand. Luke was engaged in quiet conversation with the reverend in the doorway.

Olivia said, "Well, let's have some dessert."

They all moved to take seats at the table—all except Luke. He took a step backward, toward the hall. "I'll say good night now."

Olivia stood back up. "You'll do no such thing. Get yourself in here and sit down."

For a moment he looked like he might bolt and run. Then

he slowly came in and sat in the chair next to Cole—which put him directly across from Analise.

Olivia started to cut the cake. The ticking of the hall clock sounded loud enough to shatter glass. Analise shifted in her chair.

Once the cake and coffee were served, Olivia picked up her fork. "Mimi really outdid herself. Just look at this cake."

"Delicious," Richard said as he took a bite.

"Humm," Analise managed. She wanted to stand up and shout for them to get this over with. But she took a small bite of cake that seemed to swell in her mouth.

What followed made Analise want to scream—discussion of the weather, who was in the hospital, what had happened at the last town meeting.

Finally, Olivia cleared her throat and said, "I suppose y'all have figured out I have a special reason for gathering us all together."

Analise put her hands in her lap and dug her nails into her palms. She glanced at Cole, who looked a little shaken. Had he already guessed, too?

Cole surprised her by saying, "Is this about the accident? Am I in trouble?"

Olivia's face softened. "Oh, no, dear. I'm sorry, I should have let you know that last night. I didn't even think about how you might worry."

Yeah, well, he might still need to worry. Analise headed that thought off quickly. Negativity would do no good. She must be positive. Olivia had done so much, it was little enough to give back. She breathed in and put a smile on her face. "So what is this news? Tell us." She avoided looking at Luke.

"It's family news, actually. But I wanted Richard and Luke to be here for . . . reasons you'll soon see.

"It's been a good while since I've thought about such things—"

Come on, get it over with.

"—but time catches up with us all, sooner or later."

So she's using the I'm-not-getting-any-younger approach to this decision.

Olivia glanced at Richard; then, for some odd reason, her gaze lingered on Luke. Analise glanced at him, unable to read what was on his face. It was intense, much too intense for an announcement that would mean little or nothing to him. Her gaze returned to Olivia.

"The tests from my last checkup . . . well, the cancer is back."

Analise felt as if a bucket of warm tar had been poured over her. The heat ran from her head, clogging her lungs, until it reached her feet. She seemed to be robbed of all ability to speak. Her arms and legs wouldn't move. She heard a little wheezing noise that she soon realized was coming from her own throat.

Cole shot to his feet. "No! The tests are wrong! Have the doctor do them again."

Move, get up and go to him. Say something. But Analise remained stunned, still and silent.

Olivia went to her son. Putting her hands on his shoulders, she looked up into his eyes. "No, Cole. The tests are right. I knew even before I had them. I could tell."

Analise's gaze cut from Olivia to Richard, who appeared truly pained but remained silent, his brown eyes trying to convey support, she assumed. Then she looked at Luke. Why in the hell was Luke included in this in the first place? His face was drawn, he looked sad, but in no way surprised.

Her breath was ripped away. He knew! Luke knew! He'd known for days—since that night she'd heard him and

Olivia talking. And he never breathed a word—never gave her a hint of warning of what was coming.

Cole was crying now. "You'll get the treatment like before. It made you well. They can do it again."

Olivia wrapped her arms around him. "They can't make me well. I'm not having any treatments. That's what I wanted to tell you."

Analise found her voice. "Of course there are treatments. Last time, the oncologist said there were options if you had recurrence."

Standing with her arm around a shaking Cole, Olivia turned to face her. She said softly, "I didn't say there aren't treatments. I said I'm not having any."

Analise overcame her frozen limbs and shot to her feet. "You're not serious!"

Calmly, Olivia said, "I am."

"Mom! Don't say that!"

"Let's sit back down." She pulled her chair close to his, keeping his hand held tightly in hers.

He kept trying to pull away, but she held fast. "Listen to me. The doctor says I can go through chemo again, but the outcome is doubtful."

"You have to try! You have to!" Cole said.

"Cole, listen to me. Do you remember how sick I was last time? I couldn't do *anything*. I don't want my last days with my family to be like that. I want us to live like we always do. I want to enjoy each day—as long as God gives me."

Analise asked in a shaky voice, "Exactly what did *the doctor* advise?"

Olivia looked at her, still holding tightly to Cole, as if he might try to run away—which Ana thought very possible. She knew that's just what she wanted to do.

"The doctor said it's my decision. With chemo he gives a

twenty-percent chance at remission for a period of perhaps months—there will be no cure. If I choose to go without, he'll prescribe things to make my life as comfortable and functional as it can be. I've already started taking some of them.

"You see, with chemo, I might buy some time, but this disease will claim my life. I choose to live while I can, not lie miserable for months, then die anyway."

Cole jerked away and stood. "How can you say that?" His crying was beyond quiet tears, the boy was sobbing. "How can you just give up?"

"I'm not giving up. I *want* to live. I'll do all I can to fight this thing—but I'm not going to have chemo again. I won't waste the time I have left with you in that way."

Cole collapsed back into his chair and buried his face in his hands.

Olivia went on, "Richard is my friend. I wanted him here for me, to be my support." She looked at Luke. "And Luke has proven himself to be a friend to us all."

Ana's gaze cut to Luke. He smiled thinly at Olivia, then looked at his hands in his lap, hiding what was in his eyes before Analise could read it.

"You need to get a second opinion," Analise said, trying to sound practical. "Go to Memphis, or Mayo, there are several really good clinics. We can't just let this be the verdict."

Olivia's eyes were loving when they looked upon her. "My case has been reviewed by plenty of the finest doctors. This is ovarian cancer, Ana, you know the prognosis as well as I do."

Analise tried again. "But the chemo arrested it last time. You've had four really healthy years. If you took it again—"

"I know. I can't say with certainty that it wouldn't buy me more time. But the odds . . . and the quality of the time I have left. I want us to go on with our lives, but I also appreciate the fact that I've been given enough time to prepare—I don't want to squander it.

"I know this is a shock. I just ask that you think about what I've said."

Cole got up and stalked out of the room. He thudded up the stairs. Analise jumped at the sound of his bedroom door slamming.

Olivia got up and walked around the table. She put her hands on Analise's shoulders. "Just think about it," she said, very quietly. Then she sighed. "Richard, I feel like a breath of air. Care to take a walk with me?"

The reverend smiled sadly, yet with so much warmth it almost broke Analise's heart further. "Of course. I'll get your jacket."

Olivia kissed the top of Ana's head and left the room.

For several seconds, Analise sat staring at the tablecloth, just trying to even out her breathing. She was light-headed and nauseous. The sweet cloying smell of the Black Forest cake seemed to overwhelm the room.

Somehow she found a shaky voice and said, "Could . . . could you take this cake out of here?" With a trembling hand, she pushed her plate away.

Without a word, Luke cleared all of the plates and carried the remaining cake back to the kitchen. Then he returned and sat silently in his chair. Analise didn't look at him.

She needed some air, too, but knew her legs would not carry her right now. Putting her elbows on the table, she buried her face in her hands—but she didn't cry. She was too stunned to cry. Why, oh, why couldn't the news have been of an impending marriage?

When she felt she could speak with a steady voice, she said, "You knew." She raised her eyes to meet his.

Leaning forward, Luke folded his hands on the table. "Yes."

"Why didn't you warn me? You just let me think . . ."

He drew a deep breath and exhaled slowly. "Because Olivia asked me not to."

She hardened her gaze. "Why did she tell you? I don't understand."

He shook his head. "Maybe she needed to say the words to someone a little more removed first." He paused. "She's worried about you and Cole. She wants to make this as easy as possible—"

Anger sparked. Analise got to her feet. "Easy! How in the hell can this be easy?"

"Ana." Luke got up and walked around the table. "Everyone knows there's nothing easy about this. She wants to do all she can to ease your pain, your worry."

"Then she should damn well get herself into treatment!" With those words, the tears came.

Luke stepped closer and took her in his arms. She started to pull back, saying, "Cole . . ."

He held her tight. "Shhh. He won't be back down tonight. He needs some time, too."

With that assurance, Analise let herself sob into his shirt, clinging with her fists in the fabric. He held her close and rocked her gently, cupping the back of her head with his hand. "I'm here. You don't have to do this alone."

"I'm not ready to lose her. She'd been doing so well. She deserves years and years of life after all she's suffered." She sniffed loudly and straightened up. Grabbing a napkin off the table, she blew her nose. "This is ridiculous. Of course she'll get treatment. It's just that it's such a shock. Once she gets used to—"

He put his hands on the sides of her face. "Ana, it's not the shock. She's known for weeks."

She gave a slight gasp and stepped away from him. Looking into thin air, she whispered, "Weeks? She's known for weeks and kept it to herself? How awful for her."

He said, "I think Reverend Hammond was helping her."

Her head snapped up. "Reverend Hammond isn't family. *I* should have been helping her!" Her eyes narrowed. Why did this man who walked into their lives a couple of weeks ago know more about the dearest person in her life than she did? Had the bond she'd thought she and Olivia shared been one-sided? Why hadn't Olivia confided in her—as she would certainly have confided in Olivia if the tables were turned?

Luke must have seen the change in her, because he reached out. "Ana—"

She pulled away. "Since she seems to think so highly of you"—she was ashamed of the jealousy in her voice; in a time like this it seemed petty to even consider such things as hurt feelings over who she confided in—"you can help me convince her to get treatment. First, I'll have to meet with her and her doctor to see what he's advising. Then you and I can make her see—"

"No. Ana, I can't. It's not my place."

"Bullshit!" She punched her index finger in the air between them. "She put you in that place when she told you before she told her family. She trusts you. You have to do it."

"I think we should both sleep on it and discuss it after the shock has worn off for you."

She drew a breath to argue further, but he spoke before she could. "Tomorrow. It's not like she's going to have to decide tonight. One night, that's all. Then we'll discuss this when we're more clear-headed."

She knew he thought she was the one who wasn't clear-headed. His head was clear and well ordered, since he didn't just get slammed with the news. Which gave him the advantage in this argument. So she nodded. "Tomorrow. We'll form a plan tomorrow."

He took her hand. "You look like you could use a little outside air yourself."

She glanced at the ceiling. "Cole."

Luke said, "I hear Olivia and the reverend on the front porch. He won't be alone."

Giving a single nod, she allowed him to lead her to the back door and out into the night.

They walked slowly, in silence, taking a meandering path to the metal bench. Analise drew in the cool, moist air, felt the damp film it left on her cheeks and thought how wonderful it was to be able to feel—to be alive. It just didn't seem fair that Olivia's life was being threatened. She was too young, Cole needed her—*she* needed her.

Sitting down on the bench, the cool dampness made its way through the seat of her jeans. A little chill ran down her arms, making her shiver. Luke took his long-sleeved shirt off and put it around her, leaving himself in a short-sleeved T-shirt.

"You'll freeze," she said, trying to take the shirt from her shoulders.

He stilled her hands. "I'm fine. I've slept outside in forty-degree weather wearing less."

They sat in silence, listening to the crickets and the frogs. Then Analise said, "When Layton died, I remember thinking how strong Olivia was, how I didn't know if I could begin to cope as she did if I were in her shoes. She comforted everyone else—Layton had a lot of friends and Olivia was their rock. When Calvin died, it was Olivia who held us together—it should have been me. I can't imagine what it must be like, losing a child. But Olivia held *my* hand, assured *me* that life goes on." She looked into Luke's eyes. "Where am I going to find that kind of strength? How am I going to do that for Cole?"

Luke settled his arm around her shoulders. "You know, Olivia said just about the same words to me the other night. Only *you* were the one who was strong, you helped her through the dark times."

Analise burst into tears. "She has to live! She has to fight this. I want her to see her grandchildren. God shouldn't cheat her out of that. She has so much to give. I can't . . ." The tears overcame the words, leaving the rest unsaid. But she sensed Luke understood; he understood her anger *and* her fear.

He pulled her onto his lap and held her while she cried.

Luke went to bed feeling the weight of this family's tragedy on his heart. Their trials truly seemed endless. Frustration and impotence burned in his gut. Olivia had wanted him here to support Analise and Cole—but what could he really do? He could see that Analise was going to look at him as an adversary in her campaign to convince Olivia to take chemo. And Cole was already mad at him for moving in on his brother's wife. No, he couldn't see what good he was going to be able to do at all.

Sometime in the night, he awakened from a fitful doze. He wasn't sure what had drawn him from sleep, but it had been something other than a nightmare for a change. He listened carefully. A long, thin whine came from downstairs.

He got up and pulled on his jeans. Then he moved silently through the house toward the noise. When he reached the kitchen, he saw Rufus with his nose pressed against the back door, shifting from paw to paw, his whine about to break out into baying.

He put a hand on the dog's head. "Shhh, buddy. Let's not scare anyone off," he whispered.

After making a circuit of the downstairs windows and not seeing anyone or anything out of the ordinary, he rummaged around in the refrigerator and came up with a piece of leftover beef to distract Rufus. Then he slipped quietly out the back door. Of course, Luke thought, it could be nothing more than a deer or a raccoon that got too close to the house.

As he stood on the back steps, he heard a metallic clang near the carriage house. He made his way in that direction, moving silently, sticking to deep shadow. Skirting around to the back of the building, he saw a dark form kneeling by the back door.

Employing his old skills, he moved on silent feet, maneuvering himself into a position that would prevent any attempt the man might make to sprint away. When Luke was close enough, he grabbed the man from behind, wrapping his arm around the intruder's neck. Luke threw him, face down, to the ground. The man kicked a large metal barrel next to the door, clattering it against the building before it fell on its side and rolled away.

Rufus let loose with a round of baying in the house that Luke could hear clear out here.

Luke got the man's arm wrenched behind him and applied pressure. "Hold still. You're not going anywhere." After the man stopped wriggling, Luke jerked him to his feet, but kept a firm hand on his arm. When he saw the face, he wasn't at all surprised.

Dave finally recovered his breath enough to speak. "What in the hell is wrong with you?"

"I was about to ask you the same thing." He marched Dave toward the house.

Dave sputtered, "Let go of me! I was just checking out the place."

"Yeah, you're all solicitous concern." Luke jerked him around and slammed his back against the carriage house. "I want you to listen to me very closely." He pressed harder, nearly lifting Dave off his feet. "This ends *now*. I don't care who you are, or what your position is in this county. You do anything to harm either of those women and I will make *you* disappear." He lowered his voice and said through clenched teeth, "It's all in a day's work for a man like me."

Dave's eyes grew large. "Threatening an officer—"

Luke shook him, snapping his mouth closed. "Am I clear?"

Dave's voice wasn't much more than a wheeze when he said, "I was doing my job."

"Sing that tune all you want. Nobody's going to be fooled." He jerked Dave back in front of him and marshaled him toward the house.

When they rounded the corner of the carriage house, the lights were on in the kitchen and beside the back door. Olivia's face was pressed against the glass.

As Luke got close, she opened the door and Rufus came howling down the steps. He ran in circles around Luke and Dave, baying and carrying on like he'd bagged the quarry.

"Luke? Is that you?" Olivia called, her voice broken up by Rufus's bass howl.

"Me and a little unexpected company."

Analise stepped out onto the back stoop with Olivia.

Dave jerked once more and Luke let him go. He spun on Luke. "You stupid—"

"Dave!" Olivia shouted. "What's going on?"

Dave turned to face the women. "I was just keeping an eye on things, like I always do"—he flung a finger in Luke's direction—"when this son-of . . . he jumped me."

Luke asked, "Where's your car?"

Dave shot him a killing look. "On the road. I didn't want to disturb anyone."

"Just parked at the end of the drive, then? When I walk down there, it won't be tucked away behind some bush?" Luke asked calmly. He crossed his arms over his chest to keep from putting a fist in the guy's lying mouth.

Dave ignored the question and turned on Luke. "This is ridiculous. Why were *you* out there poking around at this hour?"

"Responding to our watchdog." He pointed to Rufus, who had quieted but had his head tucked low, staring at Dave. "You normally 'check things out' using this?" Luke held up a long thin lock pick.

Dave sealed his own confession when he patted his back pants pocket, looking for the device.

Analise drew in a sharp breath, then said in a small voice, "It wasn't Roy." She and Olivia exchanged a troubled look.

Olivia said, "Oh, Dave. Did you paint Ana's car and break her window, too?" She gasped. "And poor Rufus! How could you?"

"I don't have to take this! I was just looking out for y'all." He spun around and headed down the driveway, disappearing quickly into the dark. They heard him mutter, "Bunch of ungrateful . . ."

Rufus took several steps after him, chuffing, as if getting in the last word.

Luke called after him, "Remember what I said."

After a second, Analise put a hand to her throat and said, "I wouldn't have believed it. He'd been Calvin's friend since grade school. Why? Why would he do this?"

Luke said, "For the very reason he said I was doing those things . . . he wanted you to need him. And he thought he could convince you that I was the culprit. He wanted me gone."

A new light dawned in Analise's eye. "He was jealous?"

"He wanted to be a part of this family," Luke said.

Ana shook her head and said, "I supposed we'd better call Smug in the morning. He should know."

"Yes," Luke agreed. "It'll still be our word against Dave's, no proof for charges, but the sheriff should know."

Olivia said in a sad tone, "Poor Dave. I'm so disappointed." Then she turned around and went inside.

As she'd said the words, Luke realized just how painful it would be to have Olivia use them toward him. Her disappointment would be a troublesome burden.

If she knew the truth, you'd know *the sting of those words.*

He was all too aware that he deserved them more now than on the day he'd arrived here, for he'd been letting these people believe his intentions were pure.

He tried to ignore his nagging conscience as he followed the women back inside.

Chapter 21

First thing the next morning, Analise made a difficult call to the sheriff. She explained all that had been happening. The fact that this was all news to the sheriff just confirmed that Dave was at the center of it all; Olivia had reported every incident to Dave, and there was no paperwork, no notification to his superior on any of the vandalism.

Smug said, "This puts us in a difficult spot. No evidence." He paused. "I don't think Dave is a dangerous man—a jealous one, maybe. I'll take care of things."

"Thank you, Smug. Are you going to fire him?" Wrong as he'd been, she really didn't want to think that the only thing the man had was going to be taken away from him.

"This'd be the first complaint against him. No evidence to prove he broke the law. He'll spend some time in the office instead of in a cruiser. Then we'll have to see. Y'all let me know right away if there's any more trouble."

"I'm sure there won't be, but yes, we will." She hung up the phone feeling a little safer; now that this was out in the open, that would be the end of it. Plus, she was pretty sure Luke had made a clear point to Dave last night before he brought him to the house. Dave had sputtered and denied, but she could see the fear in his eyes. He knew Luke had the ability to back up any threat he might have made.

When she entered the kitchen, Luke immediately asked, "You called the sheriff?"

"Yes. He's taking care of it."

He nodded. "Good."

As they sat down to breakfast, Analise tried to open the subject of Olivia's treatment. Luke was quiet and, although they hadn't come to any open agreement yet, she felt sure he'd back her up when the time came; he'd bolster her argument for Olivia to take a shot at chemo. It was only common sense.

Olivia quite firmly said there was nothing to discuss. She'd given careful thought to all aspects, and this was her decision. She ended by saying, "If I'd wanted family discussion, I would have informed everyone before I made up my mind."

Analise ignored the sting of that comment and pressed on. "What about Cole?" She was glad he'd already left for school; she didn't think they should have this conversation in front of him again.

Olivia's gaze honed in on her. "You think that he hasn't been at the very core of my decision?"

"He's young, he needs his mother."

Olivia nodded and sipped her coffee. "Exactly why I've decided to be his mother and not some chemotherapy patient. In another eighteen months he'll leave for college. That's not much time, I won't be an invalid and waste it. What good will it do him if I spend the entire time incapacitated? He'd feel like he had to drop everything in his life, make me the center of it." She put a hand on Ana's. "You know as well as I do, treating an illness like this is all-consuming, not just for me, but for everyone around me."

"You can't just ignore this illness. That won't make it go away!"

"Ana, *nothing* will make it go away. That's my point. I'm feeling good now. I may feel good for months and months. I don't want to deliberately make myself sicker. Don't you see?"

"No. I don't. If there's a chance that treatment could push this back into remission, I think you should try." She looked at Luke. "Tell her. Tell her what makes sense."

Luke licked his lips and leaned his elbows on the table. He ran his fingers down his coffee cup. Then he looked Analise in the eye. "I can't. It's Olivia's decision."

She felt like the air had been ripped from her lungs. "But you said you'd think about it overnight."

He nodded. "I did. And I didn't change my mind."

Analise slapped her palms against the table. "She's throwing her life away! What if it *did* cure her this time? What if in another year, they come up with a permanent cure? She has to try!"

"Ana. Ana. Don't yell at Luke about this. It's not his fault. And it's not his decision," Olivia said.

Analise stood so abruptly she jostled the table, sloshing coffee from all of their cups. "Then why did you drag him into this at all? He isn't family!"

"Because we need someone who isn't family to keep us from upsetting this boat. To help us talk it through."

Analise looked sharply at Luke. "Did you encourage this *decision*—when you knew and we didn't?"

Luke stood. "Ana—"

She interrupted, "Drive yourself to the work site today. I might need to leave." She grabbed her keys and walked out the door. She couldn't stay a second longer. She was too angry; she needed to punch the air, to scream at the top of her lungs. Which was just what she did when she was alone in the truck.

Cole waited in the school parking lot for Becca to get there. He kept himself hidden from Mrs. Baker's classroom window, just in case she looked out. Not that he cared if anyone knew he was skipping school. It didn't matter now.

Finally, he saw the old Volvo coming down the street. He sprinted to the curb and waved her down before she pulled into the lot. The second she stopped, he opened the passenger door and got in.

"Let's get out of here." He knew it was a long shot. He really couldn't imagine Becca Reynolds skipping school.

She looked at him for a long moment.

"Please," he said.

Without a word, she pulled out on the street and drove away from the school. When they'd gone a few blocks, she asked, "What's happened? You look terrible."

Cole scrubbed his hands over his face. The early morning sun stabbed at his eyes, his brain felt like it had been wrapped in fiberglass shavings and the lump in his throat suddenly made it impossible to talk.

"Cole?" There was genuine concern in her voice, which only made the lump in his throat worse.

She reached over and touched his shoulder. But she didn't ask any more questions. He looked out the passenger window and watched familiar sights pass by, feeling like he was disconnected from the world. When he realized where she was headed, he had to bite his lip to keep from crying.

A few minutes later Becca turned into the lane that led to the old plantation house. She parked her car in the same spot she had the last time they were here.

For a long time, they sat in silence. Cole was thankful

that she wasn't pushing him, badgering him like most girls would to find out what was going on.

Finally, he cleared his throat and said, "My mom's sick."

Becca made a sympathetic noise deep in her throat. "How sick?" she asked softly.

Suddenly he needed air or he was going to puke. He got out of the car and leaned against the passenger door, bracing his hands on his knees, breathing deeply.

He heard Becca's car door open and close, and her feet on the ground as she hurried around the car. When she reached him, she stood in front of him and put her hands on his shoulders.

He slid away from her touch, down the car until he was sitting on the ground with his knees bent. Putting his elbows on his legs, he ran his hand through his hair. Then he looked up at her. Her face was distorted by the tears in his eyes. "She's dying."

"Oh, Cole." She sat on the ground and put her arm around him. He leaned into her, and she took him in an embrace. Resting his head on her shoulder, he let himself cry.

Luke gave Analise all morning to cool her anger. He went about his work, watching her out of the corner of his eye as she assembled the fountain. She worked with a focused determination that seemed to be fueled by her frustration.

He wished there was something he could do or say to make her see his position. It wasn't a matter of taking sides, as she was making it. He'd already cost this family one member; he couldn't shoulder another death. Besides, he truly felt it was Olivia's decision.

Finally, just as noon approached, he walked over to Analise. "Time for lunch."

"I'm not hungry." She continued to bend copper tubing with a ferocity that bespoke her anger.

"Ana, you need to eat—and we need to talk."

She dropped the tubing with a clatter and stood to face him. Her hands were clenched at her sides and her eyes snapped with rage. "How could you? How could you do that to me?"

"What did I do *to you*?"

"The least you could have done was lend a little support. Olivia *needs* treatment!"

His patience slipped a notch. "Does she? Or do *you* just need her to go through whatever is necessary so you don't have to face being alone?"

Her sharp intake of breath told him he'd hit his mark. "That's not fair. Cole—"

"Do you really think Cole will be better off with a mother who lingers for months or even years, never fully herself? How is he to go on with his life? How is he supposed to leave for college, knowing his mother is hanging by a thread? Olivia made her choice—and I think she did it *for* Cole."

She shifted her weight and threw her hands in the air. She shouted, "You didn't have to support her in *not* getting treatment."

"I didn't. It's not my place to voice an opinion. I only supported her in the fact that it was her choice to make."

Ana braced her feet apart and leaned slightly forward. "So tell me. *If* you could *allow* yourself to voice an opinion—what would it be?"

"You mean what would I do if I were in her shoes?"

"No, what would you want if *your father* was in her shoes?"

"I hope I'd be able to support whatever choice he made.

All things considered, I think it would be the same choice that Olivia made."

She looked like he'd taken the last step in ultimate betrayal. "I see." She started walking toward her car.

"Where are you going?" he called after her.

"To see Dr. Creighton."

Since it was the lunch hour, Dr. Creighton had no patients. Analise knew from experience that the doctor didn't go out for lunch, but used the time to catch up on paperwork, eating takeout at his desk. When she entered the office, his receptionist wasn't at her station. Analise walked back into the treatment area and knocked on the doctor's private office.

"Yes?"

She opened the door to see him taking off his reading glasses and standing up.

"I'm sorry, Dr. Creighton, but I really need to talk to you."

He motioned her to a chair opposite the desk. "I expected you sooner."

Analise sat down and twisted her hands in her lap. "I would have been here sooner, but she just told me last night."

The doctor took his seat. "I see."

"I need you to tell me about her condition. I suppose you know she's decided not to have treatment."

Dr. Creighton folded his hands on his desk. "Of course, I can't discuss specifics of Olivia's case. But I'd be glad to answer any questions you have about the disease and its treatment possibilities."

"I'm her family." Analise couldn't keep an indignant edge from her voice.

"If Olivia were here with you to give her permission it would be different. Do you want to wait until we can all be together to discuss it?"

She wanted to stamp her feet and scream. "No. Tell me what you can."

"Of course, you know her history. It's very rare that we get a four-year remission with Stage III ovarian cancer, as her original diagnosis was. Even so, when there is recurrence, no matter how long the remission, it becomes a matter of staving off the illness, not curing it."

His voice left the cold facts behind and gentled slightly. "You know how poorly Olivia tolerated chemo last time. You were with her every step of the way."

Analise nodded, trying to block out the memory, telling herself that the end result was worth the misery. If Olivia had been as pigheaded last time as she was being now, she'd already be resting inside the iron fence at the old plantation. Four years. She'd gotten *four* years.

"With additional chemotherapy we see varying degrees of success—twenty to sixty percent will see some results. When there has been a longer period of remission, the chances are better we'll see some results with another round of chemo. Of course, the statistics include just an *arresting* of the progress of the disease for a short period as a response."

"You're making it sound hopeless."

He pursed his lips and shook his head. "No. Not hopeless. I'm telling you the realities—the statistics. Even in the twenty percent bracket, you never know who that twenty percent is going to be. So, no. Not hopeless."

"What about specialists? Should she see someone—not to discount your ability," she quickly added.

"I can tell you, I've had her case reviewed by the best.

The consensus is always the same. But, of course, she can go for additional opinions."

"So, if she accepts treatment, there is a chance that she could go into remission again."

"It's a possibility, although we don't see it often. More likely we buy time."

"What about new treatments? Isn't there something in the works, perhaps a clinical trial?"

"They're constantly working on new treatment. They just haven't hit on anything that gives the kind of results we'd all like to see. As for clinical trials, you'll have to discuss that with Olivia."

"She doesn't seem to be open to discussion at the moment." She stood, ready to go. Then she stopped and made herself ask the question she'd been too afraid to ask Olivia. "How long? How long will she have, if she doesn't get treatment?"

"Now we're getting into that privacy issue. I've told Olivia my educated guess." He smiled kindly as he stood and put his hands in his pants pockets. "I wish I could give you more to go on—but that would require a skill I don't have: sight into the future."

Once Cole got himself back under control, he took his time before he sat up. He wasn't sure he could look Becca in the face after crying all over her shoulder. But she kept a hand on the back of his neck, massaging lightly, and he looked into eyes that held no mockery, no condemnation.

She scooted around on her knees in front of him with her hands on the sides of his face. "I want you to tell me any-thing—anything you want. Whatever you say will stay here, in this place—your constant. I won't mention it again."

He wasn't sure he could say anything at all. His throat

felt like he'd been strangled. She must have sensed it, because her gentle fingers stroked his neck. Then she leaned close and said, "I want to help."

He wrapped his arms around her and pulled her into his lap, burying his face in her hair. But the tears were spent. He started to talk as he held her close; the words came easier when not looking at her. The things he was about to say, he'd never said to another person, not even Ana.

"I'm so scared. I don't want to be alone."

She tightened her arms around him. "I'm scared for you."

It was the most honest thing anyone had ever said to him. No, *It's going to be all right.* No, *We have to believe your mom can get well.* No, *Take one day at a time.* Becca didn't dance around the ugly facts. She came out and admitted it: He was facing something horrible. Instead of making him more frightened, it gave him strength.

"She was sick before, but the chemo worked. Now she says she won't take any more." His voice fell off to a whisper. "Why won't she try?"

"Maybe it's too hard," she whispered back. "Maybe it's just too hard."

And in that instant, he began to see how it must be for his mother. He knew she didn't *want* to die. His mother had more life in her than ten people rolled together. She didn't want to be sick—and the chemo did make her sick. He had only been twelve, but he remembered hearing her and Ana up all hours of the night as she vomited until she would be too weak to walk to the bathroom. Oh, she had always put on a smile for him, always directed their conversations away from her illness. But there was no doubt she had suffered.

For a long while, he sat there on the ground in front of the old mansion with Becca in his lap. She called this place his constant. He supposed it was. But what seemed a miracle to him was that there was another person who understood it. She seemed a part of his constant, too.

He kissed her neck, where the hair had parted to reveal skin. This seemed a much more intimate kiss than those they'd shared on the lips. She didn't pull away, as he feared. He felt her fingers slide into his hair.

When she leaned slightly away, her eyes had changed: They looked soft and inviting. As he looked into them, readying himself to kiss her again, he said, "I want this kiss to mean something. Just so you know, it *is* a big deal."

She smiled and bit her lower lip. She looked shy when she admitted, "They've *all* been a big deal to me."

As his lips met hers, he felt a whole new world open up. It was more than just wanting sex, which he'd been wanting for a long time, although he had not actually done the deed. He wanted a connection to *this* girl; he wanted to share everything with her.

Becca Reynolds. Miss Goody. Who would believe it?

On her way from Dr. Creighton's back to the park, Analise tussled with a decision. Doing what she knew she must was going to be painful, and there would be consequences for the business. But the business meant little when compared with Olivia's health.

Her chances of getting Olivia back into treatment were going to be a whole lot better without Luke constantly backing up her decision not to do it. And, Analise had to admit, she herself needed to focus on her family, not on what she should or should not be doing in the dark of night with Luke Boudreau. His presence tempted her into poor judgment. And that had to stop.

Her heart felt swollen in her chest. She knew the day was

coming for Luke to leave; it was inevitable. But now that she was faced with the reality, the thought of never seeing him again robbed her of her ability to draw a breath.

Nevertheless, she had to do what was best for her family. That was the cold truth. No sense in prolonging the torture. She had to act now, while her resolve was high.

When she pulled up to the job site, Luke was planting a grouping of azaleas on a mound that would serve as a backdrop for the fountain. He had his shirt off, damn him. There was no way she was going to do this while having to stare at his bare chest. She got out of the truck.

"Luke!" she called.

He looked up and wiped the sweat from his brow with his forearm. Way too sexy.

"Grab your shirt and come with me for a minute."

With a look of concern on his face, he did as she asked.

She didn't want to take him anywhere in the truck. She wanted to make a quick and clean break. So she stayed here; when she'd said her piece he could just climb in his car and leave. He could be packed up and long gone by the time she got home tonight—no chance for her to weaken and change her mind.

She walked toward the seclusion of the creek that ran though the park. By the time she'd begun to walk down the slope, he'd caught up with her.

"What's going on?" he asked immediately.

When she reached the water's edge, she turned to face him. She drew a breath. "I want you to leave."

"Seems to be a recurring theme around here."

She tilted her head in question.

"Cole said the same thing," he said.

She started to ask when, but decided not to let him get her off track. "Today. I want you to go today—now."

He raised a brow, but otherwise kept his emotions hidden. "We aren't going to be done with this job today."

"I know. I'll manage. With you here . . . I just can't take all of this extra tension right now. I need to focus on my family."

"The penalties—"

"Aren't your concern."

"Oh, we're back to that again, are we? Cole's not my concern. Olivia's not my concern. You're not my concern."

"That's right." She hardened her voice and her resolve.

"Well, I've got news for you. Sending me away won't stop my concern. I care about you!" He reached for her, but she stepped away.

She looked away from the hurt in his eyes. "Luke, there never was a future for us. We had stolen time. I can never *really* be with you."

"I know you're concerned about what Olivia thinks—"

"No. It's much more complicated than that."

When he just stood there staring at her, she was forced to tell him the truth. She steeled herself and said, "I can't be with you. You came because Calvin died—"

He started to say something, but she cut him off. "For years I've had a horrible, horrible thought: it would just be so much easier if Calvin never came home. Then I could have this family free and clear. So you see, we—you and I—can never be."

She was shaking, and her breath threatened to fail her, but she had to make him see. He thought she was a good woman, a wronged wife. But she was a terrible person. "I wished Calvin dead!" Her heart raced and her mouth went dry. She could hardly believe she'd finally said it out loud.

He put a hand on her. She jerked away. "Don't! You're here because of that death. Every time we make love, I compare my feelings for you against those I had for

Calvin. And God help me, what I feel for you is far deeper. It's as if I wished him away, and that wish brought you to me—I traded his life for my happiness. I can't spend the rest of my life like that." She paused and looked away. "Please, just go."

He stood there for a long moment, then said, "Look at me."

She forced herself to look him in the eye. He was angry. He saw the true woman she was. She nearly wavered, nearly begged his forgiveness. But it was better this way. Now he would leave and never want to come back. Cole needed his mother—at least for a few more years. And if she could give him those years, she'd do it.

"Ana—"

She couldn't read his eyes. She saw anger, but there was more, something else that she couldn't define. And she realized she shouldn't let herself try. "Just go."

Then he took a half-step away and said, "Just to clear your conscience, your wish didn't kill Calvin." His face looked stony. "I did."

She stood blinking, her mind in complete upheaval, as he turned around and walked back up the hill and disappeared from view. She wanted to race after him, demand he explain. But she'd achieved her goal; he was leaving. She couldn't risk talking to him anymore.

"I just can't understand why he would leave like this," Olivia said as she sat with Analise as she ate dinner. Olivia and Cole had eaten at the regular dinner hour, but Analise had worked in the park until it had grown too dark to see. "He came up with some cock-and-bull story about a family emergency. A little hard to argue with that."

Ana's head was splitting. All afternoon Luke's words had clashed and clanged around in her mind. What in the hell did he mean, he killed Calvin? The scene from the movie *Platoon,* in which Tom Berenger shot fellow soldier Willem Dafoe in the back while on a mission in a Vietnam jungle kept playing in her mind. Of course, that couldn't be what Luke had meant. Calvin died in a helicopter accident. Had Luke somehow caused the crash? She wanted to stop thinking of it, but the questions just kept popping like water splattered into hot oil.

She didn't try to discount Olivia's assessment that Luke's excuse was fabricated; that would be too obvious. Liv could always see through lies. If she even so much as suspected Analise had sent him away so she could try to get her into treatment, that would be the end of any possibility. So Ana simply said, "We really imposed on him too long, Liv. He has a life, too, you know."

She waved a hand in the air. "Yes. Yes. But this was so . . . sudden. How are we going to make that deadline now?"

Analise rubbed her temples. "We'll manage. I've asked Cole to recruit anyone from school that wants to earn some extra bucks for this weekend."

"But Cole has a soccer tournament on Saturday."

"I know. But *all* of his friends don't play soccer."

"I'll come and help."

"You need to go to the soccer game; it's especially important to Cole now. Maybe Reverend Hammond can watch the shop for you during the game, that way I can stay on the job site."

"I'm sure Richard will be glad to help for a couple of hours."

"You'll call him, then?" Analise got up from the table and put her dishes in the dishwasher.

"Yes. Tomorrow."

Analise walked behind the chair in which Olivia sat and wrapped her arms around her. "I love you, Liv."

Olivia patted her arm. "I know, Ana. It's been you and me for a long time."

"How are you feeling?" Analise felt Olivia stiffen slightly at the question, as if bracing herself for another round of argument.

"I really feel good. I'm sure the steroids are helping—I might even take up weight lifting."

Analise kissed the top of her head and straightened up. "Let's not get carried away. I don't want you looking like one of those female bodybuilders."

Olivia didn't turn around, but bent her arms in a typical muscle-flexing pose. "Don't think I've got it?"

Chuckling, glad to reopen the lines of communication with their old casual humor, Analise said, "Oh, I think you've got it. I just don't want you hitting the road, doing the competition circuit. Who would make lunch around here?"

Then she headed out of the kitchen. "I've got to get a shower. I don't know how you've stood to be near me."

Olivia's voice followed her into the hall. "You don't smell any worse than Rufus."

"Oh, thanks."

Tomorrow would be soon enough to begin her campaign for treatment. Both she and Olivia needed some time to get their feet back under them. Then she'd make Olivia see.

Analise managed to ignore the cold hole that had developed in the center of her chest until she got into bed. Then she curled on her side and mourned the loss of a man she'd tricked herself into thinking she knew. His parting words had knocked the breath out of her. Had she been as wrong about Luke as she'd been about Calvin? No matter how she played the different possibilities in her mind, she could not make Luke a killer. What in God's name had happened?

•   •   •

Luke didn't for a second think that Olivia believed his story about a family emergency in Indiana. But it really didn't matter. He was out of their lives one way or the other—the excuse was inconsequential. He'd left a note for Cole in the boy's room; he didn't want to just sneak off without a word, especially since they'd not been on very good terms of late.

He'd considered leaving Ana a note, too. But there was really nothing left to say. Obviously she would never be able to see him without tangling her feelings for him with those she had for Calvin—both the good and the bad. He really hoped that someday she would find someone to love, who could love her back in the way she deserved, someone who didn't dredge up miscast wishes and regret.

He'd been very tempted to sit Olivia down and unload the whole truth. She deserved to know her son died risking his life to save another—not in some act of mischance, a mechanical failure that caused his helicopter to crash. Calvin was a hero. Olivia should know. She should know he'd earned the same Purple Heart as his father, even though politics prevented him from receiving it.

In the end, he'd chickened out. To admit the entire story to her now would make his time here a lie. And he could easily see, lies were a near-mortal sin to Olivia. He just couldn't face the look in her eye when he admitted the truth of Calvin's death—but even worse, the fact that he'd stayed, living a lie, here at Magnolia Mile.

On his way out of town, he stopped at the Pure station for gas. After he filled the tank, he went inside to pay. Opal, Olivia's distant cousin, was at her regular post.

"Hello, young man," she said as she smiled around the cigarette hanging out of her mouth.

"This is good-bye, Opal. I'm heading out of town."

She cocked her head, looking like a hamster Luke had when he was six, all big eyes and innocence. "Say it ain't so. We were just getting used to seeing you around here."

He nodded. "Family emergency."

"So you'll be coming back, then?" The tone in her voice sounded as if she really wanted him to, that she wasn't just saying it to be polite. "We need more young men like you in this town. So many just don't come back after college. Guess we're just too boring for young folk."

"No, don't imagine I'll be back." Before she could ask any more questions, he said, "Do you have a phone book back there? I need to look something up."

"Sure." She reached under the counter and handed the book over. Then she rang up his sale. "Here's a scrap of paper if you need to make a note." She shoved a strip of blank register tape his way.

He scribbled down the number and closed the book. "Thanks." After paying for his gas, he nodded and said, "You take care, now."

As he walked out the door, she called, "You do the same." It hit him then, how much at home he'd begun to feel in this town. He was going to miss it.

You have your own town to go to, Analise's voice said in his head.

Yep, he did. But what if he couldn't find a place to fit there, either? He just couldn't bring himself to face another disappointment right now. Instead of heading north out of town, Luke took the highway west.

Cole slipped into the house unnoticed by his mother, who was working in the carriage house. He knew he needed to talk to her, but he just wanted a little time alone first. He went into his room and closed the door. For some reason, the room looked different to him—his trophies less significant, his soccer photos less important. Reaching inside his closet, he pulled out an old framed photo of his whole family, taken during those few months when it *had* been whole, and set it on his dresser. It was the first Christmas that Ana had lived with them. He stared at it for a long time. He'd only been eight years old.

Soon, there would be nothing left of that family. Nothing but photos and memories. Just like all of the Lejeunes had vanished from the plantation, there wouldn't be anyone left at this Magnolia Mile, either. It was too sad, too frightening, to consider. But the panic that had been clawing the inside of his chest had subsided. Now there was just a cold lump of fear.

As he stared at the photo, he backed up and sat down on his bed. That's when he noticed the folded sheet of paper on his pillow. He picked it up. Pandora jumped on the bed beside him, unlike her usual sneaky self, and curled up against his thigh.

Dear Cole,

I didn't want to leave without letting you know that your brother was one of the bravest men I ever served with. I know it's hard to face the uncertainty of the future without him. But you have Ana. Trust that she'll always be there for you. This family, you and your mother, mean the world to her. Nothing will make her leave you—so you might as well straighten up and stop trying to drive those who love you away with your reckless beheavior.

I bet you didn't realize I knew what you were up to—maybe you didn't even know. But I remember being a teenager, with frustrations and the fear. My mother left our family when I was ten. It never stops hurting, but, in time, it does stop bleeding.

I know you'll step up and take over the reins as the man of this family, because I've seen the same courage in you that I saw in your brother.

You are facing difficult days ahead, and I'll be thinking of all of you here at Magnolia Mile often.

Luke

For a long moment, Cole just sat there staring at the letter. He'd been furious with Luke, feeling that he'd not only betrayed his friendship, but Calvin's, by kissing Calvin's wife. Now he felt a pinch of regret. He'd acted like a baby, not thinking about how things were for Ana. Things change—the photo on his dresser told him that very clearly.

Now Luke was gone—and it was too late to do anything about it.

He promised himself he would not be making such selfish mistakes again.

Chapter 22

Three months. *Jesus Christ*. Luke ran his hands through his hair and bit back a growl of frustration.

For three months he'd made his biweekly call to Reverend Hammond, checking on Olivia. Things had been going along pretty well, some fatigue, manageable pain. She'd been working in the shop nearly every day and had been steadily making arrangements for her own passing. The very thought of planning your own funeral made Luke's stomach knot. How could someone as full of life as Olivia deal with impending death?

But now, as summer began to close its suffocating fist around the South, Reverend Hammond had called *him*. And the news wasn't good. How could Olivia's health decline so quickly? Luke could understand it if he'd been getting his updates from Olivia, who would have painted a pleasant picture, keeping the grim realities to herself. But he was relying on Reverend Hammond, who seemed to love Olivia as much as anyone did.

On the spring day that Luke had driven away from Magnolia Mile, he'd only gone as far as Memphis. He'd not been able to make himself put more distance between him and Calvin's family. He couldn't explain why he'd remained here tending bar on Beale Street, but the very thought of driving farther away was unbearable. At least bartending passed the nights; he didn't like to sleep when it was dark anymore.

He knew, if he was going to tend bar anywhere, he should have been in Indiana helping his father. But Luke had justified his decision. He didn't want to tend bar for the rest of his life, and if he started working with his dad, there would be no way to stop. Now, as he looked deep inside, he saw it for the convenient excuse it was. His father would never ask more of Luke than he wanted to give. It was the proximity to Magnolia Mile that kept his feet firmly on southern soil.

When he examined his motivation carefully, he thought it must be a masochistic streak that kept him here. The nightmares had revived themselves with a vengeance since he'd left Grover. Expanding far beyond the moment of Calvin's death, to include horrors befalling his family. Perhaps if Luke had traveled on home, put more distance between him and Magnolia Mile, if he had begun to fill his life with his own family, the nightmares would have begun to recede.

That thought froze him in midmotion as he paced his rented room, brutally clenching his cell phone as if it had been responsible for the bad news it had just delivered. He knew, until he told Olivia the truth and admitted his weakness, his duplicity, and told her of her son's heroic death, the dreams would haunt him relentlessly—no matter where he laid his head to sleep.

A matter of days. Reverend Hammond had said Olivia only had a matter of days.

It was now or never.

He quickly made a few calls to arrange being away from work. Then he stuffed his belongings into a duffel and was on the road in less than an hour.

Two hours later he was standing in the hall outside Olivia's hospital room. He'd waited until he saw Analise and Cole leave the hospital for dinner—Reverend Hammond had told Luke that he always held the bedside vigil from six to six forty-five to give the family a break.

As he stood there, gathering his courage, he realized the minutes were quickly ticking past. He knocked lightly on the partially closed door. The reverend came and opened it fully, letting him in. Then the pastor slipped quietly out.

Luke's stomach flipped upside down. He didn't know what he'd expected. A bright smile and cheerful conversation? No, he'd not been that naïve, yet seeing Olivia so . . . lifeless . . . stole his breath away.

Her eyes fluttered open, the spark of life clearly still glowing there.

She licked her dry lips. "Luke . . ." It was less than a raspy whisper, but she smiled. Then she pointed to the cup of water on her table.

He stepped closer and held the glass for her while she took a sip from the straw.

"These damn drugs, make me dry as an old onion skin." Her voice was a little stronger after the water. "I knew you'd come back." She lifted her hand and he took it, settling his elbow on the bed and sitting in the bedside chair. Her fingers were cool, too cool.

"Don't try to talk. Rest."

She sputtered. "People have been trying to shut me up for years." She grinned and he could see the spunk was still in there, beneath the pale skin and weakened body. "Pretty soon they'll have their wish. I'll have plenty of time to rest—later." Looking him in the eye, she said, "You have something to tell me."

Her gaze pierced straight to his heart. He nodded and realized that she knew—she'd always known.

She said, "I saw it in your eyes that first day." She took a shallow quivering breath and Luke wanted to caution her not to use up her strength. But he knew Olivia well enough to know that would do nothing but make her waste her breath arguing about it. "You have . . . a burden."

He swallowed. "Calvin didn't die in a helicopter crash." He couldn't see the harm to national security by telling a dying woman that her son was a hero. He could do it without giving away any of the details. Not that it mattered—Olivia wasn't going to get out of this room until her last breath had been drawn.

Closing her eyes for the briefest of moments, she nodded once. "I know."

"It was a very politically volatile mission—one of those that no one ever mentions again. I was ranking officer on the team. It was my responsibility to get everyone out safely. Our objective was to retrieve a *package*—a hostage."

As Luke closed his eyes and held her hand tightly, the whole thing came crashing over him again. The darkness of that night covered him like a suffocating blanket. He could taste the blood in his mouth, smell the gunpowder, hear the chaos on the ground that was nearly drowned out by the helicopter waiting to lift off.

For the ten-thousandth time, Luke relived the events of that night: They'd been dropped a safe distance from the target, during a dark phase of the moon. Luke and his three soldiers moved without detection to the rural building where the hostage was being held. Neither Luke nor his men knew the identity of the top-secret captive—they'd been given a photo and a description. This person had been deemed essential to national security. That was all his team needed to know in order to perform their task.

Luke signaled two of his men to circle around and approach the entrance from the other side. The building was a small single-story structure. The hostage was being held in the basement "interrogation room." Luke checked his watch. Right on schedule.

They moved cautiously forward. Luke silently dispatched the single guard on duty on the first floor of the building. There was no other resistance. The hostage was right where their directive said he would be, held only by a locked door and a pair of handcuffs. Neither presented an unanticipated problem. The man was in his thirties, probably had been physically fit when he'd been brought here. Now he was weak. He leaned heavily on Luke as they hurried up the stairs and back out into the night.

A surprisingly clean recovery.

They signaled for the chopper.

It moved in quickly. Just as it was hovering close to the ground, with its ghost ship remaining a safe distance above, the four soldiers and their recovered hostage broke cover and ran across the wide courtyard. Calvin was three steps ahead, Luke following with the hostage, and two other team members bringing up the rear.

That's when it let loose.

Luckily his team was well trained and quickly returned fire. The ghost ship took immediate action, releasing an ear-splitting round of fire, driving the enemy back into cover.

Calvin leapt into the chopper. Then he reached out and pulled in the hostage. Luke could hear the men behind him firing as he shoved the man from the rear. Within two seconds, all five were inside the chopper and it was starting to lift off.

The ghost ship continued protective fire.

They'd made it. Mission complete.

Suddenly a teenage boy ran out of the darkness, flailing his arms, screaming for them to wait.

The hostage they'd just rescued grabbed Luke's arm and shouted, "He's with me. He's dead if you leave him!"

Luke had a millisecond to make a decision. They had completed their mission—retrieved the package. Once that was done, it was time to get the hell out.

The pilot looked back at him. All he had to do was give the signal and they were gone.

The hostage scrabbled on his hands and knees, trying to get back out the door. Calvin knocked him flat on the floor of the craft.

Luke looked at the boy. He was close.

Luke jumped out, waving the kid forward.

Just thirty feet from the chopper, the boy fell to the ground, shot in the leg. He continued to try to pull himself along.

"No one leave this craft!" Luke shouted, then sprinted for the boy.

Bullets continued to streak through the air, strike the ground, splinter into trees. Just as he reached the boy, he felt a hot poker against his neck. He'd been hit, but was still moving. He grabbed the back of the kid's shirt and started to drag him along.

Three strides later, his knee was shot out from under him and he spun to the ground.

Rolling on his back, he fought the pain and signaled for the chopper to take off—leave them.

The kid on the ground next to him was screaming.

Then suddenly Calvin was there, firing like a madman. The other two soldiers grabbed Luke and the boy, dragging them to the chopper.

From the corner of his eye, Luke saw the boy's body jerk with the impact of several bullets. He stopped screaming.

Luke was shoved into the chopper.

Calvin was fifteen feet behind them, still firing. He was backing toward the chopper when a grenade hit near his feet.

The concussion knocked Luke flat on the floor and the two other soldiers off their feet. Almost before the debris stopped falling, his two uninjured men were moving toward Calvin, abandoning the dead kid's body.

They scrambled to pick up what was left of Calvin Abbott.

Luke finished telling his cleaned-up version of the event to Olivia, trembling as he spoke. "I broke protocol. The kid died anyway. I killed Calvin—and could very easily have cost the entire mission."

He didn't realize he was crying until Olivia took the back of her hand to wipe his tears. "Luke, the only thing you did was to be human. You wanted to save that boy."

Drawing in a shuddering breath, he said, "I'm a soldier. I had orders. It was not *my* choice to make." Then he added, "I should have been the one to die."

"I would say that I forgive you"—she took a breath that said she was rapidly tiring—"but there's nothing to forgive."

"But I came to your family—"

"And I thank God every day for that." She couldn't muster much volume, but there was plenty of force behind her words.

Luke grasped her hand in both of his and laid his forehead against it. His shoulders shook as he cried. It was as if a dark part of him left his body with those tears. He'd held them for so long, let them poison his soul. Maybe now he'd find some peace.

He was grateful that Olivia didn't say more, allowing him privacy in her company.

A gentle knock sounded at the door. Reverend Hammond returned and said, "I just noticed Analise pulling into the parking lot."

Luke drew in a breath and straightened up. He kept Olivia's hand in one of his and wiped his face with the back of the other. "You are an incredible woman."

She pulled his hand close, pressing it against her cheek. "You're a good man. I see it in all you've done for us. Calvin defied your order. The choice was his. I have a feeling if he had known the outcome he'd still have done the same thing."

Luke clenched his teeth together to keep his chin from quivering. There was so much he wanted to say, but no words would come.

Olivia said, softly, "I wish . . . Ana . . ." Fatigue was taking its toll. Her words were barely audible as she finished, ". . . could find . . . peace. Talk . . . to . . . her . . ."

Her eyes closed. After a moment, Luke laid her hand on the bed beside her. Then he kissed her on the forehead and left the room.

He took the stairs instead of the elevator to the first floor. He simply wasn't strong enough to see Analise right now.

The lights had been dimmed in the hospital's corridors. The night staff sat bathed in a tiny island of light at the nurses' station. Somewhere down the hall, a television droned quietly. There was the soft squeak of rubber soles on the tile floor as a nurse made her rounds. What must it be like, to come into this atmosphere every night as your employment rather than to face a deathbed vigil? Would the low lights and quiet halls bring a sense of calm instead of the gut-clenching fear that death would sneak in during the night and steal away a loved one?

Analise shifted in the recliner, adjusting her pillow and pulling the blanket over her shoulders. Cole hadn't wanted to go home. She couldn't blame him. That huge empty house echoing memories all night long would be enough to keep anyone unsettled and awake. Right now he was sleeping down the hall in an unoccupied room—which was probably against hospital regulations, but that was the great thing about a small hospital like this, the bureaucracy hadn't yet squeezed all humanity out of it.

Today they'd made a pact, she and Cole: Either they both stayed, or they both went home. There was a certain comfort in knowing that no matter what, you wouldn't be alone— either they'd both see Olivia out of this world, or they'd both bear the guilt of being somewhere else when it happened.

It seemed horrible, sitting around waiting for someone to die. But more horrible was the prospect that Olivia would meet her end alone, without the loving presence of her family to steady her soul. So they stayed.

Shortly after she'd made certain that Olivia was resting comfortably and that Cole had finally fallen to exhaustion in the other room, Analise had stretched out in the recliner. It had quickly become apparent, it didn't matter if she was here or at home, tonight sleep was going to be impossible. It wasn't that she feared Olivia would suddenly stop breathing; there was something else, something vague and nameless, bothering Analise. She tried not to fidget and make noise; Olivia seemed to be resting more comfortably than she had for a week.

She glanced at her watch. Three A.M. The darkness

seemed to drag on the hands of the clock, making minutes stretch far beyond what was natural.

Olivia began to stir. Analise waited to see if she would settle back into sleep, as she had done many times over the course of the night.

Olivia's eyes opened. She looked around the room for a second, as if she didn't remember where she was.

Then she looked at Analise and frowned. "You should be home in bed."

"I want to be here."

"I promise not to sneak out in the night. I'm ready, I'll face it headlong in the light of day."

Analise got up and moved to the chair next to the bed. "I don't doubt that for one minute. You've never backed away from anything." She adjusted Olivia's sheets. "Do you need anything?" Looking at the IV monitor, she said, "You can give yourself another dose of pain medication if you need it."

Olivia shook her head. "I want to talk with a clear head for a few minutes. It seems like there's always someone else. . . ." She pointed to her glass and Ana gave her a drink. "Better, thanks. I should have said this to you months ago—"

"Liv . . ."

"Don't make me waste my breath arguing with you, just listen."

Analise bit her lip and nodded for Olivia to continue.

"When Luke first came to us . . . and I told you not to do something you'd regret . . . I knew you misunderstood me. But I let it be."

A cascade of cold pricks ran down Analise's body.

Olivia shook her head slightly. "Your marriage to Calvin was difficult . . . a disappointment for you. I knew that."

Analise wanted to make her stop. "Liv—"

Olivia held up a pale hand. "Listen. I need you to listen." She took a shuddering breath. "I know the shortcomings in my son. It was selfish of me not to have admitted it to you years ago, released you from this family, let you find a real marriage, the married life you deserve, with someone else. But I didn't want you to leave—I love you like my own child."

Hot tears burned their way down Analise's face. She put a hand on Olivia's cheek. "I have the life I want. I chose it."

"You deserve a good husband."

Around the lump in her throat, Analise said, "Calvin wasn't a good husband—but I wasn't a good wife, either."

Olivia gave a dismissive wave of the hand. "Don't make the same mistake again. That's what I meant when I said not to do something you'll regret. You need to be sure of the man, of your feelings. Luke's a good man. I saw that right away. But I wanted *you* to see it. Maybe I should have taken a different avenue. . . ."

Analise whispered, "I sent him away."

Olivia's brow creased in question.

"I was so afraid," Analise said. "I wanted you to get treatment . . . Cole was angry . . . I couldn't deal with Luke, too. I didn't want to love him. Oh, Liv, I *can't* love him."

Much to Analise's surprise, Olivia chuckled; it was a dry, papery sound, so unlike Olivia. "Why?"

"Luke only came because Calvin died. If I love him, it's *because* Calvin died . . . don't you see?"

"Ana, it isn't as if you chose which one of them would live. Stop acting so foolish."

A little sob caught in Analise's throat. "You don't understand. I was too cowardly to step out on my own, leave this family. F-for a long time, I wished Calvin just . . . just wouldn't come home. And then, he didn't. . . ."

"And you think your wish killed Calvin?"

Covering her face in shame, Analise cried.

"Good Lord, if your wishes are so powerful, I should have had you wishing for me to win the lottery." She laid a hand on Analise's bowed head. "I think maybe you've over-estimated your powers."

Analise raised her face. "Can't you see? If I love Luke, it's like saying I'm glad Calvin is gone."

"I lost two husbands. The only reason I had the second one was because the first died. That didn't mean I was glad that Jimmy didn't come home from the war. You see, it doesn't matter who the next love is—they're always there because the first one is gone. Life takes people away from us. We have to live on. It's all right to love again. That's what keeps us alive."

Analise took Olivia's hand into hers and pressed a kiss on her fingers. "I appreciate what you've said." Her voice dropped to a hoarse whisper. "But it doesn't matter now, he's gone."

"No," Olivia whispered back, with the faintest of smiles on her lips.

Analise's gaze locked with hers. Hope and fear fought for control, creating a tangle of emotion in her throat that held her silent.

"He was here, tonight. Between the two of you, I swear you have enough guilt to sink an entire continent." She squeezed Analise's hand. "I think both you and Luke have let Calvin stand between you long enough."

After a moment, Olivia continued, "You need to talk to him." When Analise didn't immediately agree, Olivia said, "Think about it."

Analise nodded and laid her head on the bed. She fell asleep with Olivia's hand stroking her hair.

• • •

In the morning, Olivia slept quietly. Analise was left alone with her thoughts. Olivia forgave her. Even on her own deathbed, Olivia had found the grace to think of someone else.

Could Analise forgive herself? Could she ever look at Luke, accept what was in her heart and not feel the burden of guilt?

She stood before the hospital room window and closed her eyes. She wanted to. God, she wanted to.

Two days later, with Cole and Analise at her bedside and Richard Hammond saying a quiet prayer, Olivia slipped quietly away in her sleep. As she had promised, she left this world at ten in the morning, under a blazing summer sun.

It seemed odd, leaving the hospital in the middle of the day. How quickly life waiting for death had formed a routine. Now that hateful routine was broken. It left a mingling of relief and unbearable sadness that sat on the soul like a cold stone. Analise put her arm around Cole as they approached the double glass doors for the last time.

The heat hit her with a physical force as she stepped outside, making her realize just how exhausted she was. Neither she nor Cole had left the hospital in the past thirty-six hours.

The heat rose in waves off the pavement. She had to pause and look for her Explorer, as she'd forgotten exactly where she'd parked it last. As she squinted against the bright sun, she saw him, leaning against the rear gate of her car with his arms crossed over his chest.

Luke saw her at the same moment and stood, letting his arms fall to his sides. He didn't move forward, but stood waiting, as if giving her the opportunity to come to him, or turn around and walk away.

Cole said quietly, "He's back." His voice held relief, not anger.

Olivia's words had been replaying in her mind for two days. Analise still feared trusting her own feelings. This time if she was wrong, Cole would suffer, too. Still, she took Cole's hand and stepped forward, not away.

When they reached Luke, she saw he had tears in his eyes. After the briefest hesitation, he enfolded both her and Cole in his arms and drew them to his chest. She felt his tears fall on her head and heard Cole sob against his shoulder.

In a bit, when Cole's sobs quieted, they broke apart. Luke kept his hand on Cole's shoulder.

"How did you know?" she asked.

Luke said, "Reverend Hammond and I keep in touch."

In that second, she saw the true man Luke was. She'd cast him out of their lives, but he cared enough to make sure he knew of Olivia's condition. And he'd done it in a way that respected her wishes.

Looking in his eyes, she said, "Liv wants us to talk. Let's go home."

It was nearly ten o'clock that evening when the casseroles and cakes stopped arriving at Magnolia Mile. With each food offering came warm remembrances and heartfelt condolences. Analise thought it almost as exhausting as the past days at the hospital.

Now Becca Reynolds and Luke were the only two people left. Cole and Becca sat on the living room sofa, holding hands and talking softly. Analise suggested to Luke they go out on the porch for a while.

They sat next to one another on the wicker swing. Analise sighed and rotated her neck, trying to get some of the kinks out of her shoulders. She welcomed the comfort when Luke started to massage the stiff muscles there.

"Have you been in Indiana?" she finally asked.

"No. Memphis."

Her gaze snapped to his face. "Why Memphis?"

He lifted a shoulder. "Indiana was too far away from this place—from you."

In the past days, Analise's sense of security had taken a hard blow. Olivia had been her mainstay. But with a few simple words, Luke began to mend the tatters of the fabric that held her life together.

He asked, "How's Cole been? Any more signs of trouble?"

Shaking her head, she said, "Since Olivia's illness, he seems to have been focused on us, on doing whatever he can to help. Just the opposite of what I'd feared."

"Probably a good thing I was gone, then. He knew it was his responsibility to be the man around here—and he did it."

Analise drew a deep breath and forged into the conversation she'd been both dreading and anticipating. "I sent you away because I was afraid."

He nodded and his hand stilled on her shoulder.

She went on, "I hid behind Olivia's illness. Of course I wanted her to fight, to live. And for a couple of days I actually had myself convinced that I could change her mind if I got you out of here." She paused. "But there was more, and I didn't really see it until Olivia opened my eyes a couple of days ago.

"All of the time I was growing up, Grandmother made every decision for me. I always hated it, but I let her do it. Then, when I met Calvin, I made the first major decision of my life—and I screwed it up. I justified it with the fact that I got Olivia and Cole in the bargain. But that was wrong. I didn't even know Olivia when I married Calvin. What if there had been no consolation? What if I'd alienated myself from my only family and found myself totally alone? I— I've been afraid to trust myself since. When you came . . . there were so many reasons why we *shouldn't* be together . . . I still feel like I'm cheating on Calvin."

"I've had a bad case of what-ifs, too." He pulled her close against his side. "A decision I made cost Calvin his life. It's wrong for me to benefit from that by loving you." He paused. "But I do—love you."

Analise wanted to ask about that decision, but she realized if Luke could give her the details, he would have done so willingly. Instead, she tipped her chin up to look in his face. "I love you, too. Is it enough?"

"It's everything." When his lips touched hers, she realized he was right. Love was all that holds a person together.

They buried Olivia Helms Abbott Lejeune in the Lejeune family cemetery on Magnolia Mile on a blistering July afternoon. The church had been filled to capacity for her funeral service. Only those closest to her accompanied her on this final journey home. Granny Lejeune's wheelchair prevented her from making the trip to the cemetery. She said she'd be seeing it soon enough herself and went to wait at the house with Mr. and Mrs. Baker.

Dave Dunston offered to lead the procession with his cruiser. Analise hadn't talked to him since that night he walked away from Magnolia Mile. She knew he'd been to the hospital to see Olivia, the staff had told her, but he'd had the decency to do it when Analise wasn't there. She accepted his offer as his apology for his outrageous behavior during the spring.

The hearse followed his patrol car into the lane that

Analise, Cole, Becca and Luke had spent the day before clearing.

There wasn't a breath of air moving as the group gathered within the old iron fence. Analise was thankful for the shade of the ancient trees. Reverend Hammond stood at the head of the grave and gave his last words of condolence and his last gift of prayer to Olivia's spirit. Analise and Cole stood side by side, final quiet tears of good-bye on their faces. Ana felt Luke's strong presence as he stood just behind her and Cole, respectful of the fact that he wasn't actually family.

The reverend concluded the service with a final benediction. One by one, people left on the path that led back to the lane. After a few minutes, the only people left were Ana, Cole, Luke and Becca. Luke and Becca remained a step back, allowing Ana and Cole a moment alone.

When they finally turned from the grave, Cole stepped into Becca's embrace. She held him tightly for a long moment, then Cole turned to Analise and said, "I want to walk up to the old house for a minute."

Analise slipped her hand into Luke's and said, "All right. We'll be along in a bit."

After Cole and Becca left, Ana went to the large rose blanket that covered the casket. She removed a single rose, took Luke by the hand and stood by Calvin's grave. Laying the rose on the stone, she said, "I'm sorry we messed it up. I hope to have learned from our mistakes."

Luke squeezed her hand and they stood in silence, listening to the hum of nature all around them. There was a noise off to the right, on the far side of the cemetery plot. Luke and Analise both looked up at the same time. There, just at the edge of the clearing, stood Jocko, his proud antlers held high, his nose lifted to sniff the air.

"Amazing." The word was no more than a rush of breath from Luke's lips.

Analise whispered, "Olivia would be pleased."

Cole held Becca's hand as they stood in front of the old house. "My constant," he whispered. Then he turned to face her. Touching her cheek, he said, "Thank you."

She smiled. "You always knew. I just gave it a name."

"You've given me more than that. I don't know—"

She put a finger on his lips to silence him. Then she kissed him. It was a sweet kiss that said they were more than just dating, they were friends. God knew, he needed a friend. His buddies were all at the funeral, but it was Becca he needed to be close to, for she understood the quiet things— like having a constant.

They took a slow walk around the house, hand in hand. She asked, "Do you want to rebuild it? Someday, I mean."

"I don't know. There's a lot of land here. I've been thinking of something—but I have to talk to Ana about it."

Just then they came back to the front of the house. Analise and Luke were standing right where Becca and Cole had stood a few minutes ago, looking up at the front door.

Cole stopped beside them.

Analise sighed. "It seems so sad, so wasteful to just let it fall down."

Luke said, "It does. But it's pretty far gone."

Cole cleared his throat. "I've been thinking. There are over a hundred acres here. Would it be possible to donate a couple of acres to the animal shelter? Mom loved animals, and the shelter is having trouble. This way they'd have a permanent place. Maybe they'd even name it after Mom."

Analise could hardly find her voice, she was so stunned that Cole would be thinking of something so . . . giving . . .

at a time like this. "Um, maybe. They'll need a lot more than just the land, though."

Becca said, "We could maybe do some fund-raising—in Mrs. Lejeune's name—and see if we can get some volunteers."

Cole's eyes sparked with purpose. Analise realized something like this could be exactly what he needed, something positive, something outside himself, to focus on.

She smiled. "I think we just about used up our volunteer begging when we finished the park project."

Luke looked down at her. "I wondered how you were going to manage."

"It wasn't me, really. Richard put out a call, and in one weekend I had fifteen laborers. We finished on time."

"I guess you didn't need me."

"It was an emergency; I doubt I could run a business that way."

Cole said, "Yeah, but this is different. Lots of people care about animals. You don't have to be able to dig a hole or push a wheelbarrow to help with this—we could get kids, old ladies—"

"We can check into it."

"Good," Cole said. "I'm going to ride back to the house with Becca." Then he paused. "Is that okay?"

"Sure. We'll be right along." Once the kids were out of sight, she said to Luke, "Before we go back and deal with that house full of people, I need to ask you something."

He turned to face her, his face all seriousness and worry. "All right—as long as you're not going to ask me to leave again."

She smiled even though she had a thousand butterflies taking flight in her stomach. She took his hands in hers. "I know you have a family in Indiana who want you home. But

I want you to stay—with me. I'll even let you have your old job back."

"Cole? How's he going to feel about that?"

"We'll just have to deal with it as it comes. He's beginning to grow up. I can't make every decision based upon how happy it'll make Cole. Whether he knows it or not, you're good for him. Olivia saw that right away—I was the one . . ."

Things were getting all balled up, this wasn't the way she'd planned on this conversation going. She steered it back to the heart of the matter. "I'm not asking you to marry me—yet." Her heart leapt when he grinned at her. "We all need some time to adjust. But I want to try and make this work."

"I accept." He pulled her into his arms and kissed her until her toes tingled. "The job *and* the proposal."

She jerked away, startled. "I said I wasn't—"

"Too late. We're getting married. We don't have to tell anyone until you're ready—but it's gonna happen, baby."

Ten months later, on the same weekend as the groundbreaking of the Olivia Lejeune Animal Shelter, Analise stood under a newly completed metal archway on the lawn of Magnolia Mile, where Reverend Hammond joined her life to Luke's. Def Leppard played in the background. Cole served as the best man, and a freshly bathed Rufus as Analise's maid of honor. Luckily Rufus didn't know anything about weddings and his masculinity wasn't in the least offended.

About the Author

Hoosier native, Susan Crandall grew up in a small town, loving the fact that if you didn't know everyone, you at least knew of them—or their aunt, or their cousin, or the person who cuts their hair. She's taken the warmth and emotion of that sense of community and flavored her books, drawing fond memories from those who've lived in a small town and a quiet yearning from those who have not.

After a few years in the big city (Chicago), she returned to her Indiana hometown where she lives with her husband, two college-age children, a menagerie of pets, and a rock band in the basement.

Susan loves to hear from her readers. Contact her at: P.O. Box 1092, Noblesville, IN 46060. E-mail: szcrandall@ insightbb.com. Or visit her web site at www.susancrandall.net.

Molly finished out her day with a satisfied buzz in her veins. Holding new life in her hands had helped eclipse the bleakness that threatened to swamp her earlier—had pushed the dissatisfaction back behind the black curtain.

Finally, the last patient was out the door and she was free to go to the hospital and see Sarah and the baby. She was as excited as she'd been when she'd gone to see her nephew, Riley, for the first time. Having coaxed Sarah's baby's first breath, it was hard not to think of Nicholas as family.

The weather hadn't improved over the past hours. The instant Molly stepped out the door, sleet pelted her like tiny needles, stinging her cheeks and bare hands. She had to squint into the wind to protect her eyes. Despite Carmen's frequent applications of ice-melt on the walk outside the clinic, Molly didn't dare to lift her feet off the slick concrete; she did a shuffle-skate toward the parking lot at the side of the building. The sleet made a silvery halo around the street light that sat at the edge of the lot.

The lock was iced over on her car door. She gave it a couple of thumps with her fist to break the icy film so she could insert the key. Luckily all of the freezing had been on the outside of the lock and it opened fine. The cold interior creaked and crackled as she settled in the driver's seat.

"Why didn't I go to California or Arizona to med school?" she asked, her breath forming a cloud in front of her face. She could easily have relocated after graduation, but she'd stayed here in Boston, where she felt like she'd laid the groundwork for her career. What a misconception that had turned out to be.

Once the defroster had cleared the windshield enough to see, she pulled out of the near-deserted parking lot. The tires spun before they finally gripped the road; she inched along testing her brakes every so often to see how slippery the pavement was. Even though it was only seven o'clock, she found herself virtually alone on the streets. She should just drive home, forget the stop at the hospital. Even as she thought it, she turned right at the stoplight, toward the hospital, instead of the left that would take her home. She came up behind a salt truck and poked along behind him, hoping for a marginally safer road.

It took her twice as long to reach the hospital parking garage as normal. She was glad to drive inside the structure and onto the first dry pavement she'd seen all day.

She stopped in the gift shop and bought flowers; every new mother should have flowers. The thought of Sarah alone with her baby, not having anyone to share this moment, broke Molly's heart.

Stopping at the nurses' station in maternity, she asked for Sarah's room number. The duty nurse looked up from the medication cart, then shook her head as she double checked her roster. "No Sarah Morgan registered."

"Maybe they haven't moved her up here yet." Even as Molly said it a chill crept over her heart. "She delivered at my clinic today. EMS brought her here."

"You want me to call down and check?"

"No, thanks." The nurse was clearly in the middle of getting meds ready to dispense. If Sarah was downstairs, she'd have to go down there to see her anyway.

Molly's stomach was in her throat as the elevator slowly descended to the first floor. She followed the familiar corridor to the ER. Walking past the registration desk, Gladys Kopenski called, "Dr. Boudreau! You're on duty tonight?" She looked quickly at her schedule. Gladys had manned this desk for more years than Molly had been alive. The woman ran a tight ship. It really threw her to have an unexpected face show up. Molly smiled. "No. Looking for a patient. What on earth are you doing here at this hour?"

Gladys's lips pursed and she shifted in her chair. "That Cindi didn't show up again. I'm pulling a double."

Molly nodded in sympathy. Gladys had advised—to put it in mild, professional terms—against hiring Cindi Forbes in the first place. Hadn't called her anything but "that Cindi" since the first day. Gladys took a no-nonsense approach to her job and Cindi's most remarkable credentials were an impressive set of hooters—which, ironically, was the location of her last job. Dr. Michaels, director of emergency medicine, who was smack dab in the middle of a midlife crisis complete with red Porsche and new gym membership, felt Cindi was the "most qualified candidate." But Cindi had missed at least half of the work days since she'd been hired three weeks ago.

Molly said, "I'm looking for a patient brought in by the EMS around one-thirty this afternoon. Sarah Morgan, she'd just delivered a baby."

Gladys frowned. "I remember when she came in. She should be up in maternity by now."

"She's not."

Gladys started shuffling paperwork. "Things did get pretty crazy this afternoon. I hope they didn't leave that poor woman parked in a cubicle all this time." She got up and headed through the double doors, looking like she was going to extract a pound of flesh from whoever had thrown a wrench into her well-oiled machine.

Molly followed, flowers clutched in her hand. Occasionally, she'd been the recipient of Gladys's ire; it was much more entertaining when the woman had another target.

Molly's amusement quickly disappeared. Sarah wasn't in the ER. Apparently, she'd disappeared at some point in the afternoon when the victims of the bus accident, the overflow from Mass General, had flooded this facility. Her chart hung on the foot of an empty gurney. No one had seen her leave.

Had Sarah simply gotten up and carried her child out into this storm?

Molly picked up the chart. The clipboard was empty. Apparently, Sarah had had the presence of mind to take the paperwork with her. The woman really didn't trust to leave a trace of herself, even a confidential hospital record.

"Do you have an address in the computer for her?" Molly asked Gladys. She could go back to the clinic and look it up herself. But that would take another thirty minutes.

"Yes. But that's about all."

They returned to Gladys's desk. Molly laid down the flowers to make a quick notation of the address. Then she snatched them back up in a tight fist and headed to the garage. About half-way there, she realized she was swinging the bouquet at her side as she steamrolled her way toward her car, knocking the heads of the flowers against her coat, leaving a shower of petals in her wake. She felt just like Gladys had looked just minutes ago—ready to rip someone's head off. Why in the hell would Sarah put herself and her baby at risk like this?

It took Molly forty minutes on the slick streets to

get to the address on Sarah's chart. When she pulled up and stopped, she slammed her fist against the steering wheel. This was no residence. It was just one of those mail box places. She sat there for a few minutes, listening to the sleet clatter against the car and the windshield wipers thump back and forth. Had Sarah made it safely to wherever she was going? A shiver coursed down Molly's body. Somewhere in this big city, a new mother huddled with her child against loneliness and the storm. Molly prayed to God they were all right. It was the only thing she could do.

That sense of sad isolation, of cold detachment, once again covered her like an unhealthy skin. Finally, she turned around and headed home, to her own fight against loneliness.

The next day the sun shone brightly, glinting off the icy tree branches like diamonds. The cheerfulness of it didn't begin to penetrate Molly's mood. Worry had kept her awake most of the night. This morning's roads had been reduced to nasty, yet relatively safe, slush. She concentrated on its gray ugliness instead of the fairyland created by the sparkling ice coating on everything else as she drove to work at the ER.

Throughout the day she hoped against hope that Sarah and Nicholas would appear. Three different times she called the clinic to see if they'd shown up there—or at least called to tell Molly they were all right. Carmen assured her that she'd call the instant she heard anything. She never called.

By the end of her shift, it was beginning to sink in that Molly might never see either one of them again. She left work with a growing sense of loss. By the time she was warming up a can of soup for her solitary dinner, she'd managed to fall into a perfectly disgusting quagmire of self-pity.

It wasn't that she didn't love medicine. She did. But living like this wasn't enough anymore. The past days events had shone a bright light on the fact that her personal life consisted of no more than a visit home at Christmas and a single, watered-down friendship with a woman she barely knew. She really needed to rethink her life, reassess what she really wanted.

As she was going to bed, she decided, tomorrow she would decide. She would have the whole day to herself. She'd take stock, then take hold of her life and set it on a course that would deliver the fulfillment she was currently lacking. Deciding to decide delivered a measure of calm. She went to sleep certain that when she awakened her future would begin to take shape.

Just as Molly was stepping out of her morning shower, a frantic knocking sounded at her apartment door. She grabbed her robe and tied it around her as she hurried to answer it, wondering if the building was on fire. Instead of a fireman with an ax waiting for her when she opened the door, she was stunned to see a nervous-looking Sarah holding Nicholas.

Sarah didn't hesitate, but stepped right in. "Close the door."

Molly did. "What's wrong? I've been so worried about you two." She looked at Sarah. Even with cheeks reddened by the chill air, the girl looked like the walking dead, exhausted beyond normal new-mother exhaustion. "Sit down." Molly pointed to the only piece of furniture in her living room, a futon.

Sarah sat and laid the baby next to her on the futon. She unwrapped him from thick blankets. Molly looked closely at the child to assess his health. His appearance was the opposite of Sarah's, good color, alert, bright eyes.

Sarah didn't look at Molly when she said, "I need your help." She raised her blue eyes then, and the deep purple smudges beneath them were even more evident. "I need you to keep Nicholas for a day or so."

Molly drew a deep breath to silence the *What!* that was about to pop out of her mouth. Then she sat down on the floor next to Sarah's feet and said, "Tell me what's happening."

"I just have to take care of a few things—and I *can't* have the baby with me." Again, Sarah's gaze skittered away from Molly's probing expression.

"This has to do with Nicholas's father?"

Sarah nodded and ran a pale finger along the baby's cheek. Then she looked Molly in the eye. "He can't know about Nicholas. That's the only way I can protect him."

"Sarah, don't you have someone—"

Jumping to her feet, Sarah threw her arms in the air. "Don't you think if I did . . ." She stopped herself and took a breath. "I understand how much I'm asking. I don't have much time—and I don't have anywhere else to turn. Once I get this taken care of, Nicholas and I can start over . . . safe."

"My God, what kind of man is this?"

"Dangerous."

The way she said it made Molly's blood run cold. She decided if she was going to do this, she deserved more of an answer. "How could you have gotten involved with—"

"He's not what he appears. He's very convincing in his lies. The ugly truth is buried so deep . . . when I found out, it was too late. All I could do was run to protect the baby. But I can't run anymore." There was a chilling finality in her last statement.

Molly had the odd feeling she was caught up in a weeknight television drama. "Why not? If you've stayed away from him this long, why can't you just leave it this way?"

"Because I'm a liability. He can't afford liabilities. It's just a matter of time."

"You make it sound like he'll kill you."

"He will." Her voice was flat, as if fear had ground away all emotion until there was nothing left.

"If he's dangerous, you should go to the police." Molly grasped Sarah's hand; her flesh was as cold as a corpse.

Sarah looked down at her and ignored the statement. There were tears in her eyes. "Will you take him? I don't have a lot of time."

"What if I can't?"

Sarah's eyes closed briefly and she drew a breath. "Then I'll have to leave him somewhere else."

"With someone else?" Even as Molly said it, she knew that wasn't what Sarah meant.

"No. Abandon him somewhere where they'll take care of him—like the hospital . . . a church."

Molly shot to her feet. "You've got to be kidding! You'll never get him back."

Sarah blinked and a tear rolled down her cheek. "But he'll be safe."

Molly had seen plenty of kids from foster care end up in the ER. It had happened again just this week. Somehow she kept herself from saying, *Don't bet on it.* "I've got two days off. Can you be back here before my shift on Friday at three?"

Molly grabbed her into a quick, fierce hug. "Thank you." Then she stepped an arm's length away. "Promise me you'll protect him . . . no matter what. Keep him from his father."

Molly looked at her sternly. "If I knew who his father was, that'd be a whole lot easier to do."

Sarah stared hard into Molly's eyes. "No. Just the opposite."

Molly tore her uneasy gaze from Sarah to look at the baby who'd fallen asleep on the futon. She could not let this child get swallowed up in the system.

"You're sure the father doesn't know?" Molly asked.

"Absolutely."

"I still think you should go to the police."

Sarah gave Molly a quick hug. "Everything he needs is in the case. I'll be back before your shift on Friday."

"I'm worried about you," Molly said gravely.

"Don't worry about me. Nicholas is the one who matters."

Putting her hand on the door knob, Sarah paused and looked back at the baby one last time. Molly couldn't help but think she looked like a sad fairy princess; fair and beautiful, yet caught in a nightmarish tragedy.

Sarah said, "Thank you," once again, and slipped out the door.

Molly stood for a long moment, just staring at the closed door, an impotent fear filling her throat.

As Molly gave Nicholas his five a.m. bottle the next morning, she turned on the television news and discovered that Sarah was dead.

THE EDITOR'S DIARY

Dear Reader,

Like spin-the-bottle, love can be a complete game of chance. So pucker up—you never know when the bottle will stop and your Prince Charming will reveal himself. Just ask Analise Abbott and Rebecca Tremaine in our two Warner Forever titles this August.

Karen Robards raves "**Susan Crandall** is an up-and-coming star". Prepare to be dazzled for her latest, **MAGNOLIA SKY**, is going to sweep you off your feet. Luke Boudreau has been agonizing for five months over what to say to the mother of his best army buddy Calvin Abbott. After all, how do you express your regret and sorrow that someone died while saving your life? Now, finally at the door of Calvin's Mississippi home, the moment is upon him. Praying to forgive himself for surviving and find a moment's peace, Luke never expected the truth to explode like a bomb. In all the time they were together in the service, Calvin never even hinted that he was married. He certainly didn't behave that way either. Yet Analise Abbott stands before him like an angel, her green eyes full of life, her sweet smile full of warmth and the promise of something more. Torn between loyalty and temptation, can Luke open himself up to love with Analise?

Journeying from the sweet aroma of magnolia in Mississippi to the hint of desperation as a woman bolts from her wedding, we present **Julie Anne Long's THE RUNAWAY DUKE**. Mary Balogh calls this "a delightful debut novel—brimful of wit, action, passion, and romance" and she couldn't be more right. Get comfy—you're never going to want this to end. Rebecca Tremaine isn't the genteel lady her mother dreamt she'd be. She's wretched at embroidery and pitiful at the pianoforte. But when she's caught in a compromising position with a dandy, her parents have had enough. Arranging a hasty marriage, they never suspected she'd find an ally to thwart their plan. Connor Riordan has no idea how this happened. His life as a groom on the Tremaine estate was peaceful and isolated—just what this Duke of Dunbrooke "killed" in action at Waterloo needs to keep his cover. But a true gentleman never turns away a damsel in distress. As Rebecca and Connor race through the countryside, escaping Rebecca's parents, her fiancé and the highwaymen out to get them, can love catch them?

To find out more about Warner Forever, these August titles, and the author, visit us at www.warnerforever.com.

With warmest wishes,

Karen Kosztolnyik (signature)

Karen Kosztolnyik, Senior Editor

P.S. September is right around the corner, but don't put away those tank tops yet. Indian summer is about to begin with these two hot reasons to keep your A.C. plugged in: **Sue-Ellen Welfonder** pens a sensual Scottish medieval about an aloof warrior who must marry for money but never expected to lose his heart to his spirited young bride and her searing kisses in **WEDDING FOR A KNIGHT**; and **Toni Blake** delivers the sexy and heartwarming erotic romance about a man determined to get revenge, the woman he falls in love with, and her diary—his weapon of choice—in **THE RED DIARY**.